William Cullen Bryant: *The Complete Stories*

William Cullen Bryant
The Complete Stories

Edited, with Critical Commentary,

by

Frank Gado

Antoca
Hartford, VT

distributed by
University Press of New England
Hanover and London

Published by **Antoca Press**
1424 Neal Road
White River Junction, Vermont 05001

Distributed by University Press of New England
One Court St. Lebanon, NH 03766

Bryant, William Cullen, 1794-1878.
   William Cullen Bryant : The Complete Stories /edited by
Frank Gado. ~ 1st ed.

ISBN 978-1-61168-568-8 Hardcover
ISBN 978-1-61168-569-5 Paperback
ISBN 978-1-61168-570-1 Ebook

CONTENTS

With gratitude to

Above all, **Fred Fagal**, my student when I began my thirty-three years in the Union College faculty trireme. I extend appreciation beyond my means of expression. His beneficence has been unbounded, and in thanking him I must also acknowledge the forbearance of his estimable wife Janet, whom I deprived of far too many hours of spousal attention.

My dear friend since college days, **George Metes**. He read my drafts when my spirits had ebbed and renewed my faith in the value of the work I had undertaken. The nights we spent striving for sense in literature and life in our illegal subterranean apartment on Lebanon Street forged fraternal bonds that have held us fast through more storms than the log books show.

Fellow assayer of words **Nick Stevens**, always on call, a wise and constant friend.

Doris Yates, who sweetly fails to comprehend why the man who shares her days spends so many hours of the night churning words at the computer.

Laurie and **Sarah Selby**, blessed with aesthetic acumen and generous hearts, who were responsible for converting my naive concept into a professional cover.

Dan Catlin, who provided the William Guy Wall print for the cover that is a perfect match to Bryant's early stories.

Fred's former student **Lauren Tyrrell**, who sustained my hope that Bryant's fiction had appeal for an intelligent, discerning modern reader.

Sean Hunter and **Tim Bennett**, sages of Staples, who saved my bytes of chestnuts from incineration.

Exemplary librarians **Reinhart Sonnenburg** and **Bill Fontaine**, ever willing to be helpful.

Prolegomenon

GIVEN the proper respect due actuarial tables in these matters, this book stands a fair chance of being my last in literary history or criticism. Should that prove to be the case, most of the books I projected writing when I left graduate school will remain locked in my evanescing mind. For no reason that matters to my fellow man, I regret that. Immersion in the imaginations of writers who sought to spin their experience into poeïsis has enriched my life. Although even a cursory consideration of English departments belies the piety that literature ennobles its students and refines moral sentiments, I recognize that my reading over the decades has sharpened my perception of humanity. Would that I had had more years to dive deeper into the profound worlds of Herman Melville and William Faulkner, America's greatest poets.

Fate directed me instead toward a complex man who, though possibly the most intelligent of our writers, never attained the summits of true immortality. But that has not made him less intriguing to me. Perhaps because I am the child of immigrants to whom America was the full share of the heaven they dared dream of reaching, the idiosyncratic qualities of the American mind have always fascinated me, and in Bryant I met an early champion of expression of America's unique genius.

Somehow we have recognized the historical importance of Washington Irving and enshrined Poe and Hawthorne as the opposed pillars that support the tradition of the American tale, but in that reduction, we have sacrificed an appreciation of the complexity in our nascent literary history. Bryant, whose stories have been all but lost, deserves rediscovery, not only as an exhibit of the variety in the roil of a literary movement groping for purpose and definition but also for the quality of his better fiction. That, after almost a century of scholarly activity in that academic purlieu we call American Studies, Bryant's contribution to the emergence of our fiction has continued to go unnoticed is nothing short of a scandal. This volume proposes to remedy that neglect.

White River Junction, VT   Frank Gado

Introduction: From Poet to Story Writer

Stories, of varying lengths and varieties of modes, have surely existed almost as long as the rudiments of language itself, but the short story in its modern guise, however wide the latitude of its definition, only made its appearance at the end of the nineteenth century's second decade. In 1820, Sydney Smith famously scoffed in the *Edinburgh Review*, "Who in the four corners of the globe reads an American book?" Almost simultaneously, Washington Irving was contradicting the denigration with *The Sketch Book*, which not only quickly won admiration in his native land and Great Britain but also found favor throughout Europe. The publication of two of the stories it contained, "Rip Van Winkle" (written the year before) and "The Legend of Sleepy Hollow," ranks among the more consequential events of American fiction's first century. No American novel that preceded it had enjoyed greater recognition, nor could any of the short narratives padding our early magazines claim anything approaching Irving's degree of stylistic elegance.

Curiously, although our literary historians customarily delight in noting the irony in Smith's belittlement of America's prospects, they become inexplicably timid in crediting the short story's major role in establishing an emergent national literature. The campaign for literary nationalism had been waged with increasing intensity since independence. Did political separation also require expression of a discrete cultural identity, and if it did, what might it look like? Irving both helped to confirm the possibility of a distinctive, self-consciously American literature and offered a possible model for its development.

Past mention of Irving's breakthrough, attention invariably skips to Poe and Hawthorne, whose works do not start attracting readers until past the middle 1830s. The neglect of the dozen intervening years is unfortunate. While James Fenimore Cooper was whetting international appetites for sea novels and mythic frontier romances, a small group of short story writers was testing the parameters of their as-yet-unbaptised new genre as a means of asserting Americanness. None of these ignored pioneers rewards study more than a frustrated young poet who fled a deadening law practice in western Massachusetts for a literary career in New York City.

William Cullen Bryant had been impelled toward poetry soon after his birth in Cummington, a hamlet in the Berkshires, in 1794. Given a physician father who wrote poems, prided himself on an unerringly acute sense in language, revered Alexander Pope, and compiled an extensive library of verse in English – including a large selection of what his young nation had produced – the son was locked to his destiny. At nine, the precocious child composed and recited fifty-four lines in heroic couplets for his school's end-of-year ceremony; published three years later in the *Hampshire Gazette*, the poem became a favorite for declamation at similar occasions in the region. Greater celebrity came with *The Embargo*, written at thirteen, in which he hurled satiric heroic couplets of scorn on Thomas Jefferson and his administration. New England, gravely suffering the economic consequences of the recently passed Embargo Act of 1807, cheered the attack from the pen of "a mere lad" and bought the edition with such alacrity that a second edition was rushed into print, supplemented with additional poems. Shortly thereafter, his decision to prepare for entrance to Williams College at the sophomore level meant intensive tutoring in Latin and Greek – and the opportunity to study and translate from classical models. When seven months in Williamstown fell short of his expectations, he anticipated switching to Yale's more nourishing intellectual climate – until a review of family finances with his father dashed those plans. With the greatest reluctance, he then turned to reading for the law as the obvious career choice dictated by his talents and the available options. Fours and a half years later, at the very end of 1815, he began his practice, resolved to make diligence his means of subduing distaste for a profession he felt had been forced upon him.

Nevertheless, the "witchery of song" still enticed. No longer an acolyte to Pope and Neo-Classicism, Bryant was now under the spell of the Graveyard Poets and, chiefly, the freshening Romantic innovations of William Wordsworth. Despite having vowed constancy to the law that furnished him a livelihood, he continued to court the muse, much like a husband relishing the guilt of his infidelities as relief from tedium. Then, just when he seemed on the cusp of accepting a doom of small-town obscurity, a fortuity changed his future. Willard Phillips, a young scholar who had briefly resided in Cummington while cramming Latin for admission to Harvard, had shared his passion for literature with the town's doctor, Peter Bryant. The two later met again in Boston, where the elder Bryant was serving as a state legislator and Phillips, following graduation, had joined the editorial board of a new periodical, the *North American Review*. Remembering the physician-legislator's literary interests, Phillips invited submissions, and when Dr. Bryant returned to the Berkshires, he happily stuffed an envelope with both his and his son's work. On receipt, the packet triggered a burst of enthusiasm, but it was Cullen's verse that excited the editors. That initial publication quickly led to successive appearances in the *North American*, capped four years later by a summons to address the Phi Beta Kappa chapter at Harvard's commencement and the printing of a slim but impressive edition of *Poems*, his first collection of adult writing.

Now in his late twenties, Bryant was no longer just another lawyer who wrote poetry but a respected poet who practiced law to support himself and a budding family. Even so, he suffered from the impoverished cultural circumstances of Great Barrington and from plying "this beggarly profession," further degraded by the absurdities of rural justice. Longing for urban diversity, literary company, and more fruitful labor, he weighed the relative merits of Boston and New York City; with the counsel of his close friends, the remarkable Sedgwick clan, he chose the Hudson over the Charles.

It was an opportune moment in the evolution of American letters, and New York City was its quickening center. The respectability won by Irving and Cooper – both, not coincidentally, New Yorkers – reinforced convictions sometimes expressed by our literary nationalists that our role as a beacon for a new political order would have a corresponding cultural effect. Recognition abroad inspired confidence, and growing interest at home in domestic talent encouraged native writers to think it might be possible at long last to earn a living by their pens. New periodicals added to the optimism: despite their high mortality rate, some were sufficiently sanguine about their prospects to consider payment to contributors as part of their business plan. Among the more ambitious magazines, the *Atlantic* and the *North American Review* began offering writers compensation in 1824. That same year, the *United States Literary Gazette* entered the competition; gambling that quality writers would ensure success, it asked Bryant to supply an average of a hundred lines of poetry a month for an unprecedented two hundred dollars per annum. Bryant was elated. The stipend amounted to between a third and a half of his earnings at law. Moreover, the editor extended the offer apologetically, acknowledging that, although the proposed submissions would surely merit higher compensation, the magazine, regrettably, could not afford to pay according to their worth.

Neither this confirmation of esteem nor the unexpected but most welcome enhancement of his revenue solved his problem, however. No American had ever earned a living as a poet, and he fully understood that any such dream would be sheer folly, yet the thought of enduring dependence on a legal career was intolerable. A potential solution beckoned from New York City, where, in two exploratory forays, he relished the warm fellowship of its literary circle. Catharine Sedgwick, encountering him there while she was visiting her brother Henry, could scarcely believe this was the same friend she had known in the Berkshires. He was a changed man, she reported in a letter, "I never saw him so happy, nor half so agreeable." Although writing poetry would not bring enough money to live on, editing might, and the invigorating welcome Bryant received among literary comrades in the city after the depressing social conditions in Great Barrington lifted whatever small doubt that relocation would be worth the risks it carried. Henry assured him that an opening, somewhere, would occur. Catharine, too, was confident. "I think it is impossible that in the increasing demand for native literature, a man of his resources, who has justly the first reputation, should not be able to command a competency."

That desired competency quickly developed in the early spring of 1825. A swirl of complex litigation between and among competing periodicals and their schismatic editors eventually resulted in the formation of the *New-York Review and Atheneum*, a new publication in the character of a hybrid. One part, much like the *North American Review*, would be in the mold of the British reviews that featured considerations of new books, political developments, and academic questions regarding such matters as science and philosophy; its second part would present a somewhat more sophisticated version of the magazine, a miscellany in the American tradition. (*Magazine*, meaning "storehouse," was one of several terms used in the United States to refer to a periodical consisting of useful information and diverse entertainment – much of it, in earlier years, culled from European sources.) Bryant embraced the concept, and at a salary of a thousand

4

dollars a year – double his earnings in a good year as a lawyer – the appointment as editor realized his fondest hopes. Besides the financial advantage, New York's kinetic cultural opportunities tantalized, and in the magazine's "Atheneum" section he saw not only a platform for his varied interests but also, more specifically, a means to advance the nationalist cause in literature.

Unlikely as it may be that his dreams included a portent of his becoming a writer of tales, he soon recognized it as a necessity. Fortunately, a small clutch of poets had won favor in the city; Bryant's prestige lent the *Review* a measure of allure, and if what he was able to attract (and sometimes modify) from old and new poet friends fell short of his standards, he could rely on his own poems as a supplement, either extracted from the backlog he had accumulated or composed for the purpose. But to swell his number of subscribers from five hundred to the thousand necessary for the magazine to succeed as it was conceived, he needed to supply what would appeal to a broader audience – and clearly the unsatisfied hunger was for fiction. Irving and, to a lesser extent, Irving's early collaborator James Kirke Paulding, who was also now writing stories, had whetted an appetite too few cooks were well enough schooled to satisfy. Not knowing where else to turn, Bryant took the path of expedience and stepped into the kitchen himself.

For all that Bryant's ambitions fastened on poetry, the recourse to fiction was not as wild a choice as it might seem. Despite his indebtedness to Wordsworth and the British tradition in poetry (for there were no American models to build on), his advocacy for a literature expressive of our national identity inclined him to keep an attentive eye on prose in that vein. One author breaking new ground was Richard Henry Dana, the very editor at the *North American Review* who had recognized such an extraordinary talent in Bryant that he could not believe the verse he had just read was written "this side of the Atlantic." The two had become friends, and their reliance upon each other as literary guides would continue throughout their lives. Indeed, Dana was inspired to write poetry by Bryant and submitted his first poem to his one-time protégé for the initial number of the *Review*. That debut suddenly transformed Dana into a poet, but he had previously been a conspicuous hierophant for the application of Romantic precepts to fiction. Only a few years earlier, Dana ruptured his association with the *North American* over ideological differences and

5

published *The Idle Man* (1821-22), a periodical meant to be a vehicle for his stories. Young writers, notably those on college campuses, responded excitedly to what this showcase displayed, but conservative voices saw cause for moral alarm and viciously condemned it. Bryant rushed to Dana's defense, parrying the attack mounted in Boston's *Columbian Centinel* at its source. Although Bryant incorporated little of Dana's method, he sympathized with his doughty comrade's intentions as an American exploring unfamiliar dimensions.

A similar involvement on the side of the new modes of writing occurred in 1824. Hoping to promote interest in his friend Catharine Sedgwick's novel, *Redwood* (which she had dedicated to him), Bryant stepped forward to write a review speculating on American fiction's Romantic future. He had no more in common with Sedgwick than with Dana in what motivated their fictions, but the foment their writing manifested was not something he could ignore. To feel an itch to participate in that obvious development was a natural instinct for a writer suddenly thrust into the midst of a like-minded sodality. With publication of "A Pennsylvanian Legend" in late 1825, he enlisted in the sparse ranks of toilers in an emerging literary form.

Along with the arrival of spring in 1826 came the realization that the *Review* was growing too slowly to justify the effort he was pouring into it. While also preparing and delivering four major public lectures sponsored by the Athenæum library on aspects of poetry – a foundational document for the American Romantic movement – he entered into negotiations to launch a successor magazine by merging his *Review* with a publication based in Boston. Two factors drove the parties. One was economic. For the *Gazette*, the dominance of the *North American Review* in its area left meager pickings for competitors; looking to New York, its editor, James Carter, saw an increasing concentration of writers, a steadily rising population, and growing commercial power. For Bryant, the linkage gave him a means to reclaim the following he had acquired through his involvement with the *North American*, an immediate injection of additional subscribers, and the assistance of Carter, a like-minded co-editor. With one editorial leg planted in each of the two major cities of the Northeast, the combined magazines stood a chance of initially doubling sales and then, with enriched content, bidding for a larger readership than the sum of its previous subscription lists. The second motive was not wholly tainted by pecuniary considerations. Both Carter and Bryant believed in a national process of aggregation in the arts; yoking the two rival cultural centers, they hoped, might help lead the way out of provincialism. The revamped magazine proudly announced its aim "to furnish a seasonable and complete view of the progress and state of our national literature."

The original agreement stipulated an equal division of duties, with Bryant continuing as the New York editor and owning a quarter of the stock. Significantly, they also agreed to create a new name for the magazine that would avoid favoring either of the two cities. But this implicit commitment to balance immediately frayed when neither editor could quite accept the other's choice – an omen of the tensions to follow. Once operation began, the magazine's financial backers in Boston, disappointed in the return on their investment, informed Carter that they would trim his salary, whereupon he shifted his attention to seeking other employment. His replacement, Charles Folsom, an inexperienced young Harvard librarian, brought optimism to his appointment that quickly dimmed when he had to concede that he could not meet his quota of content. Thus, with the Boston base slipping into an ancillary outpost, the burden of sustaining what had finally been rechristened the *United States Review and Literary Gazette* rested mostly on Bryant, whose patience was taxed at inopportune moments. The Boston board would sometimes be recalcitrant and sometimes unresponsive, and the two editors did not hold fast to a fundamental policy: Bryant's insistence that the publication be exclusively literary had to withstand Folsom's repeated efforts to insinuate his political bias. Moreover, the ambitious initial plan to recruit and develop a talented squad of writers by paying them well for their work had to be scaled back in the face of fiscal reality. To fill the magazine's pages, Bryant ultimately had to rely on himself. In addition to his reviews, a sonnet, and a translation of a Spanish poem, he contributed the well-wrought "A Border Tradition" to the October, 1826 number. But his development in the short story was not sustained. Just short of a year later, "A Narrative of Some Extraordinary Circumstances That Happened More Than Twenty Years Since" was patently a hurried draft he surely would have held back from publication had he not been desperate to complete the September number and close down the magazine.

Despite the high mortality rate among magazines, the temptations to found them persisted, and consistent improvement in the quality of Bryant's periodicals would have made another turn as editor highly likely. But the instability in the position and low rewards it brought had dimmed the enthusiasm of a husband and father in his thirties. In the *New-York Evening Post*, owned and edited by the fiery Federalist William Coleman, he spied firmer ground. Eighteen years earlier, young Bryant had feasted on editorials in the *Post* and commended Coleman in *The Embargo* for his sallies against Jefferson. Although the youth's politics had changed almost as much as had his views on poetry, Bryant had several affinities with the legendary Coleman. Both Massachusetts natives had been lawyers in the same area of Hampshire County before fleeing to editorial work in New York. More important, they shared some similarity in sensibility. Contrary to his usual depiction, Bryant had a temper, and though he did his best to keep it under a tight lid, it occasionally would erupt. Coleman, less restrained, fulminated spectacularly. Responding to a slander by a rival editor that he had fathered a mulatto bastard, he challenged the rumormonger to a duel. When word of the challenge got out, the principals were constrained from keeping their "interview," but the matter did not end there. A political opponent spread the story that Coleman had tattled on himself in order to avoid endangering his life, whereupon the imputed coward demanded satisfaction – which he executed by killing his accuser. Bryant's pique would bring him into analogous confrontations, though fortunately, the confrontations never ended in an opponent's death.

Their strongest bond, however, was their devotion to the art of the written word. Coleman, while not himself a writer and less than deft in his editorials for his newspaper, had literary leanings that made him a key player in New York City's evolving Renaissance. In 1805, thirteen-year-old John Howard Payne had single-handedly produced a theatrical magazine and written a comedy staged at the Park, the city's prime theater; Coleman so valued the boy's talent that he assembled a group of supporters to pay for college. Later, among others he encouraged, he launched the careers of Fitz-Greene Halleck and Joseph Rodman Drake by publishing their "Croaker" poems in the *Post*. At once, they achieved celebrity for their wit and briefly reigned as the region's most admired poets. No one, however, would prove a greater beneficiary of Coleman's literary sponsorship than Bryant.

The *Post*'s editor, who had become acquainted with Bryant's writing through the *North American*, doubtless learned of his presence in New

York early on, and he went out of his way to laud the *Review*. He may also have perceived in the new arrival an opportunity to ease his own burden. A vicious pummeling at the hands of a Republican-Democrat office holder in 1819 had left Coleman partially paralyzed, and his health steadily deteriorated from that point on. After publishing Bryant's poems for about a year, he brought him to the *Post* in 1826 as an assistant editor, at a salary of seven hundred eighty dollars a year, to rewrite news reports from other sources and to revise and polish his ailing employer's editorials. Already taxed by the demands made by his struggling magazine, Bryant nevertheless accepted the additional charge as a means of propping up his finances, and Coleman, while promising not to ask more of his assistant than his other obligations would allow, believed the arrangement would not only provide him with someone to lean on but also further enhance the prestige of the *Post*.

The affiliation that buoyed Coleman, however, Bryant initially regarded as a mundane chore. When Dana had warned against the danger that "vile blackguard squabble" would distract him from poetry, Bryant replied that "politics and a belly-full are better than poetry and starvation." But appeasing the belly took a toll of the mind. "I drudge for the Evening Post and labor for the Review," he also wrote Dana, implying, in adding "I would give up one of these if I could earn my bread by the other," that it was the drudgery he would shed. Even so, it did not take long for journalism to get into his blood during his two years of widening involvement as assistant editor. By February 1828, he wrote to Dana, he had become "a small proprietor in the establishment," having signed a note for purchase of one-eighth of the company's stock. When Coleman died of an apoplectic stroke in mid 1829, the transition to full control as editor was virtually a formality. Eventually, he would own the *Post* and become, not only one of the most respected and powerful figures in nineteenth-century public life but also an astonishingly rich man. Even so, as Dana had predicted, journalism exacted a price. By embracing Andrew Jackson's Democrat Party and advocating a panoply of civic reforms for New York City, Bryant ensured that the squabbling would be unremitting.

As soon as the part-proprietor could anticipate counting on an annual income from the *Post* of more than a thousand and perhaps as much as two thousand dollars, the exigency to write stories for the sake of his magazine's survival no longer existed, yet, obviously, he had discovered satisfaction in this alternative to poetry. What began as a necessity now became a focus of recreation, and a publishing novelty presented a means of indulgence. The gift book, an adaptation of the European "almanac of the muses" – a richly illustrated literary miscellany, annually issued at the year's close for purchase as a keepsake – had arisen in Britain in 1822 in imitation of a German staple. Quickly becoming a Christmas fashion, it spawned many imitations: the *Atlantic Souvenir*, the first in America, appeared in 1826; *The Talisman for 1828*, was the second.

Elam Bliss, a failed apothecary turned book-seller (and thereby, as was often the case at the time, also a publisher) had seen the opportunity to exploit the success of this import and approached Robert Sands to assume charge of his proposed annual. Like Bryant, Sands – a Columbia graduate who had previously drawn attention as the co-author of the Romantic Indian "epic," *Yamoyden* – was earning a modest wage as assistant editor of a New York newspaper, and he saw no personal advantage in accepting the invitation, but he mentioned it to Bryant and another close friend, Congressman Gulian Verplanck. They thought it an intriguing prospect, and the more they played at what might be done, the more they warmed to it. Someone – most likely Bryant – introduced the notion of adopting the pseudonym "Francis Herbert" for the trio's merged identity – a fictitious figure in the style of Irving's Dietrich Knickerbocker or Geoffrey Crayon who would present the book's contents to his readers. Casually, but under the discipline of a deadline – the volume would have to be in bookshops for the 1827 Christmas season – the three authors started convening regularly at the Sands' Hoboken home, amusing themselves in planning for their project and collaborating on much of the composition. Bryant would later look back on their fellowship in producing the book as among the happiest days of his life.

The Talisman for 1828, for which Bryant contributed the preface and three stories, was puffed by its reviewers and well received by the public – indeed sales were still holding up during the advent of the summer solstice – and a delighted Bliss, who loved his trade but fell short when it came to transmuting ardor into profits for his firm, eagerly pursued a commitment from the pseudonymous adventurer, world traveler, and ghost writer Herbert for a second volume. "Francis Herbert" consented, but only after a long delay by Verplanck, whose political career kept him entangled in Washington. Bryant also had constraints. Perhaps distracted by heavier obligations to the *Post* and by involvement as a now dedicated Jacksonian in the turbulent 1828 presidential election process during the months when the next *Talisman* was in preparation, he contributed less prose than he had to its predecessor: "Story of the Island of Cuba" and "Recollections of the South of Spain" - the latter not a short story but a brief, charming *mise-en-scène* for what was featured as a translated ballad, "A Moriscan Romance."

Despite good reviews, the second *Talisman* did not fare as well as the first, but the fact that sales slowly rebounded in spring fanned Bliss's faith in a third volume, and again the three friends pooled their literary endeavors, though the call of other business in their crowded lives now tempered the spontaneous jollity that had characterized the loose regimen of their first Hoboken collaboration. Nevertheless, the annual's quality did not diminish; Bryant's three stories - "The Whirlwind," "The Indian Spring," and "The Marriage Blunder" - were collectively superior to his previous fiction, and two of the three were at the highest level yet achieved in the brief history of the American short story. The popularity of annuals would continue for another decade, and *The Talisman* is generally acknowledged to have been among the very best produced in this country. Yet everyone realized that Francis Herbert's days were coming to an end. Bliss, hard pressed to pay the outstanding debts accruing through his various publishing ventures, dared not imagine a fourth *Talisman*.

With the last *Talisman*, Bryant reached his pinnacle in the short story: it would not be extravagant to state that he had shown the potential for greatness in an extended devotion to writing short fiction, yet for the next two and a half years his sights veered elsewhere. Journalism was entering a more contentious era of aggressive battles to increase readership, and the *Post*, the northernmost major Jacksonian partisan, gave no quarter in its fierce advocacy of his policies in its editorials. But an even more powerful factor was his sense of having come to a critical juncture in defining himself. His thirties were slipping behind him with his poetic ambitions still unfulfilled. He was well aware that his reputation as a poet had mostly rested on a relatively small, though much praised, output that teased expectations of a substantial collection, necessary to establish broad acknowledgment of his place as America's foremost poet. His friends, Dana chief among them, feared that his status as a journalist was overshadowing the achievement in his verse, and they suspected that the next generation, led by Longfellow, was about to eclipse him. Bryant had the same perception and addressed the challenge: what time could be stolen from the conduct of his newspaper went toward protracted revision of work done and composition of fresh poems for a long anticipated successor to the slim collection with which he had first made his mark.

With the task of preparing for the publication of the new *Poems* behind him, Bryant began 1832 with a journey around the settled part of the United States, swinging into the South and then across to the country's central regions, mostly by way of major rivers, before spending time with his brothers in Illinois. What he observed and experienced in this first encounter with the lands outside the Northeast, especially with the West, deeply affected his sense of America, and of himself as an American - as the poem "The Prairie," written upon his return, would show. *Poems*, he was confident, would secure critical approbation at home, but ironically, it would be the collection's British edition, in process during this journey west, that would win accolades as among the finest expressions of the Romantic movement, thereby confirming for his own countrymen the florescence of the genuinely American literature he and his friends had striven to cultivate.

Where would Bryant next direct his ambitions? Although poetry commanded a relatively small portion of the book market, it stood at the highest perch of respect among literary genres; Dana, alert to how posterity arrived at its judgments, urged his friend to tackle a long major poem. Bryant demurred, saying he had yet to come across a vehicle for a great theme. Instead, perhaps wishing to enjoy a respite, he rekindled interest in the possibility of another volume of assembled works by friends - this one consisting exclusively of fiction.

Apparently, the initiative came from the Harper brothers, the American publishers of *Poems*, who appreciated the worth of the *Talisman* and thought their stewardship of a similar product could surpass the results poor Bliss had been able to manage. Obviously, the Harpers thought of Bryant as an accomplished short story writer as well as a poet, and they had confidence that he had established himself in that role with the public. "Francis Herbert" would not be resurrected, but the triad united under that name was to be the foundation of the new volume, and three additional friends - Paulding, Catharine Sedgwick, and William Leggett (a young poet whom Bryant had hired as assistant editor at the *Post*) - were recruited to feed in from the periphery. Originally to be issued as *The Hexade*, the book shrank from the indicated six collaborators to five when Verplanck withdrew because his chairmanship of the House Ways and Means Committee tied him to Washington. A cholera epidemic in New York that summer suggested the device, taken from *The Decameron*, of presenting the stories as having been written at a health spa by refugees from the contagion. A new title, *Tales of Glauber-Spa*, reflected that conceit (although the preposition is misleading: only the collection's headpiece concerns the Spa). Another borrowed idea, probably introduced by Bryant, asserts that the story manuscripts, left behind at the spa by their authors, are being offered for publication in order to recover whatever monetary value they might bring; contemporary readers could not have failed to recognize the allusion to the alleged Dietrich Knickerbocker manuscript in Irving's *A History of New York*. In addition to the epistolary headpiece, Bryant contributed two of his longer stories to the collection, "The Skeleton's Cave" and "Medfield." Neither is an echo of any story he had previously written; Bryant was continuing to explore strategies for the form, even though he had apparently decided at least to suspend his career in fiction and probably to retire from it altogether.

In his compilation of his father-in-law's prose writings, Parke Godwin reports: "finding himself, as he modestly said, unable to rival Irving, Cooper, and Miss Sedgwick in that field, he gave up the undertaking," but Bryant's gracious compliment to his literary friends is less than convincing. A month after Bryant published his first story, Irving was in Madrid, starting his research in the Columbus archives for what would provide material for three books published between 1828 and 1831, and in 1829 Irving was in London and being criticized by his countrymen for compromising his allegiance. In 1832, at the same time that he was securing British publication of Bryant's *Poems*, Irving produced *The Alhambra* – far afield of comparison with Bryant's fiction. Moreover, Irving's reputation as a writer of tales was declining as his interest evolved toward history and biography. If Bryant's judgment that he could not match Irving at the top of his game were a reason to withdraw from the tournament, the retirement was rather late in coming. The self-deprecation would also have been a critical misjudgment.

Cooper was a lesser rival. His popularity owed to his novels: he had written only a fraction as many short stories as Bryant, and none approached the mark of Bryant's half dozen best. Catharine Sedgwick, in contrast, occasionally demonstrated a rare attribute for the period: a knack for creating natural dialogue as an expression of character. She came closer to Jane Austen in her domestic realism than had any American writer during her lifetime. Formally, however, her stories are better as character portraits than as narratives; she seldom achieves meaning through design. Sedgwick's talent stood as a complement, not as competition, to Bryant's more innovative and varied conceptions.

Several other surmises for Bryant's suspension of writing fiction are more plausible. From 1827 on, his involvement in the short story had been associated with Robert Sands – indeed, their partnership in Francis Herbert had led to Bryant's relocation to Hoboken, where he chose a house adjoining the home Sands shared with his mother. The prospect of sustaining the social benefit of their literary relationship after the demise of the *Talisman* was a principal inducement for embarking on *Tales of Glauber-Spa*. When Sands died, crying out for his neighbor, so too did much of the pleasance of composing stories. With this blow, compounded by separation from the influence of Gulian Verplanck, the convivial third element of Francis Herbert, the time had come to turn the page on a phase of his career that, born of necessity, had become an engaging but expendable dalliance.

By 1832, the *Post* had become the foundation of lifelong prosperity and a means of wielding political and social influence, and Bryant accepted the attendant responsibilities. The share of his time that he could devote to literature he owed to his first calling as a poet. For him, poetry offered respite from the contentious struggles that were the fare of journalism; translating the emotions and moral lessons gained from the contemplation of nature into verse was restorative in a way that creating fiction could not afford. Bryant did continue to write prose, but it would be a by-product of his satisfying an appetite to experience something more of the world than the child restricted to his family and the confines of Cummington had imagined, more than the young man nettled by the petty jostling of Great Barrington dared hope would free his intellect, or more, even, than the demands on his energies posed by his drive for success in New York City would permit. In 1834, the man who had acquired half a dozen modern languages left on the first of his six trips to Europe. The edited reports of his impressions were subsequently published in popular travel books (the last of which concerned his journey to the Middle East). Fiction yielded to a form of personal journalism.

One of the impulses behind his entry into fiction had been the opportunity it furnished to advance the principles of literary nationalism. At the age of forty, he could regard that effort as generally fruitful: although the great flowering of American literature still lay ahead, the buds had been set. Whether he consciously chose to fix on more distant horizons was not something directly reflected in his correspondence, but he had clearly evolved a more cosmopolitan consciousness. It is not insignificant that Bryant died as a result of sitting in the sun at the 1878 installation in Central Park of a bust of Giuseppe Mazzini, the Italian journalist, political philosopher, and revolutionary. While abroad, Bryant had sought him out as the founder of Young Italy and Young Europe, the ideals of which had inspired Young America, a Jacksonian counterpart centered in New York City. Four decades before that fatal ceremony, Bryant had been a leader of the movement's nationalistic literary arm. Similarly indicative is the fact that, on returning from his final European journey in 1867, he dedicated himself to the crowning literary task of his life, translation of the two Homeric epics, mostly completed in the loneliness of the library in his Cummington home. It was a long way from his championing the application of Romantic principles to storytelling, his bold stride into the nascent field charted by Irving, and the ensuing camaraderie of the *Talisman*.

How telling that neither of Bryant's biographers of the past half century pays any significant attention at all to the seven-year span in which he wrote fiction! It is as though his stories were scribbles of no consequence, like advertising copy. No serious examination of that fiction justifies such oversight. For some writers, the concept of the short story emerging in those years may have been simply a truncated version of the novel – that much longer narrative form which itself had been evolving for little more than a century – but Bryant grasped that it was a game essentially unlike any played in the past, and he studied its dynamics. Remarkably, no two Bryant stories are quite the same. Within that variety, there is failure, but also flights of ingenuity that produced some of the most admirable feats in our young literature.

Stories

A Pennsylvanian Legend

IS THE WORLD to become altogether philosophical and rational? Are we to believe nothing that we cannot account for from natural causes? Are tales of supernatural warnings, of the interposition and visible appearance of disembodied spirits, to be laughed out of countenance and forgotten? There are people who have found out that to imagine any other modes of being than those of which our experience tells us, is extremely ridiculous. Alas! we shall soon learn to believe that the material world is the only world, and that the things which are the objects of our external senses are the only things which have an existence. Recollect, gentlemen, that you may carry your philosophy too far. You forget how the human mind delights in superstition. You are welcome to explode such of its delusions as are hurtful, but leave us, I pray you, a few of such as are harmless; leave us, at least, those which are interesting to our hearts, without making us forget our love and duty to our fellow creatures.

As long, however, as there are aged crones to talk and children to listen, the labours of philosophy cannot be crowned with perfect success. A dread of supernatural visitations, awakened in our tender years, keeps possession of the mind like an instinct and bids defiance to the attempts of reason to dislodge it. For my part, I look upon myself as a debtor to the old nurses and servant maids who kept me from my sleep with tales of goblins and apparitions for one of the highest pleasures I enjoy. It is owing to them, I believe, that I read, with a deep sense of delight, narratives which seem to inspire many of my enlightened and reasoning acquaintances with no feelings but that of disgust. Yet I cannot but notice a remarkable scarcity of well-attested incidents of this sort in modern years. The incredulity of the age has caused the supernatural interpositions that were once so frequent to be withdrawn; portents and prodigies are not shown to mockers, and spectres will not walk abroad to be made the subjects of philosophical analysis. Yet some parts of our country are more favoured in this respect than others. The old beldames among the German settlers of

Pennsylvania tell in the greedy ears of their children the marvellous legends of the country from which they had their origin, and to the deep awe and undoubting reverence with which these are related and received, it is probably owing that the day of wonders is not past among that people. Let the European writer gather up the traditions of his country; I will employ a leisure moment in recording one of the fresher, but not less authentic, legends of ours.

Walter Buckel was a German emigrant who came over to Pennsylvania about sixty years ago. He was of gentle blood and used to boast of his relationship to one of the most illustrious houses in his native country. Nor was this an idle boast, for he could trace his pedigree with perfect accuracy through ten generations up to a hunch-backed baron, from whose clandestine amours with a milkmaid sprung the founder of the family of the Buckels. The offspring of these stolen loves did not disgrace his birth, for he inherited all the pride and deformity of his father. So vain was he of his personal resemblance to his noble parent that he assumed the surname of Buckel, from the hump on his shoulders, and transmitted the name and the hump to his posterity. The family continued to wear this badge of their descent down to the time of Walter Buckel, and it was observed that, whenever it waned from its due magnitude in one generation, it was sure to rise with added roundness and prominence in another. As, however, the illustrious extraction of which it was the symbol grew more remote, the respect with which the neighbours regarded it diminished, and finally ceased altogether.

Walter Buckel, determined to form no connexion unworthy of his birth, had married one of his cousins, a fair, fat, flaxen-haired maiden, the purity of whose blood was attested by a hump like his own. Walter was one of those unfortunate men who are perpetually looking for respect, and perpetually disappointed, by meeting with nothing but ridicule: he had hoped to increase his consideration among his acquaintances by this marriage, but their jeers came faster and coarser, and so many rustic jokes were cracked on the well-matched couple that he almost grew weary of life. In his desperation, he sold the patrimonial estate on which he subsisted, and without bidding adieu to any of his neighbours – except the curate, who used sometimes, induced by his benevolence, to come and talk to him about the antiquity and dignity of his family, and carry home a pig, or a turkey, or a shoulder of mutton – he emigrated to America and

18

settled down upon four hundred acres of wild land in the interior of the state of Pennsylvania.

His first care was to provide a shelter for his family. His new neighbours, most of whom were recent settlers like himself, came together the morning after his arrival, and before the sun had gone down, a comfortable log house, with two rooms, was ready for their reception. It was built at the foot of a small hill, in a little natural opening of the forest under a fine flourishing tree of that species commonly called the red oak, which in favourable soils, and in the open country, grows to a great size and with a most beautiful symmetry, its long lusty boughs given off in whorls at regular distances and its smooth bark of a greenish-brown colour looking as if ready to burst with the luxuriance of its juices. The tree was one of the finest of its kind, and stood in the centre of a circle of rich turf about half an acre in extent, the circumference of which was fenced by a natural hedge of undergrowth that prevented you from looking into the darkness and solitude of the surrounding woods. A brook came down the hill and ran noisily through the cheerful spot over the round stones, among which were seen a few straggling roots of the oak, laid bare by the action of the current.

Walter, who was a thin, bilious, bustling man, went to work in the bitterness and vexation of his heart, thinking sometimes of his genealogy, sometimes of the gibes and jeers of acquaintances, and sometimes of his voluntary exile from his native country, until he had cleared the wood from all that part of the farm which lay south of the house and was judged to include about one third of the whole. The rest he suffered to lie in its wild state for the purpose of supplying with fuel the fire that roared all winter in the enormous chimney which occupied a full half of the room called the kitchen. In the mean time, his wife was not idle; before the year came round she presented him with a son, whom he named Caspar, a name which, according to the family tradition, belonged to their ancestor, the hunch-backed baron.

It has been said that marriages between relations not only perpetuate but even aggravate the physical and mental deformities of the parents in their offspring. I cannot tell if this be so; I was never willing to believe it; but whenever I think of the case of Caspar Buckel, I am staggered in my unbelief. As he grew to the age of puberty, it was remarked that he inherited the self-conceit and the uneasy temper of his father, along with the sullen taciturnity of his mother. The corpulency of the one seemed to have fixed itself in his back and belly, while the spare habit of the other was copied in his lean arms, his shrunk loins, and slender legs. The hump on his shoulders was at least two inches higher than that of either of his parents; his forehead was traversed by a thousand crossing wrinkles; his flabby cheeks were seamed with longitudinal furrows and hung down so low on each side of his peaked chin as to give him the appearance of having three chins at once. Two small dim gray eyes peeped from under two white shaggy brows; between them the nose seemed as if absorbed into the face, but re-appeared at a prodigious distance below; and above, a bushy shock of carroty hair stared in all directions.

At an early age, Caspar had an appearance of decrepitude; nobody who looked at him would have thought him younger than his father. Yet this singular being was not without his enjoyments. He had often heard his father speak of his noble extraction, and this idea became to him the occasion of great inward glorying when he looked upon the earth-born plebeians around him. But it was a pleasure of a deeper and more thrilling nature to listen to the marvellous stories doled out by a toothless old female domestic, whom his father brought with him from Germany and who was now too old and infirm to do any thing but smoke her pipe and tell old tales by the fire-side. She told him of fairies who dwell by day in the chambers of the earth and dance by night in solitary groves, of hairy wood-demons and swart goblins of the mine, till his little eyes shone with a fixed glare and his bushy hair looked as if it would disentangle and straighten itself with terror.

Caspar liked neither to work nor to go to school, and his parents were too kind to think of compelling him to do either; his boyish days were consequently passed under the great oak. He whiled away the still summer mornings in chucking pebbles into the brook; in the heat of the day he slept with the dog in the shade, or climbed up to a seat among the thick boughs and leaves and built castles in the air; and when the cooler breezes sprung up in the afternoon, he amused himself with swinging in a long rope, the two ends of which he had tied to two strong neighbouring branches. But if the tree was thus necessary to his amusements, it was also the strengthener of his superstitions. His bed was in a kind of loft just under the eaves of the house; and in the stormy autumnal nights, as he lay thinking over the legends of the old female domestic, he heard with terror the distant roar of the wind wrestling with the trees of the forest. At length he heard it fall with fury upon the oak itself, and then a storm of big rain-drops would be shaken from its boughs and a shower of acorns would rattle down and the long branches would lash the roof till it seemed to him as if all the fiends of the woodland had fastened upon the old log cabin and were going to fly away with it.

Walter Buckel now found himself growing rich, and began to be ashamed of living in a log house at a distance from the highway and under the shade of a great tree. He therefore imitated the example of some of his more prosperous neighbors and built a fine, huge, yellow house, about two hundred rods from his old dwelling, close to the public road, where there was not a bough to keep the summer heat from his door, where he might be continually stifled by the dust raised by loaded wagons and herds of cattle driven to the Philadelphia market, and where the passing traveller might look in at his windows; he then quitted his pleasant little nook, and demolished his log house. An American farmer, whether a native or an emigrant, cuts down a tree with as little ceremony as he cuts down ripe corn, and the oak would have shared the fate of the cabin it sheltered had not Caspar, who intended to swing under its boughs many an idle afternoon yet, pleaded hard in its favour.

The toothless old female domestic who had told Caspar so many goblin stories survived this transplantation of the family but two months. At first Caspar cared very little about her death, but in a few days he felt severely the want of that excitement from her wild tales that had become habitual to him, and he began to feel a sincere grief for her loss. It became irksome to linger about his father's great new house; he grew sick of seeing carts, wagons, and cattle go by the door and ramble away into the dark and still woods, like those in which the scene of most of the legends that had taken such strong hold of his mind were laid. He often remained out till the sun was down, and sometimes till the twilight was down also; and on his return, expecting at every step to be greeted by some gigantic mountain spirit, he peeped into many a dark thicket to see if it did not hide some dwarfish elf of the forest. To give Caspar his due, he did not seek these fearful interviews merely from a love of the wild and the terrible; his anticipations were all of good luck, and he considered the descendant of the hunch-backed German baron as too important and too fortunate a personage to be regarded with any other feeling than good will by these powerful but capricious beings.

At length his father and mother died, both in the same year, and were decently laid in their graves. Caspar had then just come of age, and being left master of his father's estate, which was a very comfortable one, he was unwillingly forced into contact with the world. At first his neighbours, partly from natural civility, partly from a feeling of pity, and partly also, perhaps, from a respect to his wealth, were careful to suppress the mirth occasioned by his deformity and his uncouth aspect and manners; but when they saw the undisguised contempt with which the misshapen creature treated them, they no longer kept any measures in their ridicule. The school boys chalked his figure on the board fences, the young men quizzed him, the girls ran away from him, and it was generally allowed by all who had any dealings with him that it was a capital joke to cheat him.

All these things, however, moved him less than the scorn of the beautiful Adelaide Sippel, a German beauty with an abundance of fair hair, a pair of roguish light blue eyes, and a neck and arms, none of the slenderest it is true, but of a milky whiteness. Caspar, after having fully considered the matter, had concluded to take a help-mate to assist him in the management of his estate and had signified to Adelaide his intention of conferring the honour upon her, but she only laughed in his face. Soon afterwards he made a formal declaration of his passion in a letter, the tenderest that the schoolmaster, under his special direction, could compose; but the only notice she deigned to take of it was to send, by way of answer, an exact likeness of his own figure, carved out of a rickety mangel-wortzel. This rebuff almost stunned poor Caspar, who thenceforward resolved to have as little as possible to do with such an ill-judging and disrespectful world. He resumed his lonely rambles in the woods, and sought relief from his mortification by indulging the wild imaginations that formerly possessed him.

It was in a mild summer evening, when he had been out all day in the forest and had thought more than usual of the scorn of Adelaide and the scoffs of the world, that he found himself under the great oak that once hung over his father's cabin. The twilight had just set in, and the frogs were piping in the marshes. "It is too early to go home yet," thought he, and he sat down on one of the logs of the old building that lay half bedded in the earth with wild flowers nodding over it, and began to mutter over the burden of his discontent. All at once he seemed to hear a sound as of a human voice, blended with a rustling of small boughs and leaves. He looked about him but saw nothing. Again he heard the sound; it seemed to proceed from directly above his head. He looked up and beheld, high in the tree and seemingly projecting from the side of the trunk next to him, a beautiful well-turned throat. The features were moulded in the finest symmetry – youthful, but with that look of youth which we see in Grecian statues and may imagine to belong to beings whose lives are of a longer date than ours, and which seems as if never to pass away. On each side of the face flowed down a profusion of light brown hair that played softly in the wind.

"Caspar, Caspar," said the voice.

"I am here," said Caspar, "what wouldst thou with me?"

"Art thou unhappy, Caspar?"

"Art thou a spirit, and askest that question," replied the youth; "dost thou not see my deformity, and dost thou not know that all the world laugh at me, and Adelaide slights me — and yet thou inquirest if I am unhappy."

"Caspar," returned the voice, "thou did once preserve my existence, and I have not forgotten the benefit. Wash thy hands and face in the little pool in that rivulet, and go thy way home, and thou wilt soon see that I am not ungrateful."

Caspar obeyed the direction, and returned home with a lightened heart. He went to bed, but could not sleep for thinking of the adventure of the evening. When he rose in the morning he fancied his hump was less heavy and unwieldy than the day before, and it is related that an old woman of the neighbourhood, who lived by herself in a little hut, and subsisted principally on charity, and who had come to his house to borrow, or rather beg, a bit of butter and a little tea, could not refrain from saying to him, "La! Mr. Buckel, how well you look this morning." Certain it is, however, that from that day there was a gradual and surprising change in his personal appearance. It seemed as if the superabundant bulk of his spider-like body was travelling into his shrunken arms and legs. The bridge of his nose rose from its humble level, and bent itself into a true Roman curve; his cheeks ascended to their proper place, his wrinkles went away one by one, his eyes and brightened, his brows darkened, and his chestnut hair curled the edge of a fine forehead. In a twelvemonth the transformation was complete. His shoulders had become straight, his limbs well-proportioned, and his waist, with a little reduction, would have satisfied any fashionable coxcomb that struts Broadway in a corset. His height also had astonishingly increased. Formerly he wanted just an inch of five feet, and now he wanted but an inch of six. (I myself have seen the notch where he was measured, in one of the rooms of an old house then occupied as a tavern, and I carefully ascertained its distance from the floor by means of a three-foot rattan, which I commonly carry about with me.) Caspar had formerly a great aversion to looking-glasses, but now he consulted his mirror several times a day, and whenever he approached it, he could not help bowing to the graceful stranger whom he saw there.

Caspar's neighbours would not have recognised him after this change, had he not almost from the first forgotten his misanthropy in the delight it gave him. As soon as ever he became satisfied that it was real and progressive, he almost went mad with joy, and could not forbear hugging every body he met. The elderly ladies all declared that Mr. Buckel had a strange way with him, and the young ran shrieking from these vehement demonstrations of his good will. He mingled in the rustic sports of the young men at trainings, elections, and other holidays, and though a little awkward at first, he soon became a famous leaper and wrestler, and learned to throw a ball and pitch a quoit with as much dexterity as the best of them. Every body began to take a liking to a young man so handsome, good-humoured, and rich; the farmers who had daughters told him it was high time to think of getting married; the matrons expatiated in his presence on the good temper and industry of their girls; and, the buxom fair-haired German maidens never laughed so loud as when they thought him within hearing. Caspar, however, had not forgotten his first love; and when he again proposed himself in softer phrase to Adelaide Sippel, the blushes came over her fair temples and white neck, but she did not again reject him. They were married amid such fiddling and dancing, such piles of cakes and floods of whiskey, and such a tumult and tempest of rustic rejoicings, as had never before been known in the settlement.

A man of moderate fortune, who has not acquired habits of industry and attentive management of his estate, should content himself with living idly and easily; he cannot afford to live splendidly. Caspar was not aware of the truth of this maxim: he knew that he was richer than his neighbours; but he had never calculated what expenses he could incur without lessening his estate. He was resolved that his smiling wife should wear the finest clothes, and ride to church in the finest German wagon, drawn by the finest horses in the place. He loved society, the more, probably, for having been excluded from it in his youth; and sat long and late at the taverns with merry, jesting, catch-singing, roaring blades, from the old countries. He attended all the horse-races he could hear of, at which he betted deeply, and was taken in by the knowing ones. He was fond of hunting, and bought a rifle and a couple of hounds, and went into the woods in pursuit of game, day after day, during which the concerns of his farm took care of themselves. By such judicious methods he contrived to get himself pretty deeply in debt; he was dunned; he borrowed money of one man to pay another; at length a testy creditor sued him; his other creditors followed the example, and the unfortunate man saw all the dogs of the law let loose on him at once. He had not borne his prosperity calmly, and it could not therefore be expected that he should show himself a stoic under misfortune. He grew moody and testy, and a kind of instinct drove him again to ramble in the woods without either his rifle or his dogs, as was his wont in the days of his youth and his deformity.

One evening, as he was returning, a little after sunset, he chanced to pass slowly under the boughs of the great oak. He was thinking that on the whole he had little reason to thank the kindness of his supernatural friend. "She has made me a handsome fellow," thought he, "but what of that? If I had not been handsome, I should not have run into expenses that have made me poor. A man may as well be miserable from deformity as from poverty." At that very moment, a sweet, low voice from the boughs of the tree, the well-remembered voice that three years before he had heard at nightfall on that very spot, articulated his name. He looked up, and saw the same calm features of unearthly loveliness and youth, with a smile playing about the beautiful mouth.

"I know thy thoughts, Caspar," said the apparition, "and thy misfortunes, and it shall not be my fault if thou art not happy. Dig on the north side of the trunk of this tree, just under the extremity of that long branch which points towards the ground, and there thou wilt find what, if thou art reasonable, will suffice thy wishes. Replace the earth carefully."

Caspar was of too impatient a temperament to defer for a moment the enjoyment of his good fortune. He went immediately for a spade. On his return he again looked up to the place where he had beheld the vision, but he saw only the brown bark of the tree visible in a strong gleam of twilight and the neighbouring boughs and foliage moving and murmuring in the night-wind that was just beginning to rise. He turned up the earth at the spot which had been pointed out to him and took out a large jar of money, and then shovelled back the mould and pressed the turf into its place.

On examining the coins in the jar, they proved to be Spanish and Portuguese gold pieces of a pretty ancient date, all of them at least half a century old, some still older. Among the many persons from whom I have gathered the particulars of the tradition I am recording, I have not met with one who could satisfactorily explain the circumstance of the money being found in that place. It could not be the coinage of the apparition, for it was not to be supposed that she was the proprietor of a mint, and if she were, why should the coins be so old? As to the suggestion that it was buried there by Captain Kidd, the pirate, I do not think it worthy of notice, for I hold it certain that he concealed the money elsewhere, though it is not for my interest at present to reveal the particular spot. Besides, what should the Captain be doing in the woods of Pennsylvania, more than a hundred miles from the sea coast?

Caspar, however, cared not when the pieces were coined, nor by whom; he was not accustomed to speculate upon his good fortune, but to enjoy it. He held that, if there is any pleasure in the mere exercise of speculation, there is as much opportunity for it afforded by bad luck as by good, and he chose not to confound things which appeared to him so completely different. After paying off all his creditors, he gave a grand entertainment at his house, to which all his neighbours for several miles round were invited, and among the rest, the testy creditor who had set the example of bringing a process against him. This fellow got as drunk as a lord on the whiskey of the man whom, a few weeks ago, he would have ruined, and hugged his generous entertainer with tears in his eyes. As he was altogether too far gone to find his own way home, Caspar ordered out his great Pennsylvania wagon, drawn by two spirited horses and driven by a shining-faced black fellow; the maudlin hero was lifted into the hinder seat and, nodding majestically as he went, was whirled home in that sublime condition.

It took less than half the gold of which Caspar became possessed in this extraordinary way to satisfy all his debts; and the sight of the remainder, blinking and smiling in the capacious jar, was not likely to suggest to his mind any very strong motives for leaving off his habits of idleness and expense. His only study seemed how to get rid of his money, and in this laudable design fortune seemed willing to assist him.

About this time, Nicholas Vadokin, the schoolmaster who had penned the unfortunate epistle of Caspar to Adelaide, having saved a little money by his vocation, set up shop in the neighbourhood, which he furnished from Philadelphia with dry goods and groceries, and all that miscellaneous collection of merchandise to be found in the store of a country trader. Nicholas was a cunning Hanoverian, with a shrewd hazel eye and brassy complexion. He was a prompt, ready-spoken man who could turn his hand to anything, and having come to the United States to make his fortune, he would have thought himself convicted of want of perseverance and enterprise had he suffered himself to be diverted from his object by any trifling scruples of conscience. For four years he had flogged the children of the place for a livelihood, and he now resolved to try whether any thing could be made by fawning on their parents.

To Mr. Buckel, as the richest man in the neighbourhood, he was particularly attentive and obsequious. He always offered him a glass of bad wine whenever he came to his shop; talked to him of his wealth, his horses, his wagon, and his dogs; listened with profound interest to long stories of his hunting exploits; and, though he scorned to flatter a man to his face, hinted that he ought to be a candidate for the Pennsylvania House of Representatives. He was so conscientious as to let him have all the goods for which he had occasion, at first cost; and whenever one of his loaded wagons arrived from Philadelphia, he never failed to take his patron aside and tell him of such and such articles which he had purchased expressly on his account – all which the good natured Caspar was always sure to take off his hands.

Caspar soon came to be a daily frequenter of the shop, and he never called without making a purchase, for the ingenious Nicholas had always a reason for his taking almost every article he had. One thing was necessary, another convenient; one was fashionable, another indispensable to a man of his fortune and character; this was wonderfully cheap, and that wonderfully rare; and how could he refuse to be guided by the advice of his excellent and disinterested friend, who was only so attentive to his convenience, and who let him have every thing at cost. In a short time, Caspar found the bottom of his jar; his money was gone, but his habits of expense were not easily shaken off, and being pressed for cash, he applied to his friend Nicholas. Nicholas showed himself truly his friend, for he counted out to him the sum he wanted with many smiles and protestations of delight at being able to do him a service, and took a mortgage of his estate.

The story of the mortgage soon took air, and immediately afterwards, Caspar, finding himself without money, found himself without credit also. In his embarrassment he again went to Nicholas for assistance, but his disinterested friend unfortunately had not the means of helping him further. A day or two after, he called at the shop for the purpose of beginning a new score, but Nicholas informed him, with a very solemn look, that although there was no man in the world whom he would go farther to serve than his very good friend Mr. Buckel, yet his duty to his family obliged him to give credit to those only whose circumstances justified the expectation that they would pay; he added, however, that he should be exceedingly happy to supply him with any the thing he wanted – for ready cash. Caspar stood for a moment as if thunderstruck, and the next, his rage prevailing over his astonishment, he levelled a blow at the Hanoverian, which would infallibly have knocked him down had he not wisely avoided it by ducking under the counter.

Caspar returned home to digest his mortification as he could, and the blue devils followed him and fastened upon him. He felt the thirst of Tantalus, a continual craving for expense with no means of satisfying it; it seemed to him as if all the rest of the world were rolling in wealth, buying and selling, driving fine horses, and feasting each other like princes, while he, poor fellow, had not a beggarly doit to spend. He grew meagre and hollow-eyed, and walked about with his hands in his pockets, looking vacantly at the geese nipping the grass before his door and the hens wallowing in the sand of the road and jerking it over their backs with their wings. At last he thought of the vision he had seen in the oak. "I will see her again," thought he; "who knows but she may relieve me a second time?"

He set off for the tree that very evening. It was an October night, and he lingered under it till the grass grew silvery with the frost, but she did not appear. The next evening he repaired to the same spot, and looked with a still more intense anxiety for her appearance, but he saw only the boughs struggling with the wind, and the dropping leaves. The third evening he was more successful; she was there, but her look was sad and reproachful. At times the gusts that swept by would rudely toss her hair above her forehead and against the trunk of the tree, and then, as they subsided, it would fall down again on each side of her fine countenance.

"I had hoped, Caspar," said the vision, with a mournful voice that seemed like an articulate sigh, "to have reserved for some more pressing need of thine, the last favour that is in my power to bestow upon thee. I have observed thy nightly visits to my shade; I know thy motive; I know that thou wilt be unhappy if my bounty is withheld; and I cannot forget that thou wast born under my boughs, and that thy intercession has preserved me from the axe. Between the two roots that diverge eastward from my trunk, thou wilt find a portion of what the children of men value more than all the other gifts of heaven. Replace the turf over my roots, and remember that this is the last of my benefits."

Caspar dug eagerly in the spot, for he had been provident enough to bring his spade with him, and joyfully carried home a jar of money of the same figure and capacity with the former.

It were long to tell by what methods Caspar contrived to get rid of the second donation of the lady of the oak. To do him justice, he set out with the firmest resolutions of frugality and economy, and actually kept the gold by him three days without touching a moidore. But when he came to raise the mortgage of his friend Nicholas and to satisfy some other debts that were a little troublesome, the habit of paying out money, being once re-admitted, obstinately kept possession. His old propensity to extravagance returned upon him with a violence that swept all his resolutions away. It is true that, when he saw his finances nearly exhausted, he made some praiseworthy attempts to repair them. It is whispered that he gambled a little with certain smooth-spoken, well-dressed emigrants from the country of his fathers, and it is very certain that he bought lottery tickets, drew blanks, bought others, and had the satisfaction of drawing an additional number of blanks.

(I have often thought that it was a thousand pities that Caspar did not live in these blessed times, and in this well-governed state of New-York, where the law refuses to license these pernicious institutions and prohibits the sale of the tickets of all such as are established in other states. It is true that the ghosts of old lotteries chartered long ago are raised and meet you at every turn; that lottery offices are multiplied without number and almost every tenth door holds out an invitation to try your luck; that the worthy and conscientious people who live by decoying others into this legalized gambling swarm all over our city, each provided with his poet who indites his advertisement in the sweetest of rhymes – a circumstance conveying this most beautiful moral, little attended to, I fear, by the eager adventurer who buys the ticket: that he is paying his money for a song. I say it is a pity that Caspar had not lived in these blessed times, and in this blessed state, for although he might not have been prevented from engaging as deeply as he pleased in these beneficial speculations, he could not but have admired the wise and effectual measures taken to suppress them.)

Suffice it to say that Caspar saw himself growing poor, and as he had no taste for the pleasures of such a condition, he determined to make a desperate effort to shoot beyond the circle of the whirlpool that threatened to carry him down. He was well satisfied that he should get nothing by applying to the lady of the oak, but he could not help suspecting that there was more gold under her boughs. "The two jars," said he to himself, "were concealed in different places, both near the same tree, which served as a kind of mark by which to find them again; and who knows how many more are lying scattered about the same spot? I will search at least; if there is any gold there, it is a pity it should lie useless in the earth, and if there is not, I shall lose nothing."

The very next morning, he loaded his black servant and another labourer with pick-axes, spades, and hoes and sent them to dig about and under the tree with instructions to bring him immediately whatever curious or remarkable thing they might find there. He was ashamed to go to the spot himself, for he felt that he had abused the gifts of his benefactress and was now repaying her kindness with ingratitude. In the evening the labourers returned, having found nothing but a few fragments of a glass bottle, and complained that the water from the rivulet that ran near the tree soaked through the earth and filled the excavations they were making. Caspar ordered them to dam it up a few rods nearer its source and turn it into a new channel.

It was July, and a severe drought prevailed all over the country. The pastures looked red and sun-burnt; the hardy house-plantain before Caspar's door rolled up its leaves like a segar; the birds were silent; the cattle drooped; nothing was cheerful and lively but the grasshoppers, who always swarm thickest and chirp merriest in dry seasons, and the poultry, who chased and caught them by the sides of the road. The poor oak, almost undermined and deprived of the moisture of its rivulet, was the saddest looking tree in the whole country: its leaves grew yellow and rusty and dropped off one by one, and it is said that once, when Caspar was looking towards it from one of the back windows of his house, just as the twilight set in, he fancied he saw again that fair, sad face among the boughs, and a white shadowy arm, beckoning him to approach. But he hardened his heart and turned away from the sight, and the next morning his labourers went on with their task.

One afternoon on a day of uncommon heat, as Caspar was engaged at a tavern in bargaining for a pair of horses with a jockey who had come twenty miles on purpose to cheat him, the labourers were driven from their work by a furious tempest. The woods roared and bent in the violent wind and the heavy rain, and a thousand new streams were at once formed which ran winding all over the open country like so many serpents. The brook that formerly ran by the oak broke over the barrier which diverted it from its course, and coming down the hill with a vast body of water, ploughed for itself a new channel through the excavations of Caspar's workmen and completed the undermining of the tree. At last a strong gust took it by the top and laid it on its side, with its long roots sticking up in the air. Caspar's family beheld its fall from the windows.

Two hours afterwards there was a clear sky and a bright sun shining on the glistening earth, and the wet roofs of Caspar's building were smoking in the warm rays. A little pot-bellied man, with an enormous hump on his shoulders, small, thin legs and arms, and hideous features, dressed in a suit of clothes that seemed to have been made for a man much taller and straighter than himself, the collar of his coat standing erect about a foot from his neck, entered the house and began to issue his commands to the servants with an air of authority. At first they only smiled at his conduct, supposing him to be insane, and offered him some broken victuals and a cup of cider. At this he flew into a great rage and swore he was Caspar Buckel himself, the master of the house. Finding that he grew troublesome, they sent for Mrs. Buckel, who was beginning to talk soothingly to him with a view of persuading him to leave the house, but what was her astonishment when the misshapen being insisted that he was her husband. Shocked and frightened at his proof of his madness, she ordered the labourer and the black fellow to put him out of the house, which they effected with some difficulty while he struggled, scratched, bit, foamed at the mouth, and declared, with a thousand oaths, that he was Caspar Buckel, their master. When they had got him out of the door and had disengaged themselves from him, the black gave him a stroke with the long horsewhip that he used in driving his master's horses, and calling out the dogs, set them upon him. The deformed creature scampered before them into a neighbouring wood, and then the negro called them off.

Caspar did not return that night, and the next morning Mrs. Buckel sent to the tavern to inquire for him, but without learning any thing satisfactory concerning him. The landlord recollected he was there about the middle of the tempest, but could not say when he left the house; he mentioned, also, that after the sky began to clear, a little hunch-backed man had asked at his bar for a glass of whiskey, and having paid for it, immediately went away. As for the jockey, he had gone off with his horses just before the storm began, having been unable to drive such a bargain with Mr. Buckel as he wished.

Mrs. Buckel continued her searches and inquiries for six weary months, after which she concluded that her husband was dead, and remained disconsolate for six months longer. At the end of this period she gave her hand to a young fellow from New England, who had fallen in love with her plump, round face, and well stocked farm.

As for Caspar, he was never heard of again; but the old people say that the woods north of his widow's house are haunted at twilight by the figure of a hunch-backed little man, skipping over the fallen trees and running into gloomy thickets as soon as your eye falls on him, as if to avoid the sight of man.

A Border Tradition

IN TRAVELLING through the western part of New England, not long since, I stopped for a few days at one of the beautiful villages of that region. It was situated on the edge of some fine rich meadows, lying about one of the prettiest little rivers in the world. While there, I went one morning to the top of a little round hill which commanded a view of the surrounding country. I saw the white houses under the shade of the old elms, the neat painted fences before them, and the border of bright green turf on either side of the road, which the inhabitants kept as clean as the grass plots of their gardens. I saw the river, winding away to the south between leaning trees and thick shrubs and vines; the hills, rising gently to the west of the village, covered with orchards and woods and openings of pasture ground; the rich level meadows to the east; and beyond them, at no great distance, the craggy mountains rising almost perpendicularly, as if placed there to heighten, by their rugged aspect, the soft beauty of the scene below them. If the view was striking in itself, it was rendered still more so by circumstances of life and splendor belonging to the weather, the hour, and the season. The wide circle of verdure in the midst of which I stood was loaded and almost crushed by one of those profuse dews which fall in our climate of a clear summer night, and glittered under a bright sun and a sky of transparent blue. The trees about me were noisy with birds, the bob-o'lincoln rose singing from the grass to sink in the grass again when his strain was ended, and the cat-bird squalled in the thicket in spite of the boy who was trying to stone it out. Then there was the whistle of the quail, the resounding voice of the hang-bird, the mysterous note of the post-driver, and the chatter of swallows darting to and fro. As a sort of accompaniment to this natural music, there was heard at times the deep and tremulous sound of the river breaking over a mill-dam at some distance.

There is an end of gazing at the finest sights, and of listening to the most agreeable sounds. I had turned to go down the hill, when I observed a respectable looking old man sitting near me on the edge of a rock that projected a little way out of the ground. At the very first glance I set him down for one of the ancient yeomanry of our country, for his sturdy frame and large limbs had evidently been rendered sturdier and larger by labor and hardship, and old age had only taken away the appearance of agility without impairing his natural air of strength. I am accustomed to look with a feeling of gratitude, as well as respect, on these remnants of a hardy and useful generation. I see in them the men who have hewed down the forests and tamed the soil of the fair country we inhabit, who built the roads we travel over mountains and across morasses, and who planted the hill sides with orchards, of which we idly gather the fruit. From the attention with which the old man was looking at the surrounding prospect, I judged that he was come to the hill on the same errand with myself, and on entering into conversation with him, I found that I was not mistaken.

He had lived in the village when a boy; he had been absent from it nearly sixty years, and now, having occasion to pass through it on a journey from a distant part of the country, he was trying to recollect its features from the little eminence by which it was overlooked. "I can hardly," said he, "satisfy myself that this is the place in which I passed my boyish days. It is true, that the river is still yonder, and this is the hill where I played when a child, and those mountains, with their rocks and woods, look to me as they did then. That small peak lies still in the lap of the larger and loftier ridge that stretches like a semicircle around it. There are the same smooth meadows to the east, and the same fine ascent to the west of the village. But the old dwellings have been pulled down, and new ones built in their stead; the trees under which I sat in my childhood have decayed or been cut down, and others have been planted; the very roads have changed their places; and the rivulets that turned my little machinery are dried up. Do you see," said he, pointing with his staff, "that part of the meadow that runs up like a little creek or bay between the spurs of the upland and comes close to the highway? A brook formerly came down to that spot, and lost itself in the marshy soil, but its bed, as you see, is now dry and only serves as a channel to carry of the superabundance of the rains. That part of the meadow is now covered with thick and tall grass, but I well remember when it was overgrown with bushes and water-flags, among which many old decaying trunks of trees served as a kind of causeys over a quagmire that otherwise would have been impassable. It was a spot of evil report in the village, for it was said that lights had been seen at night moving among the thickets, and strange noises had been heard from the ground – gurgling and half-smothered sounds, as of a living creature strangled in the midst of sods and water. It was said, also, that glimpses of something white had been seen gliding among the bushes, and that often the rank vegetation had been observed to be fearfully agitated, as if the earth shuddered at the spot where innocent blood had been shed. Some fearful deed, it was said, had doubtless been done there. It was thought by some that a child had been strangled and thrown into the quagmire by its unnatural mother, and by others that a traveller had been murdered there for the sake of his money. Nobody cared, after dark, to travel the road, which formerly wound about the base of this hill and thus kept longer beside the edge of the fen than it does now. I remember being drawn once or twice by curiosity to visit the place in company with another lad of my age. We stole in silence along the old logs, speaking to each other in whispers, and our hair stood on end at the sight of the white bones lying about. They were the bones of cattle who had sunk into the mire and could not be dragged out or had perished before they were found. There is a story about that spot," continued the old man, "which it may be worth your while to hear, and if you will please to be seated on this rock, I will tell it."

There was something in the old man's conversation which denoted a degree of intelligence and education superior to what I expected from his appearance. I was curious to know what sort of story would follow such an introduction; I sat down, therefore, by his side, on the edge of the rock, and he went on as follows.

"It is a story that I heard from my grandmother, a good old Dutch lady belonging to a family of the first settlers of the place. The Dutch from the North River, and the Yankees from the Connecticut, came into the valley about the same time and settled upon these rich meadows. Which were the first comers, I am unable to tell; I have heard different accounts of the matter, but the traditions of the Dutch families give the priority to their own ancestors, and I am inclined to think them in the right, for, although it was not uncommon in those days for the restless Yankee to settle in a neighbourhood of Dutchmen, yet it was a rare thing for the quiet Hollander voluntarily to plant himself in the midst of a bustling Yankee settlement. However this may be, it is certain that, about ninety years ago, a little neighbourhood had been formed of the descendants of both the emigrants from Holland and those from England. At first, the different races looked sourly upon each other, but the daily sight of each other's faces and the need of each other's kindness and assistance soon brought them to live upon friendly terms. The Dutchman learned to salute his neighbour in bad English, and the Yankee began to make advances towards driving a bargain in worse Dutch.

"Jacob, or, as he was commonly called, Yok Suydam, was one of these early Dutch planters, and Jedidiah Williams, his neighbour, one of the first Yankees who sat down on the banks of this river. Williams was a man of a hard countenance and severe manners who had been a deacon of the church in the parish he had left, and who did not, as I have known some people do, forget his religion when it ceased to be of any service to him in his worldly concerns. He was as grave in his demeanor as guarded in his speech, and as constant in his devotions as ever, notwithstanding that these qualities in his character were less prized in his new situation than they had been in Connecticut. The place had as yet no minister, but Williams contrived to collect every Sunday a few of the neighbours at his house to perform the weekly worship. On a still summer morning you might hear him doling out a portion of the Scriptures, or reading a sermon of some godly divine of the day, in a sort of nasal recitation which could be distinguished, swelling over the noises of his pigs and poultry at the distance of a quarter of a mile from his dwelling.

"Honest Yok read his Bible too, but he read it in Dutch, and excused himself from attending the meetings at Williams's house on account of his ignorance of the language in which the exercises were held. Instead, however, of confining himself to the house during the whole Sunday like Williams, he would sometimes stray out into his fields to look at his cattle and his crops, and was known once or twice to lie down on the grass under a tree in the corner of one of his inclosures, where the rustling of his Indian corn and the hum of the bees among the pumpkin blossoms would put him to sleep. The rest of the day, when the weather was fine, he passed in smoking his pipe under a rude kind of piazza in front of his house, looking out over the rich meadows which he had lately cleared of their wood, or listening to a chapter of the New Testament read to him by one of his daughters. He was also less guarded in his language than suited the precise notions of Williams; the words 'duyvel' or 'donner,' or some such unnecessary exclamation, would often slip out of his mouth in the haste of conversation. But there was another practice of Yok's which was still less to the taste of his neighbour. As was the case with most of the Dutch planters at that time, his house swarmed with negro domestics, and among the merry, sleek-faced blacks that jabbered Dutch and ate sour crout in his kitchen, there was one who could play tolerably on the fiddle. Yok did not suffer this talent to lie useless. On every New Year's eve – and not on that alone but on many a long and bright winter evening that followed it – when the snow looked whiter than ever in the moonlight and you could see the little wedges of frost floating and glistening in the air – the immense fireplace in the long kitchen was piled with dry hickory, the negro Orpheus was mounted on a high bench, and the brawny youths and ruddy girls of the place danced to the music till the cocks crew. Yok's own daughters, the prettiest maidens that ever ran in the woods of a new settlement, were allowed to acquit themselves exceedingly well on these occasions; but the performances of Yok himself extorted universal admiration. Old as he was – and he did not lack many winters of sixty – whenever he came on the floor, which was generally just before the breaking up of the revel, the youngest and most active of his guests acknowledged themselves outdone. He executed the double shuffle with incredible dexterity, drummed with his heels on the floor till you would have thought the drumming an accompaniment to the fiddle, and threw the joints of his limbs into the most gracefully acute angles that can be imagined.

"Jedidiah, of course, did not suffer these irregularities of his neighbour to pass unrebuked, and Yok always took his admonitions kindly enough, although without much disposition to profit by them. He invariably apologized by saying that he was a Dutchman, that he followed the customs of his countrymen and the practices of his fathers before him, and that it did not become the like of him to presume to be wiser or better than his ancestors, who were honest men and who, he believed, had gone to heaven. The appearance of respect, however, with which he received these reproofs went far to reconcile Jedidiah to his practical neglect of them, and a kind of friendship at length grew up between the two settlers and their families. Yok's pretty daughters came constantly to attend Williams's meetings, and Williams's son was a frequent and welcome visiter at the house of the hearty and hospitable Dutchman.

"Yok's family, with the exception of the negro domestics I have mentioned, consisted only of himself and his two daughters. Mary, the elder, was somewhat tall, with a delicate shape and a peaceful, innocent look. The climate, and three generations of American descent, had completely done away in her personal appearance with all traces of her Dutch extraction, except the fair hair and the light blue eye. She was a sincere, single-hearted creature, whom the experience of eighteen years had not taught that there was such a thing as treachery in the world. It was no difficult matter to move her either to smiles or to tears, and had she lived in this novel-reading age, she would have been inevitably spoiled. As it was, the poor girl had no book but the Bible, of which there were in Yok's family several copies in the old Dutch letter, and she was forced to content herself with weeping over the fortunes of Ruth and the resurrection of Lazarus.

"Geshie, her sister, little more than a year younger, had an appearance of firmer and more sanguine health than Mary, and all that excess of animal spirits and love of mirth with which youth and high health are generally accompanied. She was ruddier, shorter in stature, and fuller in her proportions than the elder sister, and under the shade of her thick brown hair, her bright eye shone out with a look so arch and full of mischief that, like the sun in June, it was not a thing to look long upon. The two sisters, though so little alike, were both as kind and good as the day is long, and were acknowledged to be the handsomest girls in the settlement. People, however, were divided in opinion as to which was the handsomer and more agreeable of the two. The greater number gave the preference to the blooming and sprightly Geshie, but James Williams, the son of Jedidiah, thought differently.

"Young Williams, who had come with his father to the new settlement, was a frank, high-spirited, giddy young fellow. He had given some proofs of forwardness in early youth, and his father had set his heart upon seeing him one of the burning and shining lights of the church, emulating in the pulpit the eloquence of Solomon Stoddard and the sound doctrine of Jonathan Edwards. He had sent him to Yale College to furnish his mind with the necessary worldly learning, trusting to his own prayers and to Providence for the piety that was to fit him for the work of the ministry. But his expectations were wretchedly disappointed, for the young man proved refractory under the discipline of a college and made so good a use of his opportunities of rebellion that in less than a year he was expelled. He came home to read Horace and shoot squirrels, and bear a part in the psalms sung at the meetings for religious worship held at his father's. He could not make up his mind to go back to the labors of husbandry, and yet was uncertain to what other course of life to betake himself.

"Young men who have nothing else to do are apt to amuse themselves with making love. Time hung heavy on the hands of James Williams in the new and thinly inhabited settlement. He wandered the old woods that stretched away on all sides till he was weary; he found them altogether too gloomy and too silent for his taste, and when their echoes were awakened by the report of his own fowling-piece, by the cawing of the crow, or the shriek of the hawk, he could not help thinking that these sounds would interest him more if they conveyed a human meaning. He grew tired of reading Horace in a place where nobody cared for his Latin. At length he would shut his book and lay his gun on the two wooden hooks in his father's kitchen, and walk down to the house of honest Yok Suydam, where the good Dutchman greeted him with a cordial grasp of the hand, and his daughters with smiles.

"James was soon master of Dutch enough to tell the story of his college pranks, which usually called a hearty laugh from the old gentleman, a sentence or two of kind expostulation from the elder daughter, and a torrent of good humored raillery from the younger. In return for the proficiency which the society of the family enabled him to make in their language, James offered to teach the young ladies English, and the elder readily undertook to be his pupil. As for Geshie, she had no ambition that way; it was, she said, a silken, glozing tongue – the tongue of pedlars and sharpers, fit only for those who wished to defraud and deceive; she was contented, for her part, with the plain household speech in which she had been brought up, the language of honesty and sincerity. James began to read the New Testament along with Mary, it being the only book with which she was familiar. After getting through with a few chapters, it was exchanged for a volume of Richardson's *Pamela*, which had then just made its appearance. James had contrived to possess himself of a copy of this work while at New Haven, and concealed it as carefully from the eyes of his father as the quail hides her nest from the schoolboy. He knew that if it should be discovered, the consequences could be no less than the great wrath of his father towards so graceless a son, and that the offending book would be burnt with fire.

"Geshie soon had occasion to pay her sister a multitude of sly compliments on her proficiency in English. She had never known, she said, a tutor so assiduous, nor a pupil so teachable. It was not, indeed, extraordinary that James should fancy himself in love with the prettiest girl in the settlement, nor was it more so that she should be seriously in love with him. The young couple soon understood each other, and Geshie also, although not the confidant of her sister, understood enough of the matter to anticipate a merry wedding and gay wedding-dresses.

"The language of Holland has been called barbarous and harsh; in the mouth of Mary, James thought it infinitely more musical than the Latin, and the whispers of affection in her imperfect English seemed to give new graces to his native tongue. Their studies, however, were often interrupted by the frolics of Geshie. Sometimes the volume of *Pamela* was missing for several days, and James was obliged to defer his lessons till it could be found; sometimes the master and scholar, on attempting to rise, found themselves fastened to their chairs, and their chairs fastened together. James was somewhat of a superstitious turn; he had read Mather's *Magnalia*, a copy of which by some accident belonged to his father, and had imbibed a deep respect for spirits and goblins. Geshie was not slow in discovering this weakness in his character, nor in making it contribute to her amusement. She had an abundance of stories of supernatural terrors, and always took care to relate them to James in the evening. On a moonlight night she would tell him of an apparition seen by moonlight, and on a cloudy evening, of a ghost that walked when you could not see your hand. She would then enjoy his evident alarm as it grew late, and as he looked alternately at his hat and the window. In the mean time, Geshie, notwithstanding her pretended contempt for the English tongue, was making a progress in learning it equal at least to that of her sister. In truth, she was sufficiently indifferent as long as Mary was occupied with the English Testament, but when the first volume of *Pamela* was brought to the house, her curiosity to know its contents prevailed over every other consideration. After that she lost nothing of the lessons James gave her sister; she treasured up in her memory every English phrase she heard uttered; she read *Pamela* by stealth; and her talent for mimicry soon gave her a tolerable command of the English accent.

"A year had now passed since James and Mary had become acquainted with each other. The settlement was growing every day more populous, and James had no difficulty of finding companions to cheat him of the tedious hours. There were also among the daughters of the new comers some who might be thought nearly as handsome and agreeable as Mary herself. His affection for her, by a perversity not uncommon in young men who are loved better than they deserve, began gradually to cool; his visits to her father's house became less and less frequent; the poor girl's English studies were wofully neglected, and finally discontinued altogether. Once she ventured to speak to him of his altered behaviour, but he gave her an indirect and trifling answer, and, after that she spoke of it no more. But she felt it not the less deeply; her heart bled in silence and in secret; she became melancholy, was often found weeping by herself, and seemed going into a deep decline.

"The good old Suydam, who suspected nothing of the true cause of his daughter's malady, after prescribing all the household remedies he could think of, called in the doctor, notwithstanding she protested vehemently against it. The doctor came with his saddlebags on his arm – a smock-faced young man just settled in the place who thought himself happy if his prescriptions did not aggravate the disorder. He examined the patient and seemed to hesitate about her complaint, but as he was called, he knew his duty too well not to prescribe; he therefore ordered her a little valerian, and took his leave. Geshie, who understood her sister's disorder better than the physician, and knew that it was not to be healed by medicine, threw the drug out of the window as soon as he was gone and saved her the disgust of swallowing it.

"This kind-hearted girl now undertook herself to be her sister's physician. She sung to her all the old songs she remembered, both sad and merry, composed by the mellifluous poets of Holland long ago and handed down in the American settlements from mother to daughter for a hundred years at least. She drew her forth to ramble in the meadows and to pierce the great forest around them in various directions along dark and cool paths leading to the sunny, cultivated openings lately made in its bosom. She collected for her entertainment all the gossip of her neighbourhood, mimicked the accent of the Yankees, danced, capered, and played a thousand monkey tricks to divert her. All her efforts were ineffectual to restore health and spirits to her sister, and she saw, with a sorrow almost increased to despair, that this was only to be hoped for from the return of her lover's affections.

"It was now October. The forests around this valley, where there was then little else but forest, had put on their colors of yellow, orange, and crimson and looked yet brighter in the golden sunshine of the season that lay upon them. The ripe apples were dropping from the young apple-trees by the cottages of the settlers; the chestnut, the oak, and the butternut were beginning to cast their fruit; squirrels were chirping and barking on the branches of the walnut; rabbits were scudding over the bright leaves that lay scattered below; and the heavy whirr of the partridge, as he rose from the ground, told how well he had been pampered by the abundance of the season. James Williams could not resist the temptation of such fine weather and so much game. He was absent whole days in the depths of the woods; in the morning you might hear the report of his fowling-piece in the edge of the forest, in the neighbourhood of his father's; at noon its echoes would be sent faintly from the cliffs of that long rocky ridge which bounds the valley to the east.

"One morning James passed by the house of Mary's father with his fowling-piece. He did not dare to raise his head as he went, nor to cast a look at the windows of the house, lest he should see the face of her with whose affections he had so unfeelingly trifled. He pretended to be very busy about the lock of his gun until he had fairly passed the dwelling, when he quickened his pace and was soon out of sight. Geshie observed him as he went, and determined to watch his return.

"He did not return until after sunset. It was a clear night, except some scattered banks of mist from the river; the moon was shining brightly, and Geshie discerned at some distance the well known gait of James and the glitter of his fowling-piece. She saw that this was the moment for the execution of a plan which she had formed in the hope that it might be of some advantage to her sister, but which she had communicated to no one. A few minutes afterwards a figure in white was seen stealing down from the house between some high banks so as not to be observed by James, towards the swamp of which I have already spoken, and which is now changed into that beautiful meadow.

"It was necessary for James, after passing Suydam's house, to follow the road for some distance along the edge of that swamp. The spot had already begun to have a bad name; the body of an Indian infant had been found in some bushes by the edge, and a drunken German carpenter who had straggled into the settlement had lost the road and perished there in a flood which covered the meadows, the swamp, and the road itself with the waters of the river. Among the tales of ghosts and hobgoblins with which Geshie had formerly entertained James were one or two stories of strange sights seen about this swamp – to which, I suspect, she maliciously added some embellishments of her own.

"James's heart did not beat with its usual calmness as he approached the swamp. But his timidity rose to fear, and his fear to agony, and his whole frame shook, and a cold sweat broke out at every pore as he saw a figure in white come out from the bushes and move slowly towards him. He stood rooted to the ground without the power to fly, but his hands instinctively fumbled with his fowling-piece, as though he would have used it against the object of his fears. The spectre raised its arm with a menacing gesture, and the piece fell from his hands to the ground. As the apparition drew nigh, he could perceive that it was wrapped in a linen sheet, and the white feet that showed themselves under the lower edge left him no doubt that it was the tenant of a coffin who stood before him. He essayed to speak, but his throat seemed filled with ashes; nor was it necessary, for the arm of the spectre was again raised; he saw its eye glistening under the folds of the shroud; he saw its lips move; the words came forth in clear and solemn accents; he swooned, and fell to the ground.

"The same evening, as Yok was quietly smoking his pipe by the fireside and watching the changes in the embers, Geshie entered the room, quite out of breath, with an expression of unusual agitation and anxiety on her countenance. She seated herself, and after a moment's silence, 'I have been thinking,' said she, 'that you are not a very good neighbour to Williams.'

" 'Why so, my daughter?'

" 'It is so long since you have been to see him. I hope he has taken no offence at it; but, you know, he has not called at our house lately, and James, whom you used to be so fond of, and who diverted us so much, has not darkened our doors for many a long day.'

" 'That is true, girl; I will see Williams to-morrow evening.'

" 'Why not to-night; it is a beautiful night; the sky is so clear, and the moon so bright; it may be bad weather to-morrow, you know; besides, if Williams has really taken offence at your neglect of him, the sooner it is made up between you the better.'

" 'Why that is true, again; and I will even go to-night;' – and Geshie, with a pleasure she could hardly conceal, reached him his hat, and heard him walk away in the direction of Williams's house with a pace quickened by the dampness of the evening air. On the way, Yok found James lying in the road apparently lifeless, and a man who was passing about the same time assisted in bearing him to his father's house, where, by proper applications, he was soon brought to himself. On his return, Yok related these circumstances to Geshie, who appeared as much surprised and interested as if she had known nothing of the matter.

"To the numerous questions put to him respecting the condition in which he was found, James returned no direct answer, but desired to be left to repose. Sleep did not visit his eyes that night; the event of the evening, which he had remembered but faintly on first coming out of the swoon, returned to him in all its circumstances with an impression that grew stronger every moment. Again they seemed present to him: the haunted spot, the spectre, the shroud, the white feet and hand, the gleam of its eye, the perceptible motion of its lips, and the piercing and solemn tones of its voice. Then, also, the fearful words it uttered returned, one by one, to his recollection and, as they returned, engraved themselves there as the diamond ploughs its characters on the rock; again he heard himself denounced as treacherous, faithless, and cruel, and warned to escape an untimely end by a speedy repentance. The morning found him haggard and exhausted, in a state of melancholy bordering on despair.

"It happened at this time, that the minister of the parish in which Williams had formerly lived was on a visit to his old neighbour. Williams, who had been one of the pillars of his church, had implored him so pathetically to come and dispense the word for a season in that destitute place that he could not find it in his heart to deny him. He was one of that race of excellent old clergymen – of which some specimens yet remain, I am told, in New England – renowned equally for good sermons in the pulpit and good stories out of it. His round and somewhat florid face was set off by a short fox-colored wig, and the severity of his brow tempered by the jollity of his cheeks and chin. The clergy, you know, were in those times the nobility of the country; their opinions were oracles, and their advice law. Those were good days, when the farmer sent the best of every thing he had to the minister; when every hat was doffed as he passed, and when, in every house he entered, the great easy-chair was instantly wheeled for him to the front of the fireplace, the housewife ran to comb her children, and the husband to broach the best barrel of cider in his cellar. Williams's minister was not a man to abuse the reverence in which he was held; the penitent are always ready to apply to a clergyman, but this good man was also the friend of the unfortunate and unhappy.

"In the morning, as soon as the clergyman was up, James sent for him, and communicated to him the adventure of the night. A long conversation ensued. The clergyman examined James with great minuteness concerning all the circumstances and satisfied himself of the truth of his story. He then inquired of him if there were any particulars of his late way of life which might have given occasion to so remarkable a visitation. James hesitated for a while, and at last confessed that he had loved Mary; that he believed he had won her affections; that they had talked of marriage; that he had discontinued his visits; and that he had been told she was unhappy. Another series of questions ensued, and at the end of the conference it was settled that James should immediately perform his engagement to Mary, and that the incident of the ghost should, in the mean time, be kept secret between him and the minister.

"Mary did not know to what event she owed the return of her lover, for her sister had told nobody of the part she took in the affair. She received him without a word of reproach, but with a countenance in which tears and smiles contended for the mastery. She spoke with sorrow and concern of his altered and haggard appearance, and James wondered how he could ever have ceased to love her. The parents were consulted concerning the match. Yok was pleased, because he had always liked James; and Williams because Yok was the owner of broad woodlands and goodly meadows. An early day was fixed for the marriage. The good parson came all the way from Connecticut to assist at the nuptials, and the doctor, to whose sagacious prescription Yok attributed the rapid amendment that was taking place in his daughter's health, was also of the party.

"After the ceremony was over and the minister had retired, the company adjourned to the long kitchen. A great hickory fire was blazing in the chimney, and the negro fiddler who had been provided for the occasion, with an associate, was mounted on his bench with the instrument of music at his shoulder. The couples were soon arranged; the bride and bridegroom, in the gayest attire of the day, were at the head; and old Yok himself was on the floor. A November wind was howling in the woods, the old trees creaked and groaned, and showers of the red leaves were driven against the windows; but the bluster without was unheard amidst the merriment within. The black fiddlers threw themselves into the most violent contortions and drew their bows from the head to the heel at every note. The sound of the instruments, the clatter of feet, the shouts of laughter, the jests that flew rapidly about, taken up by the shrill voices of the maidens and echoed from the sonorous lungs of the rustic beaux – made the passer by to stop in amazement. But the guests remembered that it was only a wedding, and at midnight the house was as still and dark as ever.

"James did not like the neighbourhood of the place where he had seen the spectre, and soon after his marriage, he went to settle in one of the villages on the banks of the Hudson, where he long lived quietly and respectably, and where his descendants reside to this day. Geshie was my grandmother by the mother's side, and from her lips I had the tale I have related. It is not known to many, for she never told it until she had arrived at extreme old age, when there were few in these parts who remembered either James Williams or her sister. As for the doctor who had prescribed for Mary, he rose almost immediately into great reputation and extensive practice from being supposed to have cured a patient in the last stage of a consumption.

A Narrative of Some Extraordinary Circumstances

Few PLACES in our country have any traditions of moment associated with them, and of these few a very small proportion are the objects of superstitious awe. Here and there, however, you meet with a spot memorable for one of those terrible interpositions of Providence which seem directly aimed to punish or prevent guilt. The state of religious belief in our country readily adopts these solutions of the ways of Heaven, and the freedom with which the motives of the Ruler of all things for permitting a particular event to happen is assigned, were it not for the profound sincerity and solemnity with which it is accompanied, might justly be thought daring and irreverent.

I knew one of those spots not many years since. It was in a kind of wild neglected pasture that stretched along the side of a hill worn into terraces by the paths of cattle and sheep. At one end, close to the skirt of a tall wood, was a circle of ground nearly level, in the middle of which was sunk a little hollow, four or five feet over, bordered with fragments of rock and half surrounded by bushes. I often used to visit it, for it commanded a beautiful view of the surrounding mountains, the valley between, and the river which flowed through the valley. In the northeast the smoke-wreaths from the houses that stood unseen between the hills rose as if proceeding directly from the ground, and the spire of the church looked as if planted in the midst of a green field. A little farther to the south the hills receded from each other, the meadows grew wider and wider, and the river came forth as if issuing from a chasm in the earth, and glided away, rejoicing, through the thick grass and occasional borderings of trees till its course was lost to the sight.

I became the more fond of this little nook as a kind of dread with which the neighbourhood regarded it had caused it to be abandoned to me alone. The snow at the end of winter, whether from the natural warmth of the soil or the favorable exposure, was melted away here sooner than in the neighbouring fields, and the verdure was earlier and brighter. I found the fragments of rock about the little hollow edged with the first flowers of spring. The blossoms of the liver-leaf and of the vernal saxifrage wagged their heads in the first soft winds of the season. A little later, the erythronium opened and glittered in the dew like a jewel of beaten gold for the ear of an Indian princess. I came hither in the summer to gather the black raspberry which ripened in the sun to an intense sweetness and was never plucked save by myself and the birds that built their nests unscared on the neighbouring shrubs. I loved to sit here in the long days of June and look out upon the valleys that lay in the deluge of light and heat, and watch the shadows of the clouds as they ran along the sides of the mountains. In autumn I found, on the alders and witch hazels, clusters of the wild grape which the schoolboy had left untouched. I knew well that some tradition of horror was connected with the place, but I cared not to inquire into its particulars, for I did not wish to mingle ideas of human suffering and guilt with those of the peace and innocence of nature.

At last the story was told me. One of those kind communicative beings who cannot bear that any body should remain ignorant of any thing concerning which it is in their power to afford information, one day insisted on my knowing the whole, and common courtesy obliged me to listen. I have committed his narrative to writing, relating the circumstances in my own way.

At a little distance from the spot I have described, and near the foot of the hill, were to be seen at the time of which I am speaking, and probably are to be seen yet, the ruins of an old dwelling. A square hollow showed where the cellar had been, and the shape of the old sills on which the house was built was still discernible under the green turf by which they were over-grown. A patch of tansy and a few long-lived currant bushes marked the place of the garden, and hard by was an old well, filled up with loose stones. It is now more than twenty years since that habitation was abandoned and pulled down, and the place that was once noisy with the cries of domestic animals, the hum of household industry, and the accents of the human voice, now hears no other noise than that of the neighbouring brook leaping down its stony channel and brawling all day long to the witch hopples and dwarf maples that overshadow it. Its last tenant, however, old Jacob Holmes, is still well remembered in those parts; a tall, spare, large-boned man, with a stooping figure, an ashy complexion, and thick, white, bushy eyebrows, under which a pair of grey eyes skulked in ambush, observing every thing, and themselves almost entirely screened from observation. He lived in a neighbourhood of industrious farmers, but no one of them all prospered like him; his cattle always throve, his barns and granaries were crammed till they could hold no more with the abundance of his crops. He had the art of getting more work out of his laborers than any man in the whole country, and what was still more extraordinary, he was never known to be over-reached in a bargain. On a quiet summer evening, as he sat at his window and looked out upon his farm just at the going down of the sun, his grey eyes would twinkle from their concealment with evident satisfaction as he beheld every where the signs of thrift: heavy oats, thick wheat, broad acres of Indian corn in rows of the darkest and healthiest green, sheep on well-browsed hills, and sleek kine coming home in the road with a white-haired boy and their own long shadows stalking behind them. In short, it was very evident that Holmes laid up money, and after this was once discovered, there were frequently seen about him divers men of obsequious manners who spoke in a low tone of voice. These were the people who wanted to borrow, and Holmes was not unwilling to lend on good security. But as ill luck would have it, he was never able to furnish the exact amount of money the borrower wanted, who was therefore obliged to take an old horse, a few bushels of corn, or a few loads of potatoes to make up the sum required, a process which the sagacious old usurer found to be an easier and more profitable way of disposing of this kind of property than by sending it to market. The debt thus connected was generally secured by a snug mortgage, which the creditor took care to foreclose in due time. In this way he saw his possessions gradually enlarging around him: meadow joined itself to meadow, and woodland was added to woodland, until at length he had rolled together a very considerable estate.

Among the miseries of the rich, not the least is their anxiety concerning what will become of their money after they are dead. In this country, and perhaps in others, one of two things very commonly happens to a man who has the good or ill fortune to be richer than his neighbours. Either he has a graceless son who squanders for him all he can lay hands on in his lifetime, and only waits for his last breath to begin squandering the rest; or else a wayward daughter, who falls in love with whom she pleases, marries him in spite of her honored father, and obliges the old gentleman, if he leaves his property to his own offspring, to leave it to be enjoyed by the very fellow whom of all the world he detests the most heartily. Old Holmes was under no apprehensions of the first of these misfortunes, for he had no sons; but he was in very great danger of the latter, for his only daughter, who wrote her name Elizabeth but was called by the neighbors Betsey, was one of the prettiest girls in the place, a bouncing, lively, rattling creature with big, cheerful blue eyes and cheeks as round and red as apples; kind-hearted in the main, but very much inclined to have her own way, and like the rest of her sex, somewhat fond of show and finery, or in other words, possessing a decided taste for the beautiful and elegant. I mean no disrespect to the ladies, for this passion does not perhaps naturally belong to their sex in a greater degree that to the other; it is only more unfolded and encouraged by the state of society in which we live. In a savage life there are no belles, there are only beaux. The warrior of the American wildernesses, with all his stoical virtues and all his contempt for effeminacy, bedizens himself as gaily in his own peculiar fashion as the proudest dame that flaunts in Broadway, to whom the very rainbow seems to have been made tributary, and who wears upon her head what you might take for the spoil of the fairest gardens of the earth.

Betsey's love for finery gave her father some trouble, and he could not help sometimes thinking that he should get rich faster without her. To do him justice, however, next to his money he loved his daughter; but his money was quiet and speechless, while the half-playful, half-chiding, and never discouraged importunities of his daughter enabled the weaker passion to triumph over the stronger whenever she was fully determined to have it so. So she was gratified with the gayest ribbons and finest silks worn in the place and bonnets of the newest pattern from New York, a little behind the actual mode probably, but not the less a novelty in that remote neighbourhood. The old man's heart would sometimes fail him with the dread of approaching poverty as he ran over the long account of what she had cost him. As was natural enough, however, he only placed a greater value on the object of all this expense, and resolved firmly that he would part with her upon no easy terms. "I will not," said he to himself, "give her away to the first beggarly fellow that asks for her, even though it should be Ned Hammond."

This Ned Hammond, or as Betsey was generally pleased to call him, Edward, was a young neighbor of theirs, and the most favored of all the numerous suitors by whom the good-looking heiress was besieged. Edward, had little money, but he had the wealth of a good constitution, an agreeable figure, and an excellent temper. It was a pleasure to behold

50

his strong limbs, his well spread chest, his manly countenance, and the frank steady look of his eye, and to see him moving about with that unstudied ease which belongs to those who possess the animal nature of our species in its perfection. He was the best leaper, the swiftest runner, the most dexterous swimmer, and the loudest laugher in the place. None of the young farmers excelled him at a mowing-match; none were readier to do a good office, or to retort a rustic joke. In short, no harm could be said of Edward, except that he was not rich; but as nobody was more cheerful than he, or wore a finer Sunday suit, it was perhaps no misfortune that he was not so. Betsey had preferred him to his rivals, not because she loved him exactly, for her head was too full of more important matters to be seriously in love with any body, but because she thought it a matter of course that the handsomest and best dressed young man of the place was to be her husband. His poverty was no objection to him. "My father," thought the prudent young lady, "has enough for us both. I shall be able to teaze him out of a part of it, and Edward will know how to provide the rest."

Such was her arrangement; but her father looked on the young man with other eyes. He was not well pleased with seeing him so often about his premises, and accordingly demanded an explanation of his daughter, who very frankly and with great composure admitted that she liked him.

"But you don't intend to marry him ?" said the old gentleman.

"Indeed, father, I think I shall if he asks me."

"Then you shall have none of my property; I can tell you that."

"Then we will do without."

This was too much for the old gentleman; he could have endured that his paternal authority should be slighted had the matter ended there; but the idea that his estate which he had taken so much pains to acquire, and to which he owed all the consideration he received from his neighbours, should be spoken of with contempt was more than he could bear. He therefore told his daughter in plain terms that he should turn Edward out of doors the first time he crossed his threshold, a threat which she faithfully communicated to her lover that very evening, in a tête-à-tête of half an hour held at the tender season of twilight in the old gentleman's best parlour.

Shortly afterwards an incident took place which rendered him better satisfied with his daughter. One day he had occasion to go to the village, as it was called, consisting of some half dozen buildings standing near each other, of which one was a meeting-house with its semicircle of horse-sheds, and the other a tavern. At the latter he met with a young man, whom the landlord very officiously introduced to him as a Mr. Smith of Virginia, who, as he told him in his ear, was a very nice young gentleman who had been his lodger for a couple of days and, seemed to be full of money. Holmes cast a look upon the stranger; he was too genteel-looking for his taste, and he immediately withdrew his eye in contempt; but the talkative landlord managed to keep up the conversation. Holmes happened to drop a frugal maxim; the young man, to his surprise, re-echoed it. Holmes followed it up, with a practical illustration which the young man immediately matched with another. Holmes quoted "Poor Richard," the young man quoted him also, and they soon seemed to become mutually agreeable to each other. At parting the old gentleman shook hands with his new acquaintance and, understanding that he intended to pass some time in the place, hoped that he should see him often at his house – a civility of which Mr. Smith declared that he should soon have the pleasure of availing himself.

He came the very next day. It was a beautiful evening, towards the latter end of September. The red light of the setting sun lay sweetly on the landscape: on the meadows, green with the autumnal crop of grass: on the whitening fields of Indian corn, the loaded orchards, and the woods that stretched up the sides of the mountains and here and there were spotted with scarlet and gold. The old man was sitting at his window, as was usual with him at that hour, looking out upon his farm, and Betsey was on the green before the door, engaged in the unromantic amusement of teaching a fat, waddling puppy, that was tumbling about in the grass, to play tricks for his supper. At the sudden appearance of the young man, she blushed and ran to adjust her dress, and when she returned she could not but be struck with the graceful figure and manners of the stranger. The exercise of the walk had given a ruddy glow to his dark cheek, which was yet heightened by the red lustre that lay on all objects; a pair of keen black eyes seemed to the maiden fitted to say unutterable things; and then his dress – so fashionable and quaint in its cut, and fitted so elegantly to his somewhat slight but shapely figure, his linen of such perfect purity, his waistcoat of such a spotless white, his cravat so exquisitely tied. In short, he was irresistible. Add to all this the graceful haste with which be reached her a chair, closed the window from which the air came too rudely against her neck, picked up her handkerchief, and paid her all these agreeable little attentions which are the prescriptive right of the sex, but in which the beaux of her own simple neighbourhood were not very expert. She sighed to think that Edward was not so fine a gentleman. When the stranger had departed, her father asked her, with a look of triumph, whether she did not think him worth ten of Ned Hammond. The poor girl hesitated for a while, and at last faintly answered, "No." The old man, who was accustomed to making bargains, and who knew very well when he was on the point of gaining an advantage of his antagonist, chuckled at his daughter's indecision, bid her good night, and told her that the next day she should have the shawl for which she had been teasing him the week past.

Smith saw with pleasure the impression he had made on the heart, or rather on the vanity of the young heiress, for her heart had really little to do with the matter, and he was not slow in following up the advantage he had gained. He called frequently at Holmes's, and talked for hours with the old gentleman about bonds and mortgages, about the proper mode of computing interest, the best way of securing debts, and the most profitable method of managing an estate. He had the talent, not uncommon among sharp-witted men who have seen a good deal of mankind, to seem very knowing on the subject of conversation, whatever it might he, by the help of information dexterously extracted from the person himself with whom he was talking. This talent he practised with great success on the old usurer, who was beyond measure delighted to had find him always of his own opinion, and by a natural consequence set him down as one of the most intelligent and judicious men he had ever met with. With Betsey he talked on quite different subjects, and on these he seemed more at home – the fashions, the customs of the great and gay world such as he had seen it in the large towns, and the manners of his native state. She listened eagerly and he discoursed volubly, but whether truly or not I have no means of knowing, for no record of his conversation is preserved.

Of his private history he made no secret. He told the old yeoman and his daughter that be belonged to a wealthy family in Virginia and that his mother had died a few years before, leaving him a considerable inheritance in land and slaves, of which, however, his father was entitled to the enjoyment during his lifetime. His father, he said, had married a second wife, whose ill-nature had obliged him to leave the home of his infancy. He had since resided in different parts of the

Union, and he could now hardly regret the severity that had driven him from the paternal hearth, since it had made him acquainted with a people of purer manners and severer virtue, among whom he would gladly settle for life. He intimated that, when the maternal estate came into his hands, he should immediately dispose of the land and sell, or perhaps emancipate, the slaves and take up his residence at the northward – perhaps in that very neighbourhood. His story was believed by the unsuspecting girl with implicit faith, and the wary old father, after a few shrewd questions which were satisfactorily answered, acquiesced in the same belief.

Holmes was therefore delighted with the attentions paid by Smith to his daughter; but there was another person who was far from experiencing the same satisfaction. This was Edward, who, apprised of what was going on, came several times to the house to obtain an interview. But she was either on the watch and absented herself at his approach, or else frightened him away by pretending that her father was coming and would fulfil his threat of turning him out of doors, so that he found no opportunity for an explanation. The poor fellow, who had really loved her, fell into a state of dejection; his loud, extravagant laugh grew faint and forced; he seemed not to understand the jokes that were cracked upon him, and forgot to return them as formerly; he was thrown at wrestling matches, and in a game of cricket was often observed to let the ball pass without seeing it. He took the thing so much to heart that Betsey, who knew she had used him ill, was quite angry with him. "I am sorry for him," said the sage and thoughtful maiden to herself, "but what can I do? I must have Smith if I can get him; for if one cannot have the person one likes, where is the use of marrying at all? I never exactly promised to marry Edward, and he knows very well that I cannot have every body. I wonder he will not be reasonable and let people do as they please. It is very foolish in him to take on so, and if he thinks to get me by moping and crying because I like Smith better than I do him, he is very much mistaken." She soon had an opportunity of telling him her mind on this subject.

The autumn had passed rapidly away; the leaves of the forest had been shed in the winds; all but the russet tufts of foliage, that yet hung fluttering on the young oaks, and refused, withered and sapless as they were, to be rent away by the blasts of winter. The ground had been frost-bound for a considerable time, the rattle of the carriages over the rough and iron roads was heard for miles, the brooks were transformed into long glittering trains of ice, and the keen wind from the clear northwest, which seemed to descend from the very dwelling of frost and howled continually in the woods, had beat with a steady strength against the dwellings. The school-boy put his mittens to his little scarlet nose and ran backwards against the heavy gust that swept along the road. At length the wind, as if grown weary of its ineffectual blustering, fell into a sullen silence, and the transparent blue of the heavens thickened into a dim white, through which the sun seemed to labor his way, like a traveller wading, through the deep snow. The sun at last was hidden also, and a kind of pale, woolly-looking canopy seemed to be drawn over the whole sky. One might have thought, were it not for the anachronism, that all the fleeces and flannels of the sheep owners and woollen manufacturers who sent delegates to the Harrisburg Convention in July, 1827, had been hung up between the heavens and the earth for a sign to their adversaries. Then the snows dropped down, gently at first and in scattered flakes, but faster and thicker every moment until the air was alive with the white atoms chasing each other in seeming eagerness to the earth. The farmers hastened to get their cattle and flocks under shelter, and the shrill voices of their boys and the sharp bark of the dogs came with an indistinct and deadened sound through the thick atmosphere. The snow fell all day and all night, and the next morning the country was covered with it to a great depth and the roads were filled almost to the tops of the fences. The bluff-faced yeomen yoked their oxen and sheep to the heavy sledges on which they brought wood from the forests and drove them along the highways, making a hollow and well-beaten path from house to house. Wherever the roads winded and branched from each other, you might see them urging their cattle slowly through the deep and pure snows, as far as the eye could reach. At length the paths were made, and then the sleighs and the horses loaded with bells were brought forth, and all the people of the neighbourhood were abroad under the bright golden sun, passing each other swiftly in their way over the sheet of spotless white that covered the whole country.

Edward, in a sleigh painted with all the colors of the rainbow and drawn by a spirited horse whose neck and sides were garnished with an unusual quantity of bells, called at Holmes's door, as he had been wont the winter previous, to give Betsey an opportunity of sharing in the universal amusement of the season. She came to the door, and when with a beating heart and half-cloaked voice he had told his errand, she very coolly answered that she expected to ride out with Mr. Smith. He began to murmur something which sounded like a complaint, but which Betsey did not stay to hear. Her face reddened; she told him he was a booby for coming to trouble people who did not care for him, and shut the door in his face. Edward drove off in great grief of heart, and Betsey could not but think she had treated him too harshly when she saw him from the window, at one moment suffering his horse to walk slowly with loose reins lying on his neck, and the next whipping the animal into a furious gallop.

Betsey and her lover had a charming drive that day. She declared it to be the most delightful she ever had, and it was followed by many others. Parties were made up among the young people to go to the neighbouring villages on the moonlight nights, and Smith and the young heiress were the genteelest and merriest couple of them all. On these occasions all the inhabitants of the houses along the road were attracted by the noise to the windows in order to observe the mirthful train as they passed. The sleighs glided with a hissing sound over the hard and glistening path; the bells jingled loud in the frosty air, and the light sound of laughter was left on the winds behind them. Sometimes they would pass through one of those whirling pyramids of loose snow which the wind had gathered from the surface and which, having traversed the fields like a colossal ghost in its shroud, would sweep rapidly across the road – and then all their voices were silent for a moment as the maidens bowed their faces to their muffs – for muffs were then in fashion – and the young men averted their eyes from the cold and blinding gust.

Smith was now the acknowledged lover of Betsey, and the gossips of the neighbourhood began to wonder when they would be married. An unlucky event, however, had nearly destroyed his reputation in the place and ruined his matrimonial prospects. Two young bloods in fur caps and immense camlet cloaks – very noisy, very impertinent, and calling about them with an air of great consequence, stopped at the tavern where Smith lodged, one intensely cold evening towards the end of February, and staid over night. A story obtained currency that they had passed the night in Smith's apartment, and an inquisitive chambermaid who listened half the night at the door had distinctly heard something about trumps and the ace of clubs, together with several suspicious raps on the table. The young fellows had gone away the next morning in a very ill humor, which was hardly appeased by Smith's paying their bill to the host, and the very same day the chambermaid, in pursuing her researches, brought to light a greasy pack of cards concealed in Smith's room. She engaged one of her acquaintances to assist her in keeping the secret, and before the next morning every individual in the neighbourhood knew it.

One of the deacons of the parish, a venerable old man who was held in great reverence – such a man as you may yet sometimes see in the places least visited by stage-coaches and steam boats – carrying an ivory-headed cane, and wearing a red woollen cap over his thin white hairs, called to remonstrate with Holmes on the danger to which he exposed his daughter in suffering her to marry a man of a doubtful character. Holmes was even more alarmed than the deacon, and after some consultation it was agreed that the latter should immediately call on Smith and get the matter cleared up. Smith received him with great politeness, was hurt at the slanders circulated against him; protesting his innocence, he appealed to the propriety of his past conduct, which made the accusation utterly improbable, and finished by calling in the landlord to vouch for the truth of what he said. The landlord eagerly confirmed every word he had uttered, declared the chambermaid to be a lying baggage, and, to show his sincerity, discharged her on the spot. The good deacon was the more inclined to believe in Smith's innocence as he had found him orthodox on the five points and had observed that he always touched his hat reverently to himself and the minister; that he was sufficiently punctual in his attendance at church, and scrupulously so at the conferences and Sunday evening. meetings where the deacon himself was wont to hold forth in the way of religious exhortation. Smith's cause had now obtained powerful protectors, and the calumnies uttered against his reputation were frowned down and forgotten.

Spring had come on the track of winter; the snows first grew yellow, then showed patches of the brown ground, and finally disappeared altogether; the young blade shot up through the dead grass which the burden of the snow had pressed close to the earth; the maple hung out in profusion of minute red blossoms; the budding willow filled the air with a fragrance like that of lemon groves, and resounded all day with the murmur of bees. The wild cherry, the horse-plum, and the thorn-tree put out their flowers in succession, and finally the whole country was whitened with the bloom of orchards. The birds came back and made love to each other; every living creature was happy; even Edward forgot his griefs as he whistled to his team on the hillside. But the fair Betsey was the happiest of all, for the graceful Virginian had pressed her to name the marriage day, and it had been named with her father's sanction.

It was one afternoon in this exhilarating time of the year that Smith called at Holmes's with a fowling-piece on his shoulder. He complained of melancholy, of an unusual weight of sadness on his mind which he could not shake off. Betsey tried to rally him into cheerfulness, but her efforts were ineffectual. He looked at her vacantly, and at length said that he would go and see if a little exercise would do him good, and kill a rabbit for his landlord's breakfast. He went out, and she stood gazing after him a moment and then turned to her household affairs. Smith was observed by some laborers in the neighbouring fields to go up the hill along the inclosure of pasture ground (mentioned in the beginning of this narrative) until he arrived at the little level near the skirt of the wood. It was an unusually sultry day for the season; there was not wind enough to shake the faded blossoms from the apple tree; the shriek of the tree-toad was occasionally heard from afar off; and the sound of the distant mountain brooks seemed like mysterious voices holding discourse in the air. Smith was sauntering languidly along, when the laborers heard a strange hissing sound, and looking, saw several puffs of white smoke issuing from the ground directly under his feet.

Instantly the earth seemed to be rent at that very spot with a terrible explosion; a column of stones and earth was thrown to a great height; a tongue of bluish flame shot up, and a thick dark smoke arose, enlarged, and gradually whitened as it diffused itself in the air. A moment of dead silence succeeded, and then the laborers saw the stones and clods of earth dropping back into the smoke and heard them strike heavily against the ground. After the first shock of astonishment and terror was over, they consulted for an instant together, and then hastened with mingled curiosity and fear to the spot. They were met by the smoke which was rolling slowly along the ground and of which the acrid and sulphurous odor almost took away their breath. On coming to the place they found Smith lying with his face to the earth, and the fowling-piece under him. They raised him, but he was dead; his jaw had fallen, and his countenance wore a strange expression of horror.

The body of Smith was carried to his lodgings, and a coroner's inquest was held over it. There was no appearance of any bruise or other external injury in his person, except that his eyebrows and the ends of his hair were somewhat scorched, and it seemed probable that he had perished by inhaling the fiery and deadly fume of the explosion. In his pockets were found some letters and memoranda, from the perusal of which a suspicion arose that his name of Smith was an assumed one, that the story of his Virginia family was a forgery, and that he was already married and that his wife lived in a distant part of the country. Curiosity was strongly excited; the trunks of the deceased were opened, his papers were examined with little ceremony, and their contents confirmed the suspicion beyond doubt. A strong feeling of indignation at the fraud he had practised mingled itself with the awe felt at the terrible event by which he had been cut off, and the verdict of the jury was that the deceased had come to his end by the judgment of God.

His relations were informed of his fate, and his effects were delivered to them. Further inquiries into his history showed a series of irregularities on his part which ended in his associating with a gang of sharpers in one of the Atlantic cities, from which he was at length driven by the pursuit of justice. His real name, and the place of his birth, I do not think proper to disclose, since there are probably those alive to whom the disclosure might give pain.

But the event struck a deep awe into all the neighbourhood. People spoke to each other to a subdued voice, the choleric were afraid to quarrel, and the knavish to cheat, the old warned the young, and the young forbore their usual amusements and gaieties. Even old Holmes contented himself for a while with a smaller usury, and it was long before the look of concern and the tone of fear passed away from among the good people. The little level where the event happened and the hollow where the fire broke forth from the earth – beautiful as they are, with wild flowers in spring and wild fruits in summer and autumn – still remained, and even yet remain the objects of dread.

Betsey was an heiress, and did not long remain unwooed. Edward was the handsomest young fellow left; he had remained constant in his affections, and, what was of some importance, he had always borne an excellent character. Means were found to overcome the objections of the father, and before the orchards were again in bloom, the young couple were man and wife. A numerous progeny sprung up around them, of whom I remember to have once seen a specimen in passing through the place in the stagecoach – two chubby boys of nearly the same age who, being frightened down from the back part of the coach, where they had clandestinely placed themselves, by the crack of the driver's whip, indemnified themselves by the amusement of pelting him with apples.

Preface to *The Talisman*

I AM NOT an author by profession, though I believe there are few of my countrymen whose works, if collected, would fill more volumes than mine. I have travelled much, and often in company with those whose writings have since delighted and instructed the world. It was always my custom, like other travellers, to keep a journal, in which I entered notes of uncommon or amusing incidents, descriptions of remarkable places, accounts of singular customs, and records of local traditions. My fellow-travellers often paid me the compliment of borrowing my portfolio for the purpose of refreshing their recollection of our joint observations and adventures, and I have afterwards had the pleasure of seeing what I thought my finest passages, published under great names, printed on hot-pressed wire-wove paper, illustrated with superb plates, praised and quoted in the reviews, and circulated in the newspapers wherever the English language is spoken. In this way I am sure of going down to future times, and posterity will converse with me in the works of the best describers of the manners and customs of nations at the present day.

My verses have circulated pretty freely in manuscript, and have met with a similar fate. I have seen some of them published among the miscellaneous poems of authors of no mean note, and others woven with great ingenuity into the body of some popular metrical romance. I once lent a manuscript tragedy to a friend of mine, and I am told it has since been performed with singular success and applause at the Drury Lane theatre in London, and at the Park in New-York. At Drury Lane the reputed author took a benefit, when I was last in London, which brought him four hundred and sixty pounds. I have never seen it acted, and probably never shall; especially as I learn that the gentleman who enjoys the credit of having written it, has interpolated so many ranting passages of his own, that I should be wholly unwilling to acknowledge it. Besides, I hold the stage and all its concerns very cheap, and intended my work not for the players, but as a dramatic poem.

I remained so well satisfied with this equivocal sort of notoriety, which allowed me the luxury of devouring in secret the praises bestowed on my writings, and permitted me to soothe myself under any occasional censure by the reflection that it was not aimed at me by the critic, nor applied to me by the world, that I had made a sort of resolution never to appear in public in the character of an author. But having been teased by my friends, who were pleased to speak of several of my manuscript compositions, although carelessly enough written, as being equal to any thing which my friends the poets and travellers had borrowed of me, and my bookseller having moreover offered to print them in his best manner, and to embellish them with the finest engravings he could procure, I have been prevailed upon, somewhat against my better judgment, to give them to the world in this shape. As an encouragement to the project, my friend Morse presented me with a charming original design in illustration of a favourite little piece of mine, entitled the Serenade; and Inman proffered his noble picture of Tell in chains, to be engraved as an accompaniment to a sonnet on the same subject, which I wrote in Tell's chapel, at the foot of the Righi, with the snowy pinnacles of the Alps looking down upon me. Moreover, two amiable and dutiful amateur god-sons of mine had taken the trouble to illustrate some or the scenery I had described, by original drawings. I was also promised that a drawing made by me some twenty years since from a picture of my favourite Albano, in the Florence Gallery, should be engraved; as well as some sketches made about the same period from the Greek and Etruscan antiques, all which have been done much to my satisfaction.

I have taken the fancy to call my work THE TALISMAN. I beg leave here to disclaim avowing any belief in the sciences of magic and astrology, although it is certain that their exercise has sometimes been attended with very extraordinary results. However, in the course of my travels in the East, and in particular in an overland journey which I made from India by the way of Arabia, Mesopotamia, Kurdistan, Persia, and the shores of the Black Sea to Europe, I took a little pains to inform myself of the principles of an art which has fallen into desuetude among the enlightened nations of the West. I have amused myself with getting up this volume with some attention to the forms and ceremonies with which charms and spells are usually compounded in the East. I have copied the contents with a quill plucked from a swan which I caught with my own hands, after a fatiguing chase through the meadows on the banks of Avon, and the table on which I write is spread with the skin of a royal tiger, which I happened to kill at Madras. The book was printed with virgin types; the typesetters were all born under the planet Mercury; the burines of the engravers have moved under benignant stellar aspects; and my publisher has the most auspicious and fortunate name that can be found in the whole Directory. The paper was sized with strict observation of the planetary hour, when Jupiter and Mars were in conjunction in Libra, in the seventh house of heaven, whilst Venus lorded the ascendant, culminating from the very ridge of the planetary house.

The result of all this should be, if there be any truth in astrology (which I do not positively affirm), that this volume must possess virtues similar to those ascribed by Othello to his mystic handkerchief. When given as a memorial of friendship, gratitude, respect or love, the sentiment, whatever it be, will remain indestructible and undiminished, so long as the book is kept. In justice to the art, I must add; that this mystic virtue must not be expected unless the gift be accompanied with a powerful and sympathetic co-operation of mutual sentiment.

I detest all quackery, and the examples of great men do not sanctify it in my eyes. The trick of Junius and Walter Scott to attract the public attention to their writings by making their real names a subject of mystery, always disgusted me. I therefore subscribe my name without reserve.

FRANCIS HERBERT

New-York, Dec. 1, 1827

The Legend of the Devil's Pulpit

Hy moet wel loopen die door de Duivel gedreven word.
                                                    Dutch Proverb

THERE can be but few inhabitants of the city of New-York who are not acquainted with the striking features of the Jersey shore and with the views that present themselves from the high grounds overlooking it: of the city and its islands to the south, and of the majestic Hudson pouring down from the north its "exulting and abounding" waters, covered with their seeming encampments of the white sails of river craft. I have, indeed, heard it asserted that there are some respectable native citizens who have never, during a long and otherwise well spent life, ventured their persons across the noble artery of the State of New-York, far better entitled to the epithet of King of Rivers than many streams which song has made immortal. I cannot believe it to be the fact. But for the benefit of those who have never sojourned in the London of America, it may be proper to mention that the shores of the Hudson opposite to the city, from the peninsula of Paulus Hook northward, present a singularly picturesque outline of indented coves and wood-fringed promontories, with a bold background of heights rising almost perpendicularly behind a level of meadow lands, once useless and good only for breeding moschitoes but now made valuable by human toil.

These heights are, at all times, striking in their effect as a part of the magnificent landscape which meets the eye in every direction from the favourable points on the Jersey side of the river. They attract the traveller's notice, whether they are whitened with the dog-wood flowers of spring or the accumulated snows of winter; whether glowing beneath the golden light of summer's declining sun, or burnished with the gorgeous tints which clothe his pavilion when he sinks to rest with regal magnificence, in autumn. In autumn too, at the change of the leaf before the more melancholy days of its fall are come, the woods which adorn the sides of these hills assume a variety and brilliancy of colouring which I have never seen surpassed. As you stand on the summit of some moss-grown pile of rocks – where some veteran of the forest spreads his gnarled and projecting roots beside you and extends his enormous and grotesque arms above your head while monstrous grape vines are twisting and intertwining their serpent and never-ending coils hanging in fantastic writhings and complications from one trunk or bough to another – you look down on these woods as they descend to the meadow, and the beams of the sinking sun strike through their winding alleys or glorify their many-coloured masses; and you realize more than is dreamt of in the tales of oriental enchantment. The multitudinous leaves of every conceivable hue seem transparent as they flutter in the softened light. Amidst a clump of rich evergreens stands a seeming tree of living gold, and far and wide an indescribable profusion of tints – from royal purple to sober russet, from deep crimson to the faintest tinge of red, from vivid orange to the very complexion of the sunbeams – are mingling amidst every shade of green. The graver hues have their proper distribution among the wealth and variety of colouring, for nature, unlike man, never makes her splendour become gaudy by accumulation, and her own light falling on this picture gives to it an appearance at which the painter throws down his brush and the poet abandons his vocabulary in despair. I think it would be, on the whole, advisable for me to let it alone myself. But if the tide of time should bear my name, by any chance, to posterity, I wish that it may be associated with scenes like these, where the generations who are to come will for ever repair to admire the prodigality of nature in combining all that is majestic and soft, abrupt and graceful, in the boundless variety of her works.

About a mile and a half from the Hoboken Ferry and near the celebrated Weehawken bluff – on whose summit a true poet has drunk in inspiration, and within whose shadow the blood of brave men has been shed in inglorious combat – there is a remarkable precipice called the Devil's Pulpit. I have thought it thus essential to fix its locality as it is the scene of a well-known but unrecorded tale of the olden time, which it is now my province to relate. Here the mountainous ridge I have spoken of as extending from [the] Bergen heights embraces the Swartwout meadows and descends, with its lofty semicircle of rocks and trees, to their level: the picturesque road winding at the base and beginning to climb the Weehawken hill. At this point on the eastern extremity of the ridge, just where it begins to sink towards the river, stands the precipice I have named, being a perpendicular rock of twenty or thirty feet in height in the midst of a thin clump of trees. Its top is crowned with a thick square projecting block of stone, resembling strongly a well-stuffed pulpit cushion, while a regular flight of natural stairs leads up to it from the left. From it you have glimpses through the boughs of the island of New-York – sprinkled with its villages and villas, and terminating in the city with all its spires and towers – of the intervening river and the spacious harbour, the green windings of the Jersey shores, and the distant hills of Staten Island. You see the white sails gleaming and gliding to and fro on the broad waters beneath you; you hear the quick heavy beat of paddles from the steam-boats; and when the air is more than commonly quiet, the ever-lasting murmur and coil of the great city hums drowsily on your ear.

This precipice became famous for some remarkable adventures which happened there some sixty or seventy years ago, when the city of New-York was about an eighth of its present size. From the pictures, books, and documents in my possession, I could describe it almost accurately enough for a surveyor to lay it out again according to its plan at that day, and with more than sufficient precision to enable a painter to depict it. But I am cabbined, cribbed, and confined by the limits necessity compels me to observe, and I must get along with my story, for, unlike the knife-grinder, "I have one to tell, sir."

There was, then, at this time, a tailor from London who kept a shop at the corner of Wall-street and Broadway, within the shadow of that venerable old Trinity Church whose antique magnificence, gilt cherubim, loud organ, and brass chandeliers called forth the eulogium of the historian of New-York, and whose place is imperfectly supplied by the semi-gothic structure which now occupies its site. This artist was born in the year 1736 and baptised by the name of William Vince according to the parish register of St. Giles's, Cripplegate, but he called himself Villiam Wince and assumed no small airs among the provincials on the strength of his having seen the Lord Mayor of Lunnun and "woted" at a Common Hall. But he did not find his patronage coextensive with his pretensions. All his gold lace and embroidery, stocks with gilt buckles, solitaires, flimsy silk stockings with gold clocks, faded damask and brocade, black, blue, green, crimson, scarlet and yellow silk breeches-pieces, black, green and crimson Genoa velvet, cut and uncut velvet shapes, gold and silver knee garters, &c. remained on his shelves and scarcely paid for their advertisement in the *Post Boy*. He had bought the sweepings of the shop of a bankrupt brother of his craft, but brought them to the wrong market. The stubborn burghers continued to employ Von Snick and Hoffmeyer in Crown-street or La Culotte in Hanover-square. The good and sober folks of that day preferred such coats as would keep them warm and endure so much wearing as to be often bequeathed as a rich legacy unto their issue. The dignitaries of Church and State – that is to say, the Governor, Lieutenant-Governor, Chief Justice De Lancey, Judge Ludlow, Counsellor Murray, the Rector of Trinity Church, and the collectors of his Majesty's Customs – regularly imported their apparel by the British packets.

This Cockney Prometheus of the external man had, therefore, little employment. Some young lawyer occasionally favoured him with a call who was ambitious of "going smarter" than his neighbours and who relied for funds to discharge his bill, not on obtaining his costs in a successful suit, but on getting a suit to make costs in. And sometimes a midshipman or an ensign would want to be fitted up in a great hurry, which proved to be no exaggeration, as his haste allowed him no time to settle his accounts. A crisis was approaching in the poor tailor's life, and a strange planet it was that presided over that tide in his affairs which led him to dispose of much of his trumpery.

The eldest son of the clerk of Trinity Church was named Matthew Oakes by right, but the Dutch people called him Tevas, and the English Mat and Matty. This young gentleman's father had brought him up with a noble ambition of making him his successor in his semi-sacerdotal office. But it was soon very obvious that these fond parental hopes would never be fulfilled, for master Mat was an irreverent cub who ate nuts in church and would not learn his catechism, and often forgot to take off his hat to the rector. His reading was generally such a various reading of the text as confounded all criticism, and his singing certainly resembled more the song of the sweeps than that of the seraphim. When he indulged his lungs in that exercise, the voices of the choir and the thunders of the organ were quickly silenced, to the unutterable scandal of the grave and devout audience.

He was, therefore, placed by his disconsolate father behind the counter of Mrs. Alexander (who, in silks and satins, laces and lawns, monopolized the whole fashionable custom of the city) in the hopes that he might one day become a merchant. But the quick eye of that old lady detected a great many inaccuracies in his arithmetic, with occasional fluctuations in the state of the till which could not be accounted for by corresponding variations in that of the market. One day she saw him in church, ostentatiously protruding on public attention a pair of skyblue silk stockings with red clocks. This sight gave her such painful sensations that she retired prematurely, apparently half-fainting. On examination, she found that these integuments had actually been abstracted from a parcel received by the last importation, and when Tevas returned, she very cavalierly divested him, with her own hands, of the dry-goods and turned him off, bare-legged, with a malison and a prophecy of evil import.

After this dismission Matthew led a miscellaneous life for many years. Sometimes he vouchsafed his attendance at the bar of the Blue Bell, in Sloat-lane. Sometimes he ran off errands for the Governor. Sometimes he carried invitations to funerals for the sexton. During the annual fortnight's session of the Legislature, he assisted in making fires and filling pipes for the members. He was the regular door-keeper at the school balls of Mr. Turner, the patriarch of New-York dancing masters. Though his exterior was rather ragged and dishevelled, there was a certain jauntiness about its arrangement, and what Leigh Hunt would call a viridity and leafiness in his air. He loved to dispose such ornaments as he could muster on those parts of his person where he supposed their exhibition would prove most effectual. He wore two-thirds of a three-cornered hat, with a Ramilies cock. Though his linen was filthy dowlas, his ruffles were of deep lace. If his knees seemed to indicate a curiosity to peep out of their investments, his knee-buckles were of sumptuous Bristol paste; and his stockings, though rarely whole, were always of silk. His frugal and affectionate mother often besought him to put on stout woollen hose of her own knitting, but he rejected all such overtures with unfilial contempt. The fragments of his shoes were always highly polished and garnished with buckles, one of brass, and one of steel. Such was Tevas's course of life, and such the assortment of his apparel.

By the arrival of the packet on the 30th day of December, 1760, after a short passage of seventy-nine days from Falmouth, the melancholy tidings were brought to this Dutch colony of the death of its German master, George the Second. This monarch happening to die at a lucky moment, just after the conquest of Canada, left behind him an excellent character. All England was in tears. So said the *London Advertiser*, the regular channel of intelligence to this city. With that laudable imitation of the customs of the mother country for which its citizens have ever since been distinguished, it was unanimously resolved that New-York also was much afflicted. The dignitaries before named, with others not there specified, laid aside their customary splendour of velvet, brocade, and gold lace and appeared in full suits of mourning. The sober burghers brought forth their solemn black attire from the recesses of their wardrobe, and those who were unprovided repaired to Van Snick and Hoffmeyer or to M. La Culotte.

These magnates, with all the minor members of the sartorial trade, were hard at work in making new mourning suits or in refitting and furbishing up old ones which had not been worn since the death of the last near relation or of one of the royal family. Hard at work were they all: in cutting up the fine, thick, glossy Dutch blacks of former times – to whose solidity, compactness, and lustre the boasted Regent's cloth of modern days is, in comparison, a mere web of gossamer – or in darning, piecing, patching, letting out, taking in, turning, scouring, seating, new collaring, new cuffing, and new buttoning the lugubrious livery used on former occasions.

I am not a tailor by trade – which I regret, for I have a genius that way – but I love and honour the art and sympathise in all the mishaps of its professors. I am, therefore, thus particular, because none – not even the meanest – of these jobs fell to the share of poor Vince the Cockney, who sat, some days after the arrival of the gloomy news which accompanied all these outward signs of woe, the veritable picture of woe itself – if poetical propriety would justify the personification of Woe in the shape of a tailor. He sat in his shop alone, playing with his measure and meditating on sundry wants and necessities. Among these, the most prominent was his last quarter's rent, still due, with a balance of the former one, amounting in all to fourteen pounds fifteen shillings. For living in the most frequented part of the city, his rent was proportionately extravagant.

Sadly and listlessly he felt and unrolled, for the fiftieth time, a piece of black velvet, rather shop-worn, which, having abandoned all hopes of clothing with it any of the dignitaries, from the Governor down to the Alderman of the Ward, he had that day offered, at what he called half-price, to the Dutch Church Consistory and to the vestry of Trinity for mourning hangings with equally bad success in both instances. He had almost come to the desperate conclusion of making himself a suit from the despised cloth out of respect for the memory of his departed sovereign and in keeping with the gloom of his own fortunes, and of putting himself on board the next packet.

Suddenly the door of his shop opened with a peremptory shove and an authoritative bang, and closed again with an emphatic noise. He looked up hastily, while the fear of a sheriff and the hope of a customer made his heart palpitate and his eyes incapable of accurate speculation, until, after some moments, he recognised the form of our friend Matthew Oakes, in his wonted costume but enlarged and heightened, as it seemed, by a new air of dignity or impudence.

Supposing he was the bearer of a message indicative of business from a respectable quarter (for Matthew never ran errands for low people), the tailor regarded him more complacently than usual and waited for an explanation of his embassy.

Mat seated himself, with great familiarity on the counter, kicked his heels against its supporters, folded his arms and, looking Vince in the face, with much importance said, "Cockney Bill,"

"Villiam Wince, if you please, Tevas," interrupted the astonished and angry artist, "what do you want? Get off my counter."

"Sir," replied Tevas, still more indignantly and angrily, "I would have you to know that I am Matthew Oakes, Esquire."

"Vell then, Mr. Hoakes, what do you want?" said Vince. "Get off of that 'ere counter instinctly!"

"Hold your jaw, Bill," said Tevas, drawing a red canvass bag from his pocket which he slammed on the counter, producing a jingle not unknown, though unusual to the ears of the tailor. "Hear what I have to say to you, if you please. All England is in tears for the death of our lamented sovereign. He was as brave as Solomon, and as wise as Alexander, and all York is going to be in tears, too. All the genteel people are going into mourning on this truly doleful occasion, and I want a first chop suit of black clothes, as good as you can make, to cut them all out, by the day after to-morrow."

The tailor felt strongly tempted to laugh at the wants of the shabby-genteel individual who had such loyal intentions. But as he gazed on the queer customer, the red bag with chink so delightful, and the rusty velvet which it was so difficult to get rid of, it required not the prophetic eye of genius to imagine a change in their several relations, much to his own advantage. Altering, therefore, his tone and manner very materially, he exclaimed, "Mr. Hoakes, this is the werry welwet out of what Lord Chisterfield had his last suit of court mourning

THE LEGEND OF THE DEVIL'S PULPIT

made of; and if there's any body more genteel than Lord Chisterfield, I should like for to know it."

To be brief, he measured Oakes, and promised to deliver the suit at the time required – which promise (the only instance of the kind on record in the annals of his craft) he actually performed with punctuality. Nor did he let his patient go without suggesting and supplying all the other improvements of his person which the shop afforded.

On the next Sunday, Tevas, whom we must now call Mr. Oakes, made his appearance in Trinity Church in fine new ruffles, a brilliant cocked beaver, bag, solitaire, and all the equipments of a macaroni of those days, overlaying and garnishing the mourning apparel which, albeit rusty and shop-worn, had not yet lost "all its original brightness, nor appeared less than black velvet ruined." Although Dr. Barclay preached an excellent funeral sermon on the virtues of the late British Trajan that had been, and the still greater virtues of his successor, the British Augustus that was to be, all his eloquence and learning were wasted. Not on Trajan, nor Augustus, nor Dr. Barclay, but on Mr. Oakes was the attention of the audience riveted. The gentry were not a little scandalized at the black-hilted sword which the clerk's son had mounted and wore with an air decidedly aristocratic. But they were too dignified to exhibit any other emotion than that of silent contempt.

The wonder grew, a week or two after, when Mat was seen strutting about town at a fashionable hour, in a scarlet coat with gold embroidery, with a richly laced hat and diamond knee-buckles. Two navy lieutenants whose acquaintance he had contrived to make took him with them to pay visits, and though, as you may imagine, he was received with a mixture of undefinable sensations, he was not turned out bodily any where. And he now commenced a bowing acquaintance with several ladies of fashion and was the daily subject of admiration as he perambulated William-street. He lounged every morning in Mr. Vince's shop, and rode out every day, on a strong, cantering, capering, curvetting, prancing, tall white horse with cropt ears and a switch tail, wall-eyed but of full blood and well-attested pedigree, to a tavern out of town, with the sign of the young King George III, near the site of the present Hospital. He took a room at the City Tavern, cut his father and mother and all his humble and hard-working brothers and sisters, gave dinners at the hotel, and, by way of shaking off all vulgar, familiar, and early associations, altered his name by changing Matthew into Mark, and spelling Oakes, Oques.

Mysterious was the source of his means of paying for his new and luxurious expenses. Equally mysterious seemed the way in which he gradually got into society at that time. But this would be no great matter of wonder in our days. It may be proper, however, to mention that a fashionable lady, who was fond of patronising and bringing forward young men, took a fancy to something about Mr. Oques – either his clothes, or his horse, or himself – carried him about into company, said he was an astonishing genius, and read some verses every where which he had given her as his own. Every one who knows any thing about the course of things in that part of society denominated high life knows that the Rubicon being once passed, as long as the cash seems to hold out, there is no further inquiry made as to the origin, means, or qualifications of an adopted member of the beau monde. Old women and jealous or envious rivals are alone given to making queries about the lineage, breeding, and associations of the parvenu.

So it fared with Matthew, or Mark, who lost no opportunity of making good the ground he had occupied. At a subscription ball given to Governor Monckton on his return from the conquest of Martinico, the quondam door-keeper of Mr. Turner appeared in all his glory in a rich suit of green and red Genoa velvet, lined with yellow satin, with cut steel buttons, outshining all the vestimental magnificence of the fête. He had even the assurance to ask the Duchess of Gordon (who, as all the learned in the British peerage well know, married an American gentleman) to dance a minuet with him. Supposing him to be some stray sprig of nobility, her Grace acceded to the sublimely impudent proposition, and the star of Mr. Oques became immediately one of the first magnitude. He led the mode, and his tailor profited richly by his recommendations. He became a great literary character, lounging daily at Rivington's, in Hanover-square, where he bought canes and opera-glasses and purchased all the half-dozen copies of the first two volumes of *Tristram Shandy* which had been ventured in the New-York market and which he had the pleasure of lending to all the reading people in polite society.

He sat conspicuously on the side-scenes of the theatre, directing and controlling the applauses of the audience, and boasted that he had taught Hallam how to deliver the most favourite passages in his best character. He also became a politician, and at the great contested

THE LEGEND OF THE DEVIL'S PULPIT

election between Cruger, Livingston, Delancey, Lispenard, and Bayard, manfully espoused the side which he understood to be the genteel one, and which, luckily for him, proved to be the successful and hospitable one.

Though now circulating freely in elegant society, it cannot be disguised that when Mr. Oques made any direct matrimonial demonstrations towards the only daughter or grand-daughter of some wealthy burgher, the whole family at once assumed a distant and chilling air towards the aspiring lover. If, after this, he could force his way, on a winter's evening, into the snug, oak-wainscoted little back parlour with which the rich merchants of New-York were then contented, he was received with a silent and solemn courtesy. In spite of his gorgeous apparel, the young heiress would scarcely lift her eyes from her knitting or answer more than yes or no to his gayest remarks or softest inquiries. At the least pause, the old lady would observe from her elbow chair on the right-hand of the sparkling, crackling hickory fire, "het kleed maka den man" (or else, in her other vernacular, that fine feathers make fine birds), but they would not make the pot boil. Whereupon the grave father would take his pipe from his mouth and, after pouring out a volume of smoke, add in oracular Dutch, "Spoedige Klimmers vallen schielyck."

What Mr. Oques was worth, or how he came to be worth a dollar in capital or credit, remained as great a mystery as ever. He happened, indeed, to draw a prize of two hundred pounds in the City-Hall Lottery, which accident he treated as a bagatelle. I do believe it did not come amiss, though it took place in the midst of his apparent prosperity. His tailor, who was naturally of an inquisitive temper, was perhaps most uneasy in his mind in trying to find out the cause of his patron's sudden elevation. All his indirect hints or leading questions on this topic were met by Mr. Oques with such fearful dignity that Vince dreaded the loss of his custom too much to venture any further interrogatories. Not the less, in his inmost soul, did he determine to solve the enigma.

To the early inquiries made of him concerning this new Adonis, Mr. Vince had answered that Mr. Hoaks was a cash customer. When further questioned where the cash came from, he replied that "Mr. Hoaks 'as a rich hunkle in 'Olland," &c., and he insinuated very broadly that a match was on the carpet between our hero and seventeen different heiresses. All these excursions of the tailor's extemporaneous fancy became rumours, which were magnified, mystified, and multiplied, and though, like the heads of the Lernean Hydra, they were crushed, one after another, by the Herculean club of truth, yet other little and big reports sprung up in their places, all of similar burden, that somehow or other, Tevas Oaks had got to be somebody.

As, however, Mr. Vince obtained custom, he grew less scrupulous in his conversations about the history, ways and means of him who might be called his founder, particularly as the latter began to treat him with a certain degree of distance, passed him often in the street without recognition, and grew less punctual in his visits to his shop. Vince now began to shrug up his shoulders, or give a knowing wink, when pressed upon the subject of Mr. Oques's resources. But a horrible deed was about to be done, which removed all his scruples of conscience at betraying or injuring his benefactor. At first, with a mixed sensation of incredulous wonder and alarm, and afterwards with unsophisticated indignation, he learned that Matthew, who had not called at his shop for six days, had bought two ready made French suits and ordered a brocade dress of lilac worked with rosebuds, and a pair of pea-green and yellow satin breeches of the newly arrived Mr. Peter Tims, from Cheapside, who had opened his shop in Broad-street, near the Exchange.

The barriers that held in his curiosity were now carried away. In Indian phrase the silver chain of friendship was snapt asunder. A sense of merit neglected, genius unappreciated, patronage slighted, possessed the soul of the artist. He compared Tevas to the wiper in the fable, wowed revenge, and determined to votch Mr. Hoaks.

He had for some time past noted that this gentleman was never visible on a Friday after dinner and did not appear until towards noon the next day. It happened to be on a Friday that he learned the news of Tevas's flagrant apostacy. As soon as the Dutch clock sounded the hour of two, he announced to his journeyman (for he had now the honour of having so important a personage in his shop) that he intended to walk into the country. He then planted himself at the window and began to watch the in-goings and out-goings at the door of the city tavern. It would doubtless be amusing could I record his mental observations on those whom he did and those whom he did not know as they severally entered or left the hotel, but this I leave to the reader's imagination.

Two hours passed away and Tevas did not appear. At one time Vince had made up his mind to despatch a note, requesting the honour of seeing Mr. Oques on business of importance. But indignant pride and insulted friendship forbade this step. On a sudden a figure caught his eye, wrapped in a gold-corded crimson roquelaire, which he had a right to know since he had himself given it its form and pressure. It belonged to Mr. Oques, and though the wearer walked with a stooping and slouching gait, Vince lost not a moment in throwing a brown cloak over his shoulders and scudding rapidly and guiltily across the street and down a narrow lane leading to the river, after the object of his curiosity. He lost sight of him very mysteriously ere he came to the water's edge, but again caught a glimpse of his own workmanship at a small distance, and taking the liberty of passing through a garden which bordered on the present Greenwich-street, he was enabled to dog the roquelaire along the shore till he was quite tired. He had several tumbles among heaps of brick, stone, and mortar, which he thought much more of than the occasional remarks which he was obliged to hear from the boys, boatmen, and workmen in Dutch and English, little complimentary to himself or his agility. But he had a great object in view and had bound up each corporal agent to the terrible feat of finding out "where Mr. Hoaks was a going to."

He lost sight of the roquelaire and its wearer behind a huge heap of sand, stone, and lime which showed where the present edifice of Columbia College was already begun. Scrambling over this, and bruising his shins among some large logs of timber, he paused to take breath and again saw the crimson garment disappearing at a distance in a thicket of evergreens and brambles on the banks of the river. He looked around him and saw no human being near. He had heard of the Indians, the smugglers, and Captain Kidd's ghost, and although the sun was yet half an hour high, he could not help wishing himself in his shop, but the instinct of curiosity, combined with the desire of revenge, overcame his timidity. He renewed the pursuit, plunged into the thicket, and again caught a glimpse of the roquelaire among a pile of rocks. Towards this he crept on tiptoe, keeping a careful watch on both sides as he went, and at length ensconced himself behind a massy block of granite.

Peeping through an aperture between this rock and others which lay heaped against it, he observed a little cove in which a small pettiauger was lying. It was painted black and red, and its masts, naked of sails and cordage, were of the same hue. It was an ill-looking thing to get into, and at school Mr. Vince had heard of the river Styx, its boat, and the grim ferryman who carried over the ghosts and ghostesses. The low sun was now looking red through the thick hazy air, and a streak of dusky fire quivered all along the water from the opposite shore to the pettiauger, around which the small billows seemed to form lambent tongues of forky flame of a bright but infernal ruddiness. And the cockney was all alone. Suddenly he heard a voice, which was that of Oaks, now rough and hoarse as if made husky by sulphureous and tartarean fogs. It distinctly invocated two fiends, and ugly ones too, for it called aloud, "You two black infernal devils, come up!"

Reader, if you never happened to be scared in all your life, you cannot realize how much the Londoner was frightened at these awful words, articulated in that preternatural tone made more horrible by its being a manifest exaggeration of a familiar voice and conveying the terrible intimation that the speaker was colleagued with the powers of darkness. Vince looked on the broad Hudson rolling gloomily by; he looked also at the locker or cabin of the pettiauger, just big enough for a man to lie coiled up within it. The terrible voice again sounded, and two others, harsh as the grating of the hinges of the Pandemonian gates, replied in a wild jargon, broken by shouts of horrid laughter. Again Vince beheld the roquelaire approaching, and behind it two swarthy stalwart forms in deep red jackets and caps, their black arms bare from the shoulders and their eyes shooting a demoniac and unnatural lustre. Their brawny arms brandished enormous pieces of timber, and with every volley of discordant sounds which broke from their mouths, two rows of long white grinders showed themselves which seemed able to despatch many such Christians as Mr. Vince at a luncheon.

The forms approached, the jabber became more fearfully loud, and the Cockney, scarce knowing how or why, effected a passage through the rocks and squeezed himself into the locker, pulling the door after him as close as he was able. There he lay in an uneasy posture, trembling with the presentiment of some horrible event, but he remained not long in suspense. Footsteps approached; the same grating voices were heard; the speakers leaped on board; words in the same unintelligible language were interchanged, in which Mr. Vince clearly distinguished certain appalling execrations – and the boat suddenly sprang forward as if self-impelled. A confusion of noises, like that which might be heard from the mouth of the bottomless pit, burst upon the tailor's ears. The waves, tormented by the dividing prow, lashed its sides and broke over it with a crash that seemed powerful enough to shiver adamant. The Cockney was separated only by a single plank, as Aratus says (on which passage Longinus passes a criticism of doubtful justice), from the depths beneath and the waters around; thence, as he lay uneasily with his face to the bottom of the boat, he heard a swell of booming thunders: the very voice of chaos seemed reverberating in the hollow of his ear, and along with this was a roaring as of tigers and lions, a screaming of wrath, terror, and pain – in brief, a mingling of all frightful and dolorous noises, combining the howlings of every beast of the desert with others yet more mysteriously fearful. Two huge feet, shod with spikes, were pressed against the doors of the locker, while through his peep-hole there gleamed on the prisoner's eye the apparition of four brawny black arms, with their muscles shining and swelling to a Patagonian enormity. They wielded two immense oars, and at every pull the angry river, against whose mighty current they were struggling, uttered a startling murmur, like that of a giant roused from his heavy slumbers. And they pulled and pulled, those two pair of huge black arms, and the black bark bounded on and on amidst the intolerable roar of waters while her joints groaned and creaked and gaped, and the bitter salt water leaked in, and Vince became as sick as he was frightened and he fell into a swoon. From this he did not recover in less than an hour, when he was awakened by a grating sound from below.

When he had enough strength and consciousness restored to peep through his aperture, he saw no one on board of the boat, which was now rocking in the surf by the side of a low bank, the bottom scraping and thumping upon the beach. This fact Vince knew not, but he felt the boat tossing and knocking about and wished he was out of it. He ventured by degrees to open the doors of his purgatory to protrude his head, and at last to draw out his person. The evening was cloudy, and the June twilight was obscured with unusual gloom. On one side of him, the turbid and hazy river, to which no limit could be discovered, lay moaning whilst on the surface, flakes of phosphoric light ever and anon gleamed and again vanished. On the other was a flat and dreary expanse of what seemed a heath, unbroken by any object until it was terminated by a dark rocky wall, reaching, as he thought, from earth to heaven.

No human being was to be seen, and Vince determined to quit the demon-manned bark when he might. He jumped unharmed to the shore and ran forward. A groan or grunt from behind arrested his progress, and casting his eyes backwards, he saw, at a little distance, the two infernal oarsmen. Each was sitting on a stone as big as a stoop, with his back towards Vince, whilst projecting a foot from each of their mouths was a bowl, burning red-hot with live coals, as of juniper or bright naphtha, which yields light to the kingdom of Pluto. The strong red glare thence emitted threw its lurid reflection over the bronzed swarthy side-faces of the fiendish watermen, and on their saucer-sized eyes and upon great columnar volumes of dense vapour, ascending and commingling in interminable rings of red-tinged smoke. Vince averted his eyes and ran.

He ran on until he was up to his middle in mud. How he got out I know not, but he extricated himself by that instinct which is surer than reason, and on he ran again, perhaps an hundred yards. Now the solid earth seemed to bend under his feet like a sheet of pasteboard. The ground shook and trembled, and still he ran on and on, until he ran against a rock at the base of the hills before mentioned. Well it was for him that his nose was neither a Roman nose nor a Grecian, but a pug nose, else would he have broken it. His eyes saw all sorts of many-coloured rainbow lights, and the wind swept in gusts round his ears with tones of strange import. He began to scramble up the precipice.

I despise asterisks and fragments from the bottom of my heart, but I respect truth too much to supply from fancy the chasms of authentic tradition. How Vince got up the hill, I cannot say. All that I know is that a pallid and exanimate slender man was picked up on Bergen Hill next morning by Hans Van Riper and his brother Yop, who took him to their house near Paulus Hook, whence he was ferried to the city. It was Vince. He got home about noon next day and began to tell a confused and mysterious story which nobody could make any thing of. As his senses returned, it become more coherent, though not less fantastical. He said that the devil preached over in Jersey and had a pulpit at Weehawk, that service was held there every Friday night, and that the devil talked "handsomer" than the recorder or the rector of Trinity – that Mr. Hoax had made all his money by going to hear him, and that Satan and Lucifer rowed him over to the sermon every Friday.

The tailor's shop was soon run down with a crowd of inquisitive people. He still persisted in the same story, though with variations always increasing the marvel. Still the crowd augmented, and as it grew, so did the cockney's story. At last a regular mob was collected about his door, and before old Trinity Church. Dr. Magraw came also among them, and wanted to know what brought so many fools together. But the Doctor is a person of no mean note in my story, which I must therefore suspend, to give some account of him.

Dr. M'grath, as he spelt his name, or Dr. Magraw, as others spelt it and called him, had now practised physic in New-York about fifteen years. Who, or what he was, besides being Dr. Magraw, no one knew. Some thought him a Jesuit in disguise – others a French spy – and others again, one that had dealings with the prince of darkness. A more charitable conjecture was that he belonged to one of those unfortunate Scotch families who had taken the wrong side in 1745. His name was Scotch, but he talked good, though coarse English, neither Scotch, nor Cockney, nor provincial. To perplex the curious yet more, he talked Dutch, not only to the satisfaction of the colonists, but also of their Leyden-bred pastors. He spoke French also, fluently and well, and was quite at home in various patois – Norman, Gascon, Limousin, and what not. When he talked with the Lutheran minister, it was in pure Saxon High German, yet he chatted with the humbler members of the flock in their native Hessian or Bavarian jaw-breaking dialects. So that, for aught that could be inferred from his tongue, he might be German, or Dutch, or French, as well as Scotch. One thing was certain: he was a thoroughly bred physician and surgeon, familiar with all the science of his day, had attended Boerhaave's lectures at Leyden, and walked the hospitals of Paris. In person, he was short, broad-shouldered, deep-chested, vigorous, sturdy, and stirring, with a lively, keen gray eye, sandy hair, and one of those hard-favoured visages which give no note of age. Whether he was thirty or fifty on his arrival at New-York was hard to tell – and it was equally so forty years after.

His first notoriety arose from his refusing to keep accounts and send in bills, like the other city doctors, and resolutely insisting on his guinea fees. Of these he got but few until he was called in, by sheer accident, to a consultation on a desperate case, in the family of Chief Justice Delancey, with the two most fashionable physicians of that day. One of these was a pretty, soft-spoken, mild, bowing, simpering, complimenting, news-retailing, neatly-dressed gentleman, mighty courteous to nurses and old ladies; the other was a solemn, pompous personage, who quoted Latin, called himself a Fellow of the London College of Physicians, and took snuff out of a large gold box. Magraw, at his first interview, threw the whole family into confusion by pronouncing one an old woman and the other a quack, and refusing to see the patient again unless they were both discharged. The Chief Justice, who, though unskilled in medicine, had great skill in men, saw at once (what had never occurred to him before) that Magraw was right, and gave him the command of the sick room. In a month the lady was well, and the doctor's reputation established.

After this, business flowed in upon him, and such was his skill or his luck that his reputation went on regularly increasing, although he paid court neither to the old ladies, nor to the editors, nor to the clergy, nor to the nurses. In the course of his medical career, he demolished quack after quack, regular and irregular, generally finishing them off with a sarcasm or a nick-name – sly, shrewd, scornful, and unerringly fatal. Nor did he confine this enmity to the quackery of his own art: he held all other humbuggeries and pretensions in equal aversion. If a new preacher got into vogue by tickling the ears of silly folks with big words or amazing their eyes by flourishing his hands and arms, if a young lawyer or assemblyman got the name of eloquence by rant and flummery – woe betide him if Dr. Magraw came among his audience: he was a gone man. Whilst the orator, lay or sacred as it might be, was paddling about "on his sea of glory" (as Wolsey has it) "like little wanton boys that swim on bladders," the doctor would, on the sudden, rip up the said bladders of popular applause, let out all their high-blown pride, and leave him floundering in the very mud and slime of public contempt.

He moreover extended his guardianship of the quiet little city he had chosen as his abode to the protection of it against all impostors and adventurers under the guise of style or fashion. It were long to tell of all the well-dressed swindlers whom he unmasked and routed out with as little ceremony and as sure an instinct as a terrier hauls forth the villain rat from his hole. One instance will suffice.

There arrived, just after the peace of 1763, a French marquis who turned the heads of half the pretty girls, and was received by the governor as the heir of one of the richest and noblest titles of France. He went on triumphantly until he met Magraw at a grand dinner at the Government-house. The marquis was seated between her excellency the governor's lady and General Lord Amherst. He was, as usual, gay and talkative. The ladies had scarcely left the table when the company was astounded by the doctor's asking the governor, in a most audible tone, "where he had picked up that Bordeaux hairdresser?" He had noted that the marquis's dialect was that of the Bordalese vulgar, and his gesticulation convinced him that he had been used to wield the powder-puff. Suspicion was excited, and the conjecture ascertained to be correct, just in time to prevent the Marquis of Powder-puff from quartering himself matrimonially upon the richest family in the province.

In brief, Goldsmith's epitaph upon another shrewd Scot of the same period, might, with a little variation, have served for the tomb of Magraw:

> MAGRAW here retires, from his toils to relax,
> The scourge of impostors, the terror of quacks :
> Quack doctors, quack lawyers, and quacking divines,
> Come and dance o'er the spot where your tyrant reclines.

The city had been sickly, and the doctor so busy that, though he had marked Tevas and his finery, he had had no time to pay attention to his case. He now listened to the thousand-and-one rumours bruited among the crowd, and his instinct told him at once that there was roguery in it, coupled with the agency of some quack, corporeal or incorporeal. He therefore, getting upon the church steps, made an address to the crowd, telling them, in plain words, "they were a pack of blockheads – to convince them whereof, he would hire a couple of boats, and take whoever wished to go to Weehawken over with him the next Friday," adding, that "if the devil was there, he knew how to deal with such cattle."

Friday came; and at three in the afternoon, Dr. Magraw, armed with a broad-sword and a brace of horse-pistols, appeared on the ferry-stairs accompanied by his dog Bounce, Mr. Vince, and a sergeant's guard from the fort of broad-shouldered, red-kneed Highlanders with their tartan kilts fluttering and flaunting about them. Some government barges were in waiting, together with two huge ferry-boats. The whole population of the city, except the bed-ridden and the dignitaries, poured down to witness the embarkation, and above a thousand wished to go on board, but the doctor and his guard put back the women and children and negroes and admitted none but able-bodied white adults, who embarked to the number (as stated in my documents) of two hundred and ninety-seven.

The doctor and his Highlanders led the way in the barges. The evening was fine, but there was no wind and the tide was adverse, so that, what with the delays of embarking and crossing the river, it was twilight when they arrived at the point of the Weehawken ferry. There, old Hank Zabriskie and his family met them. Hank expressed great joy at their intention, for he said he had made up his mind to quit the place, "for the spook's noises every Friday night were growing louder and louder." Hank pointed in the direction in which the lights were usually seen, but no one had any idea of the exact locality of the preacher. The woods looked black and terrific, the rocks steep and high, so that even the Highland body-guard showed symptoms of dismay and repugnance to advancing, for the Wraiths of their native mists and torrents rose in their imagination and unearthly voices murmured in their ears. The doctor swore at them in Celtic, adjusted his belt, took a powerful pinch of snuff, brandished his gold-headed orange-stick cane, and marched on, and they, at once ashamed and encouraged by his example, marched after him. Behind came the crowd, huddled together as closely as the inequalities of the ground would allow. For want of a better, they followed a kind of blind path in which fuel had been drawn to the ferry from the woody mountainous country back of the Weehawk meadows. Thousands of fire-flies twinkled in the bushes about them; owls hooted from the tall tops of trees and sailed away from their perches as they approached. Now and then they thought they heard the long howl of a distant wolf, and then came a terrifying shriek which they knew to be the panther's cry.

It seemed as if the very insects of the air were leagued to torment them. Great humming beetles flying in heavy circles came plump against their faces. They were assailed with ravenous musquitoes – not the degenerate, attenuated musquitoes which in these days are wafted over from the Bergen meadows to suck the blood of our plump citizens – but gigantic gallinipers, with a note like that of a hautboy and a proboscis that could penetrate a water-proof boot. Whether there was really anything supernatural in this relentless foray of the musquitoes, or whether it was owing to the fact of their voracity not being appeased in those days, as it is in ours, by the weekly visits of the genial and juicy members of the Turtle Club to their dominions is a subject I leave to the investigation of the learned entomologists of the Lyceum of Natural History.

These fearful sights and sounds, and the stings and insults of the creatures of the air at length exhausted the courage as well as the patience of the party. Now and then too, a straggler would be separated from the main body and would call out for his friends in fearful tones, which sounded to them like demoniac yells. At last some grew mutinous and called on the doctor to lead them back to the ferry. Their dauntless leader could not but allow the reasonableness of the request, for the intricacy of the interwisted branches of trees, the huge fragments of rocks, the brambles and creeping vines, the slippery and deceitful heaps of leaves accumulated by many autumns, [and] above all, the darkness of the woods through whose canopy a solitary star ever and anon shot a slanting, broken ray – all this made dreadful distraction in the ranks. A halt was ordered, and the party gradually collected. A deep silence came over them, and as they listened in awe to the mysterious whisperings of the breeze through the forest, the distant deep murmuring of the river, and the crackling of the dry leaves and branches under their feet, a deep dull sound, ten times repeated, was wafted to their ears by the east wind. It seemed a preternatural admonition of the late hour of night, for they had now wandered far and long.

Meanwhile Dr. Magraw was administering to each of his Highlanders a comfortable dram of Farintosh from a jug fastened to his belt, together with a double pinch of snuff out of his own mull, which refreshed and fortified them exceedingly; in both of these comforts the rest of the party expressed strong desires to participate, but the doctor resolutely refused them. Whether this partiality might not have produced overt acts of insubordination, notwithstanding the deep feeling of terror inspired by the scene and its associations and the awful respect entertained for the doctor, I cannot pretend to say. But all of a sudden, a wild and shrill sound arose upon their ears, from the woods to the south. It was an irregular chant, partaking of the solemn and the queer, a mixture of Old Hundred and Yankee Doodle interspersed with squeaks and squalls. But ever and anon it swelled to a beautiful *andante* movement, in E major, which soon changed to a spirited *allegro* in the minor of that key, in the course of which was introduced a fine *crescendo* worthy of Rossini. At one time, a beautiful chromatic passage was introduced, apparently without effort, in which the plaintive tones of an exquisite *contra–alto* were heard, producing all the power which noises of that quality have in moving the affections. Throughout the whole, the clamorous *forte* stood out in strong relief with its contrasting *pianissimo*.

The party proceeded onward, with many trips and stumblings, although fear produced something like regularity in their steps, towards that part of the woods whence this mysterious music seemed to come. They wound for some time above the brow of the hill where the trees grew less thickly together, following the light of a tin lantern borne by one of the Highlanders. But the fitful dancing pencils of light served only as a beacon, without illuminating their path. The gush of compound melody died away – not in a sadly pleasing fall – for, after the fine *baritono* had sunk into a sonorous *basso*, the strain rather basely tapered off short, with a screaming like the screech of a screech-owl, and then a smack like that of a coach whip. But as they advanced, a single voice was heard commencing a sort of incantation or hymn. Sometimes it was husky, sometimes rich and true and strong, but it was always full of learned melody – with a good shake and beautiful *appogiaturas* – and threw off its roulades with wonderful rapidity and ease. The air was in 6-8 time, but an anomalous bar of three crotchets was introduced, and often repeated, which had a curious and unpleasing effect.

Led by the sound, the doctor and his corps-de-garde continued their progress, until a high perpendicular rock obstructed the path; they turned to the left of it and wound downwards towards the precipice. Here, after a short time, streaks of red light began to break through the crevices of the grey stones and gleam among the thickets, and as they turned short round the projection of a gigantic pile of granite, a singular and startling scene broke upon their gaze. Now, as to what follows, I must beg leave to state that, like Herodotus and Walter Scott, "I tell the tale as 'twas told to me." There are too many respectable attestations of the truth of the particulars handed down to us to justify the explanation I have heard given: that the current story is a mere allegory, invented by Doctor Magraw. What I shall proceed to relate not only accords with the received tradition, but with the formal account drawn up by Dominie De Ronda and preserved in the archives of the Garden-street Dutch Church, where it may be seen on application to the pastor. It seems to me entitled to full credit from the air of historical candour and philosophical dignity with which it commences. The dominie says – "*Men mod de duivel een wassh-haars opsteeken,*" or in English, "We must give the devil his due."

The picture then presented to the eyes of these crusaders was strange, grotesque, and unnatural. In the centre of what looked like the nave of a sylvan amphitheatre, which descended, however, rather rapidly towards the river, there was a great fire of pine logs and knots blazing upwards, around which several figures were sitting, of gigantic statures, dressed in tarpaulin hats, huge heavy jackets, and trunk breeches. The dense and pitchy vapour ascending from the pyre formed an over-canopying curtain whose folds and fringes rolled up their black convolutions above the surrounding evergreens and tall old chestnuts – the whole interior of the extraordinary temple thus formed being in some places strongly illuminated by a vivid red glare in which every spray seemed of living fire, while the recesses and small arcades of the forest were thrown into a gloom deeper than darkness and black as the abysses of infinite space. Behind the fire, at the distance of some twenty feet, was a square tall block of granite and a projecting stone cushion lapping over it, with a sort of stair-way on the left side, and some rudely disposed benches of stone beneath it, on which the fire-light was thrown broadly. About two rods below this principal precipice was another, of smaller dimensions, bearing the same resemblance to the first that a clerk's desk in our churches does to the pulpit. On top of this desk, looking steadily and sagaciously at the new comers, stood a shaggy, long-eared jackass, the gravest animal of his kind, solemnly employed in whisking away and brushing off the musquitoes with his tail.

The group around the fire was as extraordinary as the scene. One figure, splendidly dressed, held in his hand a piece of timber shaped like an oar, with which, from time to time, he stirred the huge blazing coals, sending up their sparks in showers above the gloomy drapery of smoke and the tops of the woods. The rest of the human company, about twenty in number, were scattered around, seated on boxes and outlandish-looking, coffin-shaped cases. Their hue was swarthy, and their hair dishevelled and elf-like. One of the company, of a diminutive size, dressed orientally, and whose colour was a bilious mahogany, was reclining with his elbow on an uncommon looking piece of furniture with a sort of carved brass handle. Several venerable goats, of a foreign aspect, stood not far off, with their twisted horns, long beards, and bright, restless eyes glittering in the light of the fire. Nearly opposite to them, and distinguishable by fits as the flame flashed up from the crackling pile it was consuming, three mules were standing in a row whose countenances expressed great interest in the business in hand, and just at the edge of some ragged bushes were five or six cows, looking with all their big eyes quietly upon the blaze; on the neck of one of which hung a bell of a peculiar metal which emitted at times a faint and ominous and melancholy tinkling. I must not forget a large baboon with a red night-cap on his head who capered about the fire with a great stick in his paw, poking it whenever the splendidly attired figure did, and showing a row of white crooked teeth, from ear to ear, as his features were convulsed with a sardonic grin. Divers monstrous dogs, looking wise and sober and sleepy, stood between the fire and the pulpit stretching out their clumsy paws and shaking their ears. Around and above on the projecting branches, several parrots and macaws were roosting with other strange birds not of this climate, with goblin, goggle eyes and hooked beaks, the sight of which, in such a wild spot, was enough to strike terror into the boldest Christian heart.

As the numerous band which now arrived to swell the numbers of this respectable auditory defiled round the rocky promontory, the eyes of all the persons and animals present were turned upon them, and a sensation of mutual surprise seemed to keep both parties silent. Mr. Vince, passing behind the Highlanders, saw with horror, sitting cross-legged, right under the pulpit, the two black giants who had ferried him over, in their red jackets and bare arms, with the fiery bowls before their noses, fumigating the bare face of the precipice.

The form in gorgeous apparel now sprung forward from the group, and the voice of Tevas was heard. He welcomed the multitude in a subdued tone, such as one uses in a place of worship, and presently, assisted by his attendants, marshalled them all to different seats, disposing of the rabble on the stones and smooth turf but accommodating the guard with boxes and planks. But to Doctor Magraw great ceremony and politeness was shown, all of which he declined, not very graciously, choosing to fix himself aloft on the pulpit stairs, where, having adjusted himself to his liking, he took a long and a strong pinch of snuff and began to gaze with a sour and stern expression on the strange congregation. After some moments of silence, the pea-green and poppy-coloured gipsy ground out three turns of his barrel organ, and the cow rung her bell furiously. Then the great jackass brayed lustily, the mackaws screamed, the parrots whistled, the monkey chattered, the goats made a noise without a name, the dogs howled, the cows bellowed, and the mules joined in the horrible discord with a Houhyhnhnm burthen or chorus. Then Tevas gracefully waved his hand and perfumed handkerchief to enjoin silence, made a low bow to the pulpit, and sat down in an attitude of the most profound and reverential attention.

All at once there started up on the top of the cushion, and stood conspicuous in the glare of the fire, a little figure in a cocked hat (which stood off from the crown of his head as if lifted up by some protuberances) above a bushy and well powdered wig. He had a dark skinny face, with lustrous black wicked eyes, a parrotlike nose, and no chin. His form was wrapt in a short white surplice, disclosing a pair of funny looking legs cased in black silk stockings, so far as they could be seen. His arms were disproportionately long and attenuated, terminating in black silk gloves whose fingers hung depending like the pods of the Catalpa. With the left of these claws he deposited beside him a silk handkerchief, and with the right, from time to time, he applied to his physiognomy a long white cambric cloth.

He looked around him wildly and hemmed and hawed and hawked, and used his white handkerchief for some minutes and then began, in a whining tone, which produced a swinging, seesawing sound in the air, rising and falling with doleful monotonous recurrence, an harangue very much involved, and of a quaint, flourishing character, full of Johnsonian antitheses and triads but without any periods, protracted in one long, overloaded, intertwisted and inextricable series of sentences, running round and round like the lines in the puzzle which children call the walls of Troy.

At first he seemed to utter something which sounded like an apologetical exordium for his not being prepared to address so numerous and respectable an assembly; out of which modest introduction, without coming to any conclusion, he got afloat on the drift of his unintelligible argument or convoluted rigmarole, his object being, as he intimated with violent gesticulations, "to enunciate to his audience didactic precepts, calculated to evolve their energies for those aptitudes which were now ineffectual." And then he talked about soirées, races and operas; coaches, carriages and curricles; houses, horses and harnesses; diamonds, damask and drapery; fandangos, fêtes and failures. He said that large three-story houses were better than small two-story ones. That a man who could ride in a glass coach with four fat horses was better off than one who had nothing to carry him but his own two legs; and he dwelt much on some subjects thought very mystical at that day, though now familiar to every broker's apprentice, such as buying charters, flying kites, and raising the wind. On these things he expatiated at great length, and with many repetitions. He also stated that high duties were good things, because honest men might make a living by evading them.

During the latter part of these observations, Dr. Magraw disappeared from the post he had long occupied with immoveable gravity and silence. All at once, as the preacher was winding up one of his longest expectorations, or rather sliding out of it for want of breath, the doctor appeared behind him, seized him by the nape of his neck, and held him up, shaking like a scarecrow in the wind, quite off from the edge of the rock, displaying the nether part of the creature's figure more particularly than its proprietor seemed to have wished. The surplice flying all abroad discovered a little pair of red breeches, ending in a knotty pair of knees, while the crooked shanks below, in the black silk stockings, terminated in two stumpy, hoof-like, clubbed knobs, cased in a pair of black velvet bags which figured and flourished about lustily as the doctor kept their owner suspended. After holding him awhile in this manner while he screamed and hallood and begged and kicked and lost his cocked hat, he set him down again on his feet or hind paws, griping him in the same place with his left hand, and belabouring him with his huge orange walking stick, every thwack of which resounded as if the effect of its application must have been peculiarly uncomfortable to the patient.

Still brandishing this about his ears, he asked, "Are you not the same tattling devil that told the oracle in old times what Crœsus was about when he was cooking turtle soup after a bad receipt?" And he gave him a whack to enforce his attention to the question.

"Yes, my lord," said the preacher in a small voice.

"Are you not the prying, impertinent devil of Livonia that told the German ambassador to Sweden what clothes his wife had on, and what she was doing?"

"Yes, your highness," whined the goblin, as a couple of buffets made all his members rattle.

"And are you not the same poor, miserable devil that in Rabelais' time, when the great devils were raising storms to destroy armadas, was blowing a whirlwind in a parsley bed?"

"I am, indeed, your excellency." Here he got a whack that made him whimper like a whipt spaniel.

"And are you not the same helpless and contemptible devil that Paracelsus carried about in the hilt of his sword in the shape of a bluebottle-fly?"

"Alas! yes, your high mightiness!" And here he got a kick to boot, with strappadoes nowise desirable.

"And are not you the same foolish devil that troubled the people at Maçon by thumping behind the wainscots, singing filthy songs and frightening the little children, and then was decoyed by the prior of St. Deny's into an empty Burgundy bottle, where you were corked up, and soused into holy water?"

"Oh yes, your Majesty." screamed the tormented spirit, as a terrible knock half demolished his wig and discovered a crooked corneous projection growing behind a pricked up, hairy ear.

"And are not you the abominably impudent devil that for two years has been frightening my friend, the Rev. Mr. Wesley, scratching behind the children's beds, making the plates rattle on the dresser, and ringing all the bells?"

"Oh dear, yes, I and the rats," faintly replied the almost exanimate catechumen.

"And now you have come here, have you – you paltry, sneaking, despicable devil – to stuff nonsense into the heads of my poor people of New-York, and teach them, before their time comes, how to lie, and cheat, and have lotteries and banks, and to shave and smuggle?" Here he suddenly took hold of him by what seemed an extraordinary excrescence from behind, hitherto concealed by his surplice, took out of his own pocket a little book with a green cover and gilt edges which he put to the poor devil's nose, saying, "Now, Sir, I will give you a dose that will last you half a century," and then he whirled him about and dashed him down, and a crack was heard, and a light flashed before the eyes of the spectators like that produced by the galvanic battery, and the devil vanished, and a smell like that of phosphorus was perceptible, and the enormous rock of the pulpit was split from the top to the bottom, as it remains to this day. The sailors uttered a shout of horror and fear, the cow rung her bell, the jackass yelled as if he was mourning for all his relations, the macaws and parrots squalled, the monkey whooped, the dogs howled, the mules and cows uplifted a wail, and the two black ferry-men in red jackets sent up a guttural, hysterical, hoarse, demoniac laugh from their deep diaphragms, more appalling than all the other noises together.

When this uproar had subsided, Dr. Magraw was still standing on the pulpit cushion, and gave orders, in a voice of thunder, to the soldiers, to "seize those smuggling rascals," pointing to the sailor-looking men. This command was executed with business-like celerity, method, and decency. The Highlanders produced whipcords, and the surprise and terror of the smugglers at the castigation and disappearance of their preacher made them submit to be bound without resistance.

These gentry having been pinioned, and the guard having surrounded them and come to an order according to the tactics of that day, the doctor cried out, in a more solemn voice, but of equal energy, "You, Tevas Oaks, stand forward!" The summons was not to be evaded or disobeyed. With a downward look, faltering steps, and knees that knocked together with hysterical irregularity and violence, Oaks came up slowly and sneakingly in front of the judgment seat. "Get up on that stone, you puppy," said the doctor, "and take off that gilt gallipot from your skull, and hold up your face. Let us see whether or no you are worth hanging?"

With a trembling hand poor Oaks took off his gold-laced Montero cap on the assigned pedestal, shivering and shaking in all his members.

"No – upon the whole," said the doctor, after a pause, "it would grieve your old mother too much; she is a very honest woman, and one of my patients, and her rheumatism is bad enough. It would break her heart to see you strung up on Gibbet Island. Get about your business, you forlorn rascal. Sell your finery immediately. I will see that Vince allows you a fair price. Mend your manners, and try to get a living by some honest handicraft. I may lend you five pounds myself to set you up in some small way. Be off; let me see you in proper clothes to-morrow at nine."

Tevas, who, as the reader must ere this have conjectured, had been enabled to sport his fine clothes by becoming an agent or organ to certain irregular importers of contraband goods into his Majesty's provinces, departed forthwith, like a guilty ghost dismissed by the exorcist.

And here I, too, must dismiss him with a very few words. He did not make his appearance next day, according to orders, and the places which once knew him never knew him more. But I have heard, from indisputable authority, that, under another name, he afterwards kept a tavern on the banks of the Delaware, in the beautiful village of Bristol. His hotel was celebrated for its ambitious attempts at style, for its gilt china and short commons, bad beds and full-blooded bugs, Brussels carpets and smoky chimneys, lazy blackies and long bills.

The Doctor now sat himself leisurely down, with his legs hanging over the precipice, supporting himself, as he leaned backward, with his left hand while he swung his cane to and fro, and remained for some minutes in profound meditation. At length the current of his thoughts found vent in a sort of muttered prophecy.

"Yes," said he, "I see how it is. These poor people too must go the way of all flesh. Half a century hence, they will be as wicked as the Londoners. With the same vices they will have more wit. But what of that? So much the worse for them. They will have their South Sea bubbles, their land bubbles, their bank bubbles, and all manner of bubbles. They'll have their Stock Market and their New Market, and there will be bulls and bears, lame ducks, rooks and pigeons in both of them. They will have lotteries and operas and elopements and cracked poets and ballets and burlettas and Italian singers and French dancers. And every second man in a good coat will be a broker or a lawyer or an insolvent. And there will be no more cash payments, but the women will wear cashmeres, and the men will drink champagne. – And the girls, instead of learning to cook and mend clothes, will be taught to chatter bad French and worse Spanish, and to get their husbands into jail: – but there will be no jail in those days for they will have bankrupt laws, and three-quarter laws and two-third laws, and the limits will be as big as the county! There will be no more comfortable tea-drinkings and innocent dances, but they will have their balls and routes and *conversaziones* and fêtes and fiddlesticks. People will dine by candle-light of week days, and nobody will go to church on afternoons on Sundays! Folks will be knowing in wines and cookery and players and paintings and music, and know nothing of their own affairs. They will go to fashionable churches as an amusement and to fashionable gaming-houses as a business. The girls will learn to waltz of the Germans, and their mammas to flirt from the French. The boys will all be men and the old men will try to be boys. Then they will have all manner of quackery, from a patent pair of loops to hold up their breeches, to a patent way of paying off the national debt. And they will run after the heels of every quack who comes among them, and think he is the devil himself, though he has not half the sense of the dirty little devil that I have just discharged! And the doctors will quarrel about moonshine, and ruin the character of the profession and themselves by telling the truth about one another! But I shall be gone ere then: – sufficient for the day is the evil thereof!"

The doctor concluded his soliloquy, and after sitting a while in a melancholy mood, he regained his legs, took three or four huge pinches of snuff, and descended from his rostrum. Preparations were now made to return. The smugglers were guarded by the soldiers, and the multitude followed their measured tread as they set forward on their march. My narrative has reached its proper dramatic conclusion, and I shall not detain my readers with other particulars which their own imaginations will easily suggest.

Sixty-seven years have passed away, but this spot remains as wild and uncouth as it then was. The fissure made where, according to the tradition, the preacher disappeared is plainly visible, though choked with the dead leaves of many winters. The stairs are still distinguishable, though dilapidated and overgrown with moss. Should any of my readers have a curiosity to go there, they will be at no loss as to reaching the point of the road designated in the description I have given in the commencement of the story. But after they begin to climb the hill, I must confess I am puzzled as to directing them precisely how to reach the spot. I have at various times attempted it from different points; but although I have frequently visited it, yet I have as often been obliged to return without finding the object of my search. I am not naturally superstitious, but I have been sometimes tempted to believe that a kind of enchantment reigned over the place. The whole side of the hill is overgrown with bushes of cedar, witch-hazel, dogwood, and laburnum. They are tangled with the sweetbriar, the wild vine, and all the creeping plants that abound in our waste grounds, from the staff tree to the moonseed of ominous and astrologic name, and the spaces between the thickets form a labyrinth of winding passages as intricate as that of Crete.

I have more than once, just as I was giving up the search of the pulpit in despair, lifted up my eyes and beheld the old well known rock standing before me, as if suddenly placed there by magic, breathing of the strange and solemn traditions of former days. At other times having chosen, as I thought, a familiar path leading directly to the spot, I have failed in all my endeavours to find it, and have wandered among the shrubs until the light of the setting sun on the Bloomingdale shore admonished me to return. I have never been able to go back by the same path by which I reached the precipice, nor have I ever issued from the woody mazes that surrounded it at the place at which I aimed.

There is, perhaps, nothing preternatural in this, for the land-marks of the woods are uncertain, and the family likeness between the brotherhood of trees and rocks is strong. But there is a peculiar metaphysical effect produced by visiting this rock, at least on myself; which I know not whether to ascribe to the evil of my own nature, to the associations the scene brings to mind, or to the genius of the place. Dreams of wealth, projects of ambition, conceits of vanity, are there engendered in the brain. Visions of pleasure, pomp and power there come like shadows – and so depart as you descend.

The tradition that the Devil's Pulpit is haunted has been obsolete for many years, until, very recently, the people at Weehawken and Hoboken began to talk about a fantastic figure who was seen upon bright moon-shiny nights, seated on that precipice, especially during the sitting of the New Jersey Legislature. It seems to be employed in blowing immense bubbles out of a long pipe. The insubstantial globules which it forms rise and float slowly upwards, glittering with a faint and sickly mockery of the prismatic hues. Presently they dance about, above the silvery sheen of the waters, when a broad highway of molten silver is spread in honour of the mysterious queen of night as she sails above in all her regality; and so they hover among the fogs and smoke of the city, where, after throwing out strange sparks and fireworks, some of them disappear, and others are burst. And so the glory of this world passeth away; and thus ends the Legend of the Devil's Pulpit.

The Cascade of Melsingah

WHO DOES not know the little cascade of Melsingah? If any of my readers have never visited the spot, nor heard it described, let me tell them that it is situated on the east bank of the Hudson, a little below the mouth of its tributary Matoavoan, about sixty miles from New-York at the foot of the northernmost ridge of the Highlands, where it crosses the river and stretches away out of sight to the north-east. A brook comes down the crags and woody sides of this ridge and is fed by the mountain springs throughout the year. After having collected all its waters, it flows for a short distance through the forest in a narrow rocky glen, parallel to the base of the mountain, and finally pours itself in a thin white sheet over a high precipice. From this precipice the rocky banks, rising above the top of the cascade to a considerable height, recede on each side and then return in a curve towards the rivulet, forming a little circular amphitheatre having the blue pool into which the water descends at the bottom and, at the lower end, the passage by which the brook hurries off rapidly towards the Hudson. The face of the rock down which the water falls is covered with a thick mantle of green moss, which keeps its place in spite of the current passing over it and only serves to work the slender sheet to greater whiteness. Trees of the forest overhang the hollow; the maple, the bass-wood, the black ash, and the hemlock mingle their boughs, and the moose-wood rattles its bunches of green keys as you place your hand on its striped trunk. In May the dog-wood whitens the high bank with its flowers; in June the broad-leaved Kalmia hangs out its crimson-spotted cups over the stream where it comes down from the cleft above; and all around, the witch-hazel flaunts with its straw-coloured blossoms in December, like an antiquated belle in the ornaments that belong to the spring of life. Above is a small open circle among the foliage, corresponding with the shape of the banks, at which the sun looks in for a moment at noon; but the wind never descends into the hollow save in the winter, when it sweeps the loose snow into the glen and mars the fantastic frost-work of the waterfall. For three-quarters of the year the stream pours over its rock unvisited and unheard, save by the few who love what is beautiful in nature for its own sake. But in the hot months it is a place of resort for those who come to see what every body talks about, and the woody solitude is invaded by strange feet and the solemn and eternal sound of the falling water mingles with voices that have no business there. Then come the pert citizen, the spruce clerk, the matron with her bevy of giggling girls, the unfledged poet and the fashionable lady, and all whom the dog-star drives from the seat of commerce to rusticate and sport the latest fashions on the banks of the Hudson. There is no more delightful place for passing an hour or two in a summer noon: the high banks and trees create a fresh and grateful shade; there is always a cool breath from the waterfall, and its very noise seems to mitigate the heat. A tall straight birch on one side of the hollow has its bark scored with the initials of the illustrious obscure who have performed this pilgrimage, and fragments of glass bottles mingled with the pebbles on the water's edge attest the solemnities with which some of them have celebrated their exploit.

In the course of my wanderings in various parts of the world, it had been my amusement to gather up the incidents connected with the remarkable features of nature. To my mind they reflect interest upon each other; I like the story better for the scene, and the scene better for the story. A place of such frequent resort as the Cascade of Melsingah could not but furnish matter for narrative, either in the events which happened there or in the fortunes of its visitors. I have amassed a budget of these, but on running them over in my mind, I find few of them worth relating. The story of the fat gentleman whose horse broke its bridle and made off while its owner was looking at the waterfall, leaving him to trudge to his lodgings on foot; and that of the elegant young lady who slipped into the water and entirely ruined a splendid green barège, worn for the first time, are scarcely of sufficient dignity to be formally recorded. There is a more sentimental history of a young blood from Philadelphia and a dashing belle from New-York who visited the cascade together. The profound solitude, the tender twilight of the spot, and the soft sound of the waterfall penetrated their hearts; the vows of a passion which had been three days in ripening came involuntarily to their lips, and promises of eternal fidelity were exchanged, of which the rocks and trees were the conscious witnesses. The fond couple were married the next week, and the honey-moon went off quite delightfully. But he was a rake, and she was a termagant, and no people are so ill paired as these. Before the moon had again filled and emptied her horn, they found each other out and separated, and ere the anniversary of their nuptials returned, the hymeneal knot was untied in a court of law by the dextrous fingers of two Vermont attorneys. There is also a story of a long cherished passion which for years had been proof against the sneers and calumnies of the world, broken off at last and for ever in this sylvan dell. The lover and the lady visited the cascade with a party of their friends; they differed from each other a few hundred feet in their estimate of the height of the banks, and because he ventured to disagree with her, she never forgave him. It is true that about a week before, he had lost, by the failure of a commercial friend, the greater part of his property; but this could not have been the cause of the lady's behaviour, for we know that such considerations have no influence on lovers.

These are stories of modern date and exemplify the degeneracy of modern manners. Men have greatly changed within the last hundred years, or there is no truth in romances. Both the good and the bad have borrowed something from each other; the days of heroic virtue and prodigious villany are at an end; the virtuous have become prudent and discreet, and the villain aspires to be respectable. I have only one tale of the Cascade of Melsingah which I can, with a grave face, relate to the youths and maidens, and that is so old that I fear it is not more than half true. Such as it is, I give it, gathered from the lips of the aged inhabitants of the neighbourhood with whom the tradition was going to the grave.

The aborigines of North America possessed an exceedingly poetical mythology: it had much of the beauty of the Grecian, with none of its voluptuousness. Besides the Supreme Deity, the Great Master of Life, they worshipped a multitude of subordinate divinities, with whom they believed every part of the universe to be peopled. According to their creed, a Manitto dwelt upon every hill and in every valley, in every open glade and dark morass, in the chambers of every cavern and the heart of every rock, in every fountain and watery depth and running stream. These spirits were propitiated by innocent and unbloody offerings: wreaths of flowers, belts of wampum, clusters of the wild grape; shining ears of maize were spread on the mountain tops, or hung on the cliffs, or laid on the shelves of the grottos, or dropped into the waters where they were supposed to abide. As every individual among these native tribes, the females as well as the warriors, was placed under the protection of some tutelary spirit, these local divinities were often chosen as the invisible guardians to whose charge they entrusted the fortunes of their lives.

A long time ago, before a white man had settled in the county of Dutchess, the Cascade of Melsingah had also a spirit that lived in its rock and its waters, and was held in uncommon reverence. He was often seen by the Indian hunter who passed that way soon after the going down of the sun. At that time he appeared under the figure of a gigantic warrior with an abundance of the grey plumes of the eagle on his head and a grey robe of the wolf skin thrown around him, standing upright in front of his waterfall. But none were ever permitted to behold him near, and face to face. As the observer drew nigh, the figure gradually disappeared, and in its place he found only the white sheet of water that poured over the rock, falling heavily among the gathering shadows into the pool below. Sometimes also, but more rarely, he was seen in the early twilight before sunrise, and fortunate was the hunter to whom he showed himself at that hour, for it was an omen of success in the chase. None of the spirits of the surrounding country were oftener beheld in dreams by the Indians that made their haunts above the Highlands, and when the forms of the dead from the land of souls came to their friends in the visions of the night, they were often led by the hand of the gigantic warrior in the wolf-skin and the eagle plumes.

It is now almost a century and a half since there lived among the Indians who inhabited what is now the county of Dutchess a young girl, the daughter of one of their chiefs whose name is lost by the lapse of time, but the tradition of whose uncommon beauty and gentleness of character still survives. She lost her mother in early childhood, and her father, who had loved her tenderly and had brought her up with a delicacy quite unusual among the race to which he belonged, died when she was only ten years of age. A remembrance of his affection, and of the agony she had felt at his loss, seemed to have softened her heart life and rendered her an unwilling witness of the scenes of cruelty to which the customs of war among her countrymen gave occasion. After the death of her father she lived alternately in the families of the older warriors who had been his companions in arms and at the council fire. She was welcomed with kindness and affection wherever she went, endeared to them as she was by the memory of the wise and valiant man her father and by her own gentle disposition. When they spoke of her, they likened her, in their metaphorical language, to all that was beautiful, harmless, and timid among the animals – the fawn of the wood and the yellow-bird of the glades, wandering and homeless, to which they delighted to afford shelter.

The young maiden of whom I speak had beheld in her childhood the beautiful Cascade of Melsingah, and the form of the Manitto had once been revealed to her as the evening was setting in, standing in his wolf-skin robes before the waterfall. After that she saw him often in her dreams, and at a proper age she chose him for her tutelary spirit. A circumstance soon after occurred to strengthen the reverence with which she regarded him by blending it with the feeling of gratitude.

One day she went alone to his abode to pay him her customary offerings in behalf of herself, the friends she loved, and her nation. She carried in her hand a broad belt of wampum and a white honeycomb from the hollow oak, and on her way she stopped and platted a garland of the gayest flowers of the season. On arriving at the spot she went down into the narrow little glen through which the brook flowed before it poured itself over the rock, and standing near the edge, she dropped her gifts one by one into the current, which instantly carried them down the waterfall.

The pool into which the water descends was deeper than it is at present, the continual crumbling of the rocks for more than an hundred years having partially filled up the deep blue basin. The stream too, at that time, had been lately swelled by profuse rains and rushed down the precipice with a heavier torrent and a louder noise than she had ever known it to do before. In approaching more nearly to the edge and looking down to see what had become of her offerings, she incautiously set her foot on a stone covered with the slimy deposit of the brook; it slipped, and she was precipitated head-long with the torrent into the pool below.

What followed she did not recollect until she found herself lying on the margin of the pool and awaking as if from an unpleasant sleep with a sensation of faintness at the heart. She thought at first that she must have been taken from the water by somebody who belonged to her nation, and looked round to see if any of them were near. But there was no human trace or sound to be discovered: she heard only the whisper of the wind and the rush of the cascade, and beheld only the still trunks and waving boughs, the motionless rock and the gliding water.

On her return to the village where she lived, she made the most diligent inquiry to learn if any of her people had assisted her in the hour of danger, or if any thing was known of her adventure. Nobody had heard of it – none of the tribe had passed by the cascade that day – and the maiden became at length fully convinced that she had been preserved from a violent death by her guardian spirit, the Manitto of the waterfall. Her gratitude was in proportion to the benefit received, and ever afterwards she paid an annual visit to the cascade at the season when she was thus miraculously rescued, sometimes alone and sometimes in company with the young females of her age. On these occasions the dark rocks around were hung with garlands and bracelets of beads were dropped into the clear water, and a song was chanted commemorating the maiden's deliverance by the benevolent spirit of the place.

The Indians of the Hudson who lived above the Highlands, and those who possessed the country below, although belonging to the same great family of the Lenni Lennape, were not always on friendly terms. At the time of which I am speaking, a serious misunderstanding existed between them. An Indian of the tribe above the Highlands was found encroaching on the hunting grounds below and was killed in a fierce dispute which ensued. His people anxiously sought an opportunity to revenge his death, nor was it long before it was put into their hands. A young warrior of the lower tribe, ambitious to signalize himself by some act of heroic daring, boasted that notwithstanding what had happened, he would bring a deer from the hunting grounds to the north of where the great river broke through the mountains. Accordingly he set out alone, in one of the light canoes of the natives, on his way up the river.

He landed on the east bank, five or six miles above the Cascade of Melsingah, and after no long search had killed a deer, dragged the animal to his canoe, and put off from the shore. But his motions had been observed, and he had not yet gained the middle of the river when a canoe in which were five northern Indians made its appearance, coming round the extremity of a woody peninsula that projected with its steep bold shores far into the water. Immediately one of them raised his firelock to his eye and levelled it in the direction of the young Mohegan, but another who seemed to be the leader of the party placed his hand on the piece, which was immediately laid down and an oar taken up in its place.

A single glance served to show the warrior that they were all well armed, and that his only chance of safety lay in reaching the shore before them and trusting to the swiftness of his feet to effect his escape. He therefore plied his oar with great diligence, and his little vessel shot rapidly over the water, but his enemies were gaining fast upon him, and it was now evident that they must overtake him before he could reach the land.

In an instant he had leaped into the water and disappeared, but his pursuers were too well aware of his object to slacken their exertions and held on their way towards the shore. When he rose again to the surface, their canoe was at no great distance. Two of the strongest of them plunged into the river, one of whom, swimming with exceeding swiftness, soon overtook him and seized him by the hair of his head. A desperate but brief struggle ensued, in which both the combatants went down.

In a moment afterwards, the young warrior re-appeared without his antagonist, who was seen no more: but his pursuers had already surrounded him. They secured him without difficulty, carried him to the shore, and there binding his hands behind him with a strong grape vine, led him towards their village.

The warrior finding all attempt to escape useless, resigned himself with seeming indifference to his fate. At first he scarcely thought that he should be put to death, for he knew the mild character of the people into whose hands he had fallen, and he relied still more on their known dread of his own warlike and formidable tribe. However, he prepared himself for the worst and began to steel his heart against the fear of death. He did well, for soon after they began their march, his captors commanded him to sing his death-song. The youth obeyed, and in a strong deep chant began the customary boast of endurance and defiance of pain. He took up the strain at intervals, and in the pauses his conductors preserved a deep and stern silence.

At length the party came upon a kind of path in the woods, which they followed for a considerable distance and then suddenly stopped short. All at once a long shrill startling cry burst from the four savages. It was the death-cry for their drowned companion. It rang through the old woods and was returned in melancholy echoes from the neighbouring mountains.

When the last of these had died away, the party put their hands to their mouths and uttered a second cry, modulated into wild notes by the motion of their fingers. An interval of silence ensued which was at length broken by a confused sound of shrill voices at a distance, faintly heard at first, but growing every moment more audible.

In a few minutes two young warriors, who seemed to have come by a shorter way than the usual path, broke through the shrubs and took their station without speaking a word by the party who were conducting the prisoner. Presently a crowd of women and children from the village appeared in the path, shouting and singing songs of victory, and these were followed by a group of old men who walked in a grave silence. As soon as they came up, the party resumed their march and led their prisoner in triumph to the village.

The village consisted of a cluster of cabins, irregularly scattered in a natural opening of the great forest, on the banks of a stream which brawled over a shallow stony bottom between rocky banks on its way to mingle with the Hudson. The Indian appellation of this wild stream was Mawenawasigh, and it now bears the name of Wappinger's Creek.

In one respect the captive was fortunate. The chiefs and principal warriors of the tribe were absent on a hunting expedition, and it was necessary, in so grave a matter, to delay the decision of the prisoner's fate until their return, which was expected in a few days. He was therefore taken to an unoccupied dwelling, placed on a mat, bound hand and foot, and fastened with a strong cord made of the sinews of the deer to a tall post in the centre supporting the roof. It was the office of one of his captors to keep watch over him during the day time, and at night two of them slept in the cabin.

For the two first days his prison was thronged with visitors. The relatives of the drowned man and of him who was slain below the Highlands came to taunt him on his helplessness, to assure him of the certainty of a death by torture, and to exult in the prospect of vengeance. Others came and gazed at him with an unfeeling curiosity. I should have mentioned that he was of Mohawk extraction, the son of a warrior adopted into a Mohegan tribe, and that he possessed all the physical peculiarities of his noble race. They spoke to each other, commending his fine warlike air, his lofty stature and well turned limbs, and said that doubtless he would die bravely. One only seemed to regard him with sympathy. A sweet female face looked in several times at the door and turned sorrowfully away.

On the third day as the captive sat alone in the cabin, the same lovely face again showed itself at the door, and a graceful figure, just ripened to the perfection of womanly symmetry, entered. A look of surprise and pleasure shone in the features of the young warrior, but it passed away like a sunbeam in winter and was succeeded by the usual expression of indifference belonging to his race.

"Young man," said the maiden, "art thou willing to die?"

"The warriors of my tribe," he answered, "fear not death."

"But thou art yet young, and the light is still pleasant to thine eyes. It is but yesterday that thou wert received into the number of warriors, and thou hast never sat at the council fire. Thou wilt be unhonoured in the land of souls. Thou wilt go from among the warriors and hunters of thy tribe as the stranger goeth to his own country, and thy name will be no more heard. It is a pity that thou shouldst die."

The warrior cast his eyes around and was silent for a moment. "At least," said he, "I shall die like a warrior from the country whose brooks run into the great salt water lake."

When he raised his eyes the maiden had departed, but her words had engraved themselves deeply on his mind. His heart acknowledged the truth of her saying that the light was yet pleasant to his eyes. It was hard to take the long journey of death thus early, to leave his tribe, his friends, his brother warriors, the broad hunting grounds and waters of his tribe, and the plans of ambition and glory he had formed. It was hard too, to leave a world in which dwelt such lovely beings as she who had given him her sympathy. It was worth while to live were it only that he might have the opportunity of convincing her that he was not ungrateful. The artificial fortitude to which he had wrought himself in obedience to the ethics of his countrymen began to waver, and the glory of a death of torture and endurance to lose its value in his eyes.

"Would it not be better," said he to himself, "to share a long life with the beautiful maiden who has just left me, to drive the deer and the wolf for her sake, and to come home loaded with game in the evening to the hearth that she should keep brightly burning for my return?"

The night came, but brought no sleep to the young warrior until its watches had nearly expired. On awakening, he saw through the opening that served as a door to the cabin that the sun was risen and the surly savage who guarded him was standing before it. The moments passed heavily away; no one came to the cabin save an old woman who brought him his morning meal. The curiosity of the tribe was satisfied, and the relatives of the deceased were weary of insulting him. At length the shadow of a human figure fell upon the green before the door, and the next instant the well-remembered form and face of beauty made its appearance.

The maiden laid her hand on the shoulder of the sentinel and pointed to the sky where a bald eagle was sailing away to the east. The majestic bird at length alighted on the top of a tall tree at the distance of about half a mile, balanced himself for a moment on his talons, then closed his wings and settling on his perch, looked down into the village as if seeking for his prey. "If thy bow be faithful and thy arrow keen," said the maiden, "I will keep watch over the prisoner until thy return." The savage threw a glance at the captive, as if to assure himself that every thing was safe, and immediately disappeared in the forest.

The young woman then entered the cabin. She came with a plan of escape which she had formed for the captive. There was no time to be lost; the chiefs of the tribe were to return the next day, and then he must expect to be guarded with greater strictness than ever.

It were long to repeat the conversation which ensued. The young warrior implored his beautiful deliverer to accompany him in his flight. He assured her that liberty would be bitter without her and that her presence and her pity would almost compensate him for the tortures which awaited him in case he should remain. He spoke of the danger she might incur if it were known that she had aided his escape and had thus disappointed the vengeance of her tribe, and he protested that he would rather die by the death of fire than expose her to the slightest peril.

Why should I waste time in telling what has already so often been told? The conclusion was natural – it was inevitable. The heart of a young female of nineteen, in every nation and every state of society, is soft and susceptible, and when besieged at once by love and compassion, is too certain to yield. The maiden made the warrior repeat again and again his promises of affection and constancy, as if they were a security against any unfortunate consequences of the imprudence she was going to commit. She ended by believing all he said and by consenting to become his wife and the companion of his escape. "But I cannot go to thy tribe," said she; "for then thou wouldst be obliged to raise the tomahawk against my people, and I may not abide in the habitation of him who seeks to spill the blood of my friends. If thou wilt take me for the guide of thy path, I will bring thee to a hiding-place, where the arrows of thy enemies cannot reach thee, and where we may remain sheltered until this cloud of war be overpast."

The youth hesitated. "Nay then," continued she, "I may not go with thee. I will cut thy cords, and the Good Spirit will guide thee to the land of thy friends."

This was enough: love prevailed for once over the desire of warlike glory in the bosom of a descendant of the Mohawks, and it was settled that the flight should take place that night.

They had just arrived at this conclusion when the man who guarded the prisoner returned. He had been absent the longer because the eagle had changed his perch and had alighted on a tree at a still greater distance than the first. He had succeeded in bringing down the bird, and was now displaying its huge wings with evident satisfaction at the success of his aim. The maiden pulled from them a handful of the long grey feathers as the reward of having shown him to the guard and departed.

The midnight of that day found the captive awake in the cabin and his keepers stretched on a mat asleep by the door. They had begun to guard him with the less vigilance because he had made no attempt and shown no disposition to escape. He thought he heard the light sound of a footstep approaching; he raised his head, and listened attentively.

Was it the rustling of leaves in the neighbouring wood that deceived him, or the heavily drawn breath of the sleepers, or the weltering of the river on whose banks the village stood? These were the only sounds he was now able to distinguish. A ray of moonlight shone through a crevice in the cabin and fell across the bodies of his sleeping guards. As his eye rested on this, he saw it gradually widening, and soon after, the mat that hung over the opening which served for a door-way was wholly withdrawn and the light figure of the maiden appeared.

She stepped cautiously and slowly over the slumbering men, and approaching him with a sharp knife, severed without noise the cords that confined him, and stealing back to the door, beckoned to him to follow. He did so, planting his foot at every step gradually on the floor from the point to the heel and pausing between until he was out of the cabin.

His heart pounded within him when he found himself standing in the free air and the white moonlight with his limbs unbound.

They took a path which led westward through the woods, and after following it for several rods, the maiden turned aside and took from a thick clump of cedars a musket, a powder-horn, and a bag of balls, which she put into his hands. She next handed him a wolf-skin mantle, which she motioned him to throw over his shoulder, and placed on his head a kind of cap on which nodded a tuft of feathers, plucked from the wings of the very eagle his sentinel had so lately killed. She then drew forth a bow and a sheaf of arrows, and striking again into the path, proceeded with a rapid pace. It was not long before they heard the small waves of the river tapping the shore; they descended a steep bank and the broad Hudson lay glittering before them in the moonlight. A canoe, his own canoe – he knew it at a glance – lay moored under the bank, and rocking lightly on the tide. They entered it; the warrior took one oar, the maiden another; they pushed off from the shore and were speedily on their way down the river.

They glided by the shore where now stands the town of Newburgh, then a steep bank covered with tall trees, since renowned as the spot where the stern virtue of Washington awed into shame and silence the disposition that was rising among a discontented army to offer him a military crown. Far below, the moonlight dimly showed, embosomed among the mountains, a woody promontory, round which the river turned and disappeared from the view. It was the place to which we have given the name of West Point and which is now never passed without thinking of the guilt of the mercenary Arnold and the melancholy fate of the generous André. Then they neared the eastern shore and passed close to the mouth of the Mattoavoan, where it quietly and sluggishly mingles with the Hudson – so close that they could hear from the depth of the woods the incessant dashing of the stream leaping over the last of the precipices that cross its channel. High above and a little way inland rose the round, bleak, and bald summit of Beacon Hill, on which afterwards blazed the watch-fires of the American revolution when it made one of a range of signal posts reaching southward to the British lines, established to alarm the upper country in case of incursion. These are scenes now rich in historical remembrances – there were others at the time of which I am speaking, but they have passed away with the race whom we have dispossessed.

They continued to pass along under the shore until the roar of the Mattoavoan was lost to the ear. They were not far from the foot of the northernmost of the mountains washed by the Hudson that form the gigantic brotherhood of the Highlands, when a softer and lighter rush of water was heard. A rivulet, whose path was fenced on each side with thick trees and shrubs bound together by vines of the wild grape and the labrusca, came down over the loose stones and fell with a merry gurgle into the calm water below.

It was the rivulet of Melsingah. The interlacing boughs and vines formed a low arch over its mouth that looked like the entrance into a dark cavern. The young woman pointed towards it and intimated to the warrior that up that stream lay the path to that asylum whither she intended to conduct him.

At this he took his oar from the water and in a low voice began to remonstrate with her on the imprudence of remaining so near the haunts of his enemies. The parley lasted for a considerable time, during which she briefly explained to him what he had heard something of before, the profound religious reverence in which the Cascade of Melsingah, intended by her as the place of their retreat, was held, and related the interposition of its benevolent spirit in behalf of her own life. He was at length satisfied and turned his canoe to the shore. They landed, and the warrior taking the light barque on his shoulders, they passed through the arch of shrubs and vines up the path of the rivulet, and soon stood by the cascade.

The maiden untied from her neck a string of beads and copper ornaments obtained from the whites of the island of Manhadoes, dropped them into the water, and murmured a prayer for safety and protection to the Manitto of the place. On the west side of the deep glen in which they found themselves was a shelf of rock projecting from the steep bank (which has since crumbled away), and under this the warrior and his gentle guide sheltered themselves till morning.

The return of light showed the inhabitants of the Indian village on the Mawenawasigh in unwonted bustle and confusion. All the warriors were out, the track of the fugitives was sought for, discovered, and followed to the bank of the river. The print of their steps on the sand, the marks of the canoe where it had been fastened to the bank, and of the oars where they had been planted to shove it away from the shore left no doubt that the warrior had carried off the young woman to his own tribe, and they abandoned all further pursuit.

In the mean time, the warrior was occupied in constructing a habitation. A row of poles was placed against the projecting shelf of rock, which thus served for a roof; these were covered with leafy branches, and over the whole was laid a quantity of dead brushwood, so irregularly piled, as when seen at a little distance to give no suspicion of human design. The inmates of this rude dwelling subsisted on game found in the forest, on fish from the mouth of the rivulet, and on the wild fruits and roots of the soil.

The warrior's costume of the wolf-skin mantle and eagle feathers had been suggested by the idea that in case of an emergency it might enable him to pass for the Manitto of the waterfall, and on one occasion he found the convenience of his disguise. As he was sitting one day at the door of his cabin, he heard the voices of two persons in the wood who seemed to be approaching the place. He saw that if he attempted to hide himself by going in, they might enter the glen and discover the secret of his retreat. He therefore took up his bow which was lying beside him and placed himself in an upright motionless attitude on the edge of the pool in front of the water falling over the rock. In a moment two Indians made their appearance coming through the trees. At sight of the majestic figure in the grey mantle and plumes, they started and uttered an exclamation of surprise. He waved his bow motioning them away. One of them threw towards him a couple of arrow heads which he carried in his hand, and which fell into the water at the warrior's feet, sprinkling him with the spray they dashed up; and making gestures of reverence and supplication, the savages instantly retired.

Thus the time passed – swiftly and pleasantly passed – from the end of May until the beginning of September. The wants of savage life are few and easily supplied, and for the little inconveniences that might attend their situation, the tradition says that the inmates of the glen of Melsingah found a compensation in their mutual affection.

At length when the warrior had one day ventured across the ridge that rises to the south-east of the cascade and was hunting in the deep narrow valley beyond, he suddenly came upon an Indian of his own tribe, who immediately recognised him. An explanation took place, in the course of which he learned that a peace had been settled between the tribe of Mohegans above and that below the Highlands. The Mohawks, to whom both were tributary, who governed them with a rigid authority and who claimed the right of making war and peace for them, having heard of their differences, had despatched one of their chiefs to adjust them and to command the two tribes to live in friendship.

"My children," said Garrangula, the ambassador of the Confederates, in a council to which the chiefs of both tribes were called, "it is not good that ye who are brethren should spill each other's blood. If one of you have received wrong at the hands of the other, your fathers of the Five Nations will see that justice is done between you. Why should ye make each other few? Once ye destroyed yourselves by your wars, but now that ye dwell together under the shadow of the great tree of the Five Nations, it is fitting that ye should be at rest and bury the tomahawk for ever at its root. Learn of your own rivers. The streams of Mattoavoan and Mawenawasigh, after struggling and wasting their strength among the rocks, mingle at length in peace in the bosom of the father of waters, the great River of the Mountains." The council, since they could do no better, approved of the words of Garrangula; it was agreed that the relations of the hunter slain below the Highlands should be pacified by a present of wampum and shells; the chiefs smoked the pipe of peace together, and delivered belts of wampum as the memorials of the treaty.

The warrior hastened to the glen of Melsingah to communicate the intelligence to one whom he knew it would delight beyond measure. Their retreat was instantly abandoned, not, however, without some regret at leaving a place where so many happy days had been passed; the birch canoe was borne to the mouth of the rivulet, and after taking his bride, at her earnest entreaty, to visit her own tribe, the warrior descended with her to his friends below the mountains.

Adventure in the East Indies

THE ROYAL TIGER of India differs from the common tiger in his superior size and the extraordinary majesty of his appearance. His face is broader, his neck thicker and shorter, his limbs more brawny and strung with larger sinews, and his sides striped with brighter and more beautiful colours. There is a dignity in his port and a pride in his demeanour which have obtained for him the epithet of royal, and which, in the opinion of some, give him at least equal pretensions with the Lion to the title of King of Beasts. When foiled in an attempt to seize his prey, he never immediately renews the pursuit. On the contrary, he walks slowly and disdainfully away, as if too proud to expose himself to the shame of a second failure, or as if he had been unsuccessful only because he was indifferent to his prey.

Some years since, when I lived in the East Indies, I had an adventure with one of these terrible animals, and as there were some circumstances attending it which my friends were pleased to think extraordinary, I am tempted to relate it. I was then residing in the populous city of Madras, and for the sake of studying the manners of the country, I mingled more than was usual with the natives, and succeeded, in many instances, in gaining their esteem and confidence.

One morning, just as I had risen and was sitting in my virandah enjoying the fresh dewy air, so agreeable in that climate before sunrise, a Brahmin with whom I had some acquaintance came to me in great agitation, with his hand bound up and the blood trickling through the bandages. He had hardly given me time to address him with the customary salutations of the east when he told me that a royal Tiger had entered his house about the time of the morning twilight and, as he was making his escape at the door, had rushed at him and torn his hand. He had succeeded, however, in closing the door after him, which he had fastened as well as he was able, leaving the animal within. When the Brahmin had finished his relation, he looked at me very anxiously and inquired of me what I would advise should be done.

I had lived long enough in the country to know something of the dispositions of the tiger; and it seemed to me a perfect absurdity to believe that the living man whom I saw before me had ever been in the same room with one of these fierce creatures. I thought it more than probable that it was one of the hyenas which, in that part of the East Indies, often came prowling about the habitations in the night. One of them had been shot a few nights previous by a German of my acquaintance, and I had no doubt that this was another, transformed into a royal tiger by the same process of fear and obscurity which, in other countries, has been known to change a white horse into a spectre wrapt in its winding sheet. I could not, therefore, help rallying the Brahmin a little about his panic while I assured him that I would soon give an account of the creature, whatever it might be.

I exchanged my morning-gown and slippers for a hunting coat and boots, and going out, I mentioned the subject to some of my friends in the British army then stationed at Madras and found them nowise disinclined to the morning's sport of shooting an hyena. We armed ourselves with muskets, which we loaded carefully, and having picked the flints and seen that the bayonets and locks were in good condition, we set out, accompanied by two Malay servants, for the Brahmin's dwelling. Our party, including the Malays, consisted of seven persons.

On arriving, we looked in at one of the small apertures guarded with bamboo lattice-work which serve the natives for windows, and greatly to our surprise we beheld at the further end of the apartment a tiger of the largest size, quietly reposing on the floor, with one huge fore-leg stretched out before him and the other drawn up under his breast, his large eyes of a greenish yellow winking softly and sleepily in the morning light that grew stronger every moment. One of the party proposed to fire at him from the window; this was overruled on account of its height, which did not permit us to take aim with effect. I observed, also, that our Malays shuddered as the proposition was mentioned; nor do I believe that an individual of us all would have been willing to be found on the same level with the animal in case he should break from the house.

The Brahmin's habitation was built of red free-stone; it was a single story in height, with doors and lattices of bamboo. It was covered with long rods of the same plant, laid horizontally on the top of the walls, and thatched with a thick layer of the tough and durable leaves of the palmyra tree. This covering was both the roof of the house and the ceiling of the apartments, and to this, after a short consultation, we ascended. We directed the Malays to make a hole in the middle of the roof. They kneeled down and, pulling up the palmyra leaves, piled them on each side until at length they came to the horizontal rafters of bamboo, several of which they took in their hands and shoved out at one end of the roof. An opening was thus formed, through which we beheld the tiger, lying as we had seen him through the window, but it was evident that the noise we had made on the roof had excited his attention, for his head was raised and the sleepy look of his eye was exchanged for a fierce and steady glare. We put our muskets into the opening, and taking aim as well as we were able, fired together. Instantly we heard the animal spring to his feet and begin rapidly to pace the apartment.

The smoke with which the dwelling was now filled, and which came pouring out at every cranny, prevented us from taking a second aim, but each of us, as fast as he loaded his piece, discharged it through the aperture at random. Whether we had wounded the tiger or not, we were unable to judge, but it was very certain that he had become exceedingly enraged. We heard him rearing and plunging madly in the smoke, his huge tail occasionally striking the sides of the room, and his claws sometimes raking the wall from the top to the bottom as he came heavily to the floor. The bamboo rafters under our feet were several times shaken and displaced as the enormous animal sprang upwards against the wall, and once, when he struck the roof with more than usual force, our two Malays leaped down and betook themselves to flight, nor could either threats or promises induce them to return. We even began, ourselves, to fear that he might break through the roof, or, what would be still more dangerous, bring down a part of it, with those whom it sustained, into the room below. We therefore removed to a neighbouring house which, being a story higher, overlooked the dwelling where the tiger was confined, and the owner of which readily permitted us to occupy. From the top of this house our party continued to aim at the opening made by the Malays in the roof of the other, trusting that, as the animal was continually changing his place, some fortunate ball might yet give him his death-wound. More than an hour was spent in loading and discharging our pieces in this manner, without any other apparent effect than that of increasing the rage of the animal.

In the mean time the sun had risen, and the house-tops in the suburbs of Madras were tinged with the crimson light. I well remember looking about me and beholding the flat roofs, for a considerable distance thronged with the natives who stood to witness the combat. It seemed as if all the inmates of these habitations, both male and female, old and young, had gone up to their house-tops; and when I looked at their dark faces, their small but handsome figures, their flowing drapery, their motionless and eager attitudes, I could almost have thought them so many groups of statues placed on those elevated pedestals were I not occasionally reminded of their being human by the sight of a father or mother anxiously directing the attention of their child to the house we occupied. In the meantime our party received a reinforcement: two or three Europeans and several natives, armed with muskets, joined us, and a brisker fire was opened upon the building in which the tiger was confined. It did not last long, for, on a sudden, we heard a terrible shriek, accompanied with a loud crash; the door of the building was thrown to the distance of several yards, and the tiger bounded forth at liberty. A few long leaps took him beyond the reach of our fire, and he was seen moving off towards the uninhabited country.

We immediately formed a party to pursue him. We were fifty in all, and well armed with muskets, carbines, and lances. After having proceeded two or three miles, we suddenly lost track of the animal, and halted to recover it on a closer examination. We were arranged in a scattered file, along a path which followed the windings of a river close to its high and steep bank, and which was so narrow that two persons could not conveniently walk abreast. On one side of this path the ground, covered with low shrubs, descended more than twenty feet to the bed of the river, which was nearly dry, and on the other, a strip of rank tropical vegetation separated it from a luxuriant wood of acacias and trees of the palm kind, enclosed with a thick brush fence. Some of our party proceeded a few paces forward in the path, others returned a little way back, and all were intently occupied in the endeavour to discover some traces of the tiger's steps. I also lent what aid I was able to the examination, for having the misfortune to be exceedingly short-sighted, I could assist but little. I applied to my eye a glass which I always carried about me in my waistcoat pocket, suspended to my neck by a narrow black ribbon, to remedy the defect of my vision. I first looked carefully along the skirt of the wood, and scanned, one by one, the openings among the trees.

I do not remember ever to have gazed on a more quiet scene than the one which presented itself to my sight, or one more fitted to banish all apprehensions of mischief. The strong vegetation between the path and the wood bore no impression of the heavy step of the tiger, the occasional patches of sand showed no print of his feet, nor did his eye glare at me from under the boughs. It was so peaceful and so beautiful a spot that I should hardly have been surprised at hearing the innocent voices of children sporting in the recesses of the grove, or at seeing their sweet faces peeping at me from behind the shaggy trunks. The broad leaves of the fan-palm hung motionless in the blaze of the mounting sun, and the habitations of the bottle-nested sparrow which depended from the ends of the boughs and the festoons of the huge creeping plants which overran and bound together the whole summit of the wood were not moved by a breath of air. Nothing was to be heard but the occasional chatter of a monkey at a distance, or the hoarse call of some bird peculiar to the country. I then turned and looked down the bed of the river, directing my eye gradually along its course as far as it could be followed. There was no sign of life to be discovered even there, except that just below me I saw, now and then, a lizard running over the dry stones and disappearing under them. I became satisfied, for my own part, not only that the tiger was not near us, but that he had not even passed that way, and I was putting back my glass into its place, when I heard a rustling noise from the wood, which drew my attention to that quarter. I looked, and beheld the enormous animal in the air, in the very act of leaping upon me.

The creature had cleared the brush-fence and the whole space between that and the path by one of those immense leaps which the tiger is sometimes known to make, and now, with his mouth open, his eyes dilated, and his huge paws held before him a little apart from each other, was descending upon his victim with a force sufficient to crush a dozen men in pieces, and against which no weapon could be of any avail. He was already so near me that I had not time to spring from the spot where I stood. I had the certainty of death before me, and a crowd of horrible and agonizing images passed like lightning through my mind. I thought of lying half-devoured in the distant jungle to which the tiger should drag me, and the weeping faces of those whom

I had left in a distant country and whom I should never see again, came almost visibly before my eyes.

I remember that along with these there was mingled the confused idea that I would not let my brute adversary go from my death unharmed. I stood holding my musket in my left hand, with the bayonet in the air, and I had just time to raise my right to grasp the piece firmly and to give it a direction towards the animal. In doing this I suppose that I involuntarily made a step backwards towards the river, which brought me close upon the steep edge of the bank, where the soil was somewhat broken. The tiger had made his leap with unerring precision, and, as he descended, he received the bayonet between his fore-legs in the breast. At the very moment that I felt his weight upon the weapon, the ground beneath me suddenly gave way. I remember a mingled sound of shrieks and groans from those about me, a rapid downward motion, a feeling as of some heavy body passing over me, a sense of suffocation, mist and darkness and all was over.

When I came to myself, which, judging from circumstances, must have been shortly afterwards, I was at first doubtful to which world I belonged. I cast my eyes upwards, and a pure-bright sky was above me to the east, and there was the sun. I turned my head to see if it was actually on my body, and moved, one after the other, my legs and arms to assure myself that they still belonged to my person. I passed first [my] right and then my left hand over my breast and sides, and then held them up to my eyes to see if they were not covered with my own blood.

I raised myself on my elbows and found that I was lying in the dry bed of the river. A kind of wide path, reaching upwards to the edge of the bank over the low shrubs which were crushed close to the earth and covered with sand and loose stones, showed where the tiger had rolled with me down to the very spot where I lay. I then rose, and standing on my feet, found myself not only unwounded but almost unhurt. I looked about me for the fierce animal with which I had lately been in such fearful contact, but he was no where to be seen. My musket was lying at the distance of a few paces from me. I took it up and found it covered with blood. Near it were the prints of the tiger's feet where he had walked away, and these were moistened with blood also. Several of our party, all of whom had fled and abandoned me to my fate, now showed themselves on the bank above me and uttered a shout of joy at seeing me alive. They rallied their companions, and I found myself strong enough to join them in renewing the pursuit.

We soon came in sight of the tiger, moving on heavily and slowly, and staggering with the loss of blood from his wound. Before we reached him he had fallen to the ground. We despatched him without difficulty, and the natives who belonged to our party, having produced some strong cords made of the bark of the cocoa tree, which they had brought with them, tied them about the neck of the huge creature and dragged him back in triumph to Madras. As we entered the city, a large crowd of all complexions of mankind – Hindoos, Parsees, Moors, Malays, Englishmen, Germans, and Frenchmen – gathered about it and increased at every step. Even the timid Chinese artisan came to his shop-door to gaze upon the spectacle of so much fierceness tamed and so much strength overcome, and to catch a look at the man who had met the leap of a royal tiger and escaped unhurt.

The procession stopped at a kind of open square in the city. Here the animal was measured and found to exceed fifteen feet in length from the tip of the nose to the end of the tail. All who knew any thing of me in the city flocked eagerly about me; it seemed as if they could not be satisfied of my identity until they had grasped my hand. I received the cordial congratulations of my European friends. My acquaintances among the Hindoos were profuse of their florid compliments and felicitations; and as for the multitude, I thought they would never be satisfied with pressing around me and gazing at me. I withdrew as soon as I was able and sought at my lodgings the repose I so much needed. The bounty of three hundred pounds, which was the reward offered by the government of the country for killing a tiger, was paid me the next day.

If any man had ever cause of gratitude to Divine Providence for deliverance in an hour of signal danger, I am that man. I have never, since the incident I have related, ceased to cherish this feeling, and, I trust, it will not diminish in intensity to the last day of my life.

Story of the Island of Cuba

NUMEROUS as are the strangers who resort to the island of Cuba from the continent of Europe and the States of North America, few, if any, visit it from mere curiosity. The greater part are drawn thither by commerce, a few are in pursuit of health and fugitives from the severity of our northern winters; but all have almost invariably made their abode in the city of Havana, a place full of strangers and adventurers like themselves, and copying, so far as the climate will permit, the manners of the large European towns. Multitudes of these occasional residents never learn the language with sufficient perfection to speak it, or understand it when spoken, and thus are cut off from the best opportunity of becoming acquainted with the character of the native inhabitants. Thus it is that, not withstanding [that] the principal city of Cuba is the great mart for the trade of Spanish America and enjoys so large a portion of the commerce of the world, so little is yet known of the largest, finest, and most fertile of the West India Islands. All the knowledge of it exists in the minds of men too busy to write books or incompetent to literary pursuits. Geographers are at fault in searching for materials from which to compile a tolerable account of the island; and the celebrated Malte Brun, of whose work his countrymen are so proud, could do nothing better for Cuba than to give a naked translation of what was penned long ago by the old Spanish geographer Alcedo.

I also have visited Cuba, and, like others, visited it in the capacity of a man of business. I went there some fifteen years since to recover a debt due to the estate of a relation of mine, a West Indian merchant whose executor I had been appointed. Law has its delays in Cuba as well as in other countries, and being obliged to resort to legal proceedings against the debtor, I was detained longer in the island than is usual with my countrymen. I arrived there in January and passed the remainder of the winter - if so severe a name can be given to so delightful a season - pleasantly enough among its inhabitants. The acquaintances I formed in the transaction of my business introduced me into society.

I found it indeed "a web of mingled yarn," full of strong contrasts: the gentle and timid; the bold, enterprising, and unprincipled; the kind and the churlish; the acutely sensitive and shamelessly callous; disinterested honor and unblushing fraud, side by side. It was just such a state of society as our own might be were public opinion deprived of more than half its force and the opportunities of evading the laws and corrupting those who administer them a hundred-fold what they are now. Let me, however, do the Habaneros justice. Of all the citizens of Spanish America, I believe them to possess the best character. They come of a good stock – the virtuous, industrious, and poor inhabitants of Teneriffe and other Canaries [ironically] named The Fortunate were driven from Fuerteventura to the Grand Canary, from the Grand Canary to Teneriffe, and from Teneriffe to Palma by the occasional famines which afflict these islands, until they [finally] were obliged to leave their native isles altogether. Were it not for the severe laws which restrain departure, the famines would cause still greater numbers to emigrate.

In the city of Havana the rude and primitive virtues of this race are somewhat tempered by the softer and more voluptuous genius of Andalusia, but it is owing, I believe, to their extraction that so much unaffected goodness and simplicity of heart is to be found among the women. I saw them at their balls and *tertulias* in their splendid Parisian dresses; I saw them in their domestic circles in the plain but rich costume of Spain. And everywhere I found them kind, affectionate, and simple-hearted; charming in spite of the duskiness of their complexions, with the brightest and blackest eyes in the world, and forms that seemed the more graceful and bewitching from their Asiatic fulness. I talked to them in bad Spanish, and to their tuition I believe is owing the fondness I bear to their language. The people of Havana have taken some liberties with the Castilian tongue and dialect of the stately Dons. Transplanted to the delicious climate of Cuba, it has acquired an Ionic softness and volume to which it is a stranger in its original country. They have mellowed the general pronunciation, depriving it of all its harshness, and by employing on all occasions its polysyllabic superlatives and the numerous musical diminutives with which it abounds, have added to its grace what they have taken from its energy.

The warm season was advancing, and I grew uneasy at the idea of remaining in Havana, notwithstanding the hospitality with which I was treated. The odors arising from the stables in the lower stories of all the dwellings of this closely built city overpowered me, and I was wasted and debilitated by the continual heat and perspiration. I grew weary of being obliged to change my linen four or five times a day, and, what was worse, I became afraid of the yellow fever, the black vomit, and the liver complaint. I was haunted by a continual fear that I should *coger un aire*, by which phrase the people mean the contracting of half a dozen strange disorders peculiar to the hotter parts of the West Indies. I therefore resolved to take advantage of the more salubrious situations which the island offered me and accepted the invitation of a friend to pass the summer months at his coffee plantations.

The island of Cuba possesses almost every variety of temperature. Havana, on the sea-shore, lies beneath a burning sun, but you may choose your climate on the sides of that long ridge of mountains which, running the whole length of the island, lifts you at every step into a purer and cooler atmosphere. My friend had his coffee plantation in an elevated part of the island, but still within a genial though not a torrid climate. It were a vain task for me to attempt to describe these beautiful plantations in Cuba to one who has as seen nothing like them. The shrubs that produce the aromatic kernel which supplies a refreshing beverage to the whole civilized world are not trusted to the fierce sun and rude dalliance of the air. Vast groves of the most majestic trees of the island are planted to shade them from the heat and shelter them from the winds. The shrubs are disposed in squares, and the avenues between are lined with palm-trees, with mangoes, with the plantain, the banana, and the bamboo. Amid them rises here and there the gigantic cotton-tree, its vast trunk swelling out in the midst like an Egyptian column and its huge arms stretched forth in the air high above the tops of its brethren, so high that the song of the mock-bird among them is scarcely heard on the ground below. Every kind of foliage, from the slenderest and lightest to the heaviest and most massive, from the palest to that of the most intense verdure, is mingled in these delightful bowers which murmur with the continual agitation of the soft winds, blowing by day from the sea and by night from the mountains. The orange here hangs out its fragrant blossoms and no less fragrant fruit together, roses of Jericho blossom all the year, and ranks of pineapples border the intersecting alleys. The cooing of doves is blended almost continually with the soft rustling of the innumerable branches, and over all is heard at intervals the wild shriek of the catona or the guacamaya. In the midst of this beautiful garden – for such it truly is – often several miles in extent, is the residence of the proprietor and that of his slaves, surrounded by a circle of lime-trees closely planted, intermingled along its edge with flowers of the scarlet cordium and the oleander, and divided by broad openings looking along the principal avenues.

My friend's plantation was situated several miles from Havana, on a tract of ground which inclined with an easy declivity toward the north shore and was varied with gentle undulations. In the midst wound a little brook that fell into the *Rio de Puentes Grandes* and which was further increased by one or two springs breaking out at the foot of the hillocks. As you stood in the great northern avenue in front, you looked down upon the calm ocean which bathes the walls of Havana, the city itself unseen; and, turning to the south, your sight was met among the very tree-tops by the blue summits of San Salvador, a part of that mighty ridge which divides the island longitudinally, clothed to its loftiest peaks with forest of eternal verdure. How often, while I was swallowing the coffee which a domestic brought me at six in the morning, have I gazed through the windows of my bedchamber at those woody heights, red with the early sun, and thought of the majestic highlands of my native river! Let me not, however, forget to do justice to my friend's coffee, which was of the finest, raised on his own plantation, and of the quality of which he was justly proud. The seed from which the shrub was raised he had procured from the little Danish island of St. John's, where the best coffee in the world is produced – a fact known to epicures, and to which I can testify from my own experience, having often drank it at the house of a very knowing, agreeable man with whom I became acquainted in his official capacity, Counsellor Benzon, Governor of the Island of Santa Cruz.

I passed many agreeable days with my friend in this pleasant retreat, idly enough, but not without learning many things worthy of remembrance. My host was a native of Teneriffe, a dark-complexioned, stern-countenanced, deep-voiced man with the tall stature and powerful frame of his countrymen. His negroes held him in great awe, for he was one of those men who are obeyed by inferior minds, not from compulsion nor from affection but from a sort of instinct and the mere force of a determined manner. A look, a motion of .his hand, an indirect intimation of his will was with them equivalent to a command and was interpreted with a quickness and with an alacrity that surprised me. Yet he was substantially kind to them, and I believe not a single instance of corporal punishment occurred on the plantation while I remained there.

I had frequent conversations with him on the subject of the colored population of the island of Cuba. "Are you not afraid," said I to him one day, "that they will rise up in a body against their masters and make a bloody attempt to shake off the burden of servitude?"

"I have no such fears," replied he. "The blacks have no arms, and there is nobody to put arms into their hands. Our shores are lined with strong military posts all along our narrow island which would quickly put down an unarmed and undisciplined insurrection. Besides, the different classes of our colored population hate each other too cordially ever to concert together a plan of rebellion. The negro of Africa, the bravest and most spirited of them all, born a free man, detests the submissive Creole, the native of the country, and the Creole negro abhors the dogged, surly, and unchristianized African. The mulatto looks with scorn upon the negro as his inferior, and the negro regards the mulatto as a degenerate mongrel, while the quadroon, who in his own estimation is almost a white man, regards both the negro and mulatto with equal disdain. Not many years since, three Indians, from the coast of Florida, did what all the blacks of the island never did, and I believe and trust never will do – they filled the whole country for nearly three years with robbery, bloodshed, burnings, and consternation.

"The Spanish government, by virtue of some treaty or other with the Indians of Florida of which I can tell you nothing else, send them an annual present of European merchandise. A vessel is usually despatched from Havana for this purpose, and some dignitary of the Church or zealous missionary accompanies the expedition. In the last year of the last century the bishop of Havana, the venerable Tres Palacios – may God rest his soul! – made the voyage to Florida. The good priest celebrated the imposing ceremonies of our religion with so much pomp, explained its mysteries with so much clearness and eloquence, and read the Latin prayers in his missal with so much unction that the hearts of the poor savages were touched; many consented to receive baptism on the spot, and the bishop returned, bringing with him as the trophies of his peaceful victory three Indian boys, who had been delivered to him to be instructed in the learning of the white man and the doctrines of the true faith.

"The young savages were at first delighted with the change in their situation. They were highly gratified with the elegant European dresses in which they were clothed by their patron, and to which they added a multitude of trinkets received as presents and fantastically disposed on their persons. In spite of the habit of apparent indifference to everything extraordinary in which they had been educated, they could not help expressing the feeling of natural astonishment which rose in their minds as they walked the streets of Havana and beheld the various labors and devices of civilization. In a short time, however, they became familiar with the wonders around them, and with their astonishment vanished the piety which the good ecclesiastic supposed he had kindled in their hearts. He discovered that his juvenile neophytes were lazy, proud, intractable; that they loved rum and tobacco and were fond of sleeping when their stomachs were full. Sometimes they would perform their wild dances with loud and heathenish cries in the court-yard of the churchman's palace, disturbing his religious meditations.

"On one of these occasions, when the old bishop sallied forth in his night-cap, cane in hand and with a most determined demeanor to quiet the uproar, they actually had the insolence to trip up his heels and to continue their dance around the body of the sprawling dignitary, shouting and yelling with greater glee than ever. They had no objections to figuring in religious processions; they carried the blazing torches with an air and bore the standards with profound gravity and solemnity, but they resolutely refused to learn their prayers and could by no means be taught the alphabet. They would often absent themselves for several days together to wander on the woody sides of the mountains, shaping bows and arrows after the fashion of their native country, making a rude sort of lance out of a hard kind of wood, the ends of which they rendered yet harder by fire, and they would return, with their clothes fairly torn from their backs, bringing home a wild pig or a huge bunch of paroquets. In short, they were so wholly insubordinate and so decidedly savage and pagan in their habits and tastes that the bishop was forced to give up the idea of making them into good Catholics who should return to spread the light of the Gospel and the power of the Church in their native land.

"At length they committed some offence against the laws. What it was I either never heard or have forgotten, but an offence they committed for which they were apprehended, found guilty, and sentenced to imprisonment at the Arsenal in Havana. The bishop, I believe, was glad to get rid of them, for he saw that the seed he had sown had fallen upon a rock, and he was now sure that his intractable pupils would be well looked to and kept out of mischief at least. The Arsenal, you know, I suppose, is situated a little without the city, but connected with it by a gate called *Punta de la Tenaza* and surrounded by high and strong walls of its own. But if you have never visited it, you can scarcely form an idea of the activity that prevails there. It is a little town within itself. The vast magazines and storehouses, the dwellings of the officers and superintendents, the barracks of the soldiers, the dormitories of the prisoners, the shops in which various mechanical occupations are exercised, occupy the circuit of the walls with numerous buildings. Wharves extend along the edge of the water; vessels are coming and departing, taking in or discharging their cargoes; men are hurrying to and fro with packages; and a cluster of mills in the midst, turned by a canal from the river and continually employed in sawing huge trunks of the native trees of the island, fill the place with the continual noise of the machinery. Were it not that you saw here and there an officer in military uniform, sentinels pacing about, and chains fastened to the arms or legs of many of the laborers, you might fancy yourself in a common seaport. Thither the young delinquents were sent and, each being fitted with a couple of iron rings about his ankles, they were set to work in assisting to load and unload the government vessels. The employment was not much to their liking, and, after remaining there a few months, they took advantage of an opportunity to make their escape and sought refuge in *Las Vegas de Falaco.*

"The tract of country called by this name begins about twenty leagues or more to the west of Havana, on the northern shore of the island, and stretches toward Cape San Antonio as far as the settlement of Mantua and Guanes, which lie on its remotest boundary. It is fertile as the garden of Eden, and its wide extent is watered by numerous wandering rivers whose banks are encumbered with the luxuriance of their wild vegetation. A few miserable habitations are scattered here and there along the streams, or grouped into hamlets and dirty villages. In these live the herdsmen entrusted with the care of the immense droves of cattle, horses, and swine pastured in the country back of the settlements, and here also dwell the tobacco planters who cultivate patches of the rich, deep soil on the margin of the rivers. No part of Cuba is naturally finer than this, and none is peopled with a worse race. I hate the rascals, for they once stole from me the finest horse in the world, an English hunter which cost me sixty doubloons, and I was obliged to pursue my journey on a stunted, hard-trotting jade, which I purchased of a dingy mulatto who called himself a white man, and who had the conscience to ask me a hundred dollars for her. I dare say he stole the animal.

"Hither the wreckers who haunt the keys on the coast, gangs of runaway sailors who live by the plunder of the merchant ships that come into their power, resort to spend their ill-gotten wealth in gaming and debauchery. These desperadoes keep their boats moored under the thick boughs and foliage of the mangroves, whose trunks rise in the shallows out of the very brine. You might look round on the neighboring shores and sand-banks without meeting the least indication of anything in which a human being could put to sea, but let a disaster happen to a merchant vessel off the coast, and two hundred boats, perhaps, will at once make their appearance, as if they rose from the bosom of the waters. These fellows lead a merry life on shore, where they find no lack of boon companions. The dice-box rattles all day in the taverns, and the guitar begins to tinkle as the sun goes down. Brawls are kindled among them over their wine, blood is shed, and the murderer takes refuge in the keys. Sometimes one of these fellows who ventures on shore with too much money lies stark and stiff by the roadside the next morning.

"The three young savages chose the village of Guanes, situated on the river of that name, as the place of their retreat. It lies, as I have already I think mentioned, near the farther extremity of Las Vegas. Here they contrived to exchange their prison dresses for checked shirts and pantaloons, with broad-brimmed straw hats – the usual garb of the country people. They subsisted easily and lived in a manner quite to their taste among the lazy settlers. They fished a little in the streams, knocked down game in the uncultivated lands, loitered about the taverns, slept in the shade, and, when pressed by the harder necessity than usual, lent a hand in gathering and curing tobacco. I never heard that they did any harm while they remained is this part of the country; at all events, I believe they behaved themselves quite as unexceptionally, to say the least, as the rest of the inhabitants.

"Our government occasionally sends commissioners to make the circuit of the island, and to clear it of runaway criminals and of vagabonds who can give no account of themselves. The idea is a good one, in my opinion, for by this means a rogue is kept in the place where he was born and where his character is known, and when convicts who have escaped from justice repeat their crimes, they are carried back to punishment. After the three Indians had been for several months in the neighborhood of Guanes, certain of these magistrates arrived at that village. The Indians were informed against by a herdsman with whom they had some dispute. They were seized and brought before the commissioners. It appeared that they were not ancient inhabitants of the place, and they could show no passport from any other; it was, therefore, concluded that they could not be there for any good purpose. They were accordingly sent, with a guard, to Havana, where they were immediately recognized as the fugitives. They were remanded to prison, loaded with heavier chains, and condemned to severer tasks.

"Their old patron, the good Bishop Tres Palacios, was dead; there was nobody to intercede in their behalf. The prisoners bore their fate with a kind of sullen resignation, but their keepers knew little of what was passing in their minds. They had been brought back from what they most loved – idleness and liberty – to what they most hated – labor and imprisonment.The indignities with which they had been treated roused in their bosoms all the spirit of their race and filled them with an intense thirst for revenge. Their confinement was short, and it was soon rumored in Havana that they had again escaped from the Arsenal. On the second morning after their escape, a traveller, passing between Mantua and Guanes a little after sunrise, was stopped by a scene of horror and desolation. A crowd of people of all colors had gathered around the smoking ruins of a cluster of cottages which had been fired in the night. The trees by which they were once overshadowed had been scorched and seared in the fierce flame, and their half-burned leaves were dropping in the faces of those who stood below. The earth around was stained with blood, and the prints of knees and feet strongly pressed into it showed that a mortal struggle had been there. Several bodies of men, women, and children, marked with deep gashes, lay near. They had evidently been slain in the endeavor to escape by flight, for the expression of horror and fear yet stood on the faces of the dead. One or two among the group, who seemed to have been more successful in their attempts to escape and whose features were yet convulsed by fright, were telling in an agitated, incoherent manner the story of several men of hideous appearances and supernatural strength and swiftness who had put the firebrand to their houses just at daybreak and slaughtered the inmates without pity.

"While the multitude were thus intently listening, they were startled by shrill cries from a distance, growing louder every moment; all eyes were instantly turned to the quarter from which they proceeded. A dark cloud of smoke was seen rolling up from among some trees at the distance of half a league, where the spectators knew that there was a dwelling, and the next moment it was surmounted by a dozen arrowy tongues of flame shooting up in the midst. A man and a woman, each carrying a child, made their appearance, running with all their might and shrieking in an agony of terror for protection. They were pursued at some distance by three dark, strange-looking men, armed with lances, who were gaining rapidly upon them. As soon, however, as they saw the crowd, they stopped, looked at them for a moment, and, turning, went off swiftly in a direction toward the mountains in the interior of the island. In the mean time, the fugitives had reached their friends and fell prostrate on the ground in a state of exhaustion. They were immediately recognized as the family belonging to the house which was seen in flames. Fortunately, none of them were within when the ruffians came. They had observed them, however, from a little distance, and terrified by the strange fierceness and wildness of their demeanor, had concealed themselves behind some hushes until they saw them setting fire to the house, when they immediately took to flight. In their flight they had been seen and pursued, and apparently only saved by the accidental circumstance that their pursuers beheld around the ashes of the cottage a larger number of persons than they wished to encounter.

"Who were the perpetrators of these deeds of violence and bloodshed? This was a matter of intense curiosity and anxious conjecture; almost every man had his own answer to the question. Some thought that they might be a party of wreckers from the keys who had taken this method to revenge the death of a comrade slain in the village of Guanes. Some suggested that an invading force had landed on the island and was sending out small detachments to ravage the country. The greater number were of [the] opinion that they were the three Indians who had a second time escaped from imprisonment and had perpetrated these barbarities in revenge for the inhospitality which had delivered them up. This opinion was confirmed by the description given of their persons by the inmates of the destroyed cottages. But they added that, whoever they might be, it was their most solemn belief that they were in league with the powers of darkness.

Nothing else could endue them with such an irresistible strength, or render them so completely proof against all attempts to wound them, or give such a demoniac expression to their features. The idea took strong hold of the superstitious people of Las Vegas, and the voices of the group sank into a low murmur as they conferred together on this fearful subject.

"Nothing could equal the panic which prevailed in the settlements of Mantua and Guanes all that day. The families who lived in the solitary houses came into the villages, and the villagers crowded into the stronger and more defensible buildings. Every weapon that could be found was put in order: disused blunderbusses were fitted with new flints, rusty broadswords were sharpened, and an old swivel that had lain for years half buried in the earth before the *cabile*, or town-hall, of Guanes was dug out, loaded, and set upon two wooden wheels in front of the dwelling of the *Alcalde*. The rest of that day passed without any further alarm, but on the next, news was brought of other massacres and burnings in the neighborhood. On the third morning, a party of twenty men, all armed, left the village of Guanes to visit the herds in the back country. They entered several houses, the inhabitants of which lay murdered within them or before the doors. They found the herds scattered and saw many carcasses of cattle and horses lying where they had been pastured.

"In the mean time, the devastation committed by these strange beings increased the terror with which they were everywhere regarded. Wild stories were told of their exploits, of their gigantic strength and prodigious swiftness, of their swimming and fording rapid rivers which would have swept away the most powerful man on the island, of their scaling perpendicular mountains and leaping tremendous chasms, of the supernatural suddenness with which they came upon the defenceless and the astonishing swiftness with which they disappeared when the odds were against them. All the inhabitants of the district of Las Vegas followed the example of those in the neighborhood of Mantua and Guanes and removed into the villages for safety, or collected in the larger and less exposed habitations. No man would venture into the fields alone, but when the necessity of their affairs called them forth, they went in parties of a dozen or twenty men, well armed and on the watch against the enemy.

"I remember a singular instance of the extreme fear inspired by these marauders. One day a young negro slave, living at an estate called

El Rosario in the jurisdiction of Consolacion del Norte, came running home to tell that the Indians were in sight and were making toward the house. The family consisted of the master of the house, his wife and three children, his wife's brother, and a female slave with her two boys. The husband was for seeking safety by flight, his wife and her brother were for barricading the doors, and neither would follow the advice of the other. No time was to be lost. The husband left his house with a loaded musket on his shoulder and climbed a tree, hard by, of the kind we called the *guacia*, screening himself from sight among its thick boughs and tufts of pale-green leaves, while his wife and her brother bolted the door with all possible expedition.

"The ruffians were soon at the dwelling; the affrighted owner of the house saw them from his hiding-place, armed with bows and arrows slung upon their shoulders and carrying enormous lances made of the trunks of sapling trees, with an iron blade fixed in the smaller end. They were men of short stature, but broad-chested and wonderfully strong-limbed, with straight, jetty hair and round, wild eyes beneath arched and coal-black eyebrows. They first tried to open the door, and finding it fastened, without uttering a word to each other, they raised their lances to a level with their heads and drove the butt-end violently against it to beat it in. Every loud stroke went to the heart of the poor wretch in his concealment. He lay quaking with fear, just able to support himself among the branches and to keep the musket he held from dropping to the ground, but without the courage or the strength to discharge it. The door at length gave way; the brother presented himself with a musket, but was struck to the floor before he could fire, and the murderers passed into the house over his dead body.

"Shrieks and howls of agony and supplication burst from the building, and through the open door the wife and her children were seen clinging to the knees of the savages and butchered in the midst of their cries for mercy. The bodies of the two negro boys, bleeding with deep wounds, were then tossed out, and the mother, rushing forth to make her escape, was overtaken and pinned with one of their huge lances to the ground. When the work of death was finished and the house again silent, one of the murderers came out with a smoking brand in his hand, which he laid to the windward side of the building, covered it with a handful of dry sticks and twigs, and blew them into a flame. The three then departed, leaving the pusillanimous spectator of their bloody deeds half dead with horror and fear. He did not venture to come down until the house was nearly consumed, when he slipped to the ground and crawled trembling to the next village.

"I should lengthen out my story until another day were I to give you a catalogue of the murders committed by these men. All the country between the city of Havana and Cape San Antonio, called among us by the name of Vuelta Abajo, on both sides of the island, was the scene of their crimes, and was kept in a state of continual alarm. Their ravages were generally committed in the daytime, from the early dawn to nightfall, when they retired, as they also did when pursued to the woods – the ancient woods of the interior, thick, dark, and tangled with shrubs and immense vines, and full of impassable thickets. On one day their ravages would be committed on the northern shore; on the next they would have passed the mountains, and dwellings would smoke and their inmates be slaughtered on the opposite coast. The officers of justice, seeking them where their enormities had just been committed, would be apprised by messengers of still more recent crimes at the distance of twenty leagues. What occasioned no small wonder was that all the work of bloodshed and destruction was performed by them in silence. Not a word was heard to issue from their lips by any one who had been near them and yet had the good fortune to escape with his life. They gave no answer to entreaties for mercy, nor were they ever seen to confer together, though they always moved in concert. They passed from place to place as mutely and rapidly as ghosts of the dead.

"A few leagues this side of Cape San Antonio, where the island begins to grow narrow, is a remarkable cave. It passes through a continuation of the great midland ridge of the mountains and reaches from one shore to the other. At the northern entrance are several chambers that seem chiselled from the solid rock, and which, I have little doubt, are the work of the ancient inhabitants of the country. They are furnished with benches of stone, alcoves, doors passing from one to another, and roofs regularly vaulted from which the trickling of water is constantly heard in the silence and darkness. Farther on the cave is a mere cleft between rocky walls; I once visited it with some friends. We penetrated to the distance of nearly a league, till we came to where a subterraneous brook crossed the passage and a chasm above let in the light of day; but, being sickened by the strong odor of the vampires and birds of night that clung to the roof, and having come to the end of the clew which we had fastened at the mouth of the cave, we were obliged to return. In the recesses of this cave the superstitious and ignorant people of Las Vegas believed that the three Indians propitiated the devil by sacrifices of the animals they had stolen, and received the gift of irresistible strength and the power of transporting themselves in a moment to whatever place they pleased. I believe, however, that it is a mistake to suppose that they made this spot their frequent haunt, though it is certain they were often seen in the neighborhood. They were too wary to trust themselves where their retreat could be cut off, or where the fierce dogs of the island could be let loose upon them. They encamped for sleep only on the steep sides of the mountains, and never but once in the same place. Yet the idea of their subterraneous worship of the powers of darkness added greatly to the terror with which they were regarded.

"The many and horrible murders committed by these men, and the destruction of the herds, the abandonment of so many fine estates for want of tenants who would venture to occupy them, threatened the depopulation of Vuelta Abajo and drew the attention of government. Large rewards were offered, which were at length increased to five thousand dollars, for the head of each of the offenders. This measure had the effect intended. Large parties of men were collected, well armed with muskets, pistols, and broadswords, and including in their numbers a good proportion of *comisionados*, *Alcaldes*, *juezes*, *pedianos*, members of the Holy Brotherhood, and all the different officers empowered to pursue and arrest the violators of the laws. They were accompanied by the strong and fierce dogs trained in Cuba to hunt runaway negroes, one breed of which is merely employed to track the fugitive, and the other to seize and drag him down. These expeditions were wholly unsuccessful. Often did they return without having discovered the object of their search. In some instances they followed the track of the savages for whole days together, encamping, when night overtook them, in some cleft of the mountains in the wilderness of the interior, where they kept up huge fires till morning and stationed an armed watch to guard against their mysterious enemies. At length, however, their dogs led them to the hiding-place of the outlaws. After a weary march along the sides of the mountains, they found themselves at the foot of a lofty and precipitous pile of rocks which the animals, barking at the foot, in vain essayed to scale. Above, on the summit of the crags, was a thick growth of trees and mountain shrubs. The men took the dogs on their shoulders and began to climb the precipice.

"They had scarcely begun to ascend when the whole party was startled by a loud yelping, and on looking, they saw that two of the dogs had fallen from the shoulders of their bearers, struck through with arrows, and dropped to the foot of the precipice, quivering in the agonies of death. One of their number was also severely wounded by an arrow from the thickets on the summit, and as he was preparing to descend, was transfixed by a second and fell headlong from the rock on which he stood. The men at the bottom of the precipice and on the crags answered with a discharge of musketry aimed at the trees which they supposed to be the hiding-place of the enemy, but without effect. Arrows still came from above, and *chusos*, or javelins, thrown with fatal and unerring certainty – sometimes from one quarter, sometimes from another – as the savages shifted their ground to avoid the aim of their assailants. At length the whole party, discouraged by the disadvantage at which they were contending, and by the slaughter of their companions, withdrew, carrying off three of their number dead and five severely wounded, and leaving nearly half their dogs at the foot of the precipice.

"More than one attempt of the same kind was afterward made, with no better success. Nearly two years and a half had elapsed since the Indians began to devastate the island, and still their ravages continued unchecked. Impunity had not made them forget their usual caution, nor did the multitude of their murders seem to have satiated their thirst for blood. I question if ever there were three men in the world, short of the degree of monarch, who made so much havoc among their fellow-creatures in the same space of time. At length, however, a bolder and more determined band was collected than had ever before undertaken the expedition. I may justly say this, for I well knew several of the persons who joined it, and greater dare-devils were not in all the dominions of my master, the King of Spain – men who feared nothing, either in this world or in the next. They were accompanied by several relatives of persons who had been killed by the Indians, and who were resolved to lose their own lives rather than fail in the attempt to execute justice upon the assassins. Their number amounted to about a hundred and fifty, and they were accompanied by sixty of the best-trained and fiercest dogs on the island.

"After tracking the bandits for more than half a day, they approached the place of their retreat, on the steep side of a mountain covered with broken rocks, from the clefts of which sprung shrubs and small trees dwarfed by the dryness of the soil. At the foot of the place where they lay was a *quebrada*, the dry bed of a torrent, forming a ravine with precipitous sides running obliquely along the breast of the mountain. Into this ravine the party were descending, carrying their dogs down the steep banks, when they were assailed by arrows from the opposite side, by which several of the animals were killed. In all their combats with the people of the island, the outlaws aimed particularly at the dogs, whom they dreaded more than even the men, not only because they brought their pursuers to their place of retreat, but because they were so formidable and so difficult to wound in a close encounter.

"Arrived at the bottom of the ravine, the party paused for a moment to take a view of the precipice above them and to select the best places for making the ascent. It appeared that the Indians had intrenched themselves behind a kind of natural parapet of rock, through the clefts of which grew a few bushes and trees, but so thinly as not to prevent their assailants below from occasionally catching glimpses of their persons while in the act of aiming their weapons. In the mean time, their pursuers were not inactive. Every stirring of the boughs above, every appearance of a hand or face, was answered by a discharge of musketry. But the arrows and javelins still continued to come from the rocks; many of their dogs and several of their companions were already killed, and it was evident that no time was to be wasted in so disadvantageous a position. A part of the men were therefore assigned to carry the dogs, and the rest to watch the movements of the enemy; and, these being arranged so as to follow each other alternately, the whole party began to ascend by two different ways.

"The slaughter made by the Indians was now greater than ever, as they were enabled, from the near approach of the assailants, to aim their weapons with greater certainty and more deadly effect. Six of the men had already fallen dead, many were severely wounded, and more than thirty of the dogs were killed. It was horrible to hear the yells of these animals, mingled strangely with the groans of dying men, and to see their struggles when wounded, springing furiously from the shoulders of their bearers, and sometimes the animal and his bearer precipitated down the rocks together.

"But the combat was now near an end. One of the party, a *comisionado* whom I knew – a man of great strength of body, firm nerves, and keen sight – had observed through some boughs on the top of the rocks the face of one of the outlaws looking down. He kept his eye steadily fixed on the spot as he went, and shortly afterward the savage stepped forth from behind his entrenchment with an arrow fitted to his bow-string and raised it to his eye. Just as he came to the spot, the wind parted the branches before him and gave the *comisionado* a full view of his person. In an instant he levelled his piece and fired – but the arrow had already left the bow of the Indian, and both the combatants dropped dead at the same moment. A shout of triumph was raised by the whole party as they saw the body of the Indian beginning to fall heavily over the rock through the shrubs on its edge. The next moment they saw a dark, brawny arm extended after it, seizing it by the hair of the head, as if to draw it back. Twenty muskets were instantly discharged in that direction; the brawny arm suddenly let go its hold and tossed convulsively upward, and the lifeless bodies of two savages fell together down the precipice through the crashing boughs in sight of their pursuers. Encouraged by this success, they sprang with all expedition to the top of the rock, but the third Indian was nowhere to be seen.

"They now turned to examine the bodies of the outlaws who lay dead near where they had fallen. They evidently belonged to the Indian race, from the peculiarities which I have already mentioned and which the party had now an opportunity of examining at leisure. They had on no other clothing than a pair of loose trousers and a kind of belt passing over one shoulder, to which was fastened a bundle of arrows. Their forms were exceedingly muscular, bearing the signs of prodigious vigor and activity, and of that period of life when men most rejoice in their own strength. The elder, it was judged, could not be more than twenty-five years of age, and the other perhaps three years younger. The sun was already sinking when they arrived on the heights which the Indians had occupied, and weary and wounded, they encamped for a few hours of repose on the very spot without attempting any pursuit of him who had fled.

"At daybreak they set out on their return to the villages, carrying their dead and wounded, and the bodies of the slain banditti. As they entered the inhabited country, the people came flocking about them to gaze on the lifeless features and powerless limbs of those who had been so long objects of awe and affright: the swift, powerful, invulnerable beings whose crime had hitherto seemed as if destined never to meet with either check or retribution. The country people assisted in bearing the dead and wounded to the town of Consolacion del Norte, where the bodies of the *comisionado* and his companions were buried with great ceremony and every mark of respect and sorrow. The heads of the Indians were cut off, and sent from the district where they were slain to the Captain-General at Havana; their quarters were suspended by the highways; and their enormous lances, their bows, arrows, and javelins, picked up where they fell, were preserved for a memorial of the exploit, in the houses of those who led the expedition against them.

"The third Indian was never again seen in Vuelta Abajo. He passed along the midland range of mountains and shortly afterward appeared in Vuelta Arriba – which means, you know, that part of the island lying eastward of Havana. Here he renewed the work of burning and massacre among the unguarded and defenceless inhabitants and became as terrible to them as he had been to the people of the western part of the island. Warned by the fate of his companions, he never stood on the defence, but fled when threatened by a superior force. He abandoned the use of the bow and javelin, which had proved impotent to protect his comrades in their rocky fortress, and carried only his huge lance, the weapon of attack and slaughter. Hitherto, neither he nor the other two had ever been seen on horseback; now he was nearly always so. He would leap on the back of one of the horses of the country, wild and unbroken as ever ran in the forest, and ride him furiously without bridle or rein, guiding him with his lance alone,; and when the animal dropped down from fatigue, he was instantly mounted on another. Woe to the man whom he saw alone and on foot in the open country; he was sure to overtake him, and aiming a stroke at him in passing, to leave him dead on the spot. Cattle and horses without number were killed by him in the same manner – pierced between the shoulders with all the dexterity of a practiced bull-fighter. So true was his aim that, of all the animals he destroyed, not one was known to be despatched by more than a single wound. Sometimes he would dismount, and cutting out the tongues of the cattle he had killed, would hang them to his belt for future repast. Throughout the Vuelta Arriba, the inhabitants of the country bordering upon the forest or the mountains no longer thought themselves safe in the solitary houses, and like the people of the western districts, resorted to the villages for safety.

"I am sensible that the history I am giving you is an extraordinary one, and I see in your countenance the marks of incredulity. I have no answer to make to your doubts but the simple one that I am relating facts yet fresh in the memory of thousands among the people of this island. No man acquainted with Cuba and its inhabitants will pronounce it impossible that they should take place; and if they have no other fault than that of appearing a little wonderful and surprising, I hope you will not think them the less authentic.

"I am now going to relate one of the most remarkable incidents connected with the story of this man-killer. At a little distance from the town of San Juan de los Remedios resided an honest but not over-rich man, an emigrant from old Spain, named José de Pereira. He had married a native of the island, and became the father of a very pretty daughter, of whom he was extremely fond, and whom he had instructed in accomplishments somewhat above her fortune. Her beauty, her graceful manners and amiable temper won the heart of the elder son of the wealthy proprietor of a cane-plantation in the neighborhood. He paid her his addresses, which were not rejected; a match was concluded between them, and the wedding-day was already fixed. She was as happy as a young and modest woman can be who is about to marry the man of whose love she is proud; and he was as happy as a young man deeply in love always is when on the point of marriage. The father and mother were scarcely less so at seeing their daughter well settled in life, and it was thought that the good couple would stretch their means a little to celebrate the nuptial ceremonies with becoming splendor and merriment. As yet, the Indian had never appeared in the immediate neighborhood of San Juan de los Remedios, nor had the inhabitants thought of resorting to any unusual precautions for protecting themselves against his violence.

"One morning the father had gone out to look at his little plantation of bananas and maize, and the mother to talk over the approaching nuptials with a neighbor, while Anita de Pereira, the daughter, was busy in an inner apartment of the house, working with her own fair hands some article of dress to be worn at the ceremony. There was no one else in the house but a negro woman in the next room. Suddenly Anita heard a violent shriek, and the sound of footsteps passing swiftly over the floor. She rushed to the door, opened it, and saw before her a short, brawny, savage-looking man, his stiff, black hair standing upright all over his head, half naked, and carrying a long, heavy lance in his hand. She looked round instinctively for help, and beholding no one else in sight – for the negro woman who had alarmed her with the shriek had fled through a postern door – she sank to the ground in a swoon.

"In the mean time, the domestic had alarmed the neighborhood, and several men came running to the spot with arms in their hands. As they came up they saw the outlaw at some distance, on horseback, carrying the lifeless form of the young woman before him and galloping off swiftly toward the mountains. The distracted father and mother, informed of what had happened, arrived at the cottage just in time to see him disappearing with his prize over a distant eminence. The news was not slow in spreading to all the neighboring plantations, and to the town of San Juan de los Remedios, and a considerable multitude, prompted by various motives of curiosity, sympathy, and the desire of making themselves of importance, soon gathered about the old man's door. Among the rest appeared a young man of manly figure and bold and frank demeanor, but with a deep air of distress and anxiety on his countenance. The crowd that stood about the distressed father, talking loudly and earnestly to him and to each other, and offering a thousand discordant counsels, divided voluntarily to let him pass. It was Ramon de Aguarda, the intended husband of Anita. He approached and offered his hand to Pereira, who grasped it convulsively. 'We have lost Anita,' said he, in a half-choked voice.

" 'I shall find her,' answered the young man, 'and that before the sea-breeze springs up again. I will pursue the robber and bring her back, or never return.'

"The garrulous crowd were silent as they heard the strong, determined tone of Aguarda's voice, and when he finished, a low murmur ran through it as the bystanders spoke to each other, commending the fearless and resolute spirit of the young man.

" 'Who is there among you,' said he again, 'that will go with me to the rescue of Anita de Pereira?'

" 'I will go,' was the answer of many voices at once, and there arose a great struggle in the crowd among those who were pressing forward to offer their services. Every one loved Anita and respected Aguarda for his warm-hearted and generous temper.

" 'I thank you, my neighbors,' resumed the young man. 'I could not have expected less of you. Since you are so ready to accompany me, I must request such of you as have not brought your arms to send for them immediately, and that you will provide yourselves, as soon as possible, with horses, and with dogs to track the ruffian; we will set out from this place in a quarter of an hour.'

"Great was the haste and bustle in arming and preparing for the expedition. The planters willingly supplied the adventurers with dogs and horses. Several young gentlemen of the town of San Juan de los Remedios came to join the party, ambitious of distinguishing themselves in the rescue of the rustic beauty. At the appointed time a company of fifty men were assembled, armed, and on horseback, with negroes on foot, holding the dogs in long leashes. One of the animals was let loose to track the Indian, and the party, following the direction in which he had disappeared, set off under the conduct of Aguarda. They traversed the open country and arrived where the skirts of the great interior forest, stretching down the sides of the mountains toward the shore, enclose glades of pasture-ground. Here they added to their number several *monteros*, or foresters, to serve for guides in the expedition. The *monteros*, as you may perhaps know, are the keepers of the large herds which graze in this island on estates four or five leagues in circumference, and for the most part overshadowed with trees. They are as much at home in the woods of Cuba as your own Indians in those of North America. They know all the thousand intricacies and crossing paths of the forest, the ravines, precipices, and streams as well as I know the regular avenues and alleys of my own plantation. They will travel in the woods from city to city, and from end to end of the island, guiding their way by the sun, the stars, the course of the rivers, and the direction of the wind, which you know blows regularly seaward during the night, and landward during the day.

"One of the *monteros* had seen the Indian pass with his prize, and pointed out the prints of his horse's feet. The party now rode into those lofty woods along a gradual ascent toward the mountains by a broad path among old trees that had stood there ever since the conquest of the island – groves of palmetto royal, the wild cotton-tree, the pawpaw, and others of equally gigantic stature whose smooth trunks, rising to a prodigious height, uplift a close roof of thick-woven bough and massive foliage. So lofty a roof there is not in the proudest temples of Europe, nor one which more effectually excludes the sun, whose beams for ages have played upon the summit of those trees without penetrating to the ground. As they went forward, the forest, after several hours' travelling, became thicker and more choked with underwood, and the path narrower, until it could hardly be distinguished from others, made by cattle, intersecting in all directions. They were now obliged to ride one behind another, and as they ascended a little declivity they found it difficult to urge their horses between the close trunks and encroaching branches. At length one of the *monteros* made a sign for the party to stop.

" 'Here, gentlemen,' said he, 'you must dismount; the forest beyond this place will not admit of the passing of a horse and rider. And here lies a poor beast that has been ridden hard to-day, and who, if he could speak, would thank the woods for being so thick; his master could get him no farther.' As he spoke, he broke off a twig from one of the shrubs, and stripping it of the leaves, turned to the side of the path, and with a smart stroke, started up from a kind of a recess a horse covered with sweat and half-dried foam. 'This, perhaps,' continued he, 'is the horse that carried the fellow you are looking for. He has neither saddle nor bridle, and yet his back shows that he has been sat upon by a heavy rider.'

"The party pressed round to get a sight of the animal, a shaggy, wild-looking creature with a heavy, tangled mane on both sides of his neck, a long forelock hanging between the eyes, and a sweeping tail. He stretched himself for a moment, then snorted, broke through the bushes, and was out of sight.

" 'That is the Indian's horse,' said another *montero*, the same who had seen him carrying off the young woman and had showed his traces to the pursuers; 'the very beast on whose back I saw him this morning. I would swear to him before the *Alcalde*. I fancy the rider cannot be far off.' All the party were of the same opinion. A short consultation was held in which it was agreed that an attempt should be made to recover the young woman without letting loose their dogs until the rescue was effected, for fear that they might attack the captive also. They then dismounted, left the horses in the care of some negroes, and began to thread the more intricate mazes of the forest.

"They soon heard at a distance the baying of the hound whom they had let off at setting out, and proceeding for two or three miles in that direction, they came to a lofty precipice, not far from the bottom of which grew a cluster of branching trees of great height. At the foot of these trees the dog was whimpering and barking, and occasionally springing against the trunks. The party were perplexed at this circumstance; they looked up into the boughs for a solution of the mystery but could discover nothing. They called off the animal and attempted to make him recover the track which they supposed he had lost, but in vain; he immediately returned to the spot. The face of the precipice was smooth, perpendicular, nearly thirty feet in height, and quite as impossible to scale without the assistance of a ladder as the wall of a house. It stood at several paces from the trees in front, so that it seemed nobody could pass from them to its summit. Along the steeps to the right and left of it rose a thick undergrowth of young trees, filled up with thorny and interwoven vines, of that species which we call *uñas de gato*, or cat's-claws, and which formed an impenetrable barrier, stretching to a great distance on either hand and without any opening through which the outlaw could have passed with his captive. Somebody suggested that, as one of the trees was easily climbed, he might have concealed himself among the leaves and boughs of its top. A *montero* immediately sprang into it, ascended out of sight among the foliage, and called out to those below that there was no living thing in the tree but himself.

"They now became convinced that the hound had been misled by a false scent, and some proposed to go back to the place where the Indian's horse was found lying and let slip another dog upon his track. As for Aguarda, it is scarcely possible to describe his chagrin at being thus cruelly disappointed when he thought himself just upon the point of rescuing from a dreadful fate the being he most loved. The cur shall never deceive anybody else in this manner,' said he, and levelled his musket to blow out the creature's brains, when one of his companions held his arm, and pointed to where the *montero*, who had descended half-way down the tree, began to walk along one of its branches that bent with his weight to a horizontal position until, coming to the summit of the perpendicular rock at the foot of which the whole party stood, he leaped upon the top of it. The mystery was now cleared up. It was evident to all that the savage had climbed the tree with his prize and passed along the branches to the precipice before them. Aguarda caught the poor animal whose life he was just about to take and caressed it in a transport of joy.

"The *monteros* drew their *machetes*, the sharp broadswords which they usually carry about with them, and proceeded to cut a passage through the thorny and tangled fence of creeping vines on the side where it seemed thinnest and most pervious. This they did with great dexterity and quickness, and in a few minutes had formed a kind of arched passage, through which the company passed by a short circuit to the summit of the precipice. A negro carried thither the hound, and the animal was no sooner put to the ground than he recovered the track of the outlaw, darted off like lightning, and was out of sight. In a few minutes they heard him uttering a sharp and frequent bark, a sure signal that he had found the object of his pursuit. The party rushed forward and soon issued into an open glade in the forest, where the sun came in from above and a spring welled out from a stony basin and lost itself in thick grass. At the farther end of the glade rose the rocky side of a mountain, seamed obliquely with a *quebrada*, or deep ravine. The savage was seen retreating to a huge rock of stone at the foot of the mountain while the dog was running round him in swift circles and barking incessantly. You know, perhaps, that it is impossible for the runaways of our island to kill one of those nimble and quick-sighted animals without the advantage of a rock at their back. The savage, as soon as he saw his pursuers, took to flight. He sprang up the side of the mountain and disappeared over the ravine amid a shower of balls. The fierce dogs, heretofore kept in leashes, were let slip after him, but they were soon stopped by precipices which they did not venture to descend.

"The first thought of Aguarda was to look for Anita de Pereira. She was found gagged with one of her own handkerchiefs, her delicate arms pinioned, and one of them tied fast to a tree in the edge of the glade where the savage had secured her until he could kill the dog that was giving his enemies notice of his retreat. Her lover cut the cords by which she was bound and received her thanks and tears in his bosom. That night was a happy one at the house of old Pereira, and the event of that day hastened, by a fortnight at least, the ceremony that crowned the wishes of Aguarda.

"This escape of the bandit seemed to embolden him in the commission of his atrocities. I have heard many people express the opinion that all the murders, burnings, and destruction of herds committed by him and his companions during the whole time they remained in the Vuelta Abajo did not equal those committed by this man alone in the Vuelta Arriba. In addition to the price set by government upon his head, the proprietors of different *haciendas* in the island, abandoned through fear of him, offered large rewards for his death or apprehension.

"Yet this man, in the midst of his hatred of the people of the island and the bloody deeds with which he gratified his thirst for revenge, seems to have still felt some of those natural sympathies which attach us to our race and to have yearned after the pleasure of seeing a human face and hearing a human voice in peace and kindness. A short time after the adventure of Anita de Pereira he stole a little child, a daughter of a *balomer* who lived in a small hamlet between San Lorenzo and La Calidad. He kept her with him several months, treating her with great kindness, feeding her with the abundant wild fruits of the country and with the flesh of cattle which he slew on the *haciendas*. After several attempts she was at length taken from him, but not until she had contracted a strong attachment for Taito Perico, as he had taught her to call him.

"In the rescue of the little girl the savage was wounded in the thigh, a circumstance which, though it increased his shyness, did not diminish his ferocity. A little more than seven months after his first appearance in the Vuelta Arriba, a company of about thirty children from the inland city of Puerto Principe went out to gather the wild fruit we call *marañones* in the fields a little more than two miles distant from the town. It was then the month of June, and the fruit hung in its golden and ruddy ripeness on the low shrubs which, mingled with others of different species, overspread a considerable tract of land. Among the children was a fine boy, about eight years of age, named José Maria de Rodriguez. They were all busily engaged in plucking the fruit, in discovering the places where it grew in the greatest abundance, and in jostling each other away from it when discovered, and the air rung with their cheerful voices and innocent laughter. All at once one of them screamed out, 'El Indio! el Indio!' and the troop scattered off like a flock of paroquets at the discharge of a gun. José Maria stood near a clump of bushes, and thinking they afforded him sufficient concealment, crouched under them close to the ground. The savage, as ill luck would have it, rode to the spot where the boy lay trembling and powerless with fear and, observing him, checked his horse, stooped toward him, took him up by one arm, and, placing him on the animal before him, rode off to the woods.

"The mother of José Maria was a widow lady of distinction in Puerto Principe; he was her only son, and she was frantic at his loss. Her brother, Don Agostin Arias – who, I remember, was at that time an officer of the militia of Cuba, a gentleman of the true stamp and of that courage which shows itself not in words but in deeds – came to her house opposite the church of La Soledad, comforted her by representing that the Indian had not hitherto shown any disposition to destroy his captive, and pledged himself to restore her child. On the first day all endeavor to discover the track of the robber was fruitless. On the third, however, news was brought that he had been several times seen on the sides of the mountain, which then went by the name of Loma de Cubitas, whose conical summit, clothed with lofty woods to its highest peak, is seen at a distance of eight leagues from Puerto Principe. Arias immediately gave notice to an acquaintance of the name of Cespedes, a *valenton*, as we call those men who plume themselves upon the possession of extraordinary valor, and who had offered to accompany him in his undertaking to rescue the child. They set off on horseback, armed with guns and pistols, taking with them a negro who carried a weapon of the kind we call a *desjarretadera*, a steel blade in the form of a crescent, fixed in a long handle like that of a lance and used to hamstring the wild and furious animals of the herds.

"They arrived at the mountain of Cubitas, and after penetrating a little way into the old woods on its breast, dismounted, gave their horses in charge to the negro, and separated in search of the child-stealer, with an agreement that he who first heard the report of the other's gun should immediately come to his assistance. Arias had not proceeded far when he heard Cespedes discharge his piece, whether by accident, as he afterward alleged, in springing over the channel of the brook, or whether it was that his valorous soul was assailed by the ignoble passion of fear, I can not say, but the people of Puerto Principe were uncharitable enough to believe the latter. Arias turned immediately, when, as if by a miracle, he saw his nephew near him, almost at his side, sitting against the trunk of a tree, his feet bare, torn with thorns, and covered with blood.

"Arias checked the half-uttered exclamation that rose to the lips of the boy and ordered him to show him where the Indian was. He pointed up the mountain, and Arias proceeded as cautiously and as softly as possible in that direction. He soon beheld him, apparently just risen from his seat on the ground. Alarmed, doubtlessly, by the report of the gun, and still more by the noise made by the steps of Arias, he turned his face in that direction. He saw his enemy with his musket levelled – but he saw no more, for Arias fired at that instant, and the savage fell to the ground. He did not, however, let go his weapon, and, in the agony and weakness of dissolution, still seemed striving to collect his strength that he might not die passively and unavenged, and lying as he did on the slope of the mountain, with his feet toward its base, he grasped his lance in both his hands and held it before him, pointed toward his slayer. Cespedes and the negro came up to him almost at the same moment with Arias. The former valiantly sent another ball through him with one of his pistols, and the latter gave him a stroke on the face with his houghing-knife – but he had already received his death-wound.

"It was now the hour of five in the afternoon. They laid the dead body on the back of the horse which the negro had ridden, left the mountain – which has ever since borne the name of Loma del Indio in memory of the exploits of Arias – and returned to Puerto Principe, whither they arrived at ten in the evening. The body was exposed in the principal square of the city. Multitudes, of all ages, sexes, and ranks, carrying lanterns, torches, and candles, crowded to look at it, and the day broke before all the spectators had dispersed.

"I was then in Puerto Principe and was drawn by the general curiosity to witness the spectacle. I shall never forget St. Anthony's day – the day on which the Indian was killed – the thirteenth of June, I believe, in the year 1807, and the impression that sight made upon me still remains as vivid as on that night. The slain was a youth, it might be of nineteen years, of low stature, but of the marks of great strength. Shoulders of uncommon breadth; a large head, covered with coal-black hair closely shredded; round, prominent, and glaring eyes; high-arched eyebrows; a hooked nose; a brawny neck; large, muscular arms and legs; feet and hands as delicately formed as those of the ladies of our own nation – such is the picture of his person. He had on a pair of short, loose trousers, and wore a cord passing through the wound in his thigh as a kind of seton, an expedient suggested, probably, by the rude surgery of his native country.

As the mingled crowd stooped over the body to examine it, I remember well the expression of awe that stole over their features and the subdued tones in which they spoke to each other; and the fuller or fainter light thrown upon the dark face and glassy eyes of the dead as they approached and retired. Before I withdrew I saw the body nearly covered with drops of wax and tallow from the multitude of lights that had been held over it.

"The next day the boy José Maria and the little girl I have before mentioned were examined before a judicial tribunal to identify the person of the slain and to justify Arias in putting him to death. The examination was satisfactory, and the body was ordered to be hung in the public square and [then] to be drawn and quartered. A gibbet was erected, but while the ceremony of suspension was performing, the pulley by which the body was raised gave way suddenly, and it fell to the ground. The multitudes, who were not yet cured of the superstitious belief of the connection of the Indian with the powers of darkness, recoiled with shrieks and groans, and fell in heaps upon each other.

"A second attempt was made, with better success. The body was afterward dragged at the heels of a horse to a field without the city, where it was dismembered. The trunk was buried in the earth, the hands and legs set up in the public ways, and the head enclosed in an iron cage and fixed upon a pole in the neighboring village of Tanima, and the country delivered forever from the fear of one who had made such waste of human life.

"José Maria de Rodriguez is now an ecclesiastic of note in Puerto Principe, and curate of the church of La Soledad. I ought not to conceal from you that many suppose that the Indians who for three years committed such frightful ravages were of the tribe of Guachmangos, a fierce, untamable nation of Mexico, and that by some unknown means they had found their way to the island. I know not that there is any other reason for this belief than their fierceness, but I know that there is no other way of accounting for what became of those three savages from Florida than by supposing them to have been the ravagers in question."

Here ends the story of my host of the coffee plantation. It is strange enough in some of its particulars – almost to a degree of incredibility – but it rests not on the credit of my host alone. It was confirmed to me by many other inhabitants of the island, and in its substantial particulars is matter of history.

The Whirlwind

When I last visited the country beyond the Alleghanies, I travelled from Wheeling to Lexington on horseback in order to contemplate more at my leisure the beautiful scenery of that interesting region. On my way I fell in with a person, also on horseback, going in the same direction, who seemed inclined to join company with me – an arrangement to which, as I had already travelled a considerable distance alone, I felt no particular aversion. He was apparently about forty-five years of age, of a spare, athletic make, and a sallow, almost a swarthy, complexion. His eyes were of a dull hazel; they lay deep in their sockets and were surrounded by circles of a darker tinge than the rest of his face. Above them a pair of low, horizontal, coal-black eyebrows gave an inexpressibly hard and ascetic air to his countenance. He wore a black bombazette coat, the tight sleeves of which set off to great advantage his lean arms, the large joints of his elbows, his big wrists, and the heavy hands with which he grasped his beechen switch and the reins of his bridle. The remainder of his apparel consisted of a well-saved hat in that state of respectable rustiness in which that article is kept by decent people who do not often indulge themselves in the luxury of a new one, pepper-and-salt-colored satinet pantaloons over which were drawn a pair of rust-colored boots, a black-silk waistcoat, and a scanty white cravat, the sharp, spear-like ends of which projected in different directions from under his brown throat. He bestrode a tall, strong limbed, lean, black horse; across the saddle hung a well-filled portmanteau, and from under the pommel peeped a bit of sheepskin dressed with wool on, placed there to prevent the animal's back from being chafed with the journey.

He returned a civil answer to my salutation, with a broad and prolonged enunciation of the vowel sounds and a melancholy quaver of the voice. The tones, however, were full, mellow, and evidently cultivated. If I had previously any doubt of his vocation, it was now removed, and I instantly set him down for an itinerant preacher of the Baptist or Methodist persuasion. Adapting my conversation to his supposed profession, I inquired of him the state of religion in those parts. On this theme he was abundantly eloquent, and I soon found that he was a Baptist preacher who had been on a short visit to the neighborhood of Wheeling, and was now on his way to some of the villages west of Lexington, on the west bank of the Kentucky River, to perform, beside the translucent streams and under the venerable trees of that fine region, those picturesque solemnities of his sect to which they love to point as a manifold emblem of purification from moral pollution and of the resurrection from the death of sin and the sleep of the grave. He told me a checkered history of religious awakenings in some places and hundreds gathered into the fold, and of backslidings and indifference in others.

Afterward the conversation passed to other subjects. I could not help speaking of the exceeding richness of the vegetation in that country as compared with that of the Atlantic coast.

"Yes," replied my companion, the land is a land of milk and honey, and the clouds drop fatness upon it, unworthy and sinful as we are who make it our abiding-place. God maketh his sun to shine on the evil and unthankful, and sendeth rain on the just and the unjust. But are you from the Atlantic States?"

"I am."

"From New England?" inquired he, speaking more quickly than he had done before, and with something on his countenance more like a smile than I had seen him wear,

"No, from New York."

His countenance relapsed again into its former gloomy expression. "I," said he, "am from New England."

"Your friends probably live in that part of the country," said I, availing myself of that freedom of interrogation of which he had set me the example.

"Friends, if you will," answered he, "I may have there, but relations none. There lives not in all the United States, though they are my native country, a single human being with whom I can claim kindred. God has cut away, by a terrible but, as I willingly believe, a merciful dispensation, all the ties of an earthy nature that bound me to my fellow-creatures. The members of the Church of Christ, and they only, are now my fathers and mothers, and sisters and brethren."

"You allude, I perceive," said I, "to some remarkable event of your life. May I take the liberty of inquiring what it is?"

"Formerly," he replied, "it gave me pain to speak of it, but I have related it often, and it does so no longer; and moreover, I am convinced that it is sinful on my part to wish to conceal the dealings of God's providence with me from those who are willing to hear what they have been.

"You must know, then, that my father was a native of the island of Nantucket, and the only son of an emigrant pair from St. John's, on the coast of Newfoundland. My mother was from Wales. She was but a child when her father took passage for this country with her and two brothers older than herself. The vessel in which they came was wrecked off Cape Cod, and all on board perished except my mother and four of the crew, who were picked up by the fishermen of Hyannis. She was received into one of the most wealthy families on the Cape, and was brought up by the good people as if she had been one of their own children.

"My father had been a seafaring man in early life and had risen to the command of a merchant vessel. At the age of thirty-five he became acquainted with my mother, who was some fifteen years younger than himself, and made her proposals of marriage, which she would accept only on condition that he should quit the sea, which had been the grave of her family. He made the promise she required; they were married, and removed to the interior, where my father bought a farm and settled as an agriculturist.

"Our residence was on the highlands west of the Connecticut River. There was a little, decayed old dwelling on the farm when my father came to live there; he caused it to be pulled down, and had a neat white cottage built upon the spot. In this cottage was I born, and here I passed the earliest years of my life, and, speaking with respect to temporal comforts and enjoyments, the happiest. It was a lovely spot – lovely then, but now no longer so. It is bare and desolate; the besom of destruction has swept it. The winds, God's ministers, were sent against it to raze its walls and root up its shades and slay its inmates.

"I sometimes think that the distinctness with which that abode of my youth and its dear inhabitants rises before my imagination is a device of the enemy to tempt me, and to shake my resignation to the decrees of [the] Almighty. A young orchard sheltered the cottage on the northwest, and back of the orchard rose a wooded hill. On the south side of the house was our garden, which bordered on a clear, prattling brook. To the east were rich meadows and fields of grain, and pastures where I gathered strawberries and looked for birds' nests, all sloping away gently for a considerable distance, after which they sunk down out of sight into the deep glen of a river, whose shallow murmurs were often heard by us as we sat under the wild-cherry trees before our door. To the east of the river spread a wide tract of country; in full sight from our windows: farm-houses, painted red and white, with their orchards and cornfields and woodlands; steeples of distant churches, and a blue horizon of woods bounding the scene.

"Time went by pleasantly until my tenth year. Childhood is the only season of life in which happy years do not pass away swiftly. They glide softly, but they do not fly, and they seem as long as they are full of enjoyment. I had an elder sister, Jane, just arrived at seventeen: a tall, straight, blooming girl who had been my instructress in all childish pleasures. She taught me where to find the earliest blossoms and the sweetest berries, showed me where the beech shed its nuts thickest when it felt the October frosts, led me beside wild streams in the woods, read godly books with me, and taught me to sing godly hymns on Sundays under the trees of our orchard. There were two brothers, twins five years younger than myself, to whom I now performed the same office; and beautiful creatures they were, if I can trust my memory, as ever were sent into the world to be recalled in the bud of life: fair, round-faced, ruddy, good-humored, full of a perpetual flow of spirits, and, in look, gesture, and disposition, the exact copies of each other. And as they were alike in birth and mind and outward semblance, so they were alike in their lives, and in their deaths not divided. I was their constant companion, and sometimes our sister, who had now grown to maturity, would leave her sedate occupations and join our sports.

"My mother was of a delicate frame and a quiet and somewhat sad turn of mind. The calamity by which her family had perished made a deep impression upon her, and disposed her heart to religious affections. Her eyes would sometimes fill with tears as she looked at us in the midst of our pastimes, and she would often mildly check our boisterous mirth. She was our catechist; she made us read our Bibles and taught us our little hymns and prayers.

"My father was, it was thought, an unregenerate son, but he was what the world calls a good moral man, and much respected by his neighbors: he was of an even, quiet temper, never greatly exhilarated by good, nor greatly depressed by bad, fortune. I do not recollect ever seeing him apparently better pleased than when his children were noisiest in their play, when he would sit looking at us with great complacency and tell our mother how much he was like us at our age. He was what is called a silent man. He said but little, and, indulgent as he was, that little was a law to us. The neighborhood also treated him with great deference. His opinion was consulted in all difficult cases; he was made town clerk, and then sent a representative to the general court, and finally received a commission of the peace.

"My father, as I have already told you, was originally a seafaring man, and his profession had made him familiar with all the appearances of the heavens. To his knowledge of this kind, acquired on the ocean and the coast of the Atlantic, he now added that gained by a daily observation of the aspect of the heavens in the interior, until he became celebrated in those parts for his skill in discerning the face of the sky. He was looked upon as a sort of oracle on the subject of the weather, and his predictions were reverenced even more than those of the almanac. It was not always that an opinion could be extracted from him, but when obtained, it never failed of being verified. His hay never got wet while lying green on the ground, nor do I believe that he was ever overtaken by a shower in any of his excursions from home. He would pass whole hours in gazing at the sky and watching the courses of the clouds. An observation of the weather was his first business in the morning and his last at night; and if the manly placidity of his temper was ever on any occasion disturbed, it was only when the weather was more capricious than ordinary - when it refused to conform to fixed rules and failed to fulfil the promises it held forth. In this I think he was wrong as [to] questioning the providence of God, exerted in the great courses of nature; but who is without his errors?

"The country in which we lived was high and hilly. The streams by which it was intersected flowed in deep, narrow glens, unpleasant from their chilliness, shade, and mists at morning and evening; and the farms and dwellings lay on the broad, elevated country between them. Thus an ample sweep was afforded for the winds which blew over the country with as little obstruction as on the summits of the mountains. The snow was often piled in the winter to the roofs of the houses, and you might see orchards in which every tree leans to the southwest, bent and made to grow in that position by the strong and continued gales.

"In the last years of my residence in this pleasant abode, we had, about the setting in of summer, several weeks of uncommon heat and drought. God sealed up the firmament and made the heavens over our heads brass, and the earth under our feet ashes. Clouds floated over the fiery sky and brought no rain; the atmosphere was filled with a dull, dry haze, as if the finer dust of the ground had risen and mingled with it. Out of this haze the sun emerged at morning, and again dipped into it at evening, hiding his face long before he reached the horizon. The grass of the field ceased to grow, and became thin and white and dry before it ripened, and hissed mournfully whenever a breath of air passed over it. The birds chirped feebly in the trees; the cattle lowed faintly in the meadows, and gathered about the moister spots of soil. All this while the winds scarcely blew, or but softly, nor with strength enough to detach from the cherry-trees before our door the loose leaves that put on the yellowness of September and dropped of their own accord, one by one, spinning round as they descended to the earth. I had never known my father so uneasy and fidgety as at that period. He would stand for hours considering the aspect of the heavens, and after the twilight was down, he was out by the door gazing at that canopy through which the stars dimly tremble. My mother in the mean time called her children about her and taught us a prayer for rain.

"At length came a day of more perfect calm and stillness than we had experienced even in that season of calms. The leaves on the trees were so motionless that you might almost have fancied them wrought of metal to mock the growth of the vegetable world. I remember feeling uneasy at the depth and continuance of that silence, broken only by the gurgle of the brook at the bottom of our garden, where a slender thread of heated water still crept along, the sound of which fell on my ear with a painful distinctness. There was no cloud, not a speck – nothing but that thick, whitish haze to be seen in all the sky. My father went often during the day and stood anxiously looking at the atmosphere, while I crept silently near him with my two little brothers. There was something in his manner that made us afraid, though of what we knew not. My mother, too, appeared sadder than usual. Once when my father returned into the house, he told her that this was just such weather as had preceded the waterspout that overwhelmed the fishing-boat off the coast of Cape Cod thirty years before, and drowned all on board.

" 'I fear greatly,' said he, 'that some mischief is brewing for us or our neighbors, but I hope, at least, that it will steer clear of all our houses.'

"The night at length arrived, and no evil had as yet come nigh us or our dwellings. My mother saw us all in our beds, made us say our prayers, and bade us good-night in that mild, affectionate voice which I shall never forget; but for my part I could not sleep, agitated as I was with the vague and awful apprehensions with which my father's looks and words, and the strange appearances of nature, had filled my mind, and which were struggling to clothe themselves with images. Sleep at length fell upon me – a deep sleep – and with it brought visions of the night. I imagined that the profound silence was suddenly broken with strange and terrible crashings, and masses of earth and portions of sky were mingling and whirling and rolling over each other. I awoke with my limbs bathed in sweat, and it was long before my fears would suffer me to move them. When the usual current of my sensations was restored, I was comforted to find myself still in my own familiar couch, though in the midst of utter darkness, and that awful lifeless silence so deep that I could hear the clicking of my father's watch in the next room.

The sun rose as usual the next day, and the same calm and silence continued. My own apprehensions had passed away with the night, though I observed my father watching the cloudless, hazy skies with the same air of anxiety. About twelve o'clock I was in the orchard back of our cottage, amusing myself with gathering the largest unripe apples which the drought had caused to drop in great numbers from the trees, intending to carry them to my two little brothers to play with. My father had left his occupation in the field on account of the heat, and was then in the house. Suddenly I heard a crackling sound to the southwest, as of a mighty flame running among brushwood, and blown into fury by a strong wind. Looking toward that quarter, I beheld a small, dark cloud, enlarging, blackening, and advancing every instant, and under it the wood agitated with a violent motion, the tree-tops waving and tossing, the trunks swaying to and fro, bending low and then erecting themselves suddenly, as if wrestling with a furious gust. Birds were flying in all directions from the scene of the commotion, and cattle running affrighted from the wood in which they had sought shelter from the noonday heat. Then I saw broken branches, green leaves from the tree-tops, and withered ones from the ground, and dust from the dry earth, lifted together into the air in a vast column and whirled rapidly round, and heard the crash of falling trees and the snapping of the shivered trunks, as if the Prince of the Power of the Air, having received permission, had fallen in great wrath upon the forest to destroy it. Before that advancing whirlwind the trees bowed to the ground, and the next moment were raised again by the power of the gale, and drawn into the vortex and twisted off by the roots, and whirled with all their branches into the air, and tossed to one side and the other upon the summits of the surrounding wood. It was but for a moment – a brief moment of astonishment and terror – that I stood gazing on this spectacle. I turned and made for the house with my utmost speed, and as I ran I heard the roar of the whirlwind behind me, and was sensible of a sudden shade passing over the heavens. When I arrived at the house and opened the door, I saw my father, who had been engaged in reading, just rising from his seat and going toward the window, with the book in his hand, to learn the cause of the tumult without. That book was the Bible, and the recollection of this single circumstance forms a ground of consolation and hope, in the recollection of his sudden and unforewarned death, which I would not be deprived of for worlds.

"He gave a single look, the book dropped from his hand, and, before I had time to utter a word, he called out in his strong voice: 'Run – run for your lives – leave the house this instant – the whirlwind is upon us.'

"As he spoke, the sound of the gust was heard howling about the dwelling and the timbers cracked and groaned in the mighty blast. My mother had hastily gathered the children and was putting us before her to go out the door, when all at once a terrible crash was heard over our heads, the walls shook, the windows were shivered in pieces, the floor heaved under our feet, and the ceiling, bursting upward in several places, showed us the roof raised and borne off by the wind. The walls and partitions of the house were swayed to and fro like a curtain. My father was a man of great bodily strength, of the middle height, but brawny and muscular beyond most persons I have known. When I last saw him he had put his strong arms against the wall that threatened to overwhelm us and was bracing himself against it to give us an opportunity to escape. I saw also my mother, who had taken the two youngest children by the hand, her hair streaming upward in disorder, making for the door. I found myself, I know not how, without the house, and scarcely was I there when a rush of air seemed to draw my breath from my very lungs and I was lifted from the ground amid a whirl of dust and broken branches, and shingles and boards from the building. How high I was carried I know not, for I saw only the confusion around me; but shortly afterward I felt myself softly deposited among boughs and leaves.

"I must have swooned after I descended, for I recollect slowly recovering my consciousness and finding my garments wet and heavy, and the rain beating upon me. I was among the thick foliage of a maple that had been overthrown by the whirlwind. A man whose voice and mien were familiar to me, and whom, as my senses gradually returned, I recognized as one of my neighbors, came and took me off, and placed me beside him on the ground. Around me the earth was strewn with splintered branches of trees, rails, and boards, and looking westward to the hill, I beheld where fences had been swept away and stone walls scattered, and a wide path had been broken through the wood, along which masses of fresh earth appeared among the heaps of prostrate trees, and tall, shivered trunks stood overlooking their uprooted fellows. At a little distance from me was a heap of bricks and rubbish, and on my inquiring what it could be, I was told that it was the ruins of my father's house. Then flashed upon my mind the recollection of that moment of confusion, haste, and affright which passed before I left it, and in a transport of anxiety amounting almost to agony, I ran to the spot. I found the neighbors already gathered about it and busy in removing the rubbish in order to ascertain if any of the family were buried beneath; and, weeping all the while, I assisted them as far as my childish strength would allow, notwithstanding the good-natured attempts that were made to prevent me. Let me hasten over what followed. I said in the beginning that I could relate my story without any painful emotions, but I was mistaken, for when I come to this part of it I am always sick at heart. They were found – crushed to death by the fall of the chimney and the beams of the building – my father, my dear mother, and the two lovely children still in her arms. But where was my sister? Had she been fortunate as to escape? Even this hope was torn from me, for she was soon found, where the whirlwind had cast her, in the edge of the brook now swollen by rains, the water rippling against her cheek, white as snow, and her dishevelled hair floating in the current.

There are no expressions that can describe the bitterness of my grief. The bodies were carried to a neighboring house; I followed them; I remained with them all night; I refused to be comforted, but with the feverish hope which sometimes crossed my mind that the dead were in a state of insensibility from which they would awaken. I slept not, I ate not, till they were buried; I struggled madly and with moanings of agony against those who came to put them in the coffins. They were carried to the grave the next day amid a great concourse of people from all the surrounding country who filled the house and gathered in a solemn and silent multitude around the door. The hymn given out on that occasion by the minister was one my mother had taught me to repeat from memory; and when they sang the following stanza, the eyes of all were turned upon me, by reason of my passionate sobbing:

" 'Man's life is like the grass,
     Or like the morning flower;
 A sharp wind sweeps the field,
     It withers in an hour !'

"I was not allowed to see the bodies covered with earth, lest my health might suffer from the excess of my grief; but when at last they told me they were buried, I suffered myself to be undressed and led to my bed, from which I did not rise until several days afterward.

"The neighbor to whose house the bodies of my family were taken, a devout and just man of the Baptist persuasion, allowed me to remain under his roof and treated me with great kindness. He was appointed my guardian, and proved a faithful steward of the remains of my father's property. The terrible calamity with which I had been visited had engendered a sadness that hung upon me like a continual cloud; but, as I grew up, my mind was opened to receive the consolations of the Gospel. I saw that the chastisement, though severe, was meant for good, and that the Lord, by removing all whom I loved and separating me from the children of men, had enabled me to devote myself the more entirely to the work of reconciling my fellow-creatures to him. I came, therefore, to this region of the West, where the fields were white for the reaper, where the harvest was plenteous and the laborers few, and entered upon my new calling, which has not been unblessed with a cheerful and encouraged spirit."

Here the travelling preacher made an end of his story, and I had no opportunity of remarking on certain of its circumstances which seemed to me a little extraordinary, since just at that moment he found himself opposite the house of one of the brethren, a thrifty farmer, where, he said, he was under an engagement to stop.

The Indian Spring

ONE OF the adventures of my life upon which I have since oftenest reflected, and concerning which my imagination is most inclined to dispute the dictates of my reason, happened many years ago, when, quite a young man, I made an excursion into the interior of the State of New York and passed a few days in the region whose waters flow into the east branch of the Susquehanna. My readers will easily judge for themselves whether what I am going to relate can be accounted for from natural causes. For my own part, however, so vivid is the impression it has left upon my mind, and so difficult is it with me to distinguish my recollections of it from that of the absolute realities of my life, that I find it the easier belief to ascribe it to a cause above nature.

I think I have elsewhere intimated that I have great sympathy with believers in the supernatural. Theoretically, I am as much a philosopher, and have as little of what is commonly called superstition about me, as most persons of my acquaintance, but the luxury of a little superstition in practice, the strong and active play into which it calls the imagination, the fine thrill it sends through the veins, the alternate gushes of fear and courage that come over us when under its influence, are too agreeable a relief from the dull realities of the material world to be readily given up. My own individual experience also makes me indulgent to those whose credulity in these matters exceeds my own. Is it to be wondered at that the dogmas of philosophy should not gain credit when they have the testimony of our own senses against them? You say that this evidence is often counterfeited by the tricks of fancy, the hallucinations of the nerves, and by our very dreams. You are right – but who shall in all cases distinguish the false experience from the true?

The part of the country of which I am speaking had just been invaded by the footsteps of cultivation. Openings had been made here and there in the great natural forest, log houses had been built, the farmers were gathering in their first crops of tall grass, and the still taller harvests of wheat and rye stood up by the side of the woods in the clearings. It was then the month of June, and I sallied forth from my lodgings at a paltry log tavern to ramble in the woods with a friend of mine who had come with me from New York. We set out amid the warblings of the birds, scarce waiting for the dew to be dried up from the herbage. I carried a fowling-piece on my shoulder, not that I meant to be the death of any living creature that fine morning when everything seemed so happy, but because such a visible pretext for a stroll in the woods and fields satisfies at once the curiosity of those whom you meet and saves you often a world of staring, and sometimes not a few impertinent questions. I hold it right and fair to kill game late in the autumn, when the animal has had his feast of fruits and nuts and is left with a prospect of a long, hard, uncomfortable winter before him and the dangers of being starved to death. But to take his life in the spring, or the beginning of summer, when he has so many fine sunny months of frolic and plenty before him – it is gratuitous cruelty, and I have ever religiously abstained from it.

My companion was much more corpulent than I, and as slow a walker as I was a fast one. However, he good-naturedly exerted himself to keep up with me, and I made more than one attempt to moderate my usual speed for his accommodation. The effort worried us both. At length he fairly gave out, and bringing the butt of his fowling-piece smartly to the ground, stood still, with both hands grasping the muzzle.

"I beg," said he, "that you will go on at your own pace. I promise faithfully not to stir from the spot till you are fairly out of sight."

"But I am very willing to walk slower."

"No," rejoined my friend, "we did not set out together for the purpose of making each other uncomfortable, nor will we, if I can help it. Here we have been fretting and chafing each other for half an hour. Why, it is like yoking an ox with a race-horse. Go on, I beseech you, while I stop to recover my wind. I wish you a pleasant walk of it. I shall expect to see you back at our landlord's at one o'clock."

I took him at his word and proceeded. I rambled through tall old groves clear of underwood, beside rivulets broken into little pools and cascades by rocks and fallen timber, along the edges of dark, shrubby swamps, and across sunny clearings, until I was tired. At length I came to a pleasant natural glade on the slope of a hill and sat down under the shade of a tree to rest myself. It was a narrow opening in the woods, extending for some distance up the hill, and terminating in that quarter at the base of a ridge of rocks above which rose the forest.

At the lower end, near which I was, a spring rose up in a little hollow and formed a streamlet which ran off under the trees. A most still, quiet nook it was, sheltered from all winds; the leaves were not waved, nor the grass bent by a breath of air, and the sun came down between the inclosing trees with so strong a heat that, except in the shade, I felt the warmth of the ground through the soles of my shoes.

As I lay with my head propped on my hand and my elbow buried in a mass of herbage, my thoughts turned involuntarily upon the ancient inhabitants of these woods. Here, said I to myself, in this very spot, some Indian doubtless fixed his cabin; or haply some little neighborhood, the branch of a larger tribe, nestled in this sylvan enclosure. That circle of mouldering timber is probably the remains of the wigwam of the last inhabitant, and that great vine which sprawls over it was probably once supported by its walls, and when they were abandoned and decaying, dragged them to the ground, as many a parasite has done by his credulous benefactor. Here the Indian woman planted her squashes and tended her maize; here the Indian father brought forth his boys to try their bows and aim their little tomahawks at the trees, teaching – for even in the solemnity of my feelings I could not forbear the pun – teaching "the young idea how to shoot." That spring which gushes up so brightly and abundantly from the ground, yielded them, when their exercise was over, a beverage never mingled with the liquid poisons of the civilized world and gave its cresses to season the simple repast. Gradually my imagination became both awed and kindled by these reflections. I felt rebuked by the wild genius of a place familiar for centuries only with the race of red men and hunters, and I almost expected to see some Indian, with his tomahawk and bow, walk up to me and ask me what I did there.

My thoughts were diverted from this subject by my eyes falling upon an earth-newt, as red as fire, crawling lazily and with an almost imperceptible motion over the grass. I yawned by a sort of sympathy with the sluggish creature, and, oppressed with fatigue and heat, for the sun was getting high, loosened my cravat and stretched out my legs to an easier position. All at once I found myself growing drowsy, my eyelids dropping involuntarily, my eyes rolling in their sockets with a laborious attempt to keep themselves open, and the landscape swimming and whirling before me, as if I saw it in a mirror suspended by a loose string and waving in the wind. Once or twice the scene was entirely lost for a moment to my vision, and I perceived that I had actually been asleep. It struck me that I might be better employed than in taking a nap at that time of day, and accordingly, I rose and walked across the glade until I came to the foot of the rocks at the upper end of it, when I turned to take another look at the pleasant and quiet spot. Judge of my astonishment when I actually beheld, standing by the very circle of rubbish near which I had been reposing, and which I had taken for the remains of a wigwam, an Indian – a real Indian – the very incarnation of the images that had been floating in my fancy.

I will not say that I did not spring from the ground when the figure met my eye, so sudden and startling was the shock it gave me. He was not one of that degenerate kind which I had seen in various parts of the country wearing hats, frock, coats, pantaloons, and Dutch blankets but was dressed in the original garb of his nation. A covering of skin was wrapped about his loins, a mantle of the same was flung loosely over his shoulders, and his legs were bare from the middle of the thigh down to his ornamented moccasons. A single tuft of stiff, black hair on the top of his head, from which the rest was carefully plucked, was mingled with the gaudy plumage of different birds; a bow and a bundle of arrows peeped over his shoulder; a necklace of bears' claws hung down upon his breast; his right hand carried a tomahawk, and the fingers of his left were firmly closed, like those of one whose physical vigor and resoluteness of purpose suffered not the least muscle of his frame to relax for a moment. Notwithstanding the distance at which he stood, and which might be a hundred paces at least, I saw his whole figure, even to the minutest article of dress, with what seemed to me an unnatural distinctness. His countenance had that expression which has been so often remarked upon as peculiar to the aborigines of our country – a settled look of sullenness, sadness, and suspicion, as if when moulded by nature it had been visibly stamped with the presentiment of the decline and disappearance of their race. The features were strongly marked, hard, and stern: high cheekbones, a broad forehead, an aquiline nose, garnished with an oblong piece of burnished copper; a mouth somewhat wide, between a parenthesis of furrows, and a bony and fleshless chin. But then his eyes – such eyes I have never seen! Distant as they were from me, they seemed close to my own, and to ray out an unpleasant brightness from their depths, like twin stars of evil omen. Their influence unstrung all my sinews, and a gush of sudden and almost suffocating heat came over my whole frame. I averted my look instantly and fixed it upon the feet of the savage, shod with their long moccasons and standing motionless among the thick weeds, but I could not keep it there. Again my eyes returned upward; again they encountered his, glittering in the midst of that calm, sullen face, and again that oppressive, stifling sensation came over me.

It was natural that I should feel an impulse to remove from so unpleasant a neighborhood; I therefore shouldered my fowling-piece, climbed the rock before me, and penetrated into the woods. As I proceeded, the idea took possession of me that I was followed by the Indian, and I walked pretty fast in order to shake it off; but I found this impossible. I had got into a state of fidgety, nervous excitement, and it seemed to me that I felt the rays of those bright, unnatural eyes on my shoulders, my back, my arms, and even my hands as I flung them back in walking. At length I looked back, and notwithstanding I half expected to see him, I was scarcely less surprised than at first when I beheld the same figure, just at the same distance, standing motionless as then, his bright eyes gleaming upon me between the trunks of the trees. A third time I felt that flush of dissolving heat, and a violent sweat broke out all over me. I have heard of the cold, clammy sweat of fear; mine was not of that temperature: it was as the warmest summer rain, warm and free and profuse as the current of brooks in the hottest and moistest season of dog-days.

I walked on, keeping my sight fixed on the strange apparition. It did not seem to move, and as I proceeded, gradually diminished by the natural effect of distance until I could scarcely distinguish it among the thick trunks and boughs of the forest. Happening to avert my eyes for a moment, I saw, as I turned again to the spot, that the figure had swiftly and silently gained upon me and was now at the same distance as when I first beheld it. A clearing lay before me. I saw the sunshine and the grass between the trunks of the trees, and rushing forward, found myself under the open sky and felt relieved by a freer air. I looked back, and nothing was to be seen of my pursuer.

A small log-house stood in the open space with a well beside it and a tall, rude machine of the kind they call a well-sweep leaning over it, loaded with a bucket at one end and a heavy stone at the other. A boy of about twelve years of age was drawing water. The sight of a human habitation, and a habitation of white men, was a welcome one to me, and tormented as I was with heat and thirst, I rejoiced at the prospect of refreshing myself with a draught of the cool, pure element. Accordingly, I made for the well, and arrived at it just as the boy was pouring the contents of the bucket into a large stone pitcher. "You will give me a taste of the water?" said I to him.

"And welcome," replied the boy, "if you'll drink out of the pitcher, for the mug is broke and we haven't got any glasses."

I stooped, and raising the heavy vessel to my lips, took a copious draught from the brim, where the cold water was yet sparkling with the bubbles raised by pouring it from the bucket. "Your water is very fine," said I, when I had recovered my breath.

"Yes, but not so fine as you'll get at the Indian spring," rejoined he. "That's the best water in all the country - the clearest, the coldest, and the sweetest. Father always sends me to the Indian spring when he wants the best water - when uncle comes up from York, or the minister makes us a visit."

"What is it that you call the Indian spring?" I inquired.

"Oh, I guess you must have passed it, by the way you came. Didn't you see a spring of water, east of a ledge of rocks, in a pretty spot of ground where there were no trees?"

"I believe I saw something of the kind," said I, recollecting the glade in which I had thrown myself to rest shortly before, and its fountain.

"That was the Indian spring, and if you took notice, you must have seen some old logs and sticks lying in a heap and a few stones that look as if there had been fire on them. It was thought that an Indian family lived there before the country was settled by our people."

"Are there any Indians in this neighborhood at present?" I inquired, with some eagerness.

"Oh, no, indeed; they are gone to the west'ard, so they say, though I am not big enough to know anything about it. It was before father came into the country - long before. The only Indian I ever saw was Jemmy Sunkum, who came about last summer, selling brooms and begging cider."

"A tall, spare, strong-looking man, was he," asked I, "dressed in skins, and carrying a bow?" my thoughts naturally recurring to the figure I had just seen.

The boy grinned. "Not much taller than I am, and as fat as a wood-chuck; and as for the skins he wore, I never see any but his own through the holes of his trousers, unless it be a squirrel-skin that he carried his tobacco and loose change in. He wore an old hat with the crown torn out, and had lost one of his eyes - they say it was by drinking so much cider. Father swapped an old pair of pantaloons with him for a broom.

But I must take this pitcher to father, who is at work in the corn-field yonder; so good-morning to you, sir."

The lad tripped away, whistling, and I sat down on one of the broad, flat stones by the well-side, under the shade of a young tree of the kind commonly called yellow willow, which in a year or two shoots up from a slip of the size of a man's finger into a fine, shapely, overshadowing tree. I laid my hat and gun by my side and wiped my hot and sweaty forehead, upon which the wind that swayed to and fro the long, flexible, depending branches breathed with a luxurious coolness.

The Indian I have seen cannot be the one that the boy means, said I to myself, nor probably any other of which the inhabitants know anything. That fine, majestic savage is a very different being from the fat, one-eyed vagabond in the ragged trousers that the lad speaks of. It is probably some ancient inhabitant of the place, returned from the forest of the distant West to visit the scenes of his childhood. But what could he mean by following me in this manner, and why should he keep his eye fixed on me so strangely? As I said this, I looked along the forest I had just quitted, examining it carefully and with an eye sharpened by the excited state of my imagination to see if I could discover anything of my late pursuer. All was quiet and motionless. I heard the bee as he flew by heavily from the cucumber-flowers in the garden near me, and the hum of the busy wheel from the open windows of the cottage; but face or form of human being I saw not. I replaced my hat on my head and my gun on my shoulder, crossed the clearing, and entered the opposite wood, intending to return home by a kind of circuit, for I did not care again to encounter the savage, whose demeanor was so mysterious.

I had proceeded but a few rods when, a mingled sensation of uneasiness and curiosity inducing me to look over my shoulder, I started to behold the very figure whose sight I was endeavoring to avoid, just entering the forest – the same brawny shoulders clad with skins, the same sad, stern, suspicious countenance, the same bright eyes thrilling and scorching me with their light. Again I felt that indescribable sensation of discomfort and heat, and the perspiration, which had ceased to flow while I sat by the well, again gushed forth from every pore. Involuntarily I stopped short. What was this being, and why should he dog my steps in this strange manner? What were his designs, pacific or hostile? And what method should I take to rid myself of his pursuit? I had tried walking away from him without effect; should I now adopt the expedient of walking up to him and asking his business? The thought struck me that, if his designs were malevolent, this step might bring me into danger. He was well armed with a tomahawk and arrows, and who could tell the force and certainty of his aim? This fear, on reflection, I rejected as groundless and unmanly, for what cause had he to seek my life?

It was but prudent, however, to prepare myself for the worst that could happen. I therefore examined my priming, and as I had nothing but small bird-shot with me, I kicked up the dry leaves from the earth under my feet, and selecting a handful of the smallest, smoothest, and roundest pebbles from among the gravel, put two or three of them into the muzzle and lodged the rest in my pocket. As I turned, there was that face still, at the very edge of the forest, glaring steadily upon me, and watching my operations with the unchanging, stony, stoical expression of the Indian race. I replaced the piece on my shoulder, and advanced toward it.

Scarcely had I gone three paces when it suddenly disappeared behind the huge old trunk of an old buttonwood or plane tree that stood just in the edge of the clearing. I approached the tree; there was no living thing behind it or near it. I looked out into the clearing and scanned its whole extent for the object of my search, but in vain. There was the cottage ~ in which the wheel was still humming and the well with its young willow waving restlessly over it. The clearing was long and narrow and widened away toward the south, where was a field of Indian corn in which I could distinguish my friend, the lad who had given me the water, in company with a man who, I suppose, was his father, diligently engaged in hoeing the corn; and at intervals I could hear the click of their hoes against the stones. Nothing else was to be seen, nothing else was to be heard. I turned and searched the bushes about me; nothing was there. I looked up into the old planet tree above my head; the clean and handsomely divided branches, speckled with white, guided my eye far into the very last of their verdurous recesses, but no creature, not even a bird, was to be seen there.

Strange as it may seem, I found myself refreshed and cooled by this search, and relieved from the burning and suffocating heat that I felt while the eye of the savage rested upon me. My perplexity was, however, anything but lessened, and I resolved to pursue my way home with as little delay as possible and spell out, if I could, the mystery at my leisure. Accordingly, I plunged again into the woods, and after proceeding a little way, began to change my course in a direction which I judged must bring me to the spot where I had rested in the Indian glade near the spring, from which doubted not I could find my way home without difficulty. As I proceeded, the heat of the day seemed to grow more and more oppressive. There was shade about me and over my head ~ thick shade of oak, maple, and walnut – but it seemed to me as if beams of the hottest midsummer sun were beating upon my back and scorching the skin of my neck. I turned my head, and there again stood the Indian, with that eternal, intolerable glare of the eyes.

I stopped not, but went on with a quicker pace. My face was flushed, my brow throbbed audibly, my head ached, the veins in my hands were swollen till they looked like ropes, and the sweat dropped from my hair like rain. A fine brook crossed my way, clear as diamond, full to the very brim, and sending up a cool vapor from its surface that promised for the grateful temperature of its waters. I longed to strip off my clothes, and lay myself down in its bed at full length, and steep my burning limbs in its current. Just then I remembered the story of Tam O'Shanter, pursued by witches and saved by crossing a running stream. If there be any witchcraft in this thing, said I to myself, it will not follow me beyond this brook. I was ashamed of the thought as it crossed my mind, but I leaped the brook notwithstanding and hurried on. Turning afterward to observe the effect of my precaution, I saw the savage standing in the midst of the very current, the bright water flowing round his copper-colored ankles. The sight was as vexatious as it was singular and did not by any means diminish my haste.

A little opening, where the trees had been cut down and the ground sown with European grasses, came in my way, and I entered it. In this spot the red and white clover grew rankly and blossomed side by side with columbine and cranesbill, the natives of the soil ~ flowers and verdure the more striking in their beauty for the unsightly and blackened stumps of trees standing thick among them ~ a sweet, still nook, a perpetual concert of humming-birds and a thousand beautiful winged insects for which our common speech has no name, and exhaling from the herbage an almost overpowering stream of fragrance. I no longer saw my pursuer. What could this mean? Was this figure some restless shadow that could haunt only its ancient wilderness and was excluded from every spot reclaimed and cultivated by the white man?

I took advantage of this respite to wipe my face and forehead; I unbuttoned my waistcoat, took off my cravat and put it in my pocket, threw back the collar of my coat from my shoulders, fanned myself awhile with my hat, and then went on. Soon after I again entered the wood, I perceived with surprise that my tormentor had gained upon me. He was twice as near to me as when I first saw him, and the strange light that seemed to shoot from his eyes was more intense and insufferable than ever. I was in a part of the forest which was thickly strewn with the fallen trunks of trees, wrenched up, as it seemed to me, long ago by some mighty wind. I hastened on, leaping from one to another, occasionally looking back at my pursuer. The air in my face as I flew forward, seemed as if issuing from the mouth of a furnace. In leaping upon a spot where the earth was moist and soft, one of my shoes remained embedded fast in the soil. It is an old one, said I to myself; I shall be lighter and cooler without it. Immediately the low branch of a tree struck my hat from my head as I rushed onward. No matter, thought I, I will send a boy to look for it in the morning.

As I sprang from a rock my other shoe flew off and dropped on the ground before me; I caught it up without stopping and jerked it over my head with all my strength at the savage behind me. When I next looked back, I saw that he had decked himself with my spoils. He had strung both my shoes to his necklace of bears' claws and had crowded down my hat upon his head over that tuft of long black hair mingled with feathers, the ends of which stood out under the brim in front, forming a wild, grotesque shade to those strangely bright eyes. Still I went on, and in springing upon a log covered with green moss and moist and slimy with decay, my foot slipped, and I could only keep from falling by dropping the fowling-piece I carried. I did not stop to pick it up, and the next instant it was upon the shoulder of the Indian, or demon, that chased me.

I darted forward, panting, glowing, perspiring, ready to sink to the earth with heat and fatigue, until suddenly I found myself on the edge of that ridge of rocks which rose above the Indian glade where I had thrown myself to rest under a tree in the morning, before my steps had been dogged by the savage. The whole scene lay beneath my feet – the spring, the ruins of the wigwam, the tree under which I reclined. A single desperate leap took me far down into the glade below me, and a few rapid strides brought me to the very spot where I had been reposing, and where the pressure of my form still remained on the grass. A shrill, wild shout with which the woods rang in sharp echoes rose upon the air, and instantly I perceived that my pursuer had leaped also, and was at my side and had seized me with a strong and sudden grip that shook every fibre of my frame. A strange darkness came over all visible objects, and I sank to the ground.

An interval of insensibility followed, the duration of which I have no means of computing, and from which I was at last aroused by noises near me, and by motions of my body produced by some impulse from without. I opened my eyes on the very spot where I remembered to have reclined in the morning. My hat was off, my hair and clothes were steeped in sweat, my fowling-piece and shoes lay within a few feet of me, but scattered in different directions. My friend who had accompanied me at the outset of my ramble was shaking me by the shoulder, bawling my name in my ear and asking me if I meant to lie here all day. I sat up and found that the shade of the tree under which I was had shifted many feet from its original place, and that I was lying exposed to the burning beams of the sun. My old acquaintance, the red earth-newt, had made great progress in the grass, having advanced at least a yard from the place where I remembered to have seen him when I was beginning to grow drowsy, before my adventure with the savage.

My friend complained that he had been looking for me for more than an hour, and hallooing himself hoarse without effect, and that he was sure we should be late for dinner. I said nothing to my companion about what had happened until the next day, when I ventured to relate a part of the strange series of real or imaginary circumstances connected with my ramble. He laughed at the earnestness of my manner and very promptly and flippantly said it was nothing but a dream. My readers may possibly be the same opinion, and I myself, when in a philosophical mood, incline to this way of accounting for the matter. At other times, however, when I recall to mind the various images and feelings of that time, deeply and distinctly engraved on my memory, I find nothing in them which should lead me to class them with the illusions of sleep, and nothing to distinguish them from the waking experience of my life.

The Marriage Blunder

I HAVE never been able to understand the peculiar significance of the old and often-quoted maxim that matches are made in heaven, as if Providence had more to do with our marriages, and we ourselves less, than with the other enterprises and acts of our lives. The truth is that nothing we do is transacted with more deliberation than our matrimonial engagements. The talk about rashness, precipitancy, and blindness in the parties between whom the union is formed is all cant, and cant of the most ancient and stale kind. I wonder it is not exploded in an age when old theories and long-established opinions are thrown aside with as little ceremony or remorse as a grave-digger shovels up the bones and dust of past generations.

In almost every marriage that takes place, the bridegroom has passed by many a fair face before he has made his final selection, and the bride refused many a wooer. The parties are united after a courtship generally of months; the fair one defers the day of the nuptials from mere maiden coyness, and the lover must have time to provide her a habitation. Religious ceremonies, the forms of law, the preparations for the festivity of the occasion, all interpose their numerous delays. Even where the parties have nothing to do with the matter themselves, it is managed with great reflection and contrivance, with negotiations warily opened and skilfully conducted on the part of their relations. Why, the very making of these matches, which the proverb so flippantly affirms to be made without our agency constitutes nearly half the occupation of civilized society. For this the youth applies himself diligently to the making of his fortune; for this the maiden studies the graces and accomplishments of her sex. I have known persons who for years never thought of any other subject. I have known mothers who for years made it the business of their lives to settle their daughters. The premeditation of matrimony influences all the fashions, amusements, and employments of mankind. What a multitude of balls and parties and calls and visits and journeys are owing to this fruitful cause! What managing and manoeuvring, what dressing and dancing, what patching and painting, how much poetry and, eke, how much prose, what quantities of music and conversation and criticism and scandal and civility that otherwise would never have had an existence!

The result justifies the supposition of deliberation, and most marriages are accordingly made with sufficient wisdom. Talk of the risk undertaken by the candidate for the happiness of conjugal life! The man who marries is not so often cheated as the man who buys a horse, even when the bargain is driven for him by the most knowing jockey. Few are unfortunate in a wife. Marriages are comfortable and respectable things the world over, with a few exceptions. Ill-natured people torment each other, it is true, but if they were not married they would torment somebody else, unless they retired to a hermitage; while, on the other hand, good tempers are improved by the domestic affections which the married state calls forth. If marriage happened to a man without his knowledge or consent; if it came upon one unexpectedly, like a broken leg, or a fever, or a legacy from a rich relation, or a loss by a broken bank; if young men and young women were to lay their heads on their pillows in celibacy and wake the next morning in wedlock; if one were to have no voice in the selection of a wife, but were obliged to content himself with one chosen for him by lot – there would, I grant, be some propriety in the maxim I have mentioned. But in a matter which is the subject of so much discussion and deliberation as marriage, not only on the part of the youth and damsel but of all friends and acquaintances, and which is hedged round with so many forms and ceremonies, it is nonsense to talk of any particular fatality.

I recollect but two instances of people being coupled together not only without their knowledge or consent, but without even that of their friends. The marriages took place on the same day, in the same church, and from the misery in which the parties lived it might be inferred that the matches were made anywhere else but in heaven. I will relate the story, as it is rather a curious one, though, I admit, not at all romantic. I would make it more so, if in my power, for the gratification of certain persons whose fair hands will turn these pages, but I have no skill in embellishing plain matters of fact.

Some years since, when I was at Natchitoches, on the banks of the Red River, I became acquainted with a French cotton planter of the name of La Ruche, whose house stood at a little distance from the village. He was a lively, shrivelled old gentleman, dried almost to a mummy by seventy hot Louisiana summers, with a head as white as snow but a step as light as that of the deer he hunted. He loved to tell of old times, of the adventures of his youth, and of the history of his contemporaries and the country. The novelty of these subjects stimulated my curiosity and kindled my imagination, and it may readily be supposed that he found me a most willing listener. For this quality of mine he took a vehement liking to me and used to invite me to his plantation, where he would keep me, in spite of all my excuses, for days together.

La Ruche was the descendant of one of the early settlers of Louisiana, the younger son of an ancient Gascon family who came out with La Harpe in the early part of the eighteenth century and [was] made one of the colony which he led to the banks of the Red River. The father of my friend, a wealthy planter, had sent him in his youth to be educated at Paris. After an absence of six years, in which he acquired a competent share of the graces and intelligence of that polished capital, he returned to complete his education in a different school, and one better suited to the state of the country at that period. He exchanged his silk breeches for leathern ones and learned to navigate the immense rivers of this region, to traffic and hold talk with the Indians, to breed and train packs of hounds, to manage the spirited horses of the country, to pursue and kill the deer in the merry and noisy hunt by torchlight, and to bring down the fiercer bear and panther. Once he had penetrated overland to Mexico. Three times he had guided a skiff through the difficult channels of the Great Raft, as it is called, of the Red River, thirty leagues to the north of Natchitoches, where for eighty miles in length it drowns an immense extent of country, overlaying it with huge trunks of trees, above which wave the dwarf willows and gaudy March flowers, and around and under which creep sluggishly the innumerable and intricate currents.

My friend loved to make me ride out with him, and I believe he did it partly from a motive of vanity, that I might see how much better a horseman he was than I. We were commonly mounted on two fine mares of the Andalusian breed, fleet, spirited, with prominent veins and eyes that shot fire like those of an Andalusian lady. Such rides as we had in the charming month of October! – for charming it is in every region of North America. We crossed the blood-colored stream of the Red River and visited the noble prairies between it and the Washita.

Let no man talk to me of the beautiful rural scenery of the Old World;
I have seen it; it is beauty on a small scale, in miniature, in little spots
and situations; but if he would see beauty in its magnificence and
vastness – beauty approaching to sublimity, yet not losing but rather
heightening its own peculiar character – let him visit the prairies of
our southwestern country; let him contemplate the long, sweeping
curve of primeval forest with which they are bordered, where the
huge, straight, columnar trunks are wound with gigantic, blossoming
vines and upheave to an immense grassy ocean spread before him;
on the innumerable gorgeous flowers that glow like gems among the
verdure; on the clumps of towering trees planted over them at pleasant
distances, as if for bowers of refreshments; and the immense rivers
draining territories large enough for empires, by which they are often
bounded at one extremity. Here the features of the earth are in unison
with those of heaven; with the sky of tenderest blue, the edge of whose
vast circle comes down seemingly into the very grass; with the wind
that bends all those multitudes of flowers in one soft but mighty
respiration, and with the great sun that steeps the whole in his glory.

But the scene of my story lies on the western side of the Red River,
and I have no excuse for lingering thus between that stream and the
Washita, save the surpassing amenity of these gardens of God, for such
they are, laid out and planted and beautified.

One day I rode out with my ancient host toward the Rio Hondo,
a small river wandering through dark forests in a deep channel, up to
which the Spanish government formerly claimed when they extended
their pretensions to the west of the Sabine. "There," said Ruche,
pointing to a placid sheet of water over whose borders hung the peach-
leaved willows of the country, "there is the Spanish Lake, and in a
little time we shall be in the old Spanish town of Adayes, about ten
miles distant from Natchitoches. This country is the ancient debatable
ground on which the two rival colonies of France and Spain met
and planted their first settlement by the side of each other." A little
farther on my companion gave a wave of his hand. "There," said he, "is
Adayes. The inhabitants are a good sort of people – simple, hospitable,
bigoted, and ignorant – but look well to that pretty silver-mounted
riding whip of yours, or you may chance not to carry it back with you."
I looked, and saw a cluster of tall, clumsy houses, plastered on the
outside with mud, which, peeling off in many places, showed the logs
of which they were built.

We entered the town at a round pace, and then, checking our horses, passed slowly through it. The inhabitants were sitting at their doors or loitering about in the highway, for the weather had that soft, golden, autumnal serenity which makes one impatient of being anywhere but in the open air. We entered into conversation with them; they spoke nothing but Spanish, but when I looked in their faces and remarked the strong aboriginal cast of features and the wild blackness of the eye in many of them, I expected every moment to be saluted in Cherokee or Choctaw. La Ruche directed my attention to their place of worship, which stood in the centre of the village. "Look at that little church," said he, "built far back in the last century. It has four bells, two or three of which are cracked, and on the religious festivals they express the public joy in the most horrid jangle you ever heard. The walls of the interior are adorned with several frightful daubs of renowned saints which assist the devotions of the worshippers. Note it well, I beg of you, for you are to hear a story about it to-day at dinner."

We left the village and the lazy people that loitered about its old dwellings. On our way to Natchitoches we passed a fine cotton plantation, to which my friend called my particular attention. The mansion of the proprietor, with three sharp, parallel roofs and a piazza in front, stood embowered in shade, its stuccoed walls of a yellowish color gleaming through the deep-green leaves of the catalpa and the shivering foliage of the China-tree. Back of it stood, in a cluster, the comfortable-looking cottages of the negroes, built of cypress timber, before which the young, woolly-headed imps of the plantation were gambolling and whooping in the sun. Still farther back lay a confused assemblage of pens, from some of which were heard the cries and snuffing of swine; and around them all was a great enclosure for the reception of cattle, in which I saw goats walking and bleating, and geese gabbling to each other and hissing at two or three dogs that moved surlily among them. My companion stopped his horse and called my notice to a couple of fine trees of the buttonwood species, or sycamore, as they are called in the western country, planted near each other before the principal door of the house. They had not yet attained their full size, and swelled with a lustiness and luxuriance of growth that bespoke the majesty and loftiness they were yet destined to attain. My friend gave me to understand that there was some romantic association connected with these trees. "Ce sont les monumens d'un pour et tendre amour du bon vieux temps," said he, laying his hand on his heart and looking as pathetically as a Frenchman can do – but you shall hear more about it, as well as about the little old church when we are more at leisure."

That day my venerable friend dined with more conviviality than usual. He made me taste his Chateau Margaux, his Medoc, his Lafitte, etc. – for these planters keep a good stock of old wines in their cellars – and insisted on my doing him reason in a glass of champagne. I had never seen him in such fine spirits. He told me anecdotes of the French court at the close of the reign of Louis XVI and the beginning of that of his successor, and sang two or three vaudevilles in a voice that was but slightly cracked and with a sharp monotony of note. His eyes sparkled from beneath his gray eyebrows, to speak fancifully, like a bright fountain from under frost-work, and I thought I could detect a faint tinge of red coming out upon his parchment cheek like the bloom of a second youth. Suddenly he became grave. "My friend," said he, solemnly, rising and reaching forward his glass and touching the brim to mine, as is the custom of the country.

I rose also, involuntarily, awed by the earnest gravity of his manner.

"My friend, let us pledge the memory of a most excellent man, now no more, the late worthy curate of Adayes and my ancient friend, Baltazar Polo!" I did as I was requested.

"Sit down, Mr. Herbert," said the old man when he had emptied his glass; "sit down, I pray you," said he with an air which instantly showed me that he had recovered his vivacity, "and I will tell you a pleasant story about that same Baltazar Polo. I have been keeping it for you all day.

"Baltazar Polo was a native of Valencia, in old Spain, and I have heard him boast that old Gil Polo, who wrote the Diana Enamorada, was of the family of his ancestors. He was educated at the university of Saragossa. Some unfortunate love affair in early life having given him a distaste for the vanities of the world, he entered into holy orders, quitted the country of his ancestors, came to New Mexico, and wandered to the remote and solitary little settlement of Adayes, where he sat himself down to take care of the souls and bodies of the simple inhabitants. He was their curate, doctor, and school-master. He taught the children their aves and, if willing, their alphabet, said mass, helped the old nurses to cure the bilious fever, proposed riddles to the young people, and played with them at forfeits and blind-man's-buff. There his portrait hangs just before you – look at it, Herbert – a good-looking man, was he not?"

"It is a round, honest, jolly face," said I, and not devoid of expression. There is a becoming clerical stoop in the shoulders, and his eyes are so prominent that my friend Spurzheim would set him down for a great proficient in the languages. But there is a blemish in the left eye, if I am not mistaken."

"It was put out by a blow from an angry Castilian, whom he had accidentally jostled in the streets of Madrid and whom he was coaxing to be quiet. He was the gentlest and most kindly officious of human beings, full of good intentions, and ever attempting good works, though not always successfully. He was very absent, and so near-sighted with the only eye he had that his sphere of vision was actually, I believe, limited to the circle of a few inches. These defects kept him continually playing at a game of cross-purposes; and, if the tranquil and sleepy lives of the people of Adayes had ever been disturbed by any tendency to waggery, they might have extracted infinite amusement from his continual blunders. I have known him to address a negro with an exhortation intended for his master, recommending courtesy to his inferiors, and good treatment and indulgence to his slaves, enlarging upon the duty of allowing them wholesome food and comfortable clothing, and of letting them go at large during the holidays. I doubt whether this black rogue was much the better for this good counsel. The next moment, perhaps, he would accost the lazy proprietor himself with a homily on the duty of obedience and alacrity in labor. He would expostulate feelingly with some pretty natural coquette of the village (whose only pride was in her own graceful shape, lustrous eyes, and crimson petticoat, and whose only ambition was to win the heart of some young beau from Natchitoches) on the folly of staking her last rag at a gaming-table; and I once heard of his lecturing an unshaven, barefooted, shirtless old Spaniard in a poncho and tattered pair of breeches, the only ones he had in the world, on the wickedness of placing his affections on the vanities of dress.

"But, alas! there were no wags in that primitive little village, and there was no wit. The boys never stuffed with gunpowder the segars which the worthy Valencian used to smoke after dinner, nor did the men, to make him drunk, substitute brandy for the wholesome vino tinto of which, from mere absence of mind, he would sometimes, in the company of his friends, partake rather too genially. They never thought of making any man's natural oddities of manner or peculiarities of temper the subject of merriment, any more than the cut of his face. If ever they laughed, it was at what would excite the laughter of children – at palpable, rustic jokes and broad effrontery at the Punchinello, as the Spaniards call Punch, from Mexico, and at the man from New Orleans who pulled so many yards of ribbon from his mouth. On the contrary, they had as high an opinion of the Reverend Father Polo's sagacity as they justly had of his goodness. Whenever there was anything in his conduct which puzzled them, as was often the case, they ascribed it to some reason too deep for scrutiny, and only became the more confirmed in their notion of his unfathomable wisdom. Far from comprehending any ridicule on the subject of his mistakes, they would look grave, shake their solemn Spanish heads, and say they would warrant Father Polo knew very well what he was about. This confidence in his superior understanding, fortunately, served to counteract in a good degree the effects of his continual mistakes. But it was not only among the people of Adayes that he was loved and respected. The neighboring French planters found in him an agreeable and instructive companion and were glad of a pretext to detain him a day or two at their houses; nor was his reputation confined to this neighborhood alone, for I remember to have heard my friend Antonio de Sedilla, the venerable bishop of Louisiana, speak of him as a man of great learning and piety, and once in my presence the benevolent Polydras took occasion to extol his humanity.

"At the time of which I am speaking, the prettiest maiden of Adayes was Teresa Paccard, the daughter of a Frenchman who had taken a wife of Spanish extraction and settled in the village. Teresa inherited much of the vivacity of our nation and was likewise somewhat accomplished, for her father had made her learn a tolerable stock of phrases in his native language and often took her to visit the families of the French planters; and the good Baltazar had taught her to read. At the age of sixteen she was an orphan, without fortune, and, but for the hospitality of her neighbors, without a home.

"Not far from the village lived a young Frenchman who had emigrated thither from the broad, airy plains of the Ayoyelles, some hundred miles down the Red River, where he had followed the occupation of a herdsman. He had grown weary of watching the immense droves of cattle and horses belonging to others, and having collected a little money, emigrated to the parish of Natchitoches, bought a few acres, and established himself in the more dignified condition of a proprietor, with his old father, in a rude cabin swarming with a family of healthy brothers and sisters. Richard Lemoine, then in his twentieth year, was one of the handsomest men of the province, notwithstanding his leathern doublet and small-clothes, the dress of the prairies. He was of Norman extraction, fair-haired, blue-eyed, ruddy in spite of the climate, broad-shouldered, large-limbed, with a pair of heavy Teutonic wrists, of a free port and frank speech, and such a horseman is seldom seen. He saw Teresa – "

"And fell in love, of course," said I, interrupting my host.

"And fell in love, of course," resumed he; "and Teresa was not averse to his addresses. They first agreed to be married, and then the young lady consulted Baltazar Polo.

" 'Yes, my daughter,' said he, 'with all my heart. The young man is not rich, to be sure – and you are poor; but you are both industrious and virtuous; you love each other, I suppose, and I ought not to prevent you from being happy.'

"About the same time another courtship, not quite so tender, perhaps, but more prudent and well considered, was going on between a couple of maturer age and more easy circumstances. You cannot have forgotten the thrifty-looking plantation I showed you this morning, and the neat mansion with the two young sycamores before its door. There lived at the period of my story, and there had lived for eighteen years before, Madame Labedoyere, the widow of a rich planter, childless, and just on the verge of forty. She was a country-woman of yours, an Anglo-American lady, whom Labedoyere found in one of your Atlantic cities – poor, proud, and pretty– and transplanted to the banks of the Red River to bear rule over himself and his household, while he contented himself with ruling his field negroes. The honest man, I believe, found her a little more inclined to govern than he had expected, but after a short struggle for his independence, in which he discovered that her temper was best when she was suffered to take her own way, he submitted, with that grace so characteristic of our nation, to what he could not remedy, endured the married state with becoming resignation, and showed himself a most obedient and exemplary husband.

"Ten years passed away in wedlock, at the end of which my friend Labedoyere regained his liberty by departing for another world, where I trust he received the reward of his patience. Eight years longer his lady dwelt in solitary widow-hood as the sole inheritor of Labedoyere's large estates; and the features of the demure maiden had settled into that of the imperious matron – a full, square face, dark, strong eyebrows, and steady, bold, black eyes, while her once sylph-like figure had rounded into a dignified and comfortable corpulency, and her light, youthful step been exchanged for the stately and swimming gate of a duchess.

"This lady had contrived to receive the addresses of a rich old Frenchman, who lived two or three miles distant from her home, and still farther from the spot where the young Richard Lemoine had established himself with his old parents and their numerous progeny. Monsieur Du Lac was a little old gentleman of sixty years of age, an inveterate hypochondriac, and the most fretful and irritable being imaginable, with a bilious, withered face, an under-lip projecting so as to be the most conspicuous feature of his countenance, and the corners of his mouth drawn down with a perpetual grimace of discontent. No subject could be more unpromising for a woman of the disposition of Madame Labedovere, but she was weary of having nobody but a servant to govern; besides, she was a lady of spirit, and felt herself moved by a noble ambition of taming so intractable a creature as Monsieur Du Lac. She therefore began to treat him with extreme civility and deference, inquired with the tenderest interest the state of his health, sent him prescriptions for his maladies and good things from her well-stored pantry, and whenever they met, accosted him with her mildest words and softest accents and chastised the usual terrors of her eyes into a cat-like sleepiness and languor of look. The plan succeeded: the old gentleman's heart was taken by surprise; he reflected how invaluable would be the attentions, the skill, and the sympathy of so kind a friend and so accomplished a nurse as Madame Labedovere in the midst of his increasing infirmities. He studied a few phrases of gallantry, and offered her his hand, which, after a proper show of coyness, hesitation, and deliberation on a step so important to the lady's happiness, was accepted.

"Thus matters were arranged between the mature and between the youthful lovers: they were to be married and to be happy, and honest Baltazar Polo, the favorite of both young and old for leagues around, was to perform the marriage ceremony. The courtship of both couples had been in autumn, and now the chilly and frosty month of January was over and the rains of February had set in, flooding the roads and swelling the streams to such a degree that nobody could think of a wedding until finer weather. The weary rains of February passed away also, and the sun of March looked out in the heavens. March is a fine month in our climate, whatever it may be in yours, Mr. Herbert. It brings bright, pleasant days and soft airs – now and then, it is true, a startling thunder-shower, but, then, such a magnificence of young vegetation, such a glory of flowers, over all the woods and the earth! You have not yet seen the spring in Louisiana, Mr. Herbert, and I assure you it is a sight worth a year's residence in the country.

"March, as I told you, had set in; the planters began to intrust to the ground the seeds of cotton and maize; fire-flies were seen to twinkle in the evening, and the dog-wood to spread its large, white blossoms, and the crimson tufts of the red-bud to burst their winter sheaths, and the azalea and yellow jasmine and a thousand other brilliant flowers – which you shall see if you stay with us till spring – flaunted by the borders of the streams and filled the forests with intense fragrance, and the prairies were purple with their earliest blossoms. Spring is the season of new plans and new hopes – the time for men and birds to build new habitations and marry – the time for those who are declining to the grave with sickness and old age to form plans for long years to come. I myself, amid the freshness and youthfulness of nature and the elasticity of the air at this season, white as my hair is, sometimes forget that I am old and almost think I shall live forever. Monsieur Du Lac grew tenderer as the sun mounted higher, the air blew softer, and the forest looked greener; he became impatient for the marriage-day, and entreated the widow to defer their mutual happiness no longer.

" 'Ah, my dear madame!' said the withered old gentleman in a quaking falsetto voice, 'let us gather the flowers of existence before they are faded; let us enjoy the spring of life!' It was impossible for the gentle widow to resist such ardent solicitation, and she consented that the nuptial rights should be delayed no longer.

"Nearly at the same time that this tender scene was passing, Richard Lemoine also, in phrases less select but by no means less impassioned, pressed the lovely Teresa, and not in vain, to a speedy union. But it was already near the close of the carnival, and but two or three days intervened before the commencement of Lent – that long, melancholy fast in which, for the space of forty days, the Catholic Church forbids the happy ceremony of marriage. I have often thought that, if the observances of our Church had been regulated with a particular view to the climate of Louisiana, the fast of Lent would have been put a month or two earlier in the calendar, but I am no divine, and do not presume to give my profane opinion upon this delicate and sacred subject. Neither did the four lovers; but it was agreed by them all that they could not possibly wait until Lent was over, and the only alternative was to be married before it began.

"In the mean time, it seemed as if all the inhabitants of the parish of Natchitoches who had the misfortune to be single had formed the resolution of entering into the state of wedlock before the carnival ended. They came flocking in couples – of various nations, ages, and complexions – to the church of Adayes to be married by the good Baltazar Polo; and that year was long afterward remembered in the parish of Natchitoches under the name of l'an des noces – 'the year of weddings.'

" 'Do you know, Richard,' said Teresa to her lover, on his proposing that the wedding ceremony should take place the next day, 'do you know that Father Polo has promised, on the day after to-morrow, which is the last day of the carnival, to begin at four o'clock in the morning and to marry at the same mass all who shall present themselves at the church of Mayes? It is so awkward to be married with everybody staring at one, but if we are married in company with a dozen others, they cannot laugh at us, you know. Let it, therefore, be the day after to-morrow, dear Richard, and as early in the morning as you please, for the earlier we go to the church, the darker it will be, and I should like, of all things, to be married in the dark.' Richard could not but assent to so reasonable a proposal, and departed to make his little arrangements at home for the reception of his bride.

"It is somewhat remarkable that Madame Labedoyere, not withstanding she was as little liable to the charge of excessive timidity and superfluous coyness as any of her sex, should also have insisted on being married on the morning of the last day of the carnival. Her gallant and venerable suitor contended most tenderly and perseveringly against this proposal, urging the propriety of their being united in broad daylight with the decorum and ceremonies proper to the occasion, but he was forced to yield the point at last, as the lady declared that, unless the marriage took place at the time she proposed, it must be delayed until after Lent, and to this alternative Monsieur Du Lac was too gallant and impatient a lover to agree. I believe that Madame was sensible of the queer figure her withered, weak-legged, and sour-visaged Adonis would make as principal in a marriage ceremony, and was willing he should escape observation among the crowd of bridegrooms whom she expected the last day of the carnival would bring to the church of Adayes.

"At length the day arrived. At half-past three in the morning the sexton threw open the doors of the little log church and awoke the village with a most furious and discordant peal on the cracked bells. The good Baltazar Polo appeared at the appointed hour, and the building began to fill with the candidates for matrimony and their relatives. Couple came flocking in after couple. Here you might see, by the light of the lanterns which the negroes stood holding at the door, a young fellow in a short cloak and broad-brimmed palmetto hat and feathers, with a face in which were mingled the features of Spain with those of the aborigines, walking with an indifferent and listless air and supporting a young woman whose rounder and more placid, though not less dark, countenance was half covered by the manto or thick Spanish veil, which, however, was not drawn so closely over her forehead as to hide the cluster of natural blossoms she had gathered that morning and placed there. There you might see a simpering fair one, with a complexion somewhat too rosy for our climate, and a wreath of artificial flowers in her hand, stepping briskly into the church on pointed toe, leaning on the arm of her betrothed, whose liveliness of look and air needed not the help of his cocked hat and powdered locks and long-skirted coat of sky-blue to tell he was a Frenchman. In others, you might remark a whimsical blending of costume, and a perplexing amalgamation of the features of different races that denoted their mixed origin. Nearly all came protected with ample clothing against the inclemency of the weather, which, lately mild and serene, had changed during the course of the night to cold and damp, with a strong wind driving across the sky vast masses of vapor of a shadowy and indistinct outline.

"Fourteen couples at length took their place in the nave of the church in two opposite rows, with a sufficient space between them for the priest to pass in performing the marriage ceremony. Back of these rows stood the friends and relations of the parties, waiting for the moment when the rites should be concluded, to conduct the brides to the homes of the bridegrooms. The interior of the church was dimly lighted by two wax tapers that stood on the altar. A storm was evidently rising without: the sky seemed to grow darker every moment as the day advanced; the wind swept in gusts round the building and rushed in eddies through the open door, waving the flame of the tapers to and fro. As the flickering light played over the walls, it showed on one side of the altar a picture of our Lady of Grief, La Virgen de los Dolores, the very caricature of sorrow, and on the other a representation of the holy St. Anthony tempted by evil spirits, in which the painter's ingenuity had been exerted so successfully as to puzzle the most sagacious spectator to tell which was the ugliest, the saint or the devils – or, indeed, to distinguish the devils from the saint. Farther off were one or two other pictures, whose grim and shadowy faces, in the imperfect and unsteady glare of the tapers, seemed to frown suddenly on the walls, and then as suddenly shrink into the shade. The horses which the company rode – and which stood about the door, held by negroes or fastened to posts and saplings – pawed and neighed, and champed their huge Spanish bits, as if to give their riders notice of the approaching tempest.

Father Polo saw, or rather was informed by the friends of the parties, that there was no time to be lost if he intended that the brides should reach their new habitations that morning in comfort and safety. He therefore passed between the rows of the betrothed, performing the ceremony rapidly as he went, and handing over each of the ladies, as he put the wedding-ring on her finger, to the friends of her husband, who conducted her out of the church. Close together stood Monsieur Du Lac and Richard Lemoine, and opposite them, Madame Labedoyere and Teresa Paccard. The latter were both in cloaks, a circumstance sufficient in itself to cause them to be mistaken for each other by a person so absent and near-sighted as Baltazar Polo. He put the ring of Monsieur Du Lac on the hand of Teresa Paccard, and that of Richard Lemoine on the hand of Madame Labedoyere, and as they drew their cloaks over their faces, preparing to face the wind without, handed them to those whom he supposed to be the friends of their respective spouses. Madame Labedoyere was given in charge to the relatives of Lemoine. They placed her on a fleet horse, brought by the young man from the Avoyelles, and went off at a quick pace, attended by two or three of his brothers and sisters. Teresa was seated on a soft-footed, ambling nag, bought by Du Lac expressly for the use of his widow, and departed in company with an old planter, a cousin of Du Lac, a negro who rode after them on horseback, and three or four more who trotted on foot behind them.

"In consequence of the high wind, the roaring of the woods, and the haste made to escape the storm, there was little conversation between the brides and their attendants, and nothing occurred to make them suspect the mistake until they reached the habitations of the bridegrooms.

"Teresa arrived with her escort at the place of her supposed destination just as the clouds had settled into a solid mass all over the sky, and were shedding down the first drops of rain. By the imperfect light – although the sun was rising, the thickness of the gathering storm still maintained a sort of twilight in the atmosphere – she could distinguish a sort of vastness in the walls of the building she was approaching that did not agree with her ideas of the cabin of Richard: the shrubs and trees about it, waving low and sighing heavily in the violent wind, betokened the seat of an ancient dwelling. She had, however, no time to speculate upon the matter, and the temporary misgivings which these appearances forced upon her were forgotten in her eagerness to obtain a shelter. Her ancient attendant, with more briskness than the stiff formality of his figure would have warranted her to expect, alighted, and assisted her from her pony; the negro had flung himself from his horse and opened the door, and Teresa in an instant was within the house. Here she was met by half a dozen domestic negroes with shining, jetty faces, grinning and welcoming their new mistress with bows and courtesies. One took her cloak, another ushered her into a spacious apartment, a third sprang before her and placed a chair, and a fourth presented a looking-glass, by which to adjust her hair, disordered in the haste of her ride.

She threw a hurried glance at her own image, but the furniture of the room, so different from what she expected to see, more strongly attracted her attention, and she quickly handed back the mirror. She saw that she was sitting in an arm-chair, with a seat and fringe of crimson silk and the back and legs ornamented with a profusion of heavy carving and tarnished gilding. Several others of the same description were scattered around, and a large, comfortable-looking sofa, covered with faded damask, stood under a huge looking-glass, carved and gilt after the same fashion with the chairs but unluckily cracked in its voyage from France. The glass leaned majestically forward into the room, so as to reflect every inch of a floor smoothly paved with French bricks, the fashion of the day. On another side of the wall hung two family portraits in big wigs and bright armor. This magnificence was curiously contrasted with the stout cedar table in the middle of the room, with half a dozen coarse wooden chairs scattered about, and a clumsy chest of drawers, the work of some rude artificer of the country. The table, however, presented a most sumptuous déjeûner a la fourchette – coffee, claret, the delicate bar-fish, trout, duck-pies, the favorite dishes of the country, with others which I will leave you, who know something of French cookery, to imagine to yourself served up on massy old plate.

" 'Ah!' said Teresa to herself, 'this surely cannot be Richard's house, or is it possible that he has been amusing himself with my simplicity and that he is a rich man after all?'

"Her doubts were of short duration. The door opened, and a vinegar-faced old gentleman, with an olive complexion, shrunken legs, and attenuated figure, presented himself. The solemn gentleman who had hitherto attended Teresa arose, and with infinite solemnity announced Monsieur Du Lac, the bridegroom, to Madame Du Lac, the bride. The poor girl turned red, and then pale, and seemed ready to sink into the earth with embarrassment and anxiety. The old gentleman himself stood for a moment motionless with surprise, then, appearing to recollect himself, he advanced and took the hand of Teresa, who felt almost afraid to withdraw it from a gentleman so aged that he reminded her of her grandfather.

" 'Ah, madame,' said he, coughing, 'forgive my awkwardness – but I was so surprised! How much you are changed since I saw you last evening! You are more than twice as young, and ten times more beautiful.'

" 'Indeed, sir,' interrupted Teresa, eagerly, 'there is no change, I can assure you – I am the same that I ever was – there is some error here – something very extraordinary.'

" 'Extraordinary, my princess? Well may you call it so; it is one of the most extraordinary things I ever witnessed in the course of my life, and I have seen fifty years.' Here the old gentleman told the truth, though by no means the whole truth. 'Nothing less than a miracle could have produced – and yet it may be a miracle, my dear madame, the saints are so good!'

" 'Ah, sir,' said the poor girl, 'do not mock me, I pray you. I perceive here has been a sad mistake – let me go to my Richard, I entreat you, let me go to my Richard.'

"As she spoke, she arose, and made an effort to withdraw her hand, of which, however, the ancient swain retained obstinate possession. Much as he was struck with her beauty at first sight, he grew more charmed with it as he gazed upon her round, youthful figure, her polished forehead, her finely moulded cheeks, now flushed with an unusual crimson, and her full black eyes, in each of which a tear was gathering. He determined not to give up so fine a creature without an effort to retain her.

" 'May I take the liberty of inquiring,' said he, 'whom you call your Richard?'

" 'It is Richard Lemoine,' answered the young woman, 'who lives down by the Poplars. I married him this morning.'

" 'I beg ten thousand pardons, madame, but you married me this morning, and here is my ring on your finger – my grandmother's wedding ring, with the finest diamonds in the colony, and the pretty motto, Jusqu' a la mort, which I hope is a great way off; at least, I am sure it is if I can get rid of this troublesome cough. Ah, my adorable princess, we may both imagine that there is a mistake in this affair, and yet it may be all right – indeed, I am confident it is. The kind heavens have destined us for each other. I certainly expected to marry a different person, but Providence has willed it otherwise, and I am most happy to submit to its dispensations. I hope you will have as little reason to complain of them as I. We are united, I trust, for a long and happy life, and the marriage-knot, you know, is indissoluble; marriage is too solemn a thing, madame, to be trifled with, as I presume you are sensible – '

"Here Monsieur Du Lac was obliged by a violent fit of coughing, to break off his discourse. But Teresa had sunk back into the chair, and covering her face with her handkerchief, was sobbing violently. The old man tried every method he could think of to reconcile her to what he called her destiny, in which he was zealously seconded by his friend the old planter. He made her presents of necklaces and jewels, and various other fineries which he had intended as nuptial gifts to the fair widow; he enlarged on the comforts of his mansion, the extent of his plantation, the ease and opulence she would enjoy; vowed that his existence should be devoted to her service, and that her slightest wish should be the law of his conduct; and finally hinted that Richard doubtless knew very well what he was about in the affair; that he had probably intrigued with the widow, and that the perfidious beings were now in some snug corner, congratulating themselves on the success of their wicked stratagem. Monsieur Du Lac's grave old cousin re-enforced this last argument by declaring his solemn belief that it was true, and it affected what none of the others could. How could Teresa refuse to believe two such old and apparently honest men? The offended beauty dried her tears, consented to look on the rich adornments for her person presented by her venerable lover, and finally suffered herself to be led to her seat at the head of the breakfast-table.

"The widow, in the mean time, was more rapidly conveyed to her place of destination on the fine, fleet animal which Richard brought from the Avoyelles, a gentle but spirited creature, broken by him for the use of his sisters. They rode so rapidly that they seemed to leave the huge, low-hung clouds behind them, and although Richard's habitation was at a considerably greater distance from the church than that of Monsieur Du Lac, they reached home quite as soon. What was the surprise of the lady on entering the house: the room into which she was ushered was floored with loose planks; a huge naked chimney yawned in the midst, where two or three cypress-logs were smouldering; the naked rafters of the ceiling were stained with smoke; and a few old chests, a dozen joint-stools, and two clumsy arm-chairs were the only furniture of the apartment. A flaxen-haired girl assisted her to take off her cloak, and as she stood in the majesty of her rustling silk and glittering jewels, an elderly couple – a white-bearded man of sixty, in a leathern doublet, and a thin matron of ten years younger, in a coarse white-cotton cap and blue-cotton short-gown and petticoat – who had risen upon her entrance, began to bow and courtesy with an involuntary and profound respect.

" 'What a fine lady she is!' said the old woman to her husband.

" 'What an old wife Richard has got!' whispered to one of her brothers the flaxen-haired girl who had helped her off with her cloak.

"In the mean time, the stern lady stood regarding the group with a look of unutterable disdain. Her bold, black eyes flashed fire as she pushed aside the big arm-chair that was offered her. 'Where am I?' she exclaimed. 'Why am I brought to this place? I am sure this is not my husband's house; take me thither instantly.'

" 'Where is my wife?' said Richard, who just then entered the door. 'Who is that lady?'

" 'That is your wife,' answered one of the boys; that is the lady the minister handed us.'

" 'And a fine lady she is,' added Richard's mother; 'I warrant, the whole country can not show a finer.'

" 'But I am not your wife,' said Madame Labedoyere, fixing her resolute eyes on Richard. 'I demand to be taken back to my husband. I will not remain another moment in this miserable hut.'

" 'You say true,' replied Richard, 'you are not my wife. I married a younger and, thank heaven, a prettier woman. But you must consent to play the hostage here, madame, till I get her. There is some cursed blunder in the business. You claim your husband, I claim my bride – my Teresa. I declare that you shall not stir from this house until she is restored to me.'

" 'Ah, I see how it is, my son,' interrupted Richard's mother; 'the good one-eyed Baltazar has made a mistake and given you the wrong lady.'

" 'Then the good one-eyed Baltazar must give me the right one!' retorted Richard. 'What right had the old blunderer to rob me of my pretty Teresa? What business had he to give her to another man, and fob me off with a fine lady, as you call her, who is old enough to be my mother? But I will go after him and force him to make restitution – if I do not, I wish I may never mount a horse again. Brothers, look well to that lady with her silks and jewels, and do not let her leave the house till I come back.'

"So saying, Richard flung out at the door, though the rain drove in heavy torrents against the windows, and his mother screamed out to him that he would certainly catch his death by venturing forth in such a storm. He sprang upon his horse and was soon at the curate's, where he was admitted to an instant conference with Baltazar Polo. The good man tried at first to convince him that it was impossible for any mistake to have been committed, as he was very confident that he had put every particular ring upon the hand of the lady for whom it was intended and accurately handed the brides to their respective bridegrooms. This, however, only served to work up into fury the exasperation of Richard, who asked him if he supposed everybody was as near-sighted as himself, and whether he thought he could not tell a woman of forty from a girl of eighteen. The clergyman then inquired of the young man if he knew the name of the person whom the lady he had left at home intended to have married, as it was possible that Teresa might have been carried to his house by mistake. On this point Richard was wholly ignorant, having neglected to inform himself before he set out, nor did he even know the name of the lady. He saw, however, that there was a good deal of reason in Baltazar's suggestion, and departed with a determination to make the necessary inquiries of the unknown matron.

"It occurred to him, however, that he would not leave the village of .Adayes, in which Father Polo resided, without first calling at the late home of Teresa to see if its inmates could tell what had become of her. They could give him no information. They had neither seen nor heard anything of her since she left them that morning at an early hour, dressed for the marriage ceremony. He then ran to the church, which he entered with a vague hope that he might yet find her within it. Nobody was there but the sexton, and the grim, bearded, unsympathizing saints on the walls, who seemed to stare in the most unfeeling manner on his anguish. There, too, was the Virgin de los Dolores, still occupied only with her own ancient griefs, regardless of his newer and keener distress. He felt as if he could have torn them from the walls where they hung. Leaving the church, he put his horse to its full speed and came home, wet to the skin, amid a cloud of vapor arising from the perspiration of the animal.

"Madame Labedoyere, in the mean time, had borne her detention at Richard's house more patiently on account of the storm which was raging without, and which infallibly would have spoiled, or at least sadly disordered, her wedding-dress had she ventured to encounter it. Richard found her, on his return, seated somewhat sullenly in the arm-chair which she had accepted on his departure, and his mother and sisters busied in their usual occupations, though somewhat more silent than wont, for they were awed by the strange lady's imperious manner and that splendor of costume which had never before been seen within those walls. The lady's reflections, in the mean time, however, had not been much to Richard's disadvantage. If he recovered Teresa, she was sure to have Monsieur Du Lac restored to her, but if otherwise, it struck her that the young fellow's manly frame and blooming face were no inadequate compensation for the loss of the old gentleman's possessions. He was poor, it is true, but she was, in fact, rich enough for both, and she began to think that, after all, she might not be so very wretched in his society.

"Immediately on entering, Richard inquired of the lady her name and that of the gentleman whom she went to the church to marry; and a family council was held to consider what should be done, at which the stately widow graciously condescended to assist. It was finally settled that Richard should proceed with his father to the house of Monsieur Du Lac, to induce him to restore the young bride, who had doubtless been conducted thither by mistake; and, in case of the success of the embassy, Madame Labedoyere received an assurance that she should be duly conveyed to the mansion of her venerable lover.

Some time elapsed in making these arrangements, but at length the old gentleman and his son set off together. The father was a slow rider, and Richard often found himself far before him on the road and heard himself called to slacken his pace. Du Lac's house lay in a direction from the church of Adayes exactly opposite to that of Richard's, and consequently at a considerable distance from the latter. In vain the young man represented to old Lemoine that, at the rate they were travelling, it would be impossible to reach the place before nightfall.

" 'No matter, Richard,' replied the old man; 'if you get there before bedtime, it will be time enough, I take it. You know, I have never ridden any faster these ten years, and I hope you would not have your father turn jockey and break his neck in his old age. Rein in your horse, can't you, and stop kicking him in the side, and keep back along with me.'

"Oh, what a long journey that was for poor Richard! They arrived at Du Lac's house, however, while the twilight was yet in the western sky. The rain was over, and the thin, vapory clouds were crimson with the latest of those hues which foretell a fair day on the morrow. They knocked at Du Lac's door, and it was opened by a negro who told them that his master was just gone to bed with his new wife.

" 'And who is his wife?' asked Richard, quickly.

" 'A very handsome and very young woman,' said the negro in his Creole-French, 'whom master brought home with him to-day.'

"Richard's heart sank within him when he heard this answer, nor had he the voice or the courage to ask any more questions, but his father pursued the inquiry. The black informed them that the bride was a beautiful creature about eighteen years of age, that his master was married to her that very morning, that he understood her name was Teresa, that she was from the Spanish village of Adayes, that she wept very much when she first came to the house, but that before night she seemed very happy and contented.

"Richard, in the mean time, listened with feelings that are indescribable. 'Let us go home,' said he to his father. 'I see how it is; the girl has tricked me.' The old gentleman commanded him to stay, and turning to the servant, said, 'I must speak with your master.'

" 'You cannot,' answered the negro; 'he gave strict orders not to be disturbed.'

" 'Don't tell me I cannot, you black rascal!' said the old Louisianian, in a terrible voice, his blood beginning to warm in behalf of his son. 'Go and tell your master that I must speak with him immediately!'

"The black went, and soon returned with a civil message from Monsieur Du Lac, giving the Messieurs Lemoine to understand that this was his wedding-night, that he had retired to rest, and begged not to be disturbed; but that on the next morning he would be exceedingly happy to wait upon the gentlemen and execute any commands with which they might please to honor him.

"The ancient herdsman, while this message was delivering, drew himself up to his full height, which exceeded six feet, and presented a figure of weather-beaten strength such as we have few examples of at the present day – tall, bony, grim, and broad-shouldered. 'Go,' said he, in a voice which thundered through the half-open door and resounded along the passages of the dwelling, 'tell your master I will speak to him, or I will batter down his house about his ears!' The domestic again disappeared, and in a moment afterward an upper window opened, a head covered with a woollen night-cap was thrust out, and a sharp-keyed, infirm voice demanded what they wanted at that time of night.

"Old Lemoine answered that he thought it a very proper time of night and proceeded to state the nature of his errand; [he] spoke of the mistake that had occurred and the desire of his son to rectify it, said that Richard had come with him to claim his betrothed bride, and that he stood ready to restore to Monsieur Du Lac the lady whom he had intended to marry.

" 'There is no mistake whatever in the matter,' answered Du Lac from the window; 'I am well satisfied with the match as it is, and I can answer for the young lady that she makes no objections. She is my wife, regularly married to me at the church, and wears my ring on her finger at this moment. As for the widow Labedoyere, I am sure the young man is perfectly welcome to her, and I wish them a great deal of happiness.'

" 'But he does not want the widow, and is come for the young lady.'

" 'Oh, he wants my wife, does he? He is come to steal her from my bed on the wedding-night? Young gentleman, you have set out upon this errand a little too soon. It is not the custom for gallants like you to run away with other people's wives until the lady has lived with her husband a few days at least. And you, Monsieur Lemoine, as I think you call yourself, I wonder you are not ashamed of abetting your son in such a wicked business. No, no, gentlemen, my wife is my wife, and I shall keep her. I have the honor to wish you a very good-night.' Saying this, he shut the window, and the negro at the same instant fastened and bolted the door below.

"What was to be done! Old Lemoine was in a great rage, and talked of bursting open the door and penetrating into Du Lac's chamber, to ascertain from the young woman herself the truth of his story. Richard was inclined to abandon all further pursuits of one who had proved herself fickle, ungrateful, and worthless. As a sort of middle course, it was finally agreed to go to Baltazar Polo, to rate him soundly for what he had done, and see if he had any counsel to offer. The good pastor received them with his usual benignity, and listened mildly to their complaints. 'My friends,' said he, 'I should the more regret the error I have committed did I not see in it a particular and benevolent providence. I cannot alter what Heaven has done; Madame Labedoyere is your wife, and Teresa is united to Monsieur Du Lac. But come to me to-morrow morning; I will send for the other couple, and will endeavor to adjust the matter to your satisfaction.'

"The next morning early, the four newly married people were at the house of Baltazar Polo. You know, perhaps, Mr. Herbert, that, by the marital law of Louisiana, neither the husband has any title to the real or personal property of the wife, nor the wife to that of the husband; and therefore, although both Monsieur Du Lac and Madame Labedoyere were rich, yet if they had died the next day, or after ten years of matrimony, both their young spouses would have been left as poor as they were before the marriage.

" 'We have made a great blunder,' said the curate, 'by, which the original intentions of all parties have been frustrated. You,' said he, addressing himself to the old people, 'have been the gainers by this accident, and these young folks have been the losers; you must therefore make them a compensation. Let Monsieur Du Lac settle half his large estates on his young wife here, and you, madame, half yours on your young husband, and on this condition the marriages shall remain as they are.'

"None of the party seemed at first exactly pleased with this arrangement, but the curate was peremptory. Du Lac could not think of giving up Teresa; and Madame Labedoyere, when she saw the handsome Richard by the side of his withered and crooked competitor, could not help congratulating herself fervently on the exchange; a notary, therefore, was sent for, the instruments of settlement were executed on the spot, and the parties withdrew – Teresa with Du Lac, and Richard with Madame Labedoyere, now become Madame Lemoine, in whose house he was to establish himself.

186

"That very evening both the young persons had a sample of the disposition and temper of their spouses. You know something of the custom of *charivari*, which prevails in all the French colonies of North America. It is a way we have of celebrating odd, unequal, unsuitable matches. It was hardly dark when the tumult of the *charivari* was heard from a distance by the inmates of Madame Lemoine's dwelling. Horns winded, whistles blown, tin kettles beaten with sticks, a jangle of bells, and a medley of discordant voices was heard on the wind, and when the crowd came in sight, torches were seen flaming and smoking over their heads. As the procession drew near, it was observed to be headed by two grotesque masked figures – the one representing a fat, staring, bold-faced old woman, and the other a lubberly, foolish-looking young bumpkin – who at intervals kissed and embraced each other lovingly and with abundance of awkward gesticulations. A broad-chested fellow, marching after them, thundered out a halting ballad with a chorus in which the names of Richard and his spouse were duly commemorated. That fearless lady, however, took her measures with her usual spirit: she posted her negroes at the windows, gave them their orders, and was fully prepared for the arrival of the party. The procession at length reached the house and came to a halt before the door, when immediately, one dressed in a fantastic garb much like that of a clown at a theatre and who acted as marshal of the ceremonies stepped forward, and with a wand which he carried in his hand, gave a most furious rap on the door. That was the signal for the besieged to ply their weapons of defence; the windows were suddenly opened, vessels of dirty water were emptied into the faces of the procession; sticks, rotten eggs, and other missiles were thrown at them; and a couple of fowling-pieces were discharged over their heads. They fled precipitately, leaving on the field their instruments of music, which the servants afterward picked up and brought in as trophies of the victory they had gained.

"Whether it was by the same party or not, I cannot say; but the wedding of Monsieur Du Lac was celebrated with similar honors, and under more lucky auspices for those by whom they were rendered. The old gentleman submitted to the custom with so bad a grace that they were encouraged to take greater liberties: the serenaders entered his house, deafened his ears with their horrid music, drank gallons of his best wine, and one of them, a strapping young fellow, had even the impudence to snatch a kiss from the bride. It was one o'clock in the morning before these rude wassailers left the house, and then the vexation of old Du Lac, which had been so long restrained by their presence, broke forth into fury. He stormed at his negroes, cursed the neighborhood, railed at everybody whose name was mentioned or who came into his presence; nor did he even spare his wife; he told her he wished he had married Madame Labedoyere, and then none of all this trouble could have happened.

"Teresa was never destined to see him in good-humor again, He had broken, on that evening, through that reserve of first acquaintance which produces civility even in the peevish and morose, and ever afterward he treated her as he did the other inmates of the family – with an intolerable and perpetual ill-humor. In three years he fretted himself into his grave, notwithstanding all the pains which the gentle Teresa took to keep him alive, leaving her the owner of half his possessions and the mother of two children, who inherited the other half.

"As for the matron with whom Richard was paired so much against his inclination, she could never reduce the young man to that state of obedience which she esteemed the proper relation of a husband to the wife of his bosom. Richard insisted firmly on maintaining his parents in comfort and educating his sisters, and she insisted as strongly that he should not. He carried his intentions into effect, at the expense of a daily quarrel with his wife. This vain contest for the supremacy preyed upon her spirits and impaired her health, her portly figure wasted visibly, she went into a deep decline, and died at the end of five years from the time of her marriage, having also borne two children to her husband.

"And now, Mr. Herbert, you anticipate the conclusion of my story. You are right; Richard and Teresa were united at last, and the marriage ceremony was performed in the little old church of Adayes by the benevolent curate, my right worthy friend, Baltazar Polo; and never did those cracked bells ring a merrier peal than at that wedding. It was performed with more than usual precaution, for the good minister declared that no second mistake should be committed if it was possible to guard against it by human means. It took place at broad noon, on a clear, bright day, and the curate wore a new pair of concave spectacles, which he had procured from New Orleans expressly for the occasion.

"The worthy couple are now like myself – grown old. They live on the fertile plantation which formerly belonged to Madame Labedoyere, where I showed you the two fine young button-wood trees before the mansion. The children of the first marriage are provided for on the ample estates of the deceased parents, and Lemoine and his wife live surrounded by their mutual offspring in the serene old age of a quiet and well-acted life. Some years since, a French botanist, travelling in this country, claimed the hospitality of their roof. He showed them, among other matters connected with his science, how the leaf of the button-wood hides in its footstalk the bud of the next year's leaf. Richard told his wife that this was an emblem of their first unfortunate marriage, which, however, contrary to their expectations, contained within itself the germ of their present happy union and their present opulence. They adopted the tree as their favorite among all the growths of the forest, and caused two of them, of equal size and similar shape, to be planted before their door."

Glauber-Spa

Advertisement

The letter from Mr. S. Clapp which follows this announcement will sufficiently explain to the reader the manner in which the manuscripts from which the tales in these volumes have been printed came into the possession of the Publishers. Having obtained permission from Mr. E. Clapp to take time for consideration, they were inclined to believe on inspection that the handwriting of a portion of the collection was not new to them. But on applying to the quarter suspected, they obtained no admissions or information which threw any light upon the subject. They then submitted the whole to a select committee of five gentlemen, distinguished in private for their critical acumen. Their report was a singular one; inasmuch as each one unequivocally condemned, as un-typeworthy, four-fifths of the whole; but the single and separate fifths which separately pleased each of them, and on which each bestowed high commendations (no two of them agreeing), made up the entire fardel which Mr. Clapp wished to dispose of.

Under these circumstances they bethought themselves of procuring an inspection of the books kept at the Spa; and through the kind offices of a friend were enabled to ascertain that among those whose names were entered as having visited the new spring were Miss Sedgwick, Messrs. Paulding, Bryant, Sands, and Leggett. The name of G. C. Verplanck had been written, but a line was drawn through it, as if the entry had been made by mistake. There were no other names to whom suspicion could attach; and the Publishers have been unable, in reply to very polite inquiries, to obtain any light from the parties mentioned. They disclaimed, however, any right of property in the manuscripts, the contents of which are now given to the public; sanctioned, in the manner which has been mentioned, by the opinions of five gentlemen of discriminating taste. That they may afford pleasure to the reader, and some profit to Mr. Clapp, who is ascertained to be a man of exemplary character, and who has suffered so unexpectedly from the late painful affliction with which the land has been visited, is the sincere desire and hope of THE PUBLISHERS.

*Glauber-Spaw, *July* –.

To the Misters Harpers, at their store in New-York City.

This letter my son, Eli Clapp, will hand you, along with the parcel. I do not suppose you know me, though I have advertised once in one of your York papers; and the only way I came to know you was by seeing in it that you printed all the books, and I take the freedom of writing to you on the strength of it.

I have lived at Sheep's Neck since I was a boy, and so did my father before me; but we have altered the name lately to Glauber-spaw, and call the Old Ram's-alley Epsom-walk, out of a notion of the doctor's and my daughters. I will tell you how it happened, or else you would not understand how I came to write to you.

I lived on the old homestead, man and boy, and was married and had a family of children, for forty years and rising, when my wife would send my daughters to a fashionable school in Wetherville, to learn French and darning-work and the forte-piano. I cannot say I had much peace after that. From one thing to another, I was obliged to build two new wings and a back-kitchen to the old house; and when those were finished, that was pulled down and another built, as they said it was not in good taste. It tasted better to me altogether than the new place; for I was obliged to raise money on a mortgage to pay for the *willer*, as they called it, after they had cut down all the willers that were to be found upon it. They found the furniture, too, but I had to pay for it; and when it was in order, as they said, it was such a trumpery, bandbox-looking place, that I could not spit in it with any comfort.

The next thing they did, and by this time they had got my wife and youngest son all on their side (though Eli, who is a discreet lad, went and lived in the barn, and would not come inside of their shingle-shanty, as he called it), was to say that Sheep's Neck was no name at all for the farm. I told them they might call it Clapp's Folly, if they

---

* [Note accompanying the text in *Tales of Glauber-Spa*]: The orthography of Mr. Clapp, Sen., has been scrupulously preserved. – *The Publishers.*

liked; at which they turned up their noses and talked about Tully-veal-and-lamb, and Mount-Peeler and Bawl-town, and other names, to which I did not see no likeness in the premises.

Just about this time young Doctor Jodine, who had come to settle in the village, and soon got thick with my wife and daughters, began to analyze, as he called it, the waters of my spring, which we had all been drinking for ever, taking it to be plain water. But it was no such thing. The doctor made a memorandum of what it was, which he had published in a pamphlet, now for sale at the bookstore in Sheep's Neck Village. It had saline and gaseous properties, and was made out of different kinds of stuff, in which there was plenty of ox-hides and gin, as far as I can understand it, with a good deal of sulphur and soda. It is strange how the water did not seem to affect us any before the doctor had analyzed it. But after he had had the spring walled in, and let it off through logs so as to make it squirt up in a fountain, it is really astonishing how we came to find out its properties, and the kimistry of it. I take this opportunity of begging you to contradict a false tale which some of the neighbours who go to the second meeting-house got up, and which I have denied in my advertisement, that the doctor buried a barrel of oaks and potashes under the spring, which I know not to be the fact.

The kimistry of this water, after it was found out, troubled me considerable. I suffered in body and estate; as the doctor's bill was highish, and I lost a fine heifer and two or my best hogs, who drank out of the fountain by mistake. There was little left of the poor things but the hide and bristles. The doctor said that the Spaw, as he called it, was medicine-like, and must only be taken by advice, as it was good for vallydinarians. We had a fine well on the farm, in which there is no flavour of hides or potashes that ever I tasted. I took to drinking that out of the bucket, to avoid mistakes; but my wife and daughters took half a tumbler of the Spaw every morning before breakfast, by the doctor's advice, as he observed they seemed to be in delicate health – which they did. They were almost as lean as the poor heifer and swine; and are not much better off in flesh now, though they have left off drinking the Spaw, and been taking what the doctor calls tunnicks.

It was not long after he had fixed up the spring, before my neighbour Woolley Lamb, who keeps the tavern and post-office at Sheep's Neck Village, sent his son Chris one evening to tell our folks that a carriage-load of people were asking him where the Spaw was, and whether they could get boarded there. My wife and daughters overheard the message, and very much to my surprise came fluttering out, like a clothes-wash in a gale of wind. I had boarded the Yankee schoolmaster, off and on, several years before; and some high-flying girls that had been at school with mine had come to see them for a spell, after they had reformed the house, as they called it; during which I spent the most of my spare hours in the barn, along with Eli. But I had no idea of taking regular boarders, though for that matter, I did not see what else the new house was good for. Presently the doctor came up in the wagon, with my youngest son Cush, who had a load of unaccountable victuals and sauce, enough to last a whole winter. The doctor said that a member of Congress's family had come; and that two of the ladies were vallydinarians, who had been sent from away south to Glauber-Spaw, as the only place where they could get rid of their pulmonitory symptoms, and be saved from dying a natural death.

How my wife and daughters fixed it, I did not know, and hardly understand to this day. The party presently came up in a great coach and four, and a gig with two negroes a-horseback. I thought it was none of my business to help them in, as I was not allowed to hinder them from doing it. The carriages and all the cattle, as I found on coming back at evening, had been put into the barn, and poor Eli's chamber was broken up; and there was a great deal of clatter in the house, and my wife and daughters were so busy, and looked so airy, that there was no getting a word out of them. I was put down by being told by my woman, when I came to talk to her, that if I would only mind the farm, she would make a mint of money, that the girls would get well married, and that I need not trouble myself about the Spaw House, as Cush would see about it all.

Not to be too long with my story, I made myself as busy as I could with working the farm, and got my meals in the kitchen or in the fields, not troubling myself with the traps that they had up stairs, though I saw much coming and going, and some new faces. Cold weather came, and the house was empty; and some people that my wife had hired, unbeknown to me, were sent off. They looked as fine, almost, as the boarders, and had shown no more respect to me when they came straggling about, than if the land did not belong to me. As they were going out of the gate the sarciest one of the lot took off his hat in a contemptible kind of a manner, and said, "Good-by, daddy." I gave him a few kicks that sent him rather anyhow into Merino Creek, that they now called Magnesia Springs; and Eli, taking his ox-goad to the balance of them, made them "walk Spanish," as they say here. They sued us for it, and the case is not tried yet. I don't see how they are to get any witnesses.

Eli told me he was going to be married to a neighbour's daughter, and live on his farm; though he would help me to work mine for fair wages, and carry the stuff to market for me in partnership. He never asked his mother and sisters to the wedding, and so they don't speak. Presently my neighbour Colonel Cross, who had the mortgage, came for a year's interest, and part of the principal, which he had a right to ask for. My crops had been bad, and though I had cut considerable hay, what with mending fences when the high-flyers at the Spaw House had broken them, paying the hands, and getting little or nothing from the market for vegetables, as the most of them had been wasted in the house, I had not ready money enough to pay even the interest.

So I went to my wife, who had all along been blarneying me, when she got time to talk, about her great prospects. But she opened her eyes, and asked me if I was crazy, to think she could catch money at once, out of the clouds, after all the expense she had been at? I never heard her talk such hard words before, as she had picked up from the strangers she had been waiting on; and I do not wonder at it, for I heard that some of them were Nullyflyers; and I am told that those sort of people are not Christians, and are a kind of unnat'ral like. She talked about divestments, and future returns, and the goose that laid the golden eggs. This was all I understood of her new-fashioned prose; and I could not help saying rather passionate-like, "Burn my old clothes, misses, if you haven't divested me of my farm, and I won't have no footer returns to it, that's that. You're a goose yourself, and have made a gander of me, and where are the golden eggs?" Then she showed me all the bills for furniture, and groceries, and servants (she paid them vagabonds more for a month than I can make off the farm), and told me she had paid nearly half of them. And she said that next season she could make an estate, as all the company had promised to come back and bring good society with them, if she would make more room for them. And she showed me a parcel of trash that had been given to the girls, – singing-books, and old clothes, and poetry-works, and smelling-bottles, which she said were invaluable proofs of regard from the genteel ladies that would take care of Sally and Nancy.

I saw that I was in a hobble show, and I knew that Colonel Cross was twistical; but I did not know how to help myself, when he came and said that he must have money, and could not afford to wait for it; but that if I would give another mortgage for three times as much as the principal and interest came to on the whole farm, he would lift the other, as he knew a man in Wetherville who would advance it if I would make further improvements, so as to accommodate all the company that would like to come. He said my wife and daughters were smart and active; and that, as I did not know any thing about it, he would see to the improvements himself if I would give him a commission. I did not know what he meant, and told him he must go to the governor for that, but found out that he wanted to be paid for his trouble.

I had a heavy heart enough when I signed the new mortgage, and did not get a cent of the money; which the colonel put into the bank to pay for the improvements; and I spent a melancholy winter, having no good of my family, and being often driven out of doors in cold weather by the everlasting strumming that was kept up on the cracked piano, which, I was told for my comfort, was to be changed for a new one. The spring had hardly come when the whole place was covered with timber and carpenters. The colonel was boss, and I was told I had nothing to do with it, though I had made up my mind to that before. Another story was put upon the house, with long painted shanties, and sheds, and stables, and boxes with crosses and vanes upon them, all about the premises. They put one of these up on the hill we used to call Sheep's Misery which they called New 'Limpus, over Merino Creek; and in the next general rain it limped down of its own accord; and it cost more, I was told, to put it up the second time than it had done the first.

They had not got every thing painted and varnished and gilded, and cleared away the chips, and got in the wagon-loads of curosities that they bought for furniture, before we heard that the cholera morbus had come over along with twenty thousand paddies and radikles into Canada, up to the north; and the people talked about nothing but whether it would come into these parts. The doctor had newspapers and tracts which he brought every day, and said he could cure it with the Spaw. Sometimes he said it was the real sphixy that had killed so many abroad, and then he said it wasn't. And he talked about premonitories, and made us show our tongues. He wanted me to take some pills; but I told him it was out of the contract, and I did not belong to the Spaw. But my wife and daughters took them, and a sorrowful time they had of it. I believe he would have gone on physicking them, and killed them, as he did an old maid in the village, if it had not been that he would have had no patients at the house if there had been no one to keep it.

We soon heard that the cholera had got into York State. We had then but a few boarders, who all drank regularly of the water, and yet had premonitories all the time. But when the news came that it was in the city, there was in a few weeks such a run of people that the house would hold no more, and they boarded about with all the neighbours. Among them was a town doctor, who said his nerves could not stand the sight of the disease; and he too talked about nothing but premonitories. Our doctor and he at first had a quarrel, and my wife talked of turning him out of doors, when he said it would be certain death to drink the Spaw. But the two doctors soon made it up, as they seemed to be likely to have business enough for both.

Then our doctor gave notice that he would give a public lecture gratis about the disease, in the meeting-house, and we all went to it. I did not pretend to understand it, nor did I find any one who did; only it was fixed now that it was the real sphixy, and that a collapse couldn't be cured. I believed as much, for I was aboard of a steamboat when one of the flues bursted. They called it a collapse; and I am certain it was easier to make a new one than to mend that. When he came to talk about the premonitories and the spasms, there began soon to be a sighing and grunting, and finally a general groaning, for all the world like anxious meeting. Everybody, women and all, were putting their hands over their bowels; and my neighbour Slaughter, the butcher, who weighs twenty-three stone, clapped his on each of his sides, and getting up to give them a squeeze, set up a sort of a bellow like one of his own bullocks going to be killed. I felt a little squirmish myself; though I had not noticed it before.

When he came to tell what was good to eat and drink, it was curious to hear him. I did not see that he left any thing for our victuals but beef and rice. Neighbour Slaughter stroked down his jacket as if he felt a little more comfortable, when he talked of beef; but I felt more uneasy than before, thinking what was to become of all my peas, and beans, and beets, and onions, and all kinds of sauce, and corn, and watermilions, which he said it would be wilful murder to eat. All liquids he said must be avoided; and as for the Spaw, he explained how the air was so peculiar-like, that what was good physic in common times was poison now, and a kind of worked backwards. But he said that as long as the people staid quiet there, the air was better than it was anywhere else; and if they minded the premonitories, and sent for him or his friend Doctor Nervy when they got them, there was no manner of danger. He also gave notice that he would make out a list of what was proper to be eaten at the Spaw House for the benefit of strangers.

For the matter of that, though I only saw what was going on in the kitchen sometimes, they seemed to have pretty much the same cooking that they had the year before, when the Congress-people and Nullyflyers had been there; except that all the beautiful vegetables, which never looked nicer before, were left alone. I was not sorry for this, except that I could not have them cooked for myself without going over to Eli's, where I soon made a bargain to get my dinner regular and comfortable. But after he had been to market a few times, and come back complaining that he could not sell his load to the huckster-women, he returned at last with the whole load; saying he had been ordered off by the mare's men in the market; that all the shops were shut, and the streets whitewashed; and that everybody that died had eaten some premonitory or another. And being a hasty, man, who has not yet got religion, he damned the cholera morbus, and the mare, and the vegetables too, in a profane manner – though that you need not mention.

Half the people were kept half-sick, and the rest did not look well, and the two doctors had business all the time; and I began to think my wife might make something of a spec out of the business, as the boarders seemed glad enough to sleep anywhere, and fare as they could. Two or three times when I looked in by accident, at night, I saw a party in one room that were reading written papers aloud; and from what I heard my wife and daughters talking about it, I gathered that they amused themselves with it, and that it was made out of their own heads. I thought it as good a way of killing time as any, and better than strumming on the forte-piano, which was kept a-going from morning till night, till a child fell through the cover one day, and smashed all the wire-works. I was plaguy glad of this, for I didn't mind the fidells, and flutes, and tambyreens that they got to dance to, half so bad as the nasty noise, to no tune at all, that they made with the piano. Luckily there was nobody to mend it, and the poor thing stays smashed to this minute. I don't believe it will fetch much.

But to come to the marrow of the matter, after these premonitories, one night, about two weeks ago, my old negro Samboney, who lives with his wife Dinah in a little old stone house near the Spaw, complained of a great many of them. I didn't see any good the doctors did, and Samboney was awful afraid of them. He said he had drunk nothing all day but hard cider, and eat no thing but salt pork and plenty of the nice vegetables Master Eli gave him (being some of the same that would have been wasted otherwise), and some watermilions, hard biled eggs, and nice green apples. Dinah said he had taken near a pint of spirits too, which was but natural in the poor neger; for after such a mess I should have taken some myself; for all Doctor Skinner and Doctor Nervy might have said. I told him to be quiet, and Dinah to kier him up; but I had hardly sneaked into bed in the little room on the ground- floor, where my wife had put me since the company came, and begun to get asleep, when I heard Dinah screaming and thumping at the door, and bawling out, "Cholera Morbish! – Samboney has got him! – He's a kicking down the house! – Cholera! – Cholera!" loud enough to wake the dead, and scare all the vallydinarians out of all the life that was left in them.

I got up, while she kept on hollering; and when I went out, it was a curious thing to see and hear. There was all the people in the windows and piazzas to the back of the house, in their night-clothes, some screeching as if they had fits; and there was the nigger-wench in her white shimmy, dancing a Brigadoon on the grass, and pulling out her wool, and thumping herself like a possessed body in the New Testament. And when she yelled out "Cholera! – Cholera!" it put me in mind of the cry of wo set up in the streets of the old Jerusalem by a crazy man, which I used to read about in Josephus, when I had a clean place to set down in and read any thing.

There was a general mixture of noises and running about the house; but I could hear calls for Doctor Nervy, and cries of "Send for Doctor Skinner," more than any thing else. Doctor Nervy at last came out on the upper piazza in his flannel night-gown, with a blanket over it, though the nights were as hot as Tophet (as I had heard Eli profanely remark), with a bottle at his nose, and a candle in his hand, to help him see the moonshine. When he heard and saw Dinah, he looked flustrated, and said she was crazy, and must be tied and taken away, till he could attend to her in the morning. The wench was in a great passion to hear him say this, and went on screaming, "You no tie me – Come tie Samboney! – Cholera got him! – He kick down de house and bedstead! – Cholera! – Cholera! – C'lapses, spazemzes, and plemoneraries – he got um all!"

The doctor said if Dinah wasn't tied he could not answer for the health of his nervous patients; whom he besought to get into bed, as he meant to do himself. Some of the servants ran to the village for Doctor Skinner, and some went with me, at a respectful distance however, as I pushed Dinah ahead, and followed her to the house. Sure enough, poor Samboney had kicked out the foot-board of the bed, and thrown off all the clothes. He was an awful spectacle, and roared terribly. We could not keep clothes on him, or make him be quiet, until he became so of his own accord, after an hour or more. Then his nails were as blue as indigo. We could hardly say whether he breathed or not, and he lay with his eyes open, quite resigned-like, as if he had given up fighting the cholera, and meant to leave the end to Providence.

He was just so when the doctor came. He did not know, I believe, whether Sam was alive or dead. He talked a good deal of what he could do if he could get apparatus, and said he must have a consultation with Doctor Nervy. But he wouldn't come, and had locked his door, ordering from the window that no one should be let into the room who had been near the case. Doctor Skinner then stuck a lancet into Samboney, but no blood came that would trickle; and he got the whiskey-bottle, and would have crammed the muzzle into the poor fellow's mouth, but his teeth were set so tight that he only spilled it all over him. The short and long of it was, that Sam died an hour before daylight; and the peculiarest part of all was, that he began to kick again after he was a dead corpse.

When daylight did come, every carriage was ordered up to the door, and such as had none were off on foot to the village, some of them without remembering even to ask for their bills. My wife and daughters stood on the steps with real tears in their eyes; and I cannot but say, that the two latter were served shabbily enough. Mrs. Mullock had been pressing them hard to take a short jaunt with her to the Falls;

and now they wanted to go there out of pure fright. But though there was plenty of room in the carriage, she crammed it full of bandboxes and unwashed clothes, to show the impossibility of the thing, and said she depended on seeing them in Alabama next season.

Before breakfast-time not a stranger was left in the house. Doctor Nervy was one of the first who run off. And though there has been but one case in the neighbourhood since, and that five miles distant, not a soul has come to the Spaw.

What is to become of my farm and the fine house I do not know. I suppose neighbour Cross must have both.

On looking about the rooms, and at the various rubbish which had been left, I found, in one where the reading-party used to meet by themselves, a great pile of papers, making, I should say, many quires of foolscap. I thought, though they had been left as good for nothing, and were of no use to me, they might turn to some account. But I resolved to have the speculation all to myself; and on talking to Eli, he thought there would be no harm in seeing what the papers were worth. They have not been inquired after in two weeks, and I do not know whose they are; so I conclude they belong to me. If you will give any thing for them, I will trust to you to fix the price. I am an unfortunate man; and every trifle will help me that I can come by in an honest way. There were other scraps and blotted papers about the house, and some love-letters and verses; but I take it for granted they are not worth any thing.

Your very humble servant,

SHARON CLAPP

The Skeleton's Cave

Chapter I

Qual è quella ruina che, nel fianco
 Di quà da Trento, l'Adige percosse.
O per tremuoto, o per sostegno manco,
 Che, da cima del monte onde si mosse,
Al piano è si la rocca discoscesa,
 Ch' alcuna via darebbe a chi su fosse—
Cotal di quel burrato era la scesa.
— DANTE, *Inferno*

WE HOLD our existence at the mercy of the elements; the life of man is a state of continual vigilance against their warfare. The heats of noon would wither him like the severed herb; the chills and dews of night would fill his bones with pain; the winter frost would extinguish life in an hour; the hail would smite him to death, did he not seek shelter and protection against them. His clothing is the perpetual armour he wears for his defence, and his dwelling the fortress to which he retreats for safety. Yet even there the elements attack him; the winds overthrow his habitation; the waters sweep it away. The fire that warmed and brightened it within seizes upon its walls and consumes it, with his wretched family. The earth, where she seems to spread a paradise for his abode, sends up death in exhalations from her bosom, and the heavens dart down lightnings to destroy him. The drought consumes the harvests on which he relied for sustenance; or the rains cause the green corn to "rot ere its youth attains a beard." A sudden blast ingulfs him in the waters of the lake or bay from which he seeks his food; a false step or a broken twig precipitates him from the tree which he had climbed for its fruit; oaks falling in the storm, rocks toppling down from the precipices are so many dangers which beset his life. Even his erect attitude is a continual affront to the great law of gravitation, which is sometimes fatally avenged when he loses the balance preserved by constant care and falls on a hard surface. The very arts on which lie relies for protection from the unkindness of the elements betray him to the fate he would avoid, in some moment of negligence or by some misdirection of skill, and he perishes miserably by his own inventions. Amid these various causes of accidental death which thus surround us at every moment, it is only wonderful that their proper effect is not oftener produced – so admirably has the Framer of the universe adapted the faculties by which man provides for his safety to the perils of the condition in which he is placed. Yet there are situations in which all his skill and strength are vain to protect him from a violent death by some unexpected chance which executes upon him a sentence as severe and inflexible as the most pitiless tyranny of human despotism. But I began with the intention of relating a story, and I will not by my reflections anticipate the catastrophe of my narrative.

One pleasant summer morning a party of three persons set out from a French settlement in the western region of the United States to visit a remarkable cavern in its vicinity. They had already proceeded for the distance of about three miles through the tall original forest, along a path so rarely trodden that it required all their attention to keep its track. They now perceived through the trees the sunshine at a distance, and as they drew nearer they saw that it came down into a kind of natural opening at the foot of a steep precipice. At every step the vast wall seemed to rise higher and higher; its seams and fissures and inequalities became more and more distinct; and far up, nearly midway from the bottom, appeared a dark opening under an impending crag.

The precipice seemed between two and three hundred feet in height, and quite perpendicular. At its base, the earth for several rods around was heaped with loose fragments of rock which had evidently been detached from the principal mass and shivered to pieces in the fall. A few trees, among which were the black walnut and the slippery-elm, and here and there an oak, grew scattered among the rocks and attested by their dwarfish stature the ungrateful soil in which they had taken root. But the wild grape vines which trailed along the ground and sent out their branches to overrun the trees around them showed by their immense size how much they delighted in the warmth of the rocks and the sunshine. The celastrus also here and there had wound its strong rings round and round the trunks and the boughs till they died in its embrace and then clothed the leafless branches in a thick drapery of its own foliage. Into this open space the party at length emerged from the forest and for a moment stopped.

"Yonder is the Skeleton's Cave," said one of them, who stood a little in front of the rest. As he spoke he raised his arm and pointed to the dark opening in the precipice already mentioned.

The speaker was an aged man, of spare figure and a mild, subdued expression of countenance. Whoever looked at his thin gray hairs, his stooping form, and the emaciated hand which he extended might have taken him for one who had passed the Scripture limit of threescore years and ten, but a glance at his clear and bright hazel eye would have induced the observer to set him down at some five years younger. A broad-brimmed palmetto hat shaded his venerable features from the sun, and his black gown and rosary denoted him to be an ecclesiastic of the Romish faith. The two persons whom he addressed were much younger.

One of them was in the prime of manhood and personal strength, rather tall and of a vigorous make. He wore a hunting-cap, from the lower edge of which curled a profusion of strong dark hair, rather too long for the usual mode in the Atlantic States, shading a fresh-coloured countenance lighted by a pair of full black eyes, the expression of which was compounded of boldness and good-humour. His dress was a blue frock-coat trimmed with yellow fringe and bound by a sash at the waist, deer-skin pantaloons, and deer-skin mocasins. He carried a short rifle on his left shoulder and wore on his left side a leathern bag of rather ample dimensions, and on his right a powder-flask. It was evident that he was either a hunter by occupation or at least one who made hunting his principal amusement – and there was something in his air and the neatness of his garb and equipments that bespoke the latter.

On the arm of this person leaned the third individual of the party, a young woman apparently about nineteen or twenty years of age, slender and graceful as a youthful student of the classic poets might imagine a wood-nymph. She was plainly attired in a straw hat and a dress of russet-colour, fitted for a ramble through that wild forest. The faces of her two companions were decidedly French in their physiognomy; hers was as decidedly Anglo-American. Her brown hair was parted away from a forehead of exceeding fairness, more compressed on the sides than is usual with the natives of England, and showing in the profile that approach to the Grecian outline which is remarked among their descendants in America. To complete the picture, imagine a quiet blue eye, features delicately moulded, and just colour enough on her cheek to make it interesting to watch its changes as it deepened or grew paler with the varying and flitting emotions which slight cause will call up in a youthful maiden's bosom.

Notwithstanding this difference of national physiognomy, there was nothing peculiar in her accent as she answered the old man who had just spoken.

"I see the mouth of the cave, but how are we to reach it, Father Ambrose? I perceive no way of getting to it without wings, either from the bottom or the top of the precipice."

"Look a few rods to the right, Emily. Do you see that pile of broken rocks reaching up to the middle of the precipice, looking as if a huge column of that mighty wall had been shivered into a pyramid of fragments? Our path lies that way."

"I see it, Father," returned the fair questioner, "but when we arrive at the top, it appears to me we shall be no nearer the cave than we now are."

"From the top of that pile you may perceive a horizontal seam in the precipice extending to the mouth of the cave. Along that line – though you cannot discern it from the place where we stand – is a safe and broad footing, leading to our place of destination. Do you see, Le Maire," continued Father Ambrose, addressing himself to his other companion, "do you see that eagle sitting so composedly on a bough of that leafless tree which seems a mere shrub on the brow of the precipice directly over the cavern? Nay, never lift your rifle, my good friend; the bird is beyond your reach, and you will only waste your powder. The superfluous rains which fall on the highlands beyond are collected in the hollow over which hangs the tree I showed you, and pour down the face of the rock directly over the entrance of the cave. Generally, you will see the bed of that hollow perfectly dry, as it is at present, but during a violent shower, or after several days' rain, there descends from that spot a sheet of water, white as snow, deafening with its noise the quiet solitudes around us and rivalling in beauty some of the cascades that tumble from the cliffs of the Alps. But let us proceed."

The old man led the party to the pile of rocks which he had pointed out to their notice and began to ascend from one huge block to another with an agility scarcely impaired by age. They could now perceive that human steps had trodden that rough path before them; in some places the ancient moss was effaced from the stones, and in others their surfaces had been worn smooth. Emily was about to follow her venerable conductor, when Le Maire offered to assist her.

"Nay, uncle," said she, "I know you are the politest of men, but I think your rifle will give you trouble enough. I have often heard you call it your wife, so I beg you will wait on Madame Le Maire and leave me to make the best of my way by myself. I am not now to take my first lesson in climbing rocks, as you well know."

"Well, if this rifle be my spouse," rejoined the hunter, "I will say that it is not every wife who has so devoted a husband, nor every husband who is fortunate enough to possess so true a wife. She has another good quality – she never speaks but when she is bid, and then always to the point. I only wish for your sake, since I am not permitted to assist you, that Henry Danville were here. I think we should see the wildness of the paces that carry you so lightly over these rocks a little chastised while the young gentleman tenderly and respectfully handed you up this rude staircase, too rude for such delicate feet. Ah, I beg pardon, I forgot that you had quarrelled. Well, it is only a lover's quarrel, and the reconciliation will be the happier for being delayed so long. Henry is a worthy lad and an excellent marksman."

A heroine in a modern novel would have turned back this raillery with a smart or proud reply, but Emily was of too sincere and ingenuous a nature to answer a jest on a subject in which her heart was so deeply interested. Her cheek burned with a blush of the deepest crimson as she turned away without speaking and fled up the rocks. But though she spoke not, a tumult of images and feelings passed rapidly through her mind. One vivid picture of the past after another came before her recollection, and one well-known form and face were present in them all. She saw Henry Danville as when she first beheld and was struck with his frank, intelligent aspect and graceful manners: respectful, attentive, eager to attract her notice and fearing to displease; then again as the accepted and delighted lover; and finally, as he was now, offended, cold, and estranged. A rustic ball rose before her imagination: a young stranger from the Atlantic States appears among the revellers; the phrases of the gay and animated conversation she held with him again vibrate on her ear; and again she sees Henry standing aloof, and looking gloomy and unhappy. She remembered how she had undertaken to discipline him for this unreasonable jealousy by appearing charmed with her new acquaintance and accepting his civilities with affected pleasure – how he had taken fire at this, had withdrawn himself from her society and transferred his attentions to others. It was but the simple history of what is common enough among youthful lovers, but it was not of the less moment to her whose heart now throbbed with mingled pride and anguish as these incidents came thronging back upon her memory. She regretted her own folly, but her thoughts severely blamed Henry for making so trifling a matter a ground of serious offence, and she sought consolation in reflecting how unhappy she must have been had she been united for life to one of so jealous a temper. "I am confident," said she to herself, "that his present indifference is all a pretence; he will soon sue for a reconciliation, and I shall then show him that I can be as indifferent as himself."

Occupied with these reflections, Emily, before she was aware, found herself at the summit of that pile of broken rocks, and midway up the precipice.

Chapter II

I'll look no more,
Lest my brain turn.— *King Lear.*

The ecclesiastic was the first of the party who arrived at the summit. He had seated himself on one of the blocks of stone which composed the pile, with his back against the wall of the precipice, and had taken the hat from his brow that he might enjoy the breeze which played lightly about the cliffs and the coolness of which was doubly grateful after the toil of the ascent. In doing this he uncovered a high and ample forehead, such as artists love to couple with the features of old age when they would represent a countenance at once noble and venerable. This is the only feature of the human face which Time spares: he dims the lustre of the eye; he shrivels the cheek; he destroys the firm or sweet expression of the mouth; he thins and whitens the hairs; but the forehead, that temple of thought, is beyond his reach, or rather, it shows more grand and lofty for the ravages which surround it.

The spot on which they now stood commanded a view of a wide extent of uncultivated and uninhabited country. An eminence interposed to hide from sight the village they had left, and on every side were the summits of the boundless forest, here and there diversified with a hollow of softer and richer verdure where the hurricane, a short time before, had descended to lay prostrate the gigantic trees, and a young growth had shot up in their stead. Solitary savannas opened in the depth of the woods, and far off a lonely stream was flowing away in silence, sometimes among venerable trees, and sometimes through natural meadows, crimson with blossoms. All around them was the might, the majesty of vegetable life, untamed by the hand of man and pampered by the genial elements into boundless luxuriance. The ecclesiastic pointed out to his companions the peculiarities of the scenery; he expatiated on the flowery beauty of those unshorn lawns, and on the lofty growth and the magnificence and variety of foliage which distinguish the American forests, so much the admiration of those who have seen only the groves of Europe.

The conversation was interrupted by a harsh stridulous cry, and looking up the party beheld the eagle who had left his perch on the top of the precipice, and having passed over their heads, was winging his way towards the stream in the distance.

"Ah," exclaimed Le Maire, "that is a hungry note, and the bird is a shrewd one, for he is steering to a place where there is plenty of game to my certain knowledge. It is the golden eagle – the war eagle, as the Indians call him – and no chicken either, as you may understand from the dark colour of his plumage. I warrant he has gorged many a rabbit and prairie hen on these old cliffs. At all events, he has made me think of my dinner: unless we make haste, good Father Ambrose, I am positive that we shall be late to our venison and claret."

"We must endeavour to prevent so great a misfortune," said Father Ambrose, rising from the rock where he sat and proceeding on the path towards the cavern. It was a kind of narrow terrace, varying in width from four to ten feet, running westwardly along the face of the steep solid rock and apparently formed by the breaking away of the upper part of one of the perpendicular strata of which the precipice was composed. That event must have happened at a very remote period, for in some places the earth had accumulated on the path to a considerable depth, and here and there grew a hardy and dwarfish shrub, or a tuft of wildflowers hanging over the edge. As they proceeded, the great height at which they stood and the steepness of the rocky wall above and below them made Emily often tremble and grow pale as she looked down. A few rods brought the party to a turn in the rock where the path was narrower than elsewhere, and precisely in the angle a portion of the terrace on which they walked had fallen, leaving a chasm of about two feet in width, through which their distance from the base was fearfully apparent. Le Maire had already passed it, but Emily, when she arrived at the spot, shrunk back and leaned against the rock.

"I fear I shall not be able to cross the chasm," said she in a tone of alarm. "My poor head grows giddy from a single look at it."

"Le Maire will assist you, my child," said the old man, who walked behind her.

"With the greatest pleasure in life," answered Le Maire, "though I confess I little expected that the daughter of a clear-headed Yankee would complain of being giddy in any situation. But this comes of having a French mother, I suppose. Let me provide a convenient station for Madame Le Maire, as you call her, and I will help you over." He then placed his rifle against the rock where the path immediately beyond him grew wider, and advancing to the edge of the chasm, held forth both hands to Emily, taking hold of her arms near the elbow. In doing this he perceived that she trembled.

"You are as safe here as when you were in the woods below," said Le Maire, "if you would but think so. Step forward now, firmly, and look neither to the right nor left."

She took the step, but at that moment the strange inclination which we sometimes feel when standing on a dizzy height, to cast ourselves to the ground, came powerfully over her, and she leaned involuntarily and heavily towards the verge of the precipice. Le Maire was instantly aware of the movement, and bracing himself firmly, strove with all his might to counteract it. Had his grasp been less steady, or his self-possession less perfect, they would both inevitably have been precipitated from where they stood. But Le Maire was familiar with all the perilous situations of the wilderness, and the presence of mind he had learned in such a school did not now desert him. His countenance bore witness to the intense exertion he was making: it was flushed, and its muscles were working powerfully; his lips were closely compressed; the veins on his brow swelled, and his arms quivered with the strong tension given to their sinews. For an instant the fate of the two seemed in suspense, but the strength of the hunter prevailed, and he placed the damsel beside him on the rock, fainting and pallid as a corpse.

"God be praised," said the priest, drawing heavily the breath which he had involuntarily held during that fearful moment while he had watched the scene, unable to render the least assistance.

Chapter III

A hollow cave,
Far underneath a craggy cliff ypight,
Dark, doleful, dreary, like a greedy grave.
— SPENSER

Beneath whose sable roof, ghostly shapes
  Might meet at noontide, – Fear and trembling Hope –
Silence and Foresight, – Death the Skeleton,
And Time the Shadow. – WORDSWORTH

Some moments of repose were necessary before Emily was
sufficiently recovered from her agitation to be able to proceed. The
tears filled her eyes as she briefly but warmly thanked Le Maire for his
generous exertions to save her and begged his pardon for the foolish
and awkward timidity, as she termed it, which had put his life as well
as her own in such extreme peril.

"I confess," answered he, good-naturedly, "that had you been of as
solid a composition as some ladies with whom I have the honour of an
acquaintance, Madame Le Maire here would most certainly have been
a widow. I understood my own strength, however," added he, for on
this point he was somewhat vain, "and if I had not, I should still have
been willing to risk something rather than to lose you. But I will take
care, Emily, that you do not lead me into another scrape of the kind.
When we return I shall, by your leave, take you in my arms and carry
you over the chasm, and you may shut your eyes while I do it, if you
please."

They now again set out, and in a few moments arrived at the
mouth of the cavern they had come to visit. A projecting mass of rock
impended over it, so low as not to allow in front an entrance to a
person standing upright, but on each side it receded upwards in such a
manner as to leave two high narrow openings, giving it the appearance
of being suspended from the cavern roof. Beneath it, the floor, which
was a continuation of the terrace leading to the spot, was covered, in
places to a considerable depth, with soil formed by the disintegration
of the neighbouring rocks, and traversed by several fissures nearly

filled with earth. As they entered by one of the narrow side openings, Emily looked up to the crag with a slight shudder. "If it should fall!" thought she to herself, but a feeling of shame at the idle fear she had lately manifested restrained her from giving utterance to the thought.

The good ecclesiastic perceived what was passing in her mind, and said, with a smile, "There is no danger, my child; that rock has been suspended over the entrance for centuries, for thousands of years perhaps, and is not likely to fall today. Ages must have elapsed before the crags could have crumbled to form the soil now under our feet. It is true that there is no place sacred from the intrusion of accident; everywhere may unforeseen events surprise and crush us, as the foot of man surprises and crushes the insect in his path; but to suppose peculiar danger in a place which has known no change for hundreds of years is to distrust Providence. Come, Le Maire," said Father Ambrose, "will you oblige us by striking a light? Our eyes have been too much in the sunshine to distinguish objects in this dark place."

Le Maire produced from his hunting bag a roll of tinder, and lighting it with a spark from his rifle, kindled in a few moments a large pitch-pine torch. The circumstance which first struck the attention of the party was the profound and solemn stillness of the place. The most quiet day has under the open sky its multitude of sounds – the lapse of waters; the subtle motions of the apparently slumbering air among forests, grasses, and rocks; the flight and note of insects; the voices of animals; the rising of exhalations; the mighty process of change, of perpetual growth and decay, going on all over the earth, produces a chorus of noises which the hearing cannot analyze – which, though it may seem to you silence, is not so, and when from such a scene you pass directly into one of the rocky chambers of the earth, you perceive your error by the contrast. As the three went forward they passed through a heap of dry leaves, lightly piled, which the winds of the last autumn had blown into the cave from the summit of the surrounding forest, and the rustling made by their steps sounded strangely loud amid that death-like silence. A spacious cavern presented itself to their sight, the roof of which near the entrance was low, but several paces beyond it rose to a great height, where the smoke of the torch, ascending, mingled with the darkness, but the flame did not reveal the face of the vault.

They soon came to where, as Father Ambrose informed them, the cave divided into two branches. "That on the left," said he, "soon becomes a low and narrow passage among the rocks; this on the right leads to a large chamber, in which lie the bones from which the cavern takes its name."

He now took the torch from the hand of Le Maire, and turning to the right guided his companions to a lofty and wide apartment of the cave, in one corner of which he showed them a human skeleton lying extended on the rocky floor. Some decayed fragments, apparently of the skins of animals, lay under it in places, and one small remnant passed over the thighs. But the bones, though they had acquired from the atmosphere of the cave a greenish yellow hue, were seemingly unmouldered. They still retained their original relative position and appeared as never disturbed since the sleep of death came over the frame to which they once belonged. Emily gazed on the spectacle with that natural horror which the remains of the dead inspire. Even Le Maire, with all his vivacity and garrulity, was silent for a moment.

"Is any thing known of the manner in which this poor wretch came to his end?" he at length inquired.

"Nothing. The name of Skeleton's Cave was given to this place by the aborigines, but I believe they have no tradition concerning these remains. If you look at the right leg you will perceive that the bone is fractured: it is most likely the man was wounded on these very cliffs, either by accident or by some enemy, and that he crawled to this retreat, where he perished from want of attendance and from famine."

"What a death!" murmured Emily.

The ecclesiastic then directed their attention to another part of the same chamber, where he said it was formerly not uncommon for persons benighted in these parts, particularly hunters, to pass the night. "You perceive," added he, "that this spot is higher than the rest of the cavern, and drier also – indeed, no part of the cavern is much subject to moisture. A bed of leaves on this rock, with a good blanket, is no bad accommodation for a night's rest, as I can assure you, having once made the experiment myself many years since, when I came hither from Europe. Ah, what have we here? Coals, brands, splinters of pitch-pine! The cave must have been occupied very lately for the purpose I mentioned, and by people, too, who, I dare say from the preparations they seem to have made, passed the night very comfortably."

"I dare say they did so, though they had an ugly bedfellow yonder," answered Le Maire; "but I hope you do not think of following their

211

example. As you have shown us, I presume, the principal curiosities of the cave, I take the liberty of suggesting the propriety of getting as fast as we can out of this melancholy place, which has already put me out of spirits. That poor wretch who died of famine! – I shall never get him out of my head till I am fairly set down to dinner. Not that I care more for my dinner than any other man when there is any thing of importance in the way, as, for example, a buffalo, or a fat buck, or a bear to be killed; but you will allow, Father Ambrose, that a saddle of venison, or a hump of buffalo and a sober bottle of claret are a prettier spectacle, particularly at this time of day, than that mouldy skeleton yonder. I had intended to shoot something in my way back just to keep my hand and eye in practice, but it is quite too late to think of that. Besides, here is Emily, poor thing, whom we have contrived to get up to this place, and whom we must manage to get down again as well as we can."

The good priest, though by no means participating in Le Maire's haste to be gone, mildly yielded to his instances, particularly as they were seconded by Emily, and they accordingly prepared to return. On reaching the mouth of the cave, they were struck with the change in the aspect of the heavens. Dark heavy clouds, the round summits of which were seen one beyond the other, were rapidly rising in the west, and through the grayish blue haze which suffused the sky before them, the sun appeared already shorn of his beams. A sound was heard afar of mighty winds contending with the forest, and the thunder rolled at a distance.

"We must stay at least until the storm is over," said Father Ambrose. "It would be upon us before we could descend these cliffs. Let us watch it from where we stand above the tops of these old woods: I can promise you it will be a magnificent spectacle."

Emily, though she would gladly have left the cave, could say nothing against the propriety of this advice, and even Le Maire, notwithstanding that he declared he had rather see a well-loaded table at that moment than all the storms that ever blew, preferred remaining to the manifest inconvenience of attempting a descent. In a few moments the dark array of clouds swept over the face of the sun, and a tumult in the woods announced the coming of the blast. The summits of the forest waved and stooped before it, like a field of young flax in the summer breeze – another and fiercer gust descended – another and stronger convulsion of the forest ensued. The trees rocked backward and forward, leaned and rose, and tossed and swung their branches in every direction, and the whirling air above them was filled with their leafy spoils. The roar was tremendous – the noise of the ocean in a tempest is not louder. It seemed as if that innumerable multitude of giants of the wood raised a universal voice of wailing under the fury that smote and tormented them.

At length the rain began to fall, first in large and rare drops, and then the thunder burst over head and the waters of the firmament poured down in torrents, and the blast that howled in the woods fled before them as if from an element that it feared. The trees again stood erect, and nothing was heard but the rain beating heavily on the immense canopy of leaves around, and the occasional crashings of the thunder, accompanied by flashes of lightning that threw a vivid light upon the walls of the cavern.

The priest and his companions stood contemplating this scene in silence when a rushing of water close at hand was heard. Father Ambrose showed the others where a stream, formed from the rains collected on the highlands above, descended on the crag that overhung the mouth of the cavern, and shooting clear of the rocks on which they stood, fell in spray to the broken fragments at the base of the precipice.

A gust of wind drove the rain into the opening where they stood and obliged them to retire farther within. The priest suggested that they should take this opportunity to examine that part of the cave which in going to the skeleton's chamber they had passed on their left, observing, however, that he believed it was no otherwise remarkable than for its narrowness and its length. Le Maire and Emily assented, and the former taking up the torch which he had stuck in the ground, they went back into the interior.

They had just reached the spot where the two passages diverged from each other when a hideous and intense glare of light filled the cavern, showing for an instant the walls, the roof, the floor, and every crag and recess with the distinctness of the broadest sunshine. A frightful crash accompanied it, consisting of several sharp and deafening explosions, as if the very heart of the mountain was rent asunder by the lightning, and immediately after a body of immense weight seemed to fall at their very feet with a heavy sound and a shock that caused the place where they stood to tremble as if shaken by an earthquake. A strong blast of air rushed by them, and a suffocating odour filled the cavern.

Father Ambrose had fallen upon his knees in mental prayer at the explosion, but the blast from the mouth of the cavern threw him to the earth. He raised himself, however, immediately, and found himself in utter silence and darkness, save that a livid image of that insufferable glare floated yet before his eyeballs.

He called first upon Emily, who did not answer, then upon Le Maire, who replied from the ground a few paces nearer the entrance of the cave. He also had been thrown prostrate, and the torch he carried was extinguished. It was but the work of an instant to kindle it again, and they then discovered Emily extended near them in a swoon.

"Let us bear her to the mouth of the cavern," said Le Maire; "the fresh air from without will revive her."

He took her in his arms, but on arriving at the spot he placed her suddenly on the ground, and raising both hands, exclaimed with an accent of despair, "The rock is fallen! – the entrance is closed!"

It was but too evident. Father Ambrose needed but a single look to convince him of its truth – the huge rock which impended over the entrance had been loosened by the thunderbolt and had fallen upon the floor of the cave, closing all return to the outer world.

Chapter IV

Had one been there, with spirit strong and high,
Who could observe as he prepared to die;
He might have seen of hearts the varying kind,
And traced the movements of each different mind;
He might have seen that not the gentle maid
Was more than stern and haughty man afraid.
— CRABBE

Before inquiring further into the extent of the disaster, an office of humanity was to be performed. Emily was yet lying on the floor of the cave in a swoon, and the old man, stooping down and placing her head in his lap, began to use the ordinary means of recovery and called on Le Maire to assist him. The hunter, after being spoken to several times, started from his gloomy revery, and kneeling down by the side of the priest, aided him in chafing her temples and hands and fanned her cheek with his cap until consciousness was restored, when the priest communicated the terrible intelligence of what had happened.

Presence of mind and fortitude do not always dwell together. Those who are most easily overcome by the appearance of danger often support the calamity, after it has fallen, with the most composure. Le Maire had presence of mind, but he had not learned to submit with patience to irremediable misfortune. Emily could not command her nerves in sudden peril, but she could suffer with a firmness which left her mind at liberty to employ its resources. The very disaster which had happened seemed to inspire both her mind and her frame with new strength. The vague apprehensions which had haunted her were now reduced to certainty; she saw the extent of the calamity and felt the duties it imposed. She rose from the ground without aid and with a composed countenance, and began to confer with Father Ambrose on the probabilities and means of escape from their present situation.

In the mean time, Le Maire, who had left them as soon as Emily came to herself, was eagerly employed in examining the entrance where the rock had fallen. On one side it lay close against the wall of the cavern; on the other was an opening of about a hand's breadth which appeared, so far as he could distinguish, to communicate with the outer atmosphere. He looked above, but there the low roof, which met the wavering flame of his torch, showed a collection of large blocks firmly wedged together; he cast his eyes downwards, but there the lower edge of the vast mass which had fallen lay imbedded in the soil. He placed his shoulder against it and exerted his utmost strength to discover if it were moveable, but it yielded no more than the rock on which it rested.

"It is all over with us," said he at length, dashing to the ground the torch, which the priest, approaching, prudently took up before it was extinguished. "It is all over with us, and we must perish in this horrid place like wild beasts in a trap. There is no opening, no possible way for escape, and not a soul on the wide earth knows where we are, or what is our situation." Then, turning fiercely to the priest and losing his habitual respect for his person and office in the bitterness of his despair, he said, "This is all your doing – it was you who decoyed us hither to lay our bones beside those of that savage yonder."

"My son – " said the old man.

"Call me not son – this is no time for cant. You take my life, and when I reproach you, you give me fine words. You call yourself a man of God – can you pray us out of this horrible dungeon into which you have enticed us to bury us alive?"

"Say not that I take your life," said Father Ambrose mildly, without otherwise noticing his reproaches. "There is no reason as yet to suppose our case hopeless. Though we informed no person of the place to which we were going, it does not follow that we shall not be missed, or that no inquiry will be made for us. With to-morrow morning the whole settlement will doubtless be out to search for us, and as it is probable that some of them will pass this way, we may make ourselves heard by them from the mouth of the cavern. Besides, as Emily has just suggested, it is not impossible that the cave may have some other outlet, and that the part we were about to examine may afford a passage to the daylight."

Le Maire caught eagerly at the hope thus presented. "I beg your pardon, Father," said he, "I was hasty – I was furious – but it is terrible, you will allow, to be shut up in this sepulchre, with the stone rolled to its mouth, and left to die. It is no light trial of patience merely to pass the night here, particularly," said he with a smile, "when you know that dinner is waiting for you at home. Well, if the cave is to be explored, let us set about it immediately; if there is any way of getting out, let us discover it as soon as possible."

They again went to the passage which diverged from the path leading to the skeleton's chamber. It was a low, irregular passage, sometimes so narrow that they were obliged to walk one behind the other, and sometimes wide enough to permit them to walk abreast. After proceeding a few rods it became so low that they were obliged to stoop.

"Remain here," said Le Maire, "and give me the torch. If there be any way of reaching daylight by this part of the cavern, I will give an account of it in due time."

Father Ambrose and Emily then seated themselves on a low bench of stone in the side of the cavern while he went forward. The gleam of his torch appearing and disappearing showed the windings of the passage he was treading, and sometimes the sound of measured steps on the rock announced that he was walking upright, and sometimes a confused and struggling noise denoted that he was making his way on his elbows and knees. At length the sound was heard no longer, and the gleam of the torch ceased altogether to be descried in the passage.

"Father Ambrose!" said Emily after a long interval. These words, though in the lowest key of her voice, were uttered in such a tone of awe and sounded, moreover, with such an unnatural distinctness in the midst of that perfect stillness that the good Father started.

"What would you, my daughter?"

"This darkness and this silence are frightful, and I spoke that you might reassure me by the sound of your voice. My uncle is long in returning."

"The passage is a long and intricate one."

"But is there no danger? I have heard of death-damps in pits and deep caverns, by the mere breathing of which a man dies silently and without a struggle. If my poor uncle should never return!"

"Let us not afflict ourselves with supposable evils while a real calamity is impending over us. The cavern has been explored to a considerable distance without any such consequence as you mention to those who undertook it."

"God grant that he may discover a passage out of the cave! But I am afraid of the effect of a disappointment, he is so impatient – so impetuous."

"God grant us all grace to submit to his good pleasure," rejoined the priest; "but I think I hear him on the return. Listen, my child, you can distinguish sounds inaudible to my dull ears."

Emily listened, but in vain. At length, after another long interval, a sound of steps was heard, seemingly at a vast distance. In a little while a faint light showed itself in the passage, and after some minutes Le Maire appeared, panting with exertion, his face covered with perspiration, and his clothes soiled with the dust and slime of the rocks. He was about to throw himself on the rocky seat beside them without speaking.

"I fear your search has been unsuccessful," said Father Ambrose.

"There is no outlet in that quarter," rejoined Le Maire sullenly. "I have explored every winding and every cranny of the passage and have been brought up at last, in every instance, against the solid rock."

"There is no alternative, then," said the ecclesiastic, "but to make ourselves as tranquil and comfortable as we can for the night. I shall have the honour of installing you in my old bed-chamber, where, if you sleep as soundly as I did once, you will acknowledge to-morrow morning that you might have passed a worse night. It is true, Emily, that one corner of it is occupied by an ill-looking inmate, but I can promise you from my own experience that he will do you no harm. So let us adjourn to the skeleton's chamber and leave to Providence the events of the morrow."

To the skeleton's chamber they went accordingly, taking the precaution to remove thither a quantity of the dry leaves which lay heaped not far from the mouth of the cave to form couches for their night's repose. A log of wood of considerable size was found in this part of the cavern, apparently left there by those who had lately occupied it for the night; and on collecting the brands and bits of wood which lay scattered about, they found themselves in possession of a respectable stock of fuel. A fire was kindled, and the warmth, the light, the crackling brands, and the ever-moving flames, with the dancing shadows they threw on the walls and the waving trains of smoke that mounted like winged serpents to the roof and glided away to the larger and loftier apartment of the cave, gave to that recess, lately so still, dark, and damp, a kind of wild cheerfulness and animation which, under other circumstances, could not have failed to raise the spirits of the party.

They placed themselves around that rude hearth, Emily taking care to turn her back to the corner where lay the skeleton. Father Ambrose had been educated in Europe; he had seen much of men and manners, and he now exerted himself to entertain his companions by the narrative of what had fallen under his observation in that ancient abode of civilized man. He was successful, and the little circle forgot for a while in the charm of his conversation their misfortune and their danger. Even Le Maire was enticed into relating one or two of his hunting exploits, and Emily suffered a few of the arch sallies that distinguished her in more cheerful moments to escape her.

At length Le Maire's hunting watch pointed to the hour of ten and the good priest counselled them to seek repose. He gave them his blessing, recommending them to the great Preserver of men, and then, laying themselves down on their beds of leaves around the fire, they endeavoured to compose themselves to rest.

But now that each was left to the companionship of his own thoughts, the idea of their situation intruded upon their minds with a sense of pain and anxiety which repulsed the blessing of sleep. The reflections of each on the events of the day and the prospects of the morrow were different; those of Emily were the most cheerful, as her hopes of deliverance were the most sanguine. Her imagination had formed a picture of the incidents of her rescue from the fate that threatened her, a little romance in anticipation which she would not for the world have revealed to living ear, but which she dwelt upon fondly and perpetually in the secrecy of her own meditations. She thought what must be the effect of her mysterious absence from the village upon Henry Danville, whose very jealousy, causeless as it was, demonstrated the sincerity and depth of his affection. She represented him to herself as the leader in the search that would be set on foot for the lost ones, as the most adventurous of the band, the most persevering, the most inventive, and the most successful.

"He will pass by this precipice to-morrow," thought she. "Like others, he has heard of this cave; he will see that the fall of the rock has closed the entrance, his quick apprehension will divine the place of our imprisonment, he will call upon those who are engaged in the search, he will climb the precipice, he will deliver us, and I shall forgive him. But should it be my fate to perish – should none ever know the manner and place of my death – there will be one at least who will remember and regret me. He will bitterly repent the wrong he has done me, and the tears will start into his eyes at the mention of my name."

A tear gushed out from between the closed lids of the fair girl as this thought passed through her mind, but it was such a tear as maidens love to shed, and it did not delay the slumber that already began to steal over her.

Sleep was later in visiting the eyes of Le Maire. The impatience which a bold and adventurous man accustomed to rely on his own activity and address for escape in perilous emergencies feels under the pressure of a calamity which no exertion of his own can remedy had chafed and almost maddened his spirit. His heart sank within him at the thought of the lingering death he must die if not liberated from his living tomb. Long and uneasily he tossed on his bed of leaves, but he too had his hopes of deliverance by the people of the village who would unquestionably assemble in the morning to search for their lost neighbours, and who might discover their situation. These thoughts at length prevailed over those of a gloomier kind, and the fatigues of the day overcoming his eyes with drowsiness, he fell into a slumber – profound, as it seemed from his hard-drawn breath, but uneasy and filled with unpleasant dreams, as was evident from frequent starts and muttered exclamations.

When it was certain that both were asleep, Father Ambrose raised himself from his place and regarded them sorrowfully and attentively. He had not slept, though from his motionless posture and closed eyes, an observer might have thought him buried in a deep slumber. His own apprehensions, notwithstanding that he had endeavoured to prevent his companions from yielding themselves up to despair, were more painful than he had permitted himself to utter. That there was a possibility of their deliverance was true, but it was hardly to be expected that those who sought for them would think of looking for them in the cavern, nor was it likely that any cry they could utter would be heard below.

The old man's thoughts gradually formed themselves into a kind of soliloquy, uttered, as is often the case with men much given to solitary meditation and prayer, in a low but articulate voice.

"For myself," said he, "my life is near its close, and the day of decrepitude may be even yet nearer than the day of death. I repine not, if it be the will of God that my existence on earth, already mercifully protracted to the ordinary limits of usefulness, should end here. But my heart bleeds to think that this maiden, in the blossom of her beauty and in the springtime of her hopes, and that he who slumbers near me in the pride and strength of manhood should be thus violently divorced from a life which nature perhaps intended for as long a date as mine. I little thought, when the mother of that fair young creature in dying committed her to my charge, that I should be her guide to a place where she should meet with a frightful and unnatural death.

Accustomed as I am to protracted fastings, it is not impossible that I may outlive them both, and after having closed their eyes who should have closed mine, I may be delivered and go forth in my uselessness from the sepulchre of those who should have been the delight and support of their friends. Let it not displease thee, O, my Maker! if, like the patriarch of old, I venture to expostulate with thee." And the old man placed himself in an attitude of supplication, clasping his hands and raising them towards heaven. Long did he remain in that posture motionless, and at length lowering his hands, he cast a look upon the sleepers near him, and laying himself down upon his bed of leaves, was soon asleep also.

Chapter V

A dull imprisoned ray,
A sunbeam that hath lost its way,
And through the crevice and the cleft
Of the thick wall is fallen and left.
The Prisoner of Chillon

Of course the slumbers of none of the party were long protracted. They were early dispersed by the idea of their imprisonment in that mountain dungeon which now and then showed itself painfully in the imagery of their dreams. When Emily awoke she found herself alone in the skeleton's chamber. Her eyes, accustomed to the darkness, could now distinguish most of the objects around her by the help of a gleam of light which appeared to come in from the larger apartment. The fire, kindled the night previous, was now a mass of ashes and blackened brands, and the couches of her two companions yet showed the pressure of their forms. She rose, and not without casting a look at the grim inmate of the place whose discoloured bones were just distinguishable in that dim twilight, passed into the outer chamber. Here she found the priest and Le Maire standing near the mouth of the cavern where a strong light, at least so it seemed to her eyes, streamed in through the opening between the well and the fallen rock, showing that the short night of summer was already past.

"We are watching the increasing light of the morning," said the priest.

"And waiting for the friends whom it will bring to deliver us," added Le Maire.

"You will admit me to share in the occupation, I hope," answered Emily. "I am fit for nothing else, as you know, but to watch and wait, and I will endeavour to do that patiently."

It was not long before a brighter and a steady light through the aperture informed the prisoners that the sun had risen over the forest tops, and that the perfect day now shone upon the earth. To those who could look upon the woods and savannas, the hills and the waters around, that morning was one of the most beautiful of the beautiful season to which it belonged. The aspect of nature — like one of those human countenances we sometimes meet with, so radiant with cheerfulness that it seems as if they had never known the expression of sorrow — showed in the gladness it now put on no traces of the tempest of the preceding day. The intensity of the sun's light was tempered by the white clouds that now and then floated over it, trailing through a soft blue sky, and the light and fresh breezes seemed to hover in the air, to rise and descend with a motion like the irregular and capricious course of the butterfly, now stooping to wrinkle the surface of the stream, now rising to murmur in the leaves of the forest, and again descending to shake the dew from the cups of the opening flowers in the natural meadows. The replenished brooks had a livelier warble, and the notes of innumerable birds rang more cheerfully through the clear atmosphere. The prisoners of the cavern, however, could only distinguish the beauty of the morning by slight tokens - now and then a sweep of the winds over the forest tops, sometimes the note of the woodthrush or of the cardinal bird as he flew by the face of the rocks, and occasionally a breath of the perfumed atmosphere flowing through the aperture. These intimations of liberty and enjoyment from the world without only heightened their impatience at the imprisonment to which they were doomed.

"Listen!" said Emily. "I think I hear a human voice."

"There is certainly a distant call in the woods," said Le Maire after a moment's silence. "Let us all shout together for assistance."

They shouted accordingly, Le Maire exerting his clear and powerful voice to the utmost, and the others aiding him as well as they were able, with their feebler and less practised organs. A shrill discordant cry replied, apparently from the cliffs close to the cave.

"A parrokeet," exclaimed Le Maire. "The noisy pest! I wish the painted rascal were within reach of my rifle. You see, Father Ambrose, we are forgotten by mankind, and the very birds of the wilderness mock our cries for assistance."

"You have a quick fancy, my son," answered the priest; "but it is yet quite too soon to give over. It is now the very hour when we may expect our neighbours to be looking for us in these parts."

They continued therefore to remain by the opening, and from time to time to raise that shout for assistance. Hour after hour passed, and no answer was returned to their cries, which indeed could have been but feebly heard, if heard at all, at the foot of the precipice. Hour after hour passed, and no foot climbed the rocky stair that led to their prison. The pangs of hunger in the mean time began to assail them, and, more intolerable than these, a feverish and tormenting thirst.

"You have practised fasting," said Le Maire to Father Ambrose, "and so have I when I could get nothing to eat. In my hunting excursions I have sometimes gone without tasting food from morning till the night of the next day. I found relief from an expedient which I learned of the old hunters, but which I presume you churchmen are not acquainted with. Here it is."

Saying this, he passed the sash he wore once more round his body, drawing it tightly, and securing it by a firm knot. Father Ambrose declined adopting, for the present, a similar expedient, alleging that as yet he had suffered little inconvenience from want of food except a considerable degree of thirst, but Emily, already weak from fasting, allowed her slender waist to be wrapped tightly in the folds of a silk shawl which she had brought with her. The importunities of hunger were thus rendered less painful, and a new tension was given to the enervated frame, but the burning thirst was not at all allayed.

The cave was then explored for water: every corner was examined, and holes were dug in the soil which in some places covered the rocky door, but in vain. Le Maire again ventured into the long narrow passage which he had followed to its termination the day previous, in the hope of now discovering some concealed spring, or some plane where the much desired element fell in drops from the roof, but he returned fatigued and unsuccessful. As he came forth into the larger apartment, a light fluttering sound, as of the waving of a thin garment, attracted the attention of the party. On listening attentively it appeared to be within the cavern, but what most excited their surprise was that it passed suddenly and mysteriously from place to place, while the agent continued invisible in spite of all their endeavours to discover it. Sometimes it was heard on the one side, sometimes on the other, now from the roof, and now from the floor, near, and at a distance. At length it passed directly over their heads.

"It is precisely the sound of a light robe agitated by the wind, or by a swift motion of the person wearing it," said Emily.

"It is no sound of this earth, I will depose in a court of justice," said Le Maire, who was naturally of a superstitious turn, "or we should see the thing that makes it."

"All we can say at present," answered the priest, "is that we cannot discover the cause, but it does not therefore follow that it is any thing supernatural. What is perceived by one of our senses only does not necessarily belong to the other world. I have no doubt, however, that we shall discover the cause before we leave the cavern."

"Nor I either," rejoined Le Maire with a look and tone which showed the awe that had mastered him. "I am satisfied of the cause already. It is a warning of approaching death. We must perish in this cavern."

Emily, much as she was accustomed to rely on the opinions of the priest, felt in spite of herself the infection of that feeling of superstitious terror which had seized upon her uncle, and her heart had begun to beat thick, when a weak chirp was heard.

"The mystery is resolved," exclaimed Father Ambrose, "and your ghost, my good friend, is only a harmless fellow-prisoner, a poor bird which the storm doubtless drove into the cave, and which has been confined here ever since." As he spoke, Emily, who had looked to the quarter whence the sound proceeded, pointed out the bird sitting on a projection of rock at no great distance.

"A godsend!" cried Le Maire. "The bird is ours, though his little carcass will hardly furnish a mouthful for each of us." Saying this, he took up his rifle, which stood leaning against the wall of the cavern, and raised the piece to his eye. Another instant and the bird would have fallen, but Emily laid her hand on his arm.

"Cannot we take him alive," asked she, "and make him the agent of our deliverance?"

"How will you do that?" said Le Maire, without lowering his rifle.

"Send him out at the opening yonder with a letter tied to his wing to inform our friends of our situation. It will at least increase the chances of our escape."

"It is well thought of," answered Le Maire. "And now, Emily, you shall see how an experienced hunter takes a bird without harming a single feather of his wings."

Saying this, he went to the mouth of the cave and began to turn up, with a splinter of wood, the fresh earth. After considerable examination he drew forth a beetle, and producing from his hunting-bag a quantity of packthread, he tied the insect to one end of it, and having placed it on the point of a crag, retired to a little distance with the other end of the packthread in his hand. By frequently changing his place, he caused the bird to approach the spot where he had laid the insect. It was a tedious process, but when at length the bird perceived his prey, he flew to it and snapped it up in an instant, with the eagerness of famine. By a similar piece of management he contrived to get the thread wound several times about one of the legs of the little creature, and when this was effected, he suddenly drew it in, bringing him fluttering and struggling to his hand. It proved to be of the species commonly called the cedar bird.

"Ah, Father Ambrose," cried Le Maire, whose vivacity returned with whatever revived his hopes, " we have caught you a brother ecclesiastic, a *recollet*, as we call him from the gray hood he wears. No wonder we did not see him before, for his plumage is exactly of the colour of the rocks. But he is the very bird for a letter: look at the sealing-wax he carries on his wings." As he spoke he displayed the glossy brown pinions, the larger feathers of which were ornamented at their tops with little appendages of a vermilion colour, like drops of delicate red sealing-wax.

"And now let us think," continued he, "of writing the letter which this dapper little monk is to carry for us." A piece of charcoal was brought from the skeleton's chamber, and Le Maire having produced some paper from his hunting-bag, the priest wrote upon it a few lines, giving a brief account of their situation. The letter, being folded and properly addressed, was next perforated with holes, through which a string was inserted and tied under the wing of the bird. Emily then carried him to the opening, through which he darted forth in apparent joy at regaining his liberty.

"Would that we could pass out," said she, with a sigh, "as easily as the little creature which we have just set free. But the recollet is a lover of gardens, and he will soon be found seeking his food in those of the village."

The hopes to which this little expedient gave birth in the bosoms of all contributed somewhat to cheer the gloom of their confinement. But night came at length to close that long and weary day – a night still more long and weary. The light which came in at the aperture began to wane, and Emily watched it, as it faded, with a sickness of the heart which grew almost to agony when finally it ceased to shine altogether. She had continued during the day to cherish the dream of deliverance by the sagacity and exertions of her lover and had scarcely allowed herself to contemplate the possibility of remaining in the cavern another night. It was therefore in unspeakable bitterness of spirit that she accompanied the priest and Le Maire to the skeleton's chamber, where they collected the brands which remained of the fire of the preceding night and kindled them into a dull and meager flame. That evening was a silent one – the day had been passed in various speculations on the probability of their release, in searching the cave for water, and in shouting at the entrance for assistance. But the hour of darkness – the hour which carried their neighbours of the village to their quiet and easy beds in their homes, overflowing with abundance, filled with the sweet air of heaven, and watched by its kindly constellations – that hour brought to the unhappy prisoners of the rock a peculiar sense of desolation and fear, for it was a token that they were, for the time at least, forgotten; that those whom they knew and loved slumbered and thought not of them. They laid themselves down upon their beds of leaves, but the horrible thirst which consumed them like an inward fire grew fiercer with the endeavour to court repose, and the blood that crept slowly through their veins seemed to have become a current of liquid flame. Sleep came not to their eyes, or came attended with dreams of running waters which they were not permitted to taste; of tempests and earthquakes, and breathless confinement among the clods of earth and various shapes of strange peril, while their friends seemed to stand aloof and to look coldly and unconcernedly on, without showing even a desire to render them assistance.

Chapter VI

My brother's soul was of the mould
Which in a palace had grown cold,
Had his free breathing been denied
The range of the steep mountain side.
The Prisoner of Chillon

Shall Nature, swerving from her earliest dictate,
Self-preservation, fall by her own act?
Forbid it Heaven! let not, upon disgust,
The shameless hand be foully crimsoned o'er
With blood of its own lord.
— BLAIR, *The Grave*

On the third day the cavern presented a more gloomy spectacle than it had done at any time since the fall of the rock took place. It was now about eleven o'clock in the morning and the shrill singing of the wind about the cliffs and through the crevice, which now admitted a dimmer light than on the day previous, announced the approach of a storm from the south. The hope of relief from without was growing fainter and fainter as the time passed on, and the sufferings of the prisoners became more poignant. The approach of the storm, too, could only be regarded as an additional misfortune, since it would probably prevent or obstruct for that day the search which was making for them. They were all three in the outer and larger apartment of the cave. Emily was at a considerable distance from the entrance, reclining on a kind of seat formed of large loose stones and overspread with a covering of withered leaves. There was enough of light to show that she was exceedingly pale, that her eyes were closed, and that the breath came thick and pantingly through her parted lips, which alone of all her features retained the colour of life. Faint with watching, with want of sustenance, and with anxiety, she had laid herself down on this rude couch which the care of her companions had provided for her, and had sunk into a temporary slumber. The priest stood close to the mouth of the cave leaning against the wall with his arms folded, himself scarcely changed in appearance except that his cheek seemed somewhat more emaciated and his eyes were lighted up with a kind of solemn and preternatural brightness. Le Maire, with a spot of fiery red on each cheek, his hair staring wildly in every direction and his eyes bloodshot, was pacing the cavern floor to and fro, carrying his rifle, occasionally stepping to examine the priming, or to peck the flint, and sometimes standing still for a moment, as if lost in thought.

At length he approached the priest and said to him, in a hollow voice, "Have you never heard of seamen on a wreck, destitute of provisions, casting lots to see which of their number should die that the rest might live?"

"I have so."

"Were they right in so doing?"

"I cannot say that they were not. It is a horrid alternative in which they were placed. It might be lawful – it might be expedient that one should perish for the salvation of the rest."

"Have you never seen an insect or an animal writing with torture, and have you not shortened its suffering by putting an end to its life?"

"I have – but what mean these questions?"

"I will tell you. Here is my rifle." As he spoke, Le Maire placed the piece in the hands of Father Ambrose, who took it mechanically. "I ask you to do for me what you would do for the meanest worm. You understand me?"

"Are you mad?" demanded the priest, regarding him with a look in which the expression of unaffected astonishment was mingled with that of solemn reproof.

"Mad! Indeed I am mad, if you will have it so: you will feel less scruple at putting an end to the existence of a madman. I cannot linger in this horrid place, neglected and forgotten by those who should have come to deliver me, suffering the slow approaches of death - the pain - the fire in the veins - and, worst of all, this fire in the brain," said Le Maire, striking his forehead. "They think, if they think of me at all, that I am dying by slow tortures. I will disappoint them. Listen, Father," continued he, "would it not be better for you and Emily that I were dead? Is there no way? Look at my veins, they are full yet, and the muscles have not shrunk away from my limbs; would you not both live the longer if I were to die?"

The priest recoiled at the horrid idea presented to his mind. "We are not cannibals," said he, "thanks be to Divine Providence." An instant's reflection, however, convinced Father Ambrose that the style of rebuke which he had adopted was not proper for the occasion. The unwonted fierceness and wildness of Le Maire's manner, and the strange proposal he had made, denoted that alienation of mind which is no uncommon effect of long abstinence from food. He thought it better, therefore, to attempt by mild and soothing language to divert him from his horrid design.

"My good friend," said he, "you forget what grounds of hope yet remain to us; indeed, the probability of our escape is scarcely less to-day than it was yesterday. The letter sent out of the cave may be found, and if so, it will most certainly effect our deliverance; or the fall of the rock may be discovered by some one passing this way, and he may understand that it is possible we are confined here. While our existence is prolonged there is no occasion for despair. You should endeavour, my son, to compose yourself, and to rely on the goodness of that Power who has never forsaken you."

"Compose myself!" answered Le Maire, who had listened impatiently to this exhortation. "Compose myself! Do you not know that there are those here who will not suffer me to be tranquil for a moment? Last night I was twice awakened, just as I had fallen asleep, by a voice pronouncing my name, as audibly as I heard your own just now; and the second time, I looked to where the skeleton lies, and the foul thing had half-raised itself from the rock and was beckoning me to come and place myself by its side. Can you wonder if I slept no more after that?"

"My son, these are but the dreams of a fever."

"And then, wherever I go by myself, I hear low voices and titterings of laughter from the recesses of the rocks. They mock me, that I, a free hunter, a denizen of the woods and prairies, a man whose liberty was never restrained for a moment, should be entrapped in this manner and made to die like a buffalo in a pit, or like a criminal in the dungeons of the old world – that I should consume with thirst in a land bright with innumerable rivers and springs – that I should wither away with famine while the woods are full of game and the prairies covered with buffaloes. I could face famine if I had my liberty. I could meet death without shrinking in the sight of the sun and the earth, and in the fresh open air. I should strive to reach some habitation of my fellow-creatures; I should be sustained by hope; I should travel on till I sank down with weakness and fatigue, and died on the spot. But famine made more frightful by imprisonment and inactivity, and these dreams, as you call them that dog me asleep and awake, they are more than I can bear. – Hark!" he exclaimed after a short pause and throwing quick and wild glances around him; "do you hear them yonder – do you hear how they mock me! You will not, then, do what I ask? Give me the rifle."

" No," said the priest, who instantly comprehended his purpose. "I must keep the piece till you are more composed."

Le Maire seemed not to hear the answer, but laying his grasp on the rifle, was about to pluck it from the old man's hands. Father Ambrose saw that the attempt to retain possession of it against his superior strength would be vain; he therefore slipped down his right hand to the lock, and cocking it, touched the trigger and discharged it in an instant. The report awoke Emily, who came trembling and breathless to the spot.

"What is the matter?" she asked.

"There is no harm done, my child," answered the priest, assuming an aspect of the most perfect composure. "I discharged the rifle, but it was not aimed at any thing, and I beg pardon for interrupting your repose at a time when you so much need it. Suffer me to conduct you back to the place you have left. Le Maire, will you assist?"

Supported by Le Maire on one side and by the priest on the other, Emily, scarcely able to walk from weakness, was led back to her place of repose. Returning with Le Maire, Father Ambrose entreated him to consider how much his niece stood in need of his assistance and protection. He bade him recollect that his mad haste to quit the world before called by his Maker would leave her, should she ever be released from the cavern, alone and defenceless, or at least with only an old man for her friend who was himself hourly expecting the summons of death. He exhorted him to reflect how much, even now, in her present condition of weakness and peril, she stood in need of his aid, and conjured him not to be guilty of a pusillanimous and cowardly detection of one so lovely, so innocent, and so dependent upon him.

Le Maire felt the force of this appeal. A look of human pity passed across the wild expression of his countenance. He put the rifle into the hands of Father Ambrose. "You are right," said he. "I am a fool, and I have been, I suspect, very near becoming a madman. You will keep this until you are entirely willing to trust me with it. I will endeavour to combat these fancies a little longer."

Chapter VII

A burst of rain
Swept from the black horizon, broad descends
In one continuous flood. Still overhead
The mingling tempest weaves its gloom, and still
The deluge deepens. — THOMSON

In the mean time the light from the aperture grew dimmer and dimmer, and the eyes of the prisoners, though accustomed to the twilight of the cavern, became at length unable to distinguish objects at a few paces from the entrance. The priest and Le Maire had placed themselves by the couch of Emily, but rather, as it seemed, from that instinct of our race which leads us to seek each other's presence than for any purpose of conversation, for each of the party preserved a gloomy silence. The topics of speculation on their condition had been discussed to weariness, and no others had now any interest for their minds. It was no unwelcome interruption to that melancholy silence when they heard the sound of a mighty rain pouring down upon the leafy summits of the woods and beating against the naked walls and shelves of the precipice. The roar grew more and more distinct, and at length it seemed that they could distinguish a sort of shuddering of the earth above them, as if a mighty host was marching heavily over it. The sense of suffering was for a moment suspended in a feeling of awe and curiosity.

"That, likewise, is the rain," said Father Ambrose, after listening for a moment. "The clouds must pour down a perfect cataract when the weight of its fall is thus felt in the heart of the rock."

"Do you hear that noise of running water?" asked Emily, whose quick ear had distinguished the rush of the stream formed by the collected rains over the rocks without at the mouth of the cave.

"Would that its channel were through this cavern," exclaimed Le Maire, starting up. "Ah! here we have it - we have it! - listen to the dropping of water from the roof near the entrance. And here at the aperture!" He sprang thither in an instant. A little stream detached from the main current, which descended over rocks that closed the mouth of the cave [and] fell in a thread of silver amid the faint light that streamed through the opening; he knelt for a moment, received it between his burning lips, and then hastily returning, bore Emily to the spot. She held out her hollowed palm — white, thin, and semi-transparent, like a pearly shell used for dipping up the waters from one of those sweet fountains that rise by the very edge of the sea, and as fast as it filled with the cool, bright element, imbibed it with an eagerness and delight inexpressible. The priest followed her example; Le Maire also drank from the little stream as it fell, bathed in it his feverish brow, and suffered it to fall upon his sinewy neck.

"It has given me a new hold on life," said Le Maire, his chest distending with several full and long breathings. "It has not only quenched that hellish thirst, but it has made my head less light and my heart lighter. I will never speak ill of this element again - the choicest grapes of France never distilled any thing so delicious, so grateful, so life-giving. Take notice, Father Ambrose, I retract all I have ever said against water and water-drinkers. I am a sincere penitent, and shall demand absolution."

Father Ambrose had begun gently to reprove Le Maire for his unseasonable levity, when Emily cried out, "The rock moves! The rock moves! Come back - come further into the cavern!" Looking up to the vast mass that closed the entrance, he saw plainly that it was in motion, and he had just time to draw Le Maire from the spot where he had stooped down to take another draught of the stream when a large block which had been wedged in overhead gave way and fell in the very place where he left the prints of his feet. Had he remained there another instant, it must have crushed him to atoms. The prisoners, retreating within the cavern far enough to avoid the danger, but not too far for observation, stood watching the event with mingled apprehension and hope. The floor of the cave just at the edge, on which rested the fallen rock, yawned at the fissures where the earth with which they were filled had become saturated and swelled with water, and unable any longer to support the immense weight, settled away, at first slowly, under it, and finally, along with its incumbent load, fell suddenly and with a tremendous crash to the base of the precipice, letting the light of day and the air of heaven into the cavern. The thunder of that disruption was succeeded by the fall of a few large fragments of rock on the right and left, after which the priest and his companions heard only the fall of the rain and the heavy sighing of the wind in the forest.

Father Ambrose and Emily knelt involuntarily in thanksgiving at their unexpected deliverance. Le Maire, although unused to the devotional mood, observing their attitude, had bent his knee to imitate it when a glance at the outer world now laid open to his sight made him start again to his feet with an exclamation of delight. The other two arose also, and turned to the broad opening which now looked out from the cave over the forest. On one side of this opening rushed the torrent whose friendly waters had undermined the rock at the entrance and now dashed themselves against its shivered fragments below. It is not for me to attempt to describe how beautiful appeared to their eyes that world which they feared never again to see, or how grateful to their senses was that fresh and fragrant air of the forests which they thought never to breathe again. The light, although the sky was thick with clouds and rain, was almost too intense for their vision, and they shaded their brows with their hands as they looked forth upon that scene of woods and meadows and waters, fairer to their view than it had ever appeared in the most glorious sunshine.

"That world is ours again," said Le Maire, with a tone of exultation. "We are released at last, and now let us see in what manner we can descend."

As he spoke, he approached the verge of the rock from which the severed mass had lately fallen and saw to his dismay that the terrace which had served as a path to the cavern was carried away for a considerable distance to the right and left of where they stood, leaving the face of the precipice smooth and sheer from top to bottom. No footing appeared, no projection by which the boldest and the most agile could scale or descend it. Le Maire threw himself sullenly on the ground.

"We must pass another night in this dungeon," said he, "and perhaps starve to death after all. It is clear enough that we shall have to remain here until somebody comes to take us down, and the devil himself would not be caught abroad in the woods in the midst of such a storm as this."

The priest and Emily came up at this moment: "This is a sad disappointment," said the former, "but we have this advantage: that we can now make ourselves both seen and heard. Let us try the effect of our voices. It is not impossible that there may be some person within hearing."

Accordingly they shouted together, and though nothing answered but the echo of the forest, yet there was even in that reply of the inanimate creation something cheering and hope-inspiring to those who for nearly three days had perceived that all their cries for succour were smothered in the depths of the earth. Again they raised their voices, and listened for an answering shout a third time – and they were answered. The halloo of a full-toned, manly voice arose from the woods below.

"Thank heaven, we are heard at last," said Emily.

"Let us see if the cry was in answer to ours," said the priest, and again they called, and again a shout was returned from the woods. "We are heard – that is certain," continued he, "and the voice is nearer than at first – we shall be released."

At length the sound of quick footsteps on the crackling boughs was heard in the forest, and a young man of graceful proportions, dressed, like Le Maire, in a hunting-cap and frock, emerged into the open space at the foot of the precipice. As he saw the party standing in the cavity of the rook, he clapped his hands with an exclamation of surprise and delight. "Thank heaven, they are discovered at last! Are you all safe – all well?"

"All safe," answered Le Maire, "but hungry as wolves, and in a confounded hurry to get out of this horrid den."

The young man regarded the precipice attentively for a moment, and then called out, "Have patience a moment, and I will bring you the means of deliverance." He then disappeared in the forest.

Emily's waking dream was, in fact, not wholly unfulfilled. That young man was Henry Danville; she knew him by his air and figure as soon as he emerged from the forest, and before she heard his voice. He had been engaged, with many others belonging to the settlement, in the pursuit of their lost curate and his companions from the morning after their absence, and fortunately happened to be at no great distance when the disruption of the rock took place. Struck with astonishment at the tremendous concussion, he was hastening to discover the cause when he heard the shout to which he answered.

It was not long before voices and steps were again heard in the wood, and a crowd of the good villagers soon appeared advancing through the trees, one bearing a basket of provisions, some dragging ladders, some carrying ropes and other appliances for getting down their friends from their perilous elevation. Several of the ladders being spliced together and secured by strong cords were made to reach from the broken rocks below to the mouth of the cavern, and Henry ascended.

My readers will have no difficulty in imagining the conclusion. The emotions of the lovers at meeting under such circumstances are of course not to be described, and the dialogue that took place on that occasion would not, I fear, bear to be repeated. The joy expressed by the villagers at recovering their worthy pastor brought tears into the good man's eyes, and words are inadequate to do justice to the delight of Le Maire at seeing his old companions and their basket of provisions.

My readers may also, if they please, imagine another little incident, without which some of them might think the narrative imperfect: namely, a certain marriage ceremony which actually took place before the next Christmas, and at which the venerable Father Ambrose officiated. Le Maire, when I last saw him, was living with one of Emily's children, a hale old man of eighty, with a few gray hairs scattered among his raven locks, full of stories of his youthful adventures, among which he reckoned that of his imprisonment in the cave as decidedly the best. He had, however, no disposition to become the hero of another tale of the kind, since he never ventured into another cave, or under another rock, as long as he lived, and was wont to accompany his narrative with a friendly admonition to his youthful and inexperienced hearers against thoughtlessly indulging in so dangerous a practice.

Medfield

Obey !
Thy nerves are in their infancy again,
And have no vigour in them.—*Tempest.*

TWO OR three years ago I passed a few weeks, about the end of summer and beginning of autumn, at a pleasant village within a few days' journey from the city of New-York. Here I became acquainted with a gentleman residing in the place, of the name of Medfield, one of the most interesting men I have known. He lived on a beautiful and well-cultivated farm and was said by his neighbours to be in the possession of an easy fortune. I, for my own part, found him possessed of leisure, knowledge, and courteous manners. He showed me many civilities; he introduced me to all the pleasant walks and drives for miles round; he led me to all the picturesque spots in the neighbourhood, both those sheltered and retired places whose beauty is in themselves and those which are beautiful from the scenery they command; he made me acquainted with the vegetable and mineral riches of the region, rare plants and curious fossils; he related the local traditions and told me something of the state of society, with which, however, as I gathered from his conversation and from the account given me by others, he mingled little, except in occasional acts of kindness.

Even now, while I write, I think I see him standing before me, a man who with little license of speech might be called handsome, rather tall of stature, and somewhat slenderly but elegantly shaped; his garb, though negligent, adjusting itself to his person with a natural and unavoidable grace – an oval countenance, a complexion fair and somewhat pale, a finely arched forehead, on the upper edge of which the lapse of thirty-five years had somewhat thinned the light brown hair that curled over it, a clear gray eye, and the remaining features moulded with more than usual regularity. There was, however, an unsettled and often unpleasant expression which almost neutralized the agreeable effect of this symmetry of features. In the midst of an animated conversation you would all at once perceive that his thoughts were wandering; a shade of alarm would pass over his countenance, and a shudder over his frame, and he would shrink as if from contact with some object which he wished to avoid. From these peculiarities of manner I was prepared to expect some eccentricities, not to call them by a worse name, in his way of thinking. Nothing of the kind, however, appeared, although he discoursed freely on all subjects and our conversation took in a large variety. On questions of politics and religion, his opinions were as rational as those of most men. He was a philanthropist after the fashion of the age, but he was no more an enthusiast in his plans of benevolence than some hundreds of worthy persons of my acquaintance. Of foreign and ancient literature he knew as much as most well-educated men in this country, and of old English literature something more; and his remarks on the authors he had read were those of a man of taste and judgment. Many of the fine old ballads in our language he knew by heart, as well as the imitations of them produced by modern authors; and he would repeat to me, as we sat together in the twilight, the ballad of Thomas the Rhymer with the additions by Scott, and Coleridge's "Ancient Mariner," in a fine impressive manner that even now vibrates on my nerves whenever I recall it to mind.

Among his neighbours Medfield had the reputation of great judgment and equity, as well as benevolence. He had formerly acted as a magistrate, but since the death of his wife, which happened a few years before I knew him, he had ceased to employ himself in that capacity, though his neighbours still referred their disputes to his friendly decision. Since that event his manners, formerly cheerful, and sometimes, when earnestly bent on gaining a favourite point, imperious to a fault, had, as I was told, undergone a change. Always kind and generous, he was now more so than ever; all sternness was gone from his temper, which was now marked by a uniform grave tenderness. Some even acknowledged to me that "the squire had some strange ways with him lately," a specimen or two of which I was shortly to witness.

I have no great passion either for angling or shooting; the former is a dull inactive sport, the latter a fatiguing one, and I am exceedingly awkward at both; but at the time I mention I was seized with the ambition of acquiring some skill in their exercise. I had therefore provided myself, before I left town, with an excellent fowling-piece, chosen for me by a good judge of such matters, and an ample and neatly-assorted store of hooks, lines, flies, and other implements for angling. With this apparatus I frequently went out, and sometimes solicited Medfield to accompany me, but without success. He pleaded sometimes an engagement, and always an aversion to these sports, and once or twice he ridiculed them so effectually that I was half-persuaded to throw my flies into the fire and make a present of my fowling-piece to a ragged boy with a crownless hat who looked at it most wishfully whenever I met him, and whom I once saw, when I had placed it against a tree, walking round it and contemplating it with an appearance of intense interest. I could not, however, yet give up a favourite project I had formed of performing some exploits in this line worth telling of when I should return to the city.

I well remember the first and only time that I walked out in company with Medfield with my gun on my shoulder. I was to visit a spot of much picturesque beauty, to which he undertook to be my guide. We set out from his house, and on our way passed by my lodgings. Begging him to wait at the door for a moment in order to give me an opportunity of drawing on a pair of boots, I entered the house, and when I came out I had my fowling-piece on my arm.

"Let me beg of you," said Medfield, "if you value your own comfort, to leave that unwieldy thing at home. You will be fatigued enough, I assure you, before you return, without encumbering yourself with any unnecessary burden."

"What!" I answered, "would you have us to go scrambling over stiles and fences, and traversing fields without any apparent purpose, like a couple of boys looking for birds' nests? Or do you mean to alarm the worthy farmers by leading them to suppose that we are going to rob their orchards or cornfields? Or would you have us pass for a lawyer and sheriff, coming with a still more unwelcome design upon somebody's real estate? This fowling-piece assures them of the contrary, and clears up the mystery. I dare say I shall have no occasion to use it – at all events I shall not look out for any."

Medfield desisted from any further objection, though somewhat reluctantly, as I could see by his subsequent gravity and silence. Our path at length brought us to the place of which he spoke. It was a long level passage, three or four rods in width, between two parallel rows of steep precipices, while from the rich mould on the shelves and in the interstices grew gigantic butternut and hickory trees, throwing their broad rough coated arms across the path and forming a verdant canopy overhead. Below, the ground was carpeted with grass, and squirrels were leaping and chirping among the boughs above. One of these, a fine little animal, was very busily employed in shelling a half-ripe nut which he had gathered from one of the trees, stopping occasionally to utter a short sharp bark of defiance and scorn. The temptation was irresistible; I raised my piece and fired with better fortune than usual, for the creature fell dead at my feet. On turning to look for my friend, I perceived he had left me, and casting my eye down the embowered avenue, I caught a glimpse of him hurrying out of sight. I followed, however, walking as fast as I was able and sometimes running a little, and in a few minutes had overtaken him. My game was in my hand, and I swung it about with an air of some ostentation.

"Well," said he, "you have killed a squirrel, I see; may I ask what you are going to do with it?"

"A good shot, was it not? A part of the charge went through the head. Why, I may throw it away, or give it, perhaps, to my landlord's dog."

This answer drew upon me a rebuke, mild in its terms but somewhat severe in its import, for taking the life of a happy, harmless creature from mere wantonness. I defended myself as well as I was able, but came to the conclusion that whatever might be my friend's other accomplishments, he was certainly, as I had heard him before acknowledge, no sportsman.

It was not long after this that I had engaged a black fellow to procure me a box of earth-worms, or "angle-dogs," as he called them. They were brought me in the morning; I put them in my pocket along with my fishing-tackle, and going out I met with Medfield, who asked me to accompany him and look at some improvements he was making on his estate. After a walk of some length about his grounds, we sat down under the shade of a large buttonwood-tree which stretched its long arms over a brook pent in a narrow channel, full of little cascades and rapids, and pools boiling with the force of the current that rushed into them. It was, in short, a very trout stream. My friend's attention was occupied for a moment in giving directions to a labourer while I, tempted by the appearance of the brook, had cut off a long tapering bough from the tree, and fastening upon it my fishing-line, had taken out my box of worms and began very leisurely to impale one of them on the hook. Just then, Medfield, who had dismissed the labourer, turned towards me. As his eye fell upon me, he started with a look of horror.

"In the name of mercy what are you doing?" asked he.

"Only going to try my luck at angling a little in this brook," answered I, quietly. "It looks like a capital stream for trout. I prepared myself this morning on purpose for a fishing excursion."

"But if you must follow that idle sport," returned Medfield, "can not you do it in a manner less inhuman and disgusting? Have you forgotten the admonition of the poet of "The Seasons"

'Let not on thy hook the tortured worm,
Convulsive, twist in agonizing folds!' "

He went on to repeat in his fine way the whole of the passage and finally persuaded me to commit my whole stock of worms to the bosom of the great mother from which they were taken, and to make him a kind of promise that if I continued to follow the profitless diversion of angling, I would do it in a less exceptionable manner.

Other instances of similar behaviour about this time fell under my observation. At one time I saw him buy a supper from a butcher for a strange dog that had come into the village, a lame, half-starved, snappish tyke whose bad manners, my friend said, were evidently owing to his having nothing in his stomach. On another occasion he gave a wagoner a crown for lightening a load apparently too heavy for his horses. But what most surprised me was the equanimity with which he bore all kinds of reproaches. I once saw him stopped in the street by a person of rather decent appearance, who appeared to enter immediately into earnest and rapid conversation, and as I came up I could perceive that he was censuring him, for some action of his, in terms of greater severity than were exactly consistent with good breeding. Medfield answered him mildly, which appeared only to exasperate him the more, and he replied with a torrent of abuse and malediction. My own blood, I confess, was hot with indignation at such epithets applied to my friend, but Medfield heard them with as much serenity as if he had been listening to his own praises until, finding that the man would hearken to no explanation, he put his arm within mine and walked away.

"Poor fellow," said he, "I cannot greatly blame him. He thinks himself injured by an act which I was obliged to perform as a magistrate some years since, and now whenever he sees me, which is not often, he makes a point of telling me, as he says, 'what he thinks of me.' I only wish that the composure with which I hear his opinion of me did not irritate him so much."

One day I took the liberty of remarking to my friend upon the peculiarity of character indicated by the examples I have already mentioned. He acknowledged immediately that his humanity might seem in many instances overstrained and excessive, and sometimes perhaps affected.

"It is, however, no virtue of mine," continued he, "if a virtue it be, for I cannot do otherwise than practise it. I have been disciplined to it by a mysterious cause apparent to no one but myself. You have been witness to so many of my actions, which must have struck you as exceedingly singular, that I have been thinking I ought, as a matter of justice to myself, to give you the explanation of my behaviour. I have deferred it the longer on account of the unpleasant nature of some of the incidents of my story, and perhaps, after all, it may not be worthy of your attention."

I assured Mr. Medfield, with perfect truth, that I should be not only a willing, but an interested listener, and that I should hardly forgive him were he not now to gratify the curiosity he had excited.

"By what I am about to relate," said he, "I run the risk of losing ground in your good opinion. I wish you therefore to understand, once for all, that I am naturally by no means a credulous or superstitious man. On the contrary, my disposition has always been to examine and to doubt, rather than to admit and believe. An early fondness for mathematical studies gave my mind the habit of insisting, even too much perhaps for the common purposes of life, on strict demonstration of whatever was proposed for my belief. I took delight in sifting the grounds of a received opinion and rejecting it peremptorily when it seemed to me supported by incomplete evidence. On some knotty and controverted points I merely contented myself, like the worthy Bishop Watson, with keeping my opinion in suspense, but my general inclination was to believe too little rather than too much. If, therefore, any parts of my narrative should strike you as incredible, you will do me the justice to suppose that the incidents which you find too extraordinary for belief appeared as repugnant to my notions of the laws of nature as they now do to yours, and that it was only on testimony too strong to be resisted that I acquiesced in the idea that they were not a delusion.

"About five years ago I was in many respects a different man from what you find me at present. At that time I was the husband of a most beautiful and gentle woman, and the father of a little daughter of three years of age, the loveliest of children. I was a man of strong passions, and a temper that brooked no control and kindled at the slightest opposition. I was allowed to be generous, and my generosity gained me many friends, but I often lost them by that fierce and imperious temper. If an insult was offered me, I returned it with insults still more intolerable; I repaid scorn by bitterer scorn; I yielded every thing to humble entreaty, but nothing to a frank and bold claim of right, however just. These peculiarities of manners and character I was, however, by no means disposed to tolerate in others; nothing so soon roused my indignation as any conduct which exhibited them, and I was instantly on terms of hostility with any one who had the misfortune to resemble me in this respect. In short I was one of those men of whom if the whole world were composed, society would be a state of perpetual warfare, or at best an armed truce, and who are only tolerated because on important occasions their pugnacious spirit may be turned to use, and because in matters of minor importance the prudent and peaceable part of the community find it a lesser evil to let them have their way than to wrangle with them to prevent it.

"My wife lamented this defect in my character and endeavoured to persuade me to correct it, but in vain. She produced some impression, however, when she showed me how my little daughter, whom I loved with a doting fondness, and who also really bore to me a strong affection, shrunk and trembled before me when in my sterner moods, and a glow of shame came over my cheek when I witnessed that look of terror in the countenance of so artless and innocent a being – and of terror at me. The manners which could produce such an effect, I felt, must be essentially unamiable and repulsive, but this reflection was followed by no material amendment.

"My little daughter died, the sweetest blossom ever mown down by the scythe of death, and my wife in a little time followed her. On her death-bed she desired all to withdraw but myself.

" 'My dear Charles,' said she, 'I have a last request to make of your kindness. If you grant it, I shall die in peace.'

"Such an appeal could not be resisted; I answered that the request should be fulfilled if it was within the compass of human power.

" 'It may cost you some effort,' returned she, 'but you will make it, I am persuaded, both for my sake and your own. Promise me that you will keep a strict watch against that severity and impetuosity of temper which make you less useful and less beloved in the world than the qualities of your mind and heart would otherwise make you.'

"I made the promise in sincerity of heart and in tears.

"Her remains were laid beside those of her little daughter, and I was left the prey of a grief which I will not attempt to describe. So strong was the feeling of desolation which took possession of me that it sometimes actually seemed to me as if that it was I who had died, and that I had been translated to another world: strange, cold, and lonely, and haunted by the tormenting remembrance of enjoyments fled for ever. The proud, stern manners of my prosperous days at first prevented any sympathy with my affliction, but mankind are good-natured; I at least have found them so, since they bore so patiently with my caprices and tallies; and at last, when they saw the sincerity, the depth, the extremity of my sorrow, their behaviour towards me became visibly kinder and more considerate.

"For awhile this sorrow absorbed every other feeling, and the usual violence and haughtiness of my temper seemed to be subdued; but life has its duties and its cares, which none of us are at liberty to decline, and to which we must all return from the seclusion of mourning. As I again came forth into the world, I began to assume my former manners.

"Before my late calamity I had consented to become a candidate for a public office. I was now attacked in a newspaper with that coarse invective too much indulged in by the press of this country; allusions the most unwarrantable and unjustifiable were made to my personal character and history; and actions the most innocent were, by an artful mixture of truth and falsehood, perverted into crimes. I was fiercely indignant; I knew that the shaft came from the hand of a rival candidate, and I resolved that I would send it back to his bosom with tenfold force. I went into my study, and with the obnoxious article before me, sat down to pen a reply which my adversary must feel if the sense of indignity were not extinct within him. I had already written part of an article, intended for publication, in which I briefly and explicitly disclaimed the charges brought against me, and I now proceeded to retort the attack. Already thoughts and feelings of supreme and intensest scorn filled my mind; the fitting words came crowding to my pen – phrases of the bitterest derision, coined by my very heart – when I felt a touch softly laid on my right arm. I started, and looked round me, but saw nothing. Again I began to write, and again the touch was felt – more strongly than before; again I started, rose, and surveyed the room, but it contained no living thing except myself. A third time I began, and a third time I felt that mysterious prepare. The table at which I was writing stood not far from the window, but at such a distance that I could not easily be reached by an arm from without. The door was closed, and there was no furniture in the room under which a person could effectually conceal himself. Going to the door, I opened it, and looked in every direction, but saw no one; I listened attentively for the sound of retreating footsteps, but heard only the chirp of grasshoppers in the summer-noon.

"Returning to my study, I carefully scanned a second time every corner of the apartment, removed the table further from the window, and again sat myself down to write. I mused a while to recover the train of ideas which the interruption had caused me to lose; and when I had done so, again attempted to proceed. Before I had finished a single sentence, I felt on the hand which was employed in guiding the pen a distinct, palpable pressure, but at the same time a gentle and delicate one, as if the fingers of a female hand were laid on my own. It was impossible to resist the inclination to turn my head and to inspect narrowly the room around me in order to be certain whether any person was standing by my side or behind me. There was no one – all was silence and emptiness. I strove again to write – the pressure grew firmer. I brought my left hand over and passed it along the back of my right – my hair rose on end – and my blood grew cold in my veins, when I seemed to feel an invisible human hand lying closely on mine. With a convulsive start I dropped the pen, and my hand was instantly released. You may well suppose that I was now in a state of mind which unfitted me from proceeding with the article, even if I had not been restrained by the dread of that mysterious interposition.

"The more I reflected on that incident, the more it embarrassed me. I laboured to convince myself that the sensation I had experienced was owing to some outward cause, independent of the state of my mind, but I was unable satisfactorily to account for it in this manner. That it was an illusion arising from the state of high mental excitement in which I was while writing the article was a supposition which, independent of other considerations, my pride would not suffer me to embrace. I determined, therefore, to settle the point for myself by the fullest and most deliberate examination.

The next day I went again into my study, closed carefully the door and windows, looked under the table and examined the room thoroughly to satisfy myself that no person was concealed there. I then sat down to the table, took up the unfinished manuscript, and beginning where I had broken off the day before, proceeded to complete it. In a moment I perceived the well-known pressure of the arm, slight and gentle at first - then firmer - but I disregarded it and continued to write. Then came the sense of compression and restraint on the fingers of my right hand which I had experienced the day previous, and which now impeded their motion. Applying my left hand to the investigation, I found a set of fingers passing over and clasping my own. I subjected, to the examination of the touch, finger after finger, and joint after joint of that invisible hand; it was delicately moulded, the fingers were tapering, plump and soft, the articulations small and feminine, and it was joined to a round and slender wrist, but beyond that I could feel nothing. I attempted to scrutinize it with my eye, but the sight could not shape for it even the faintest and most shadowy outline. I bowed my forehead towards it, and touched flesh that was not my own. You may judge of the feeling of awe which filled my mind while I was making this investigation. At length, with a shudder, I quitted my grasp of the pen, and immediately I perceived that the invisible hand was gone.

"My perplexity was now greater than ever. I had hoped that a deliberate and careful examination would have dispelled the mystery, but it ended in setting the evidence of my senses, or rather of one of them, in opposition to the conclusions of my reason. Was I to believe or to distrust that evidence? Was not what I had experienced a reality to me, a substantial verity, whatever it might be, or appear, to the rest of the world? Then, as to the agent in this mysterious interposition, could it be that the spirit of her to whom I had given the solemn promise of watching over my temper was permitted to remind me of the obligation I had taken by this appeal to my outward sense? Must I believe what was so repugnant to the whole tenor of my previous opinions? I determined a third time to make the experiment, and it was followed by precisely the same result as in the instances I have already related. Taking the unfinished paper in my hands, I tore it in pieces, and abandoned my design of replying to the attack which had been made upon me.

"For several days the strange event which had happened afforded me food for reflection - reflection deep, continual, absorbing. Firm as were the convictions of my reason that the spiritual part of our nature cannot, without the help of material organs, act upon the perceptions of one to whom it does not belong, I could not, I would not believe, that what I had witnessed was owing to a cause above nature. Still, the uniform recurrence of the same sensation, under the same circumstances, perplexed and confounded me. To divert my thoughts from this subject, I took my fishing-rod and strolled out to the fine noisy brook that flows through my farm. It was a beautiful day in July: the sun was warm, but not powerful, and clouds were now and then floating lazily over his orb. As I approached the stream, which hurried from one clump of softly-waving trees to another, I thought of the lines in the "Castle of Indolence":

> — Softly stealing, with your watery gear.
> Along the brooks, the crimson spotted fry
> You may delude-the while amused you hear
> Now the hoarse stream, and now the zephyr's sigh,
> Attuned to the birds and woodland melody.

"I felt a sort of relief from the images of mingled motion and repose, of activity and ease, of change without effort, which belong to a fine day in this fine season of the year, and my mind began to partake, in some sort, of the serenity of the scene around me. Standing on the green bank in the shade of a thicket, I dropped my line into the water. It was a clear and glassy little pool of the brook, save at the upper end where it was agitated with the current that fell into it over a mossy rock, and I saw the fish playing in its transparent depths, noiselessly, and with that easy, graceful motion which belongs to most creatures of their element. I was leaning intently forward, waiting for one of them to approach the fatal hook, when I felt a touch, a distinct touch, laid on my right arm.

"So unexpected was this, in the silence and quiet and utter solitude of the scene around me and in the pursuit of amusement which I had never regarded as otherwise than innocent - and so irritable had my nervous system become in consequence of the late extraordinary incidents – that I started at the sensation with the quickness of lightning, wheeling suddenly to the right and jerking involuntarily the line from the water. There was nothing in sight that could have touched me – and the only living sound to be heard was my own hard breathing through distended nostrils, mingling with the murmurs of the water and the sighs of the wind. For a while I stood lost in astonishment, but at length recovering, I searched the thicket in the shade of which I stood to discover whether it concealed any person who was idle enough to amuse himself in this manner at my expense. In this search I was, as usual, unsuccessful.

"I sat on the bank a while to recover my composure. 'I must not,' said I to myself, 'leave the cause of this interruption in uncertainty. I will, if possible, discover whether it be accidental, or whether it be of the same nature with what I have experienced in other instances.' Accordingly I arose and again swung the bait over the stream and suffered it to sink into the water. At that instant I felt the monitory touch on my right arm just above the elbow. Turning my head in that direction, I suffered the butt-end of the fishing-rod to press against my breast, keeping firm hold of it with my right hand only and applying my left to the spot where I felt the pressure. There I found the same invisible hand which I had so closely examined the day previous, the same delicate and tapering fingers, gently yet firmly grasping my arm. I threw away my fishing-rod and have never attempted the sport of angling since. The admonition I had received, whether real or imaginary, induced a train of reflections which brought me to the conclusion that, however justifiable it may be as an occupation, it cannot be defended as an amusement.

"It was at this time that a view of the subject occurred to my mind which, at length, more than any thing else decided my opinion. Of all our senses the touch is the least liable to delusion or mistake. It is the most direct of all our channels of perception; it brings its objects to the closest and minutest scrutiny; it is the least under the control of the imagination, the least liable to be acted upon by delicate and evanescent influences. I never heard of an instance in which the touch became subject to an illusion while the eye remained faithful to reason and the truth of things. In all the idle and silly stories of ghosts and apparitions, in which I believe as little as you do, the supposed supernatural visiter always addresses itself to the eye or the ear; the haunted person sees its form or distinguishes its voice; he rarely ever feels its substance. The spirit is generally said to elude the touch; a blow passes through it as through empty air, the arms stretched to embrace it meet in the midst of its shadowy outlines. The touch is the test by which we prove the truth of the information furnished us by the other senses, and in its decisions the mind acquiesces with undoubting confidence. So universally and fully is this axiom admitted that some of the commonest phrases in our own and other languages are founded upon it. When we speak of palpable truth, or truth demonstrated by the touch, we mean reality which admits of no dispute; while to the unsubstantial pictures of the imagination which impose upon us by the mere semblance of reality, we give the name of visions, or things apparent to the sight only.

"True it was that in my own case I had the testimony of but one of my senses, but it was that sense which corrects the errors of the others, and which is never deceived alone. Had the others concurred with it, my perplexity, I thought, would have been less. Had those fallible, organs, the eye and the ear, presented to me the one a definite form, and the other an audible voice, I might have concluded that what wore the appearance of a supernatural interposition was but the hallucination of disturbed nerves, or the phantom of a disordered mind, and I might have inferred that the touch was deceived by a natural sympathy with the other senses. But now my case admitted of no such explanation.

"I again recurred to the arguments which were familiar to me, and which had hitherto appeared to my mind conclusive against the sensible interference of the spirits of the departed in matters of human action. Shall I confess to you that they appeared to me to have lost somewhat of their force when I considered the question as one of experience and testimony? The moral purposes which such an interference might serve were apparent; and was it not, I asked myself, as presumptuous in the philosophers of this age to say that they were contrary to the laws of nature as it would be, in a generation during whose existence a comet had never appeared, to deny that such bodies, eccentric as were their courses, belonged to the system of the universe?

"I see that you do not agree with me; well, I pray that you may never have reason to do so from your own experience. Do not mistake me, however; I did not immediately pass from disbelief to credulity. I was determined to keep my opinion in suspense until the number and uniformity of instances should leave me no other way of accounting for what had happened than by ascribing it to a cause above nature.

"The incidents I have related took place in solitude, in places and at moments when there was no one to witness the effect they produced upon me; but I was now to experience the same extraordinary interposition in the midst of a crowd of my fellow-men. In the election to which I have already alluded, I had been unsuccessful, principally, I believe, on account of the unpopularity of my manners. My antagonist, the writer of the attack on me in the public prints, who was all smiles and suavity, was returned by a large majority. I had some friends, however, who adhered to me firmly, and who wished to give me a testimony of their respect by the customary compliment of a public dinner. This I declined, alleging, as a principal reason, my late domestic calamities, but offered to meet them in another manner at any time they might appoint. A day was fixed upon, and I made my appearance before an assembly of those who had given me their suffrages. If you have never been a candidate at a country election you can have no idea of the warmth of that feeling of good-will and confidence which subsists between the candidate and his supporters – the hardy, intelligent, independent masters and cultivators of the soil. I looked round on their strong-featured, sunburnt, honest faces, and shook their hard hands with a pleasure which I cannot describe.

"In obedience to the general expectation, I addressed the meeting. I thanked my friends for the zeal they had shown in my behalf; fruitless though it had been, it gave them no less a claim on my gratitude than if it had been attended with the accident of success. I alluded to the accusations which had been brought against me – slanders worthy, I said, of the source from which they had proceeded. I vindicated myself from them briefly and concisely, for I was anxious to arrive at a point in my discourse on which I intended to dilate more at length – namely, the conduct of my antagonist and his party. Having come to this topic, I felt myself inspired by that degree of excitement which gives force and fluency of language and the power of moving the minds of others, and I thought to utter things which should be remembered, and repeated, and felt by those against whom they were leveled.

I had already begun my philippic, and was proceeding with a raised voice and some vehemence of gesture, when I felt myself plucked by the sleeve. Pausing for an instant, I looked round, but saw no one who touched, or appeared to have touched me. I proceeded, and the signal was repeated. It occurred to me that there was probably some creature of my adversary near me who wanted to interrupt and confuse me, and I cast brief and fierce glances to the right and the left, which made my worthy friends who stood near me recede with looks of anxiety and almost of alarm. Again I began, raising my arm as I spoke, but at that moment it seemed clogged with the weight of a mill-stone and fell powerless to my side.

"Eager only to proceed, and careless from what quarter the interruption might come, provided I got clear of it, I made a strong effort to shake off the encumbrance, raising at the same time my voice and attempting to finish in a full sonorous tone the sentence I had begun. Instantly I felt at my throat a cold rigid grasp, as of a hand of iron – a grasp quite different from the gentle and apparently kind pressure I had sometimes before experienced, choking the voice as it issued from my lungs and forcing me down into my seat. So completely had I been absorbed in the subject of my harangue that I did not, until the moment that I found myself in my chair, conjecture the real cause of the interruption. The idea then flashed upon my mind that this was an interference of the same nature with that which had withheld me from replying to the newspaper attack of my antagonist. My emotions of awe, alarm, and discouragement at this stern and mysterious rebuke were overpowering, and it was with difficulty that I collected myself sufficiently to whisper to a friend who was near me, requesting him to apologize, as well as the case would admit, for my inability to proceed. He arose and attributed what had happened, I believe, to a sudden indisposition, while I retired hastily from the assembly.

"Arriving at my house, I gave myself up to various and distracting reflections, asked myself whether I, who had ever prided myself on my superiority to vulgar prejudices and superstitions, who had scoffed at stories of supernatural visitations, must now surrender myself to the belief that the ordinary laws of nature were daily broken for my sake, and that I was the object of constant solicitude and care to a being of the other world, who was disquieted for me in the midst of that eternal repose prepared for the spirits of the good? Was not this interference of such a nature as to destroy all liberty of action, and to reduce me to a state little short of servitude? Was I to be withstood even in obeying the instinct of self-defence which forms a part of the moral constitution of all the nobler animal existences, and which was so emphatically a part of my own? Could it be the will of the Supreme Father, could it be the desire of the loved and lost one, whom haply he permitted to return to this world in order to watch over and admonish me, that I should be reduced to a pusillanimous passive being, submitting tamely to every injury, and leading a life of mere sufferance and inaction, like the plants of the soil or the animals who are but a degree above them?

"I did not at that time reflect – I did not even know how little the utmost malice of slander avails against an established reputation for integrity – how the plain tale of the honest man, related without passion, puts down the foul calumny of the unprincipled, and how little it gains, or rather how much it loses, by being coupled with a retaliatory attack, with words of anger and phrases of vituperation.

"This restraint upon what seemed to me the necessary liberty of a rational being, this hindrance in the way of actions which I esteemed justifiable and laudable, raised my impatience to a tremendous pitch. I walked my room rapidly until the sweat started from every pore; I chafed like a wild beast caught in the toils. What is life, said I to myself, if it is to be held on these conditions? To suffer every indignity from your enemy, and when you strive to repel him, to be smitten with impotence, and to retire with defeat, disappointment, and shame from the contest – nay, more, to be bound hand and foot, and thrown in his path to be buffeted and trampled on, without escape, and without redress. Even if the interference were to a good end, of what value is the virtue which is the fruit solely of coercion? What merit is there in not doing what I am continually struggling to do, and find myself restrained?

"Several days and nights passed away in a state of sleepless dejection, from wounded pride, impatience of restraint, and the perplexity arising from the unresolved mystery of my condition. When I went out, I observed that men seemed to look at me with an air of curiosity, as upon one to whom something extraordinary had happened; and it was manifest that my appearance furnished them with a new topic of conversation. I was wasted almost to a shadow, and I started when I saw myself in the glass, so pale, emaciated, and hollow-eyed. My friends entreated me to take exercise, and I was persuaded to provide myself with a horse, a fleet animal in the harness which the man who brought him to me assured me, honestly enough, was the best creature in the world, bating some caprices of temper which only required a little wholesome castigation. 'When the horse refuses to go,' said he, you have nothing to do but to take a whip and whip the devil out of him.'

"The horse was put into a light sulky, and I drove out daily. The rapid motion, and the quick succession of objects, were a sensible relief to the gloomy monotony of my reflections. My excursions comprehended a considerable extent of country lying in the sober and mature beauty of September, and the deep hush of the scene and the season began to communicate somewhat of a correspondent tranquillity to my feelings. My horse had as yet shown none of the caprices of which the seller had given me notice, and I began to think that they were occasioned merely by unskilful management on his part, when at length, one day as I was returning in some haste from a morning drive of greater length than usual, he gave me a specimen of his humours. All at once he stopped short in the middle of the road. I shook the reins over his neck, cracked the whip about his ears, touched him with the end of the lash, spoke to him, chirrupped, whistled and used every means of encouragement and stimulus usual in such cases, but in vain. The only effect they had was to make the animal break, at times, into a short bouncing gallop which he performed with such a wonderful economy of space as not to get forward more than a rod in a minute. I had engaged a friend to dine with me that day, and remembering the prescription of the owner of the horse, I got out of my carriage in no little indignation to 'whip the devil out of him.'

"I struck him smartly with the lash, and as I did so I felt the monitory pressure on my arm, but I paid no attention to it at the time, thinking it occasioned by some accidental entanglement of the reins which I was holding. The animal answered the blow by running a few steps backward. Taking the whip in my left hand, I wound the lash spirally round the handle, and restoring it to the right, I raised it to deal a series of heavier and severer blows with the stock, but immediately I perceived a force which I could not resist pulling it down to my side. Shuddering, I desisted from my intention, and after a pause of a few moments, to recover from the shock caused by this new interposition, I took the animal by the bridle to lead him forwards; he obeyed the motion without hesitation, and after leading him a few rods I again got into the carriage, and he proceeded at his usual pace.

"After this I took little pleasure in my rides, in consequence of the perpetual apprehension of a check from my invisible monitor, fearing as I did to urge my horse beyond his voluntary speed, lest I should incur a repetition of these ghostly admonitions of which I now entertained a kind of nervous dread, and which, instead of becoming more indifferent to them as they grew more frequent, I only regarded, with greater terror. Instead of driving out, therefore, I began to take long walks, wandering into unfrequented places, traversing forests, and climbing mountains.

It was a fine season, about the beginning of October; a few light early frosts had fallen, the days were soft and sunny, and the woods glorious with the splendours of their annual decay. My walks, begun at early sunrise, were often protracted to nightfall. Sometimes I carried a fowling-piece, but I had not yet thought of using it, when once straying into a deep unfrequented wood, I observed, not far distant from me, sitting on the prostrate trunk of a tree, a partridge or pheasant ~ as it is differently called in this country, though like neither of the birds known in England by these names.

"The shy and beautiful bird, unaware of my near approach, yet roused to attention by the rustling of the leaves, stood with his crested head and ruffed neck erect, as if listening to the sound in order to determine whether it boded danger. I raised my fowling-piece to my eye and levelled it, and immediately I felt the muzzle drawn towards the ground as if loaded with a sudden weight. I raised it again, taking fresh aim, but before I could discharge the piece, it was drawn downwards a second time. Was this the effect of an excited imagination, or of my own want of skill, or was it in fact a supernatural admonition? The worst certainly could not be so painful as this state of doubt; and in conformity with the habit and inclination of my mind, I instantly resolved that I would obtain all the certainty of which the case admitted. Kneeling down, therefore, I rested my fowling-piece on a log which lay before me, and placing my hands, one on the stock and the other under the lock, with forefinger on the trigger, I directed the muzzle towards the object. Before I could take accurate aim, I felt my right arm suddenly pulled back, the piece was discharged, and the ball passed over the head of the bird, which, spreading its mottled wings, rose with a whirr from the ground, and flying a few rods, alighted and ran from my sight.

"Here was what appeared to me a clear interposition of some external power which had caused me to discharge the piece before I was prepared. But who or what was the agent by whom I had been restrained? In the present case it was an interposition of benevolence, and effected its end by mild methods. But what was I to think of the chill and iron grasp which had stifled my utterance, and nearly deprived me of the breath of life when I strove to speak in my own defence? And in what light should I regard the force which but a day or two previous had struck my arm powerless to my side? Could it be that the gentle being who once shared my fortunes was the agent of such violence – or was another employed in the ungrateful task of subduing my more obstinate moods, while to her was left the care of admonishing me by light pressures and soft touches of her own delicate hand?

"There was nothing less fitted to awaken or keep up the idea of communication with the supernatural world than the aspect of nature around me. The woods were all yellow with autumn, or rather the prevailing colour was a bright golden tinge, here and there interspersed with flushes of crimson, purple, and orange. There was no shadow throughout this wide extent of forest – at least there appeared to be none, for the light came through the semi-transparent leaves, or was reflected from their glowing surfaces, with the same golden hue as when it left the orb of the sun. It was a scene of universal warmth and cheerfulness. In the broad glare of the common sunshine, to an imagination excited by the idea of a spectral visitant, the sight of one's own shadow keeping pace with him and mimicking all his actions has something in it actually frightful. The wild motions of the clouds also, on a stormy day, have the same effect; and from the uncertain outlines of things seen by a feeble light, the alarmed fancy shapes for itself images of terror. But here was no shadow, no dimness; all was brightness and glory around me. Yet even here, said I to myself, alone as I seem, I have my companions. Invisible beings are ever at my side; they glide with me among the trunks of these trees; they float on the soft pulsations of the air which detach the yellow leaves from the boughs; they watch every motion of my frame, and every word of my lips. Never was prisoner, suspected of having formed a plan to escape from his captivity, so vigilantly guarded and observed.

"As I walked slowly homeward, I came to an opening in the forest on the top of a little eminence, where I stopped and turned to take a last look of the sun as he descended. His mild golden rays were streaming with a sweet and sleepy languor, as if the lids of that great eye of heaven were half-closed over it, softening but not veiling its brightness, while beneath, the earth slept in Sabbath stillness, as if yielding itself up to the sole enjoyment of that genial splendour. I sighed as I thought of the contrast thus presented between my own enthralled and agitated spirit and the repose and liberty of every thing around me. As I proceeded, sunset came on, and twilight stole over the woods. Sometimes I passed through a gloomy thicket of evergreens, and as darkness always heightens the feeling of the marvellous, I almost expected to descry some dim half-defined form in the shadow, the visible presentation of my ghostly attendant. I saw, however, nothing; powerfully as I had been affected by the incident I have just related, my imagination refused to body forth a visionary shape from the indistinct outlines of things around me; but I reached home in state of extreme excitement.

"I went to my chamber, but I was too much agitated to think of sleep. For hours I paced the floor, revolving in my mind circumstances of the mysterious visitation of which I was the subject. I watched the moon as she rose, and saw her climb the zenith, and I said to myself, though half ashamed of the thought, 'Will not the dead of night, the witching hour at which our forefathers believed the dead were permitted to leave their graves and walk the earth visible to men, show me the form of that being which keeps perpetual watch over me? Must even the light of the moon, powerful as it is to endue things with strange shapes – that light which the Mantuan poet called malignant from its being peopled with terrifying phantoms – show me only the accustomed and familiar objects of day? Shall I never be permitted to behold the external shape of the mysterious existence which so often manifests itself to another of my senses that I may determine with more certainty its nature, and whether its interposition be for good or evil? But it must be for good, for it interposes only to prevent some act of cruelty or passion.'

"These reflections, it will easily be imagined, did not dispose me to slumber. It was not until the stars began to grow pale that a sense of fatigue compelled me to throw myself on the bed, nor even then were my eyes soon closed in sleep. It was late, however, very late when I awoke, the light streaming into my windows pained my eyes as I opened them. My black man – an honest, faithful creature who had grown old in the family of my wife's father, and whom at her request I had taken into my service – was just opening the door.

" 'What o'clock is it?' said I." 'Look at my watch on the table.'

"He took up the watch, but appeared to find some difficulty in distinguishing the hour.

" 'Hand it to me, you stupid creature,' said I, 'and let me see for myself.'

"I looked at the dial, which informed me that it was half-past ten o'clock.

" 'Rascal!' exclaimed I, 'have you not been positively directed never to neglect calling me at seven o'clock if I were not already up?'

" 'Yes, master, but I thought you might have need of rest. I am certain that I heard master walking his room till very late, and I was afraid he would not like to be disturbed.'

" 'What business had you to set your thoughts or your fears against my orders? How did you know that I had not some appointment to keep, or some important business to transact before this hour? I had actually an appointment, and your negligence has caused me to break it. But I will take care to teach you a lesson that you will remember. Leave the room instantly, call again in half an hour, and I will pay you your wages, and you shall –'

"I was going to add that he should immediately quit my service, but at that moment I felt the bedclothes, which lay across my shoulders and the lower part of my face, pressed over them so tightly and closely, and with such a prodigious weight as to smother my voice, or at least to reduce it to sounds choked and inarticulate. In vain I struggled to free myself; the sheets seemed, as we sometimes fancy them in a fit of the nightmare, to be thick plates of the heaviest and hardest of metals, and lay upon me with an immoveable rigidity. The black man retreated from the room with a face of blank astonishment, but as soon as he was gone, the enormous weight ceased to press upon me, and I again breathed freely. I arose and put on my clothes; in a short time the negro presented himself, and I paid him his wages up to that morning. He looked surprised, but I sent him about some ordinary service, without entering into any explanation.

"It might be thought that these successive admonitions, manifest as their design had become, would have made me cautious of transgressing the bounds of a just moderation of temper and have restrained me from every act bordering on inhumanity. I was not yet, however, wholly cured. One day, as I was returning from one of my usual walks, I chanced to pass by a farm of which I was the proprietor. I had been of late so entirely absorbed in other matters that I had not visited it to inspect its condition, but I now observed that the house was in bad repair, the shutters dropping from the hinges, the windows broken and patched with rags, and the fences everywhere falling down. The tenant had taken the farm on condition of rendering me half the annual product. The portion I had already received was not equal to my expectations, and the autumnal crops, then ready for gathering, exposed as they were to the depredations of animals, I thought would be little or nothing.

"I sent for the man as soon as I got home. He made no haste to come; but in a day or two, after a second message, he deigned to make his appearance. He was a stout, broad-shouldered, dark-complexioned man, with a blackguard cast of the eye, and a resolute demeanour. His beard was of some ten days' growth; he wore a tattered hat and an old greatcoat tied round his middle with a fragment of an old silk handkerchief. In short, he had every mark of being an idle, saucy, good-for-nothing fellow, and a very unpromising subject for a quarrel.

" 'Johnston,' said I to him, 'I fear you do not keep your farm in the best order.'

" 'I do the best I can, squire,' was the laconic answer.

" 'But I saw the fences down the other day, and observed strange cattle feeding in my meadows and spoiling the next year's crop of grass.'

" 'I have nothing to do with the next year's crop, squire, till I know whether I am to stay another year on the place.'

" 'That you may know from this moment. Your lease is from the twentieth of November to the twentieth of November, so you may make up your mind to leave the premises the very day your lease expires, for I am determined that so worthless a tenant shall remain on the farm no longer.'

"The man laughed in my face. 'I rather guess, squire,' returned he, 'that you will be troubled to git me out quite as soon as you expect. I believe there was no writing in the business; and as for the law about them matters, I know what it is as well as you, for I heard the judge lay it down once in court. No, squire, I thank you; I shall not budge a foot; I shall stay in that house for the winter. I will not be turned out, wife and children and all, in the cold weather, just because you ha'n't made so much money by me as you meant to do – and what is more, you can't turn me out. I know what the law is as well as you.'

"I was provoked beyond measure at the man's insolence. 'Scoundrel!' said I; 'do you set me at defiance? Did I not put you on that farm out of charity?'

" 'And now you would turn me into the street to starve - out of charity, I s'pose. There is just as much charity in one ease as in the other. I was needy, and you thought to take advantage of my situation for your own profit; you have been disappointed, and now you want to be rid of me.'

" 'Fellow,' said I to Johnston, 'your dishonesty and ingratitude are bad enough, but your ill-manners are past all bearing. Leave the house instantly.'

"I shall never forget the look of cool impudence which the man gave me as he answered that, having come at my request on a of business, he should not think of taking his leave until it was settled; that he was no lackey of mine, to come and go at my bidding, and that having entered the house by my special invitation, he should take his own time for leaving it.

"Then I must endeavour to quicken your speed,' said I, reaching my hand to the wall near me, where hung a large horsewhip with which, in the extremity of my anger, I resolved to chastise the insolence of the plebeian. Immediately I felt a soft pressure on the wrist, as if a gentle hand strove to detain my awn. This was no time, however - nor was I in a mood - to be withheld from my purpose by any thing short of irresistible force. There stood the insolent and ragged rascal who had provoked me, who had thrown off his great-coat and stood in the only garments left, a tattered shirt and pantaloons, placing himself in an attitude of defence, looking as if ready to spring upon me and watching me with a quick eye and a determined look, which, however, indicated no more passion than might give firmness to his purpose and vigour to its execution.

I broke impatiently from the soft restraint which impeded me, raised my hand to the whip, seized it, and had already lifted it over Johnston's head when I felt my arm suddenly arrested by a firm, rigid, painful grasp. I strove to move forward, but could not: it seemed as if every part of my frame was imprisoned with bars and shackles of iron; I felt them on my breast, my sides, my arms, and my thighs. No words can describe the tumult of feelings in my bosom - indignation, surprise, disappointment, all wrought to the highest pitch, and all subsiding into horror. Johnston, who was waiting to repel and return my blow, and who evidently intended to fell me to the earth, if possible, had I struck him, grew pale as he looked at me, and walked away, turning once or twice as he left the room to fix his eyes upon me. I heard afterward that he had acknowledged that, fearless as he was, the expression of my countenance daunted him – with such a frightful and demoniac energy did it speak of the violent passions which raged within me.

"I was now left alone, but not as formerly was I released as soon as the occasion for restraint had ceased. On the contrary, the rigid pressure still continued to impede my motions on every side. My left hand, however, was at liberty, and as somewhat of my presence of mind returned, I began to investigate the nature of the strange invisible shackles which confined me. That powerful grasp was still on my tight arm. I searched it – it was not a hand of flesh – I felt the cold-articulations of a skeleton. The gentle being who had given me the first admonition had resigned me for the time to severer guardianship. I endeavoured to move my hand forward and towards either side; – it was obstructed by a kind of irregular lattice-work which, on [my] examining it closely, proved to be the bones of a skeleton. I felt the parallel ribs; I passed my hand through them and touched the column of the spine. Words cannot describe my horror. I did not swoon; I did not lose consciousness; but with dilated eyes and erected hair and cold shudderings passing over my whole frame, I explored the mysterious objects which surrounded me; I continued the examination until not a doubt remained, and I came to the conclusion that I was surrounded by a group of skeletons, one of which held my arm, and another clasped me in its horrible embraces. Shortly afterward my arm was released – the stricture around my chest was gone, and I could move my limbs without difficulty. In a state of extreme exhaustion, I sank down upon the nearest seat.

"My incredulity with respect to these interpositions had previously to this, as I think I have intimated, been overcome, and it now remained for me to consider whether I would incur a repetition of such admonitions as the last, administered doubtless in that terrible manner because it was manifest that milder means had no effect upon me. I began to watch all my actions and words, to abstain from the utterance of every thing unkind or angry and from the doing of every thing which could give pain to a living creature. I have in some measure reaped the reward of my circumspection in the complacent feeling which attends the overcoming of temptation, or, in perhaps better phrase, the sense of gratitude at having been preserved from odious and mischievous actions. My life has since been passed with great tranquillity, though still saddened with the memory of my loss. Yet I confess to you that with this perpetual restraint upon my actions, this sense of a presence which checks and chastises what is wrong, I am far from happy. I feel like a captive in chains, and my spirit yearns after its former freedom, My sole desire and hope is that, by a patient submission to the guidance appointed me, I may become fitted for a state where liberty and virtue are the same, and where in following the rules of duty we shall only pursue a natural and unerring inclination."

Here Medfield ended. I endeavoured to reason with him on the subject of his story, and to show him that what he had experienced was only a delusion of the imagination, a monomania, as it is termed by the physicians – though I did not venture to call it by that name – a diseased relation between the mind and one of the senses, to which a man of the soundest and clearest judgment might be subject.

He heard me for a little while, and then interrupting me, said, "All that you say is only what has occurred to my own mind. I am willing to believe you as ingenious in argument as most men, but I can scarcely suppose that you will advance any thing new in favour of incredulity on this point, which I have not already considered, and to which I did not sedulously endeavour to allow its utmost weight. It was all in vain. Skeptical as I naturally was on such subjects, I could not bring myself to set aside the evidence of the most scrutinizing and least fallible of our senses, the sense which conveys to us the most certain information of the world about us. You will only weary me by the revival of a dispute which I long ago settled for myself. Let us, my dear sir, talk of something else."

After some conversation on indifferent topics, I parted from Medfield with a full conviction that his melancholy had produced some alienation of mind. I returned in a few days afterward to New-York. In the course of the winter I had a letter from him, somewhat melancholy in its tenor. He spoke of ill-health and impaired spirits, and complained of the monotony and weariness of the season. In the month of June afterward, as I was looking over the columns of a newspaper, I saw announced in the obituary the death of Charles Medfield, of ——————, aged 36 years.

Commentary

A Pennsylvanian Legend

Published at a time when evaluation of fiction seldom extended beyond brief description of content coupled with an adjective or two in summary judgment, Bryant's short stories elicited no critical scrutiny when they first appeared. Later, after he abandoned the genre, they were eclipsed by his reputation as a poet and as the influential, politically powerful owner-editor of the *New York Evening Post*. In the twentieth century, modernism heedlessly devalued his poetry and time's passage faded his journalistic accomplishments, but the stories took the greatest blow: their very existence was virtually forgotten. Even in the decades when academe finally (if grudgingly) bestowed respectability on the study of American literature and its past attracted close reconsideration, Bryant's fiction was ignored. Yet, in their variety, they arguably constitute the most intriguing body of work produced during the first dozen years of an evolving new class of literature.

What slight notice has been paid to Bryant's debut as a story writer owes solely to assumed similarities to Washington Irving's "Rip Van Winkle" – and it has suffered for the comparison. Bryant's biographer, Charles Brown, could not have been more dismissive – or more inaccurate – in invidiously pairing them: "A Pennsylvania [sic] Legend," he supposes, merely "attempted to do for the Pennsylvania Germans what Irving had done for the Dutch in the Catskills." And as imitation, he adds, "it gave neither Irving nor Paulding cause to worry about their public. ... A nation that had taken Rip Van Winkle to their hearts could not do as much by [Bryant's protagonist,] Caspar Buckel." (An odd comment, as Caspar is not meant to be loved.) Was Bryant only applying a different coat of paint to a borrowed Catskills template? Not at all. The two stories are radically dissimilar, as is the function of their settings. For Irving, evoking Rip's life in his Knickerbocker village was crucial; for Bryant, who had not yet crossed the Delaware, the designation of Pennsylvania as a location is arbitrary: the setting is irrelevant.

To distinguish "A Pennsylvanian Legend" from "Rip Van Winkle," however, is not to gainsay that Bryant consciously operated in Irving's wake. Even while Romanticism was gaining adherents during the previous decade, skeptics scoffed at the cry for "Americanness," declaring that our young, practical nation had no instinct for wonder and lacked the shadows of history to stimulate the oneiric imagination. Irving had a decisive effect on overcoming such prejudices. He showed the value of incorporating surroundings into stories and, by treating his characters with wit, managed to situate the Gothic in American settings that lacked remnants of a distant past. Bryant immediately responded to Irving's example, and actually proved more inventive in his exploration of the story form than the man who had inspired him.

"A Pennsylvanian Legend" is unique among Bryant's stories in being cast in the mold of the traditional European folktale. That importation to advance the cause of a singularly American literature of course presents an inescapable irony – and Bryant sports with it in the opening paragraphs. Lamenting the tyranny of rationality and the belief "that the material world is the only world," the narrator recalls the delight in childhood's scares and superstitions, and he draws comfort from their survival through the old German beldams who "tell in the greedy ears of their children the marvellous legends of the country from which they had their origin." But, after acknowledging a debt to Germany, he then feistily dismisses it: "Let the European writer gather up the traditions of his country; I will employ a leisure moment in recording one of the fresher, but not less authentic, legends of ours." That "not less authentic" holds an obviously ambivalent meaning – and Bryant no doubt privately enjoyed the ambiguity. On the one hand, the legend it prefaces is a figment, "authentic" only in its fidelity to the analogous European tradition. On the other – and the more interesting of the two – the "fresher," American version of a German fairy tale is in large measure "authentic" autobiography, in camouflage.

The Buckels, an aristocratic German family who cross the Atlantic to Pennsylvania, parallel the author's antecedents. Like Walter Buckel and his wife, Bryant's parents were "emigrants" – not from Germany as in the tale, of course, but from Bridgewater, a town close by Plymouth, to newly-settled Cummington in the state's northwest corner. The Buckels make much of their "gentle blood"; both sides in Bryant's lineage trace to an American equivalent, Plymouth's Pilgrim settlers. Stephen Bryant arrived in 1632; the Snells, still earlier as part of the original company that sailed on the Mayflower – indeed, the Snell lineage included the storied couple John Alden and Priscilla Mullins. Walter Buckel's description as "a thin, bilious, bustling man [who] went to work in the bitterness and vexation of his heart" points to Ebenezer Snell, the dour, stubborn, combative, and righteous grandfather Bryant remembered all his life with conflicted emotions. More specifically, the date assigned for the Buckels' departure to the New World corresponds to the Snells' relocation in Cummington. But the most persuasive evidence is the name he chose for the fictional family: snell, in American English – particularly in early nineteenth-century New England – referred to a type of buckle.

Such insertion of personal markers is not rare – writers often play secret games simply for private enjoyment – but here the surname's personal reference is compounded in its use as the story's pivotal conceit. Buckel, the author reminds the reader, is German for "hump," and we are then told that the family believes its hereditary humpback manifests its aristocratic superiority. The analogy to Squire Ebenezer Snell's Calvinist convictions of being among God's elect – a presumption reinforced by his relative wealth and his standing as deacon and theological authority of the community's Puritan church – is evident. Peter Bryant evinced a similar pride. A Harvard alumnus and ardent Federalist who, in addition to being a physician, was a master of Greek and Latin, wrote erudite poetry, and possessed an extensive knowledge of botany, Bryant's father was a man of great self assurance not given to suffering fools. Contrary to what one might infer from his subsequent election as his district's representative in the state legislature, he was seen as an alien intruder during his early years in Cummington. Townsmen shrank from what they regarded as an overweening bearing, and, rather like Walter Buckel, he reciprocated by being properly formal toward the more ordinary folk.

Being Peter Bryant's son could not have been easy. Ironically, the sartorially correct "Boston gentleman," described by his son as having "a certain metropolitan air" that bespoke lofty sophistication, fell prey to scandal. Perhaps to rise above his tough-minded father-in-law's disparagement, Peter rejected Squire Snell's warning not to invest in a risky mercantile venture and borrowed large sums of money to increase his stake. The gamble failed; he fled his creditors and went into hiding. Hoping to mitigate his debts, he then signed on as a ship's surgeon. That scheme led to a fiasco when the French seized the ship and detained it for a year in Mauritius. On his return to the United States, only his father-in-law's financial intervention saved him from enduring shame. The tale of the Buckels presents a plausible analogy: the hump they wear with hauteur also makes them the objects of their neighbors' ridicule. Young Cullen might very well have contended with mixed feelings about his similar position.

Once the narrative turns from Walter the father to Caspar the son, the symbolism of the Buckel hump also shifts, from the family's pretensions to the grotesque boy's isolation. Here too, the protagonist corresponds to the author. From the age of four and a half, when Cullen began living in the Snell house, until he entered Williams College, his human contact had mainly been limited to his siblings and adult members of his family. He read prodigiously, both for idle pleasure and to study major works of Western culture. *Robinson Crusoe*, the account of a marooned man who eventually finds one true friend to share his state, was a telling favorite. Asked decades later to reminisce about his boyhood, Bryant wrote that he could not summon the happy memories customary in such retrospection. It may be significant that he suspended the memoir (which was eventually published in *St. Nicholas Magazine*).Though hardly a chronicle of Dickensian horrors, it revisited a conspicuously solitary existence.

A painful episode during Bryant's late adolescence may have triggered the story's plot. He was seventeen when a prominent Rhode Islander arrived in Cummington on a visit to his father. Cullen met the daughter and was smitten. How far his infatuation reached and to what extent she encouraged it is unknown, but passions ignited and poetic surrender to her "syren's song" filled envelopes for about two years. Then, as often happens in the course of young love, something happened: his affection, he wrote to her, had crashed on the rocks of her "fraud and guile and faithless art." In the tale, the comely Adelaide Sippel responds to Casper's overture to wooing her by laughing in his face and mocking the hump with a carved mangel-wortzel copy of it.

The story's next phase continues to draw from its author's life. Cullen's first home in Cummington was a rough-hewn log cabin overlooking a stony brook at the hamlet's edge and flanked by one of the many red oaks that still dot the area's meadows. When he was three and a half, the family moved to a second Cummington home, and just short of a year later, to another, two-thirds of a mile away, owned by his grandfather. Although his parents lived in the house and his father contributed financially to a remodeling for a medical office and more private quarters for his family, Squire Snell maintained his suzerainty. He let it be known that he expected more respectful subordination and gratitude for keeping his daughter's husband out of debtor's prison. One can easily surmise, during Peter Bryant's months of absence to serve in the Boston State House, that Snell's characteristic barbed wit found occasions to remind his daughter of his disapproval of her husband's choices. Cullen, a keenly intelligent, sensitive boy, surely sensed the persistent currents of tension.

Biography's contribution to the fairy tale is unmistakable. As soon as Walter Buckel's wealth allows, he builds "a fine, huge, yellow house, about two hundred rods from his old dwelling, close to the public road" – and moves to demolish the family's log former residence and cut down the red oak that sheltered it. Clearly, Walter Buckel here figures as the stand-in for the severe grandfather whose Calvinism-besotted regimen gave Cullen's childhood in the fine yellow Snell house close to a public road a hellish tint. In an unpublished poem, Bryant years later remembered immersion in evangels of death twined with sin and damnation – "a fearful creed," in which "the strong fear / Of death o'ermastered me and visions came – / Horrible visions such as I pray God / I may not see again."

For all of Bryant's personal investment in his protagonist and his ancestry, however, it is Caspar's literal and figurative transformation after the death of his parents that impels the story. That transition begins with Caspar's proposal to Adelaide. Strangely, he is motivated not by her fair hair, roguish blue eyes, or the milky whiteness of her arms and neck, but by his conclusion, "after having fully considered the matter, ... to take a helpmate to assist him in the management of his estate." Caspar would seem to have no sexual consciousness at all. No longer a child, he is confused by adulthood. Adelaide's rebuff sends him recoiling into "lonely rambles in the woods" and "the wild imaginations that formerly possessed him."

He returns instinctively to the razed house where he once "heard with terror" the sounds of storms that "seemed to him as if all the fiends of the woodland had fastened upon the old log cabin and were going to fly away with it." Why revisit that "terror"? Because the beldam's story-telling intermediated for the "wild" manifestations of his psychological turbulence. Re-entering the fairytale realm, Caspar seeks guidance in his quest.

Sitting at the foot of the red oak he had spared his father's axe, the disconsolate humpback sees, "seemingly projecting from the side of the trunk next to him, a beautiful well-turned throat." Presumably, the maternal hag has metamorphosed transformed into a female deity: "The features were moulded in the finest symmetry – youthful – but with the look of youth which we see in Grecian statues, and may imagine to belong to beings whose lives are of a longer date than ours, and which seems as if never to pass away." But there is nothing stone-like in the profuse flow of light brown hair "that played softly in the wind": the vision evokes what is implicitly a sexual awakening.

To repay Caspar for saving her life (here the feminine pronoun becomes imperative), the oak instructs him to wash his face and hands in the pool of the rivulet beside his house – patently a baptism confirming his rebirth. The next morning, it seems his hump has shrunk, and day by day, he grows taller, better-proportioned, more handsome, athletically proficient, and socially adept – culminating in marriage to Adelaide Sippel. But external transformation does not confer judgment. After three years of profligacy have put him deeply in debt, he resumes his rambles in the woods and is drawn to the oak. Shamelessly, he blames her for his woe: "If I had not been handsome, I should not have run into expenses that made me poor."

At this point, the narrative becomes more highly charged with sexually suggestive metaphor than anything previously published in America. Like a woman hoping that an obtuse prospective lover will get the message he previously missed, the oak tells Caspar that she knows his thoughts and "it shall not be my fault if thou art not happy"; he has only to dig beside her trunk to find what "will suffice thy wishes." He assumes she is offering treasure – which is literally true – but Bryant's language intimates a different reward, one that he is too callow to recognize. Calling him to her, the oak again displays "the same calm features of unearthly loveliness and youth, with a smile playing about the beautiful mouth" she had initially presented. Though unwittingly, he complies with her disguised invitation by fetching a spade to penetrate the turf. The seductive undertones continue in the description of his return to the oak: "only" her bark (skin) is "visible in a strong gleam of twilight," and he responds to her "boughs and foliage moving and murmuring in the night-wind that was just beginning to rise" by "turn[ing] up the earth at the spot which had been pointed out to him" (as though at a lover's cue). He then pulls out the money-filled jar (itself sexually allusive), and after shoveling back the mould, "press[es] the turf into its place" to protect the tree and hide his act.

The erotic subtext takes on even sharper definition when Caspar, having dissipated the trove, again solicits help from his benefactress, and she grants it. "I cannot forget that thou wast born beneath my boughs," she says, adding, "Between the two roots that diverge eastward from my trunk, thou wilt find a portion of what the children of men value more than all the other gifts of heaven." Once more, she punctuates her instructions with a reminder to "replace the turf over my roots." The graphic image of the red oak, at once voluptuous and maternal, emphasizing her two diverging roots and the jar between them is so plain in its reference that it needs no gloss. The circuitous characterization of the jar as that which "will suffice thy wishes" and "what the children of men value more than all other gifts of heaven," however, merits some explication. Caspar understands it to mean money, but, as the motive behind his extravagance shows, he is really a profoundly insecure man who spends to acquire respect. To the oak, who, in the tradition of oracles, speaks enigmatically, it represents love – as both eros and agape, the Christian concept of the greatest gift of heaven, salvation through Jesus's love of man.

The story's concluding segment elaborates this theme. Caspar, blinded by his fixation on money, destroys the oak he had once saved – and with her destruction, insures his own perdition. Destitute a third time and too ashamed to face the oak, he orders others to his fateful birthplace to dig for anything of value. Monomaniacal excavation leads to damming the rivulet (Bryant's recurrent symbol of life's renewal); deprived of irrigation, the oak withers. One evening, in the twilight that Bryant reminds the reader once revealed a vision of impassioned beauty, the oak's wanton "son" looks down from a window of the yellow house and fancies he sees her sad face and a white arm "beckoning him to approach." But Caspar's obsession with the elusive treasure has so hardened his heart that he averts his eyes. Eventually, like a fever breaking, "a furious tempest" follows July's drought: it whips the woods and looses a deluge that ruptures the dam, releasing the rivulet's pent up "vast body of water." A final wind gust, the blow of reality, topples the oak; dead as the possibility of redemptive love the tree symbolized, it lies "with its long roots sticking up in the air."

The fairy tale's spell has broken, and all reverts to the conditions of life before love lent its voice to the oak. In the coda. Caspar, having suddenly resumed his former shape, is driven from his own yellow house. Adelaide, who has not recognized the crazed, deformed man as her husband, searches for him for six months before yielding to a marriage proposal from a New England youth "who had fallen in love with her plump, round face and well-stocked farm." Apparently, the new husband is humble enough to enjoy what should suffice his wishes. And Caspar? He becomes a legend, said to haunt the woods at twilight, "skipping over the fallen trees and running into gloomy thickets ... as if to avoid the sight of man."

As the story consistently employs wilderness and the forest to represent confusion sown by the threatening demonic impulses in the psyche, Caspar's isolation stands as a judgment. But is the purpose to avoid being seen by other human beings, or to avoid seeing them? Is it, in some uncomprehended way, a response to shame over his liaison with the oak, or an expression of repugnance over what he has learned lies in the human heart? As in many of the tales Hawthorne would write in subsequent decades, an irreducible ambivalence persists in "A Pennsylvanian Legend." Although Caspar precipitates his own doom, he is also a victim. That his humpback signifies an isolation through arrogance is patent from the beginning, but at a deeper level the deformity suggests original sin, subject to cleansing through the baptism the oak offers. For the baptism to be effective, however, Caspar must be able to love and to accept the gift of love – and that ability, Bryant implies, is crippled by what the next century would label Oedipal guilt. Each of the tale's three women – the beldam who is a mother surrogate, the red oak, and Adelaide – shares some identifying feature with another, and the physical resemblance between the oak and Adelaide is striking. Is Caspar's human failure rooted in an existential incapacity to define himself as a man through his relationship to women?

What seems on the surface a simple adaptation to the conventions of the fairy tale reveals, with closer study, an intricate psychological weave. Although Bryant's turn at fiction, when noted at all, has been denigrated as a marginal effort, the sophisticated attention evident in his debut belies that inference. Had his readers been more insightful in perceiving and appreciating what he brought to this young art, Bryant might have developed the tendencies of "A Pennsylvanian Legend" far beyond anything the American imagination had conceived and become, more than a precursor to Hawthorne, a rival in shaping moral fables. Instead, this first story is sui generis. With his next story, he would adopt a markedly different approach, while setting the bar no lower.

A Border Tradition

Still eager to accommodate his subscribers' interest in fiction, Bryant again assigned himself the task with his second tale, "A Border Tradition." Bryant later said he got the idea for it during his return to Great Barrington to close down his law office. If so, it was an ironic moment of inspiration. While residing and practicing law in that town for a decade, Bryant had come to disdain its inhabitants as querulous, bigoted, and narrow-minded – "an extremely excitable and not very enlightened population" with whom, he wrote to Richard Henry Dana, "it cost me more pain and perplexity than it was worth to live on friendly terms"; his relocation in Manhattan loomed as nothing less than a liberation. But now, intent on the survival of his recently merged magazine, he recognized an opportunity in the history of these same townsmen, the mingled descendants of Dutch settlers from the New Amsterdam patents and their English counterparts who had moved west from the Connecticut River. A benign story of a courtship encounter between the two groups would appeal to subscribers in both Anglo-Saxon Boston and Dutch New York. Furthermore, and of greater importance than the subject matter's immediate, practical advantage, it exactly suited his broad prescriptions as an advocate of literary nationalism. In earnest rebuttal to critics who denigrated America's prospects in the arts as lacking themes worthy of attention, Bryant argued that a rich array of ethnic communities invited the imagination of aspiring writers and piqued the curiosity of readers. A truly national literature thus depended on cultivation of what was unique to the local.

Bryant's good friend Catharine Sedgwick may also have influenced the choice of subject. Reviewing *Redwood* the previous year to promote interest in her writing, Bryant speculated on what the future held for American fiction. Sentimental novels from abroad had captured a large female audience, and American imitators had so hewn to the model that their subliterary, treacly titillations cultivated no distinctively American characteristics. But Bryant saw intriguing possibilities in Sedgwick's investigation into the yearnings of the female heart. He declared her "specimen" the first "highly meritorious" account to be "descriptive of the manners of our countrymen"; it stood "as a conclusive argument that ... works of fiction, of which the scene is laid in familiar and domestic life, have a rich and varied field before them in the United States." Bryant's second story would mine the same vein.

How to render stories so as to make them American, however, was not quite the simple a matter it may seem from a distance of two centuries. To many literary nationalists, "Americanness" could be as uncomplicated as incorporating description of our unique scenery, native animals and plants, and perhaps an occasional local oddity. Bryant disagreed. He argued for American stories that not only drew upon the native scene but also fostered an American consciousness. What he was contending, in effect, was that reading "Rip Van Winkle" changed the perception of the Catskills, that shaping the imagination alters the reality. As a corollary of that view, he looked to superstition and the supernatural – given their primitive, instinctive appeal – as useful means to aesthetic involvement. A key factor in Washington Irving's popular success, Bryant grasped, was his ability to tap the vestigial penchant for the eerie under the cover of a nimble style and wit extending from the language of Addison and Steele. Later described as "sportive gothic," this combination is evident in "A Border Tradition," the most Irving-like of all his fiction. In addition, Irving's light supernatural infusions abetted the impression of a historical moment at a further remove than the actual thirty years. No American writer was as adept as Irving in overcoming the notion that America lacked the sufficiently deep sense of the past required by the Romantic imagination, and Bryant aimed for a comparable effect.

Bryant set his tale still earlier, but he also devised a more complicated strategy in layering time to enhance the sense of separation from the present. A traveler first speaks directly to the reader and paints the immediate scene about him. Everything he sees from a hilltop is idyllic: white buildings under the shade of old elms; neat fences; a road as clean as the gardens; profuse dews that glitter under a bright sun and transparent blue sky. Presently he meets an old man, an evocation of the pioneers who "hewed down the forests and tamed the soil of the fair country we inhabit"; in contrast to the traveler's perception of beauty, the old man stresses decay. Although the river and mountains are as they were when he was a boy in the village, the rest has succumbed to time: the houses he knew have been pulled down, the trees under which he sat as a child have rotted, roads have disappeared, rivulets have dried up. At the end of this roll of mutability, however, he points his staff toward the sun-lit meadow that was once a shadowy marsh, figuratively directing his audience to a past he now begins to evoke through a narrative set the his own birth. The tale that initially associates the marsh with death and dark deeds then swings comically to marriage and renewal; it concludes with the revelation that he is the grandson of the long-dead woman who engineered that marriage. Like the scene that opens the story by arresting the traveler's notice (and, vicariously, ours), and like the passage through life's stages, the narrative has come full circle. In the process, the landscape selected as the story's platform for his story has acquired a human enrichment.

At its core, "A Border Tradition" is an epithalamion that pivots on a trick. Ruses have appealed to storytellers since the art was first practiced because they lend themselves to plot design. Traditionally tied to bawdy themes (one need only think of Boccaccio and Chaucer), they continued to be useful when more modern fiction veered from coarseness toward milder comic treatment of genteel romantic relationships. "The Legend of Sleepy Hollow" is an obvious example, and Bryant, who admired it, surely had the Hessian Horseman at some level of his mind when planning his own story. But just as the idea of the ghostly imposture is not the measure of Irving's genius, Bryant's skill lies in the dramatic interplay of the five personalities he arranges.

The story progresses at a slow pace, casually linking character portraits in the village's social tapestry. Jedidiah Williams and Yok Suydam represent the Yankee and Dutch inhabitants, two "races" that, over their ninety years as neighbors, have been brought to friendly terms through "the need of each other's kindness and assistance." Yet language remains a barrier: "The Dutchman learned to salute his neighbour in bad English, and the Yankee began to make advances towards driving a bargain in worse Dutch." Contrasting religious attitudes also divide them. Williams clings to his puritan faith: having no minister in the village, he conducts services in his home. But Yok shrugs off the Yankee's invitations to join in worship. He prizes life's comforts, enjoys a free-spirited party at which he outlasts the young men in dancing, and allows swearing to roll from an unhobbled tongue. His house swarms with black servants (probably slaves, although that goes unstated), whom he joins as a comrade in their easy revelry. Williams considers it his Christian duty to "rebuke" his neighbor for his "irregularities"; Yok counters by noting that he is a Dutchman behaving as his ancestors did, and to change his ways would imply that he thinks himself wiser than they.

Bryant devotes fully a sixth of the story to introducing these two fathers. Given their ancillary roles, this much attention might seem excessive, but it actually serves a cunning strategy of indirection. Focusing on the families' linguistic hurdle sets up the English lessons that lead to the marriage uniting the two ethnic groups at the conclusion – the story's overarching theme. Similarly, counterposing Calvinist discipline and Dutch self-indulgence foreshadows the question of moral conduct on which the resolution depends. Could Bryant have eliminated this entire curtain raiser? Of course. But that would have elevated the ghost deception, thereby diminishing attention to those very elements that most interested its author and made it an American fiction.

Early in his residence in New York, Bryant, who had previously demonstrated an uncommon talent for drawing, forged close ties with the city's young artists, particularly with Thomas Cole, Asher Durand, and Samuel Morse, leaders in the rebellion against John Trumbull's domination of the New York Academy of Fine Arts. The insurgents, inclined toward the same philosophical view of nature that Bryant's poems reflected, argued for a graphic art based, not on the imaging of an event – the function assumed by Trumbull's faction – but on the broader effect produced through compositional arrangement within the field. The names the breakaway group chose for themselves – first the New-York Drawing Association, and then, months later, the National Academy of the Arts of Design – indicated their emphasis on design and arrangement in its subtle elements. Bryant's lectures to the Academy served to buttress its commitment; indeed, he was embraced by the artists as a key figure in the movement for a new American aesthetic. Defining that aesthetic in poetry in one of his lectures, he stated that the poet "selects and arranges the symbols of thought" to stimulate the imagination to delight. "A Border Tradition," begun at about the same time he was delivering the lectures, implies a similar attention to arrangement in application of compositional principles to fiction.

The hinged descriptions of Jedidiah and Yok are mirrored by panels of their offspring showing the parental values in reverse. The stern Calvinist dreams of hearing his son speak from the pulpit with "the eloquence of Solomon Stoddard, and the sound doctrine of Jonathan Edwards"; instead, the "refractory" James cultivates idleness and pleasure, resulting in his expulsion from Yale. "Young men, who have nothing else to do," the old narrator observes, "are apt to amuse themselves with making love," and so James, "frank, giddy, high-spirited" – and bored – recites tales of his college pranks for an audience at the Suydam house. Soon he is teaching Yok's elder daughter English. Mary, as demur and innocent as her father is outgoing and worldly, is easily snared once James smuggles *Pamela* into the house: its moralistic provocation of erotic fancies bespeak lessons James might teach of a kind more exciting than the New Testament's. Whether the novel enables her seduction is left unstated, but Bryant hints as much: she is, after all, the stereotypical blonde of nineteenth-century fiction who unwisely yields to a trifler's dulcet words. Fortunately she has a younger sister, Geshie – a sensible brunette, also true to fictional convention – to protect her interests. Geshie has an instinct for penetrating to reality; raised in "plain, household speech, ... the language of honesty and sincerity," she distrusts glibness, especially in English, "a silken, glozing tongue ... fit only for those who wished to defraud and deceive." She is James's opposite, and thus his natural adversary; herself a prankster, she will turn the tables on him. Just as he relies on *Pamela* to wrest advantage from Mary's weakness, she exploits his weakness: "a deep respect for spirits and goblins" born of reading Cotton Mather's *Magnalia Christi Americana*. Evening after evening, she grips his imagination with stories of supernatural terrors, all the while secretly studying *Pamela* to learn the English words and phrases useful in undermining his reason.

A writer with a lesser affinity for the art of fiction might have ended with the simple accomplishment of Geshie's purpose through her masquerade as the ghost, but Bryant extracts an additional effect with another pairing of opposites. When Mary's broken heart threatened her survival, the doctor, though unable to diagnose her malady, "knew his duty too well not to prescribe." Similarly, when James, "in a state of melancholy bordering on despair" after his encounter with the ghost, calls for a minister to doctor his soul, the minister, upon examining his patient, confirms the ghost's existence. Both the physician and the minister, the author wittily suggests, are humbugs who profit from their delusions and rise in esteem because of people's credulousness. But Bryant – a homeopath who mistrusted traditional medicine, as well as a transcendentalist who eschewed traditional religion as a dangerous exploitation of superstition – is a gentle observer, not a scourge. Like Mr. Spectator, he observes human foibles with compassion and a dollop of humor. James is not morally perfect, and Mary, a frail soul, is susceptible to the titillation pandered by Samuel Richardson, but they serve to build a community and bear the American children who unite their Yankee and Dutch strains. As in Bryant's previous tale, his next, and most of those to come, the life force prevails – here overwhelming the penchant for folly to ensure procreation of the next generation

"A Border Tradition" is missing the novelty and curious emotional appeal of "A Pennsylvanian Legend," and our familiarity with the numerous local color stories that dominated American short fiction after the Civil War may blunt appreciation of the subtle strengths lost in that abundant brummagem, but it reveals a superior craftsman who has done more with less. A year after his debut in fiction, Bryant exhibited uncommon control over the elements of his story and a technical sophistication unsurpassed by any of his contemporaries – including Irving. Had critics exercised a similar level of sophistication, had the economics of the literary profession permitted, and had Bryant been able to convince himself that prose matched the challenge of poetry, he might today be as celebrated a master of fiction as a select few American writers. Destiny, however, determined a different course.

A Narrative of Some Extraordinary Circumstances

Busy as he had been while writing "A Border Tradition," Bryant had to contend with greater pressure and more distractions while fitfully working on what would be his last story for his rechristened *United States Review and Literary Gazette*. His appointment as editorial assistant at the *Evening Post* in July of 1826 had grown in responsibility, leading to part ownership and promotion to joint editor in December of 1827. Acquitting those duties and simultaneously continuing his battle to make the periodical profitable enough to meet urgent family needs was impossible. Moreover, the Boston leg of the enterprise, forced to prune expenses, suffered from disarray. Practicality dictated ceasing publication. Personal matters hardly offered refuge from uncertainty. While arranging an orderly demise for the *Review*, he was forced to relocate his wife and five-year-old Fanny to affordable new quarters in lower Manhattan; with sadness, he informed Frances that they would have to endure the inconveniences of another boarding house.

July's heat oppressed the city, and he was alone. Meanwhile, Frances and their daughter summered in Fishkill, N.Y., dissatisfied with their accommodations. Partisan fervor also contributed to his discomfort: an article published by the Boston co-editor of their merged periodical praised Henry Clay, raising hackles among the fervidly pro-Jackson crowd tied to the *Evening Post*. Such strain between his conservative counterpart and his own increasingly liberal positions added to the burden the *Review* imposed, even in its declining days. Yet, welcoming the prospect of happier circumstances in which to exercise his literary interests, in August he joined his friends Robert Sands and Gulian Verplanck in creating a gift annual. Its contents were to be planned, written, and sent to the printer within four months.

The story for the *Review* was now very much "old business," but Bryant was not one to renege on an obligation, however noisome it had become. "I am yet hard at work writing my tale for the next number of the *Review*," he told Frances in a letter of August 1. "It is the story of a man killed by an explosion of fire and water from the ground like that which happened at Alford a few years since on old Patterson's farm. I hope I shall get it finished in season, but I find it slow work." Ten days later, though unsure as to whether his co-editor was still at his post, he mailed to Boston an incomplete "A Narrative of Some Extraordinary Circumstances That Happened More Than Twenty Years Since." Along with the explanation that it "has given me some trouble to write," he promised, "A page or two more will be sent on next Monday, which will finish it."

As his own extraordinary circumstances in 1827 imply, what he submitted fell well below the standard set in his previous stories, even though it reprises elements of both. An epithalamion tale like "A Border Tradition," here the sex of the discarding lover is reversed. And as in "A Pennsylvanian Legend," Bryant begins by addressing the reader, as though to open a conversation his narrative will illustrate. More closely analogous to the introit of the Catholic mass than to the true frame of a conventional tale, this introduction declares that "few places in our country have any traditions of moment associated with them, and of these few a very small proportion are the objects of superstitious awe." Clearly, the reader is about to be told how one such rarity came to be.

Again employing the handoff used in "A Border Tradition," Bryant installs a second narrator to relate the history tying the supernatural

275

to this otherwise ordinary spot. Jacob Holmes, a clever usurer, has amassed a large estate – and thereby been afflicted with one of the "miseries of the rich": anxiety over the money to be passed on after death. Holmes loves his money, but he also loves his daughter, who loves to spend it. Presumably, the narrative will unravel that complication and culminate in the revelation of how the unraveling has led to imbuing "the inclosure of pasture ground mentioned in the beginning of this narrative" with its awesome quality. But that is not quite what happens.

When Jacob tells his daughter, Betsey, that he will not give her away to the first suitor who calls, "even though it should be Ned Hammond," the reader intuits that miserly Jacob believes Ned is a fortune hunter who would spend the Holmes inheritance, and that Betsey will fall in love with the handsome, witty, athletic, popular youth and marry him over her father's objections. In fact, Ned, though poor, is no fortune hunter: he truly loves Betsey. And though Betsy announces her intention to marry Ned, the willful girl does so to spite her father, "not because she loved [Ned] exactly." She really loves only herself; the most desirable of the eligible young men, she thinks, should belong to her as a matter of course. At this point, our perceptive reader surmises that Ned will grow rich by outsmarting Jacob in a deal, thereby winning his approval, and Betsey, humbled, will recognize Ned's virtues, change her values, and rejoice that he wants to wed her despite what she now sees is her unworthiness of his love. Or something of that sort. Instead, evidently more concerned with preparing for the extraordinary circumstance at the finish than dramatizing the interplay among Ned, Betsey, and the cupidinous Jacob, Bryant ushers Mr. Smith onstage.

Both the absence of a Christian name and the fiery association with his surname are surely significant – the reader can almost smell the brimstone as Smith walks into the Holmes house with "a ruddy glow to his dark cheek, which was yet heightened by the red lustre that lay on all objects; a pair of keen black eyes seemed as to the maiden fitted to say unutterable things." Given the heat generated by those inferred unutterables and Smith's fanning of her vanity, Betsey's goose is cooked, and Ned is, literally, out in the cold. The self-centered heiress and worldly stranger announce their engagement.

At this point in writing the story, Bryant apparently lost his bearings. Although he had to reveal Smith's depravity as so extreme as to deserve the extreme punishment that sprang the idea for the story, the best he could come up with was the arrival of two uncouth young men who spend the night with Smith at his tavern lodgings. What they do together is not stated, but a pack of greasy cards left behind is sufficient to launch a scandal. What purpose Bryant had in mind with this episode, however, is occluded by the ease with which Smith restores his reputation among the gullible citizenry – a disparagement of human behavior that, deserved or not, is gratuitous in this context. The abrupt finale is equally incongruous: Smith, suffering, for unknown reasons, from melancholia, goes to the Holmes farm, where a hiss, an eruption, and a column of smoke spell his death. What is this *coup de théâtre* supposed to mean? An inquest determines "that the deceased had come to his end by the judgment of God," but what was the indictment? Being a card sharp and a fortune hunter? Censurable as these may be, they scarcely warrant capital punishment by a spectacular divine intervention. Perhaps to correct the imbalance in justice's scales, Bryant adds, in a coda, that the bounder was preparing to commit bigamy, and that his name wasn't really Smith, but because the reader has certainly inferred this information pages earlier, the pyrotechnic punishment appears emphatically de trop.

The ending for which Bryant settled departs significantly from his original intention. The introit focuses on the site of the "terrible interposition of Providence" as serving, according to the "state of religious belief in our country," as a reminder of God's wrath, "directly aimed to punish or prevent guilt." The coda returns to this thought by telling us that, for a brief period, the "deep awe" elicited by the extraordinary event changed the community's conduct: "People spoke to each other in a subdued voice, the choleric were afraid to quarrel, and the knavish to cheat, the old warned the young, and the young forbore their usual amusements and gaieties. Even old Holmes contented himself for a while with a smaller usury, and it was long before the look of concern and the tone of fear passed away from the good people." But pass it did, and when it did, all reverted to their former comportment. If this cynical assessment attests the ultimate fecklessness of God's wrath, what values does the story affirm? Indeed, it is not only God's moral scheme that the story challenges but the author's as well. Aside from Smith's evanescence, no one pays a price for bad character. Why should Holmes, a usurer who puts money ahead of his daughter's happiness, be spared the consequences of his behavior? Why rescue Betsey, whose haughty selfishness has gone uncorrected? And why, as a result of the extirpation of his fiendish rival, marry All-American Boy Ned to Princess Betsey? From what we have been shown of this narcissist, marriage would seem more a sentence than a reward.

Nevertheless, the start of the story's last sentence, "A numerous progeny sprung up around them," would have us smile at their blessing by heaven; the sentence concludes with the narrator's recall of seeing their "two chubby boys" while his stagecoach was "passing through the place" – presumably, the spot where holy vengeance was visited on Smith. The driver cracked his whip to frighten them off the back of the coach, and they "indemnified" themselves by pelting him with apples. Once again, Bryant closes by gently expressing faith in futurity: the boys' venial misbehavior suggests the life force's triumph over Smith's demonism. But by the same token, it also subtracts from the gravity of what was announced to be the reason for the tale.

The improvisational carelessness resulting from the pressure to meet a deadline makes it easy to dismiss "A Narrative of Some Extraordinary Circumstances," but even this basically flawed story is not without its merits. As in his previous fiction, the clever acerbic quips scattered throughout the account reveal a Bryant similar to the writer of the *Evening Post* editorials and rather unlike the one reflected by his poetry; this is a writer quick to pierce human vanities and expose the foibles with wry humor. His descriptive passages, too, delight with their virtuosity, even when they prompt the thought that the author would prefer such painterly exercises to the task of advancing the action. Bryant's first two stories were auguries of a brilliant career in a protean new form of literature; his third was a cautionary notice of the danger in subordinating talent to expediency. The near future would test his capability for securing his grasp of what he might achieve in short fiction.

The Legend of the Devil's Pulpit

As the prime contributor to *The Talisman*, Bryant wrote three stories, apparently in less than four months. Except that the weight of responsibility for the *Review* had lifted, his schedule remained as crowded as ever; what, then, explains a greater burst of fiction in the fall of 1857 than the sum of his production over the previous two years? Undoubtedly, the mutual stimulation of congenial spirits played a major part. Bryant himself spoke of the remarkable ease of blending his gifts with those of Robert Sands and Gulian Verplanck in giving life to their joint venture, *The Talisman*. One of the trio might mention an idea, a second would roll it forward in polished sentences, a third speedily turn it into copy. Or so Bryant remembered the experience.

The *Talisman* presents itself as the creation of Francis Herbert, supposedly a world traveler whose writings, published as the works of famous other authors, have won resounding praise. In fact, he was as much an invention as the contents of "his" annual. More than a pseudonym but less than a hoax, Herbert was conceived as a corporate entity, though not really for the purpose of fooling anyone. The idea almost certainly came from Bryant. In 1809, William Coleman, through his *Evening Post*, had been complicit in stirring interest in Irving's *A History of New York* by publishing a report that its fictive author, Dietrich Knickerbocker, had vanished. In 1827, as Coleman's right-hand man and associate editor at the same paper, Bryant published similar "verification" of Herbert's existence as part of a sly advertising campaign to fan rumors and thus promote curiosity about the book. But the question of Herbert's true identity verged on being an open secret. It was a lark, and the trio invested much care and energy in keeping it aloft, not only for publicity but also simply for their own fun. Within a not-so-tight inner circle, "Francis Herbert" was understood to be Bryant, yet all three addressed each other with the name or spoke of him in the third person as though their fantasy existed in an independent reality.

But how much fact lay behind the light-hearted ruse? Were Herbert's stories joint confections, not reliably assignable to single authors? Given their camaraderie, one can imagine an occasional moment of composition in the manner Bryant described, perhaps when a paragraph refused to submit to an intention and the writer would enlist assistance, or when a draft being read aloud was interrupted to offer improvement. Under the pressure to squeeze the most out of their meetings at the Sands home in Hoboken before returning to the demands of their jobs, the pretense that a single pen and personality was responsible for the work probably fed on itself, and retrospect tended to exaggerate the extent of fusion. That seamless collaboration was a sustained, normal practice, however, is rather improbable. Significantly, mentions of a story's title in their correspondence take the singular possessive pronoun, not the plural, and each story shows its author's idiosyncratic marks.

The fractured nature of "The Legend of the Devil's Pulpit" fed the hypothesis of multiple hands at work, but it takes only minimal scrutiny to collapse the claim. Although his three stories for the first *Talisman* differ from each other, each bears Bryant's distinct stamp. Like the earlier stories, "Devil's Pulpit" opens with an introit that conducts the reader into the past – here, "sixty or seventy years" back – and like the previous two, the introit implies a climax that will bestow the glamor of the supernatural to a specific geographical location. This time the setting is not rural Massachusetts (or "Pennsylvania") but the landscape on the two sides of the Lower Hudson River, particularly Weehawken, Hoboken, and the unsettled stretches of the old Dutch Bergen settlement. The narrator, Francis Herbert, is an erudite New Yorker. He traces back to Irving's personas, but his satirical bent probably owes more to Bryant's good friend and eminent Knickerbocker, Fitz-Greene Halleck. Bryant had published Halleck's "Marco Bozzaris" in the first number of the *New-York Review*, thereby establishing his credentials as a serious poet, but it was the delighted response to the "Croakers" (written jointly with Joseph Rodman Drake), followed by the phenomenal popularity of his *Fanny* (published in 1821 and, with thirty additional stanzas, again in 1823) that confirmed New Yorkers' great appetite for satiric derision of their fellow citizens. Surely mindful of Halleck's conquest of New York, Bryant saw the advantage of including a similarly tart *amuse-bouche* in the launch of the gift annual. .

After guiding a leisurely tour of New Jersey's portion of the Hudson basin, the discursive Herbert reminds himself to "get along with my story." The death of George II causes a run on black velvet for mourning clothes that brings Matthew Oakes, a shabby-genteel petty thief and social climber, to the shop of William Vince, a Cockney tailor. The suit Vince sews for Oakes, made of an expensive brocaded cloth that the fashionable set had shunned, inexplicably starts a fad that boosts the fortunes of both – and sparks jealousy that lays the foundation for Part Two of the story. (The division is emphasized by a separation, in the book, by other content.) In the continuation, however, the tailor becomes a secondary character, and is replaced as protagonist by Dr. Magraw (whose personality as well as his disdain for quackery and religious flummery invite comparison with Peter Bryant). Informed by Vince that Oakes has gained his wealth through league with the devil in New Jersey, Magraw leads an expedition of truthseekers across "the Meadows" to the Devil's Pulpit, a rock formation purported to be the site of the satanic rites. There he uncovers a smuggling operation and hurls the devil who heads it against the rock, thereby splitting the basaltic column down its entire vertical length. The tale ends with Magraw atop the Pulpit, delivering a prophecy of the follies New York City will be embracing in the future – the present in which Herbert is telling the story.

If, as has been said, "Devil's Pulpit" is a jumble, that is not because the story lacks transparency but because Bryant never settled on what it is about. Part One satirizes the asininity of fashion; Part Two attacks religious humbug. Oakes's acquisition of wealth through smuggling is the tie between the two, but (if one can dare a pun) the thread between foppery and smuggling is too slender for the strain. Equally problematic, Part One is Herbert's show; the characters are largely incidental to his repartee. In Part Two, Herbert has slipped into the background; Magraw's take on society dominates, and unlike Herbert the detached observer, he directs the action. Their two sensibilities are unrelated, and the tale's conclusion does not correspond to its beginning. Indeed, there is an obvious disjunction between the beginning of Part Two – where Magraw is the avatar of science and reason– and the end –where he fights a devil and exerts force enough to cleave a tower of igneous rock. Bryant also creates a difficulty for himself by having two accounts of the same route to the Devil's Pulpit: the first by Vince, the second by Magraw and his expedition. Instead of heightening suspense, Magraw's trek across the Meadows merely repeats what the reader already knows. Finally, Herbert's need of a much sharper editorial pencil is sometimes egregiously evident. The running joke in Oakes's alterations in the spelling of his name as his pretensions swell, for example, grows wearisome, and the recital of the devil's history of tricks at the end is too long, too obscure, too trivial, and utterly extraneous.

For all its ramshackle composition, "Devil's Pulpit" did not damage the new annual's appeal. The Talisman enjoyed a most encouraging reception, despite its late entry as a rival to The Atlantic Souvenir in the competition for holiday sales and the fact that it was marketed on terms generally unfavorable to booksellers. Bryant's attempt to lend a fume of Gothic fancy to the "wilds" across the river seems to have found particular favor among New Yorkers – a reflection, perhaps, of the period's as yet unsophisticated standards for American fiction. Retrospective judgment cannot be so generous. "Devil's Pulpit" has to be the low point in its author's story writing career. Its very weakness, however, may be a sign that Bryant was in the process of stretching his talent to new conceptions. Although each of his previous tales had shown flashes of the satirist, "Devil's Pulpit" marks the first time he gave free rein to the impulse. The fiasco to which it led forced him to consider other modes of fiction. The debut of *The Talisman* should be seen as a laboratory for testing alternative approaches in a field in which there were few models and little consideration of the possibilities.

The Cascade of Melsingah

Whether recipe, or habit, Bryant's penchant for anchoring a story to a specific place recurs in this romance of Indian lovers. Writing as Francis Herbert, Bryant articulates a key concept in his view of storytelling: "In the course of my wanderings in various parts of the world, it had been my amusement to gather up the incidents connected with the remarkable features of nature. To my mind they reflect interest upon each other; I like the story better for the scene, and the scene better for the story." What he meant by "story," however, should not be understood narrowly as plot.

Early in Bryant's thinking as a critic about fiction, he expressed distaste for plot. Structure – the schema by which the various parts of a narrative relate to each other to confer meaning – was obviously necessary, but that design expressed by action should express the story's characters; he disdained gimmickry that put a premium on mere cleverness. Above all, the conjunction of scene and story should be realized through poetically tempered language rendering beauty and insight. Words and sentences should be to the writer of fiction what paint and brush are to the artist. Herbert's musing in the introit to "The Cascade of Melsingah" about which of several stories about the Cascade he might write reflects the views Bryant had been expressing before he himself started writing fiction – and began foregoing his own advice. Herbert briefly mentions four possibilities, then rejects them. He claims it is because they "exemplify the degeneracy of modern manners," but, even though all of Bryant's stories to this point were set in the past, the excuse is not credible. None of the possibilities is time-bound, and "degeneracy" had not been a disqualifier before for either Bryant or his persona. The more likely reason may be that all four alternate options depend on sudden reversals at the end. Perhaps, after two startling finales, Bryant chose to elaborate a situation and rely on an exquisite verbal palette instead of working with a set of characters in complicated relationships.

That he would turn to an Indian story was practical. During the preceding decade, while the US government was slaughtering Indians in the West and bearing down on the "Five Civilized Tribes" in the South, depictions of the native peoples as noble and heroic grew steeply in popularity, both in the United States and in Europe. Robert Sands's collaboration with James Eastburn in the romance-epic *Yamoyden* had caught that wave on the rise in 1820, and response to publication of the first three novels in Cooper's Leatherstocking series in 1823, 1826, and 1827 certified the arrival, at last, of a distinctively American literature. That Bryant – who had been writing poems with Indian themes for years, had become a good friend of Cooper through his Bread and Cheese club, and shared an identity with Sands in Francis Herbert – would try his own hand at an Indian tale verged on the inevitable.

Bryant biographer Charles Brown supposes that he obtained the legend on which he based his narrative from Gulian Verplanck, whose family home was in Fishkill, NY (also known by its Indian name, Melzingah). But Bryant, through his association with Verplanck, was himself well acquainted with the area, and the supposed "legend" is probably more indebted to Shakespeare's Romeo and Juliet than to Indian lore. Nothing in it smacks of uniqueness: except in its painterly rendering of nature, it does not notably differ from the general stamp of Indian narratives that had suddenly spread through the poetry and prose of the preceding decade. But that says more about the quality of the genre than about Bryant's specimen. By comparison, it outshines in all respects "An Indian Tradition," the only Indian story Bryant thought fit to publish in the Review, and an English publisher, a year later, paid it the compliment of plagiarizing it (with a new introduction replacing the Herbert comments) in a multi-volume collection of supposedly genuine "Indian" tales. Strong demand in the marketplace stimulates sameness, not originality, and as in the case of most producers of these depictions of braves and their invariably comely maidens, Bryant gained his knowledge of the race from the printed page, not from experience.

"Cascade" consists of Herbert's recitation of a sequence of actions; the characters, who go unnamed, lack any significant interiority. When the protagonist, captured after poaching on another clan's territory, contemplates his fate, he resolves to "die like a warrior," but a very short interview with a maid who visits his tent swiftly changes his mind: " 'Would it not be better,' said he to himself, 'to share a long life with the beautiful maiden ... ?' " The juxtaposition is unintentionally comic. The same problem attaches to the conversion of the "beautiful maiden" from captor to betrayer of her tribe. Despite the captive's protest that "he would rather die by the death of fire than expose her to the slightest peril," he readily accepts her aid in the escape, and she precipitously severs her ties to kith and kin, apparently from the moment her eyes register "the physical peculiarities of his noble race" – particularly "his lofty stature and well-turned limbs." In an aside, Herbert asks, "Why should I waste time in telling what has so often been told? The conclusion was natural – it was inevitable." The peculiarities of this coupling, however, surely demand more than consignment to a cliche.

The conclusion to the tale is still more unsatisfying. Bryant could not just back away from the pair to let them live out their lives in their hideaway. His solution was to remove the very impediment that had required their retreat from the world. An intervention arrives from outside the terms of the love story: a deus ex machina – or, more accurately, a pax ex machina – in the form of an accidental meeting that brings news of peace having been concluded between the warring Mohawk factions. The lovers can now wed, and presumably continue doing what they have done all along. It is as though Romeo and Juliet were to learn on the eve of Friar Lawrence's stratagem that the Capulets and Montagues had decided to mend their feud, forget about Tybalt's death, and dole out the food catered for Juliet's wedding to Prince Paris among the citizens of Verona for a grand picnic.

After an auspicious beginning, Bryant's fiction was in a slump. He had understood that he needed to move beyond Irving's example, but he had to find and master his own genius. The third narrative in the 1828 *Talisman* would signal reassessment and renewal.

Adventure in the East Indies

Of the three tales in the first *Talisman*, Francis Herbert's account of killing a royal, or bengal, tiger is the most remote in geography and the furthest removed in technique. At first glance, one might think it a hurried, half-hearted effort to fill an empty quarter signature in the book, and the fact that it runs counter to Bryant's tenets for an American literature suggests expedience. It deserves a second glance – and more respect.

As the chief actor in the incidents Herbert recounts in first person, his role as narrator differs radically from that which Bryant presented in all his tales to this point. No longer the observer-interpreter, he is now simply the instrument of recall, recreating an unusual event with no apparent stake or purpose beyond that of the telling itself. That shift contributes to Bryant's development of an entirely new category of short story, one having no plot at all.

Anecdotes about uncommon happenings had often appeared in early periodicals, frequently as "miscellany" or under the guise of news oddities. One such report, Defoe's "A True Relation of the Apparition of One Mrs. Veal," published in 1705, is frequently cited as the first short story in English. Yet no one thought of the few hundred words in a report of a bear stowing away on a fishing boat or of a snake lured from within a man's chest as a story, and even the manifestation of Mrs. Veal to Mrs. Bargrave on the day after her death, though much longer, does not qualify as a story in the modern sense. But "Adventure in the East Indies" is clearly recognizable as a short story, and conceived as one, despite the fact that the emergent genre – labeled variously as "tale," "legend," "narrative" and "story," among other, more exotic designations – had not yet acquired a set of defining features.

Francis Herbert had lived on the Asian subcontinent, but Bryant had not – indeed, he had no experience of anywhere remotely similar to the East Indies. That fact itself promoted inclusion of details peculiar to the setting – Bryant had to convince himself as to the authenticity of his description in order for Herbert to convince the reader. But there was another motive as well. "Adventure" evinces the simplest degree of contrivance imaginable: because a tiger bites a man, a hunting party pursues the beast and kills it. Absent the intricacies of plot and any consequent recourse to anagnorisis, the author must find other means to engage the reader's interest. Bryant's solution is to link a series of moments, each precisely riveted to the reader's imagination to convey the mutual peril to hunter and hunted. The progress toward the death of the tiger is inevitable, yet the suspense is constant and immediate.

Bryant tested the technique in detailing the crossing of the Jersey Meadows in "The Legend of the Devil's Pulpit," but here it is the story's entire axis. Evidently, the result satisfied him, for he would modify the technique the following year in his sole fiction for the second *Talisman*. But the experiment anticipates more than the next phase of a poet's progress in exploring the possibilities of an embryonic literary strategy. Without expounding any manifesto or theory of fiction, Bryant was beginning to practice a creed that would surface among some of the Naturalists near the close of his century. From "Adventure" to the earliest of Stephen Crane's stories – particularly to such instances as "Killing His Bear" and "A Clerk's Holiday" – is a very short step. Indeed, the fact that Herbert is awarded a bounty and cheered as a hero even the tiger's death is the result of an accident anticipates Crane's Naturalistic interest in debunking the glory of heroism. This is not to say, of course, that Bryant was an influence on the future of the short story. Unfortunately, his reconnaissance of its domain would soon be forgotten, but it is a gauge of the seriousness and intelligence he brought to the short story in its nascent decade.

Story of the Island of Cuba

Bryant's fascination with things Spanish in general and with Cuba in particular dates from residence in two lower Manhattan boarding houses run by Adelaida de Salazar and her Spanish husband, from March 1828 to June 1830. Bryant took advantage of his situation to study Spanish, and he may have acquired some of the information used in "Story of the Island of Cuba" from the Salazars' Caribbean visitors. The result was an incomparable success. American writers, lamenting what they perceived to be an absence of exploitable materials in their native land, had often imported foreign elements; the great challenge for the first part of the nineteenth century, however, had been to realize the potential of an infant nation to create its own literature. No one devoted more to that task or came closer to its unambiguous accomplishment than Bryant. How ironic, then, that in "Cuba" he would limn what may be argued is the most convincing depiction of a non-English-speaking country an American pen had yet produced. Francis Herbert writes so knowingly of aromatic coffee shrubs, cottonwoods like Egyptian columns, orange bowers, the odor of stables invading the lower apartments of houses and the scent of oleander mixing with lime blossoms in the garden, the movements of air along mountain ridges, and so much more that natives omit in conversations with strangers. Who could doubt that he had lived in Cuba and known its people? What rival among his countrymen would dare write at such length and painstaking particularity, and with such confidence, of a place where he had never set foot?

Contrary to what it may initially seem, the author's purpose was not to purvey an impressionistic travel piece about an imagined Cuba, nor was it to transcribe a gruesome history of three desperadoes – as some suppose it had been told to him during an evening at the Salazars. The reader engages the story at two narrative levels. The first is that of Francis Herbert, the well-educated surrogate traveler who mirrors the cultural background and values of the story's readers. The second narrator, Counsellor Benzon, is a native of Teneriffe in the Canary Islands, hence also an outsider, a Spaniard whose wealth derives from ownership of a New World coffee plantation; he represents the colonist class. Finally, there is also a third level of perceiving reality, one which has to be inferred from Benzon's account of the three Indians.

Although Bryant's Cuban tale did not influence Joseph Conrad's *Heart of Darkness*, they are fundamentally similar, not only in confronting civilization with savagery, but also in the "unreliability" of their narrators. The three Indians come to Havana as the end result of colonial events over which they have no control. "By virtue of some treaty or other" – the implication of arrogance and arbitrariness is telling – Cuba's Spanish overlords had sent a boatload of European goods to the Florida Indians. Bishop Don José de Tres-Palacios, who accompanied the shipment, so impressed the natives with his pomp, mysteries, and Latin prayers that many received baptism and awarded him three Indian boys as "trophies of his peaceful victory." (Bryant does not mention – but it is worth noting – that this first bishop of Havana, highly respected for his moral rectitude, had been appointed to beat back "secularist tendencies" in the rule of the island. The historical reason for the trip to Florida was the bureaucratic enlargement of his diocese to include Florida and New Orleans.) European clothes and trinkets seduce the "young savages," but their refusal, or inability, to learn prayers or the alphabet, neither of which relates to their culture, sets in motion a train of disobedience followed by punishment that drives them to their ultimate deaths.

To understand the story, the reader at some point needs to realize that all information about racial relationships is filtered through Benzon's European values. For example: unlike Bryant, a constant opponent of slavery throughout his life, Herbert seems untroubled by his encounter with slavery or his host's bias on this, or any other, issue. The New Yorker, presumably a Protestant of some stripe and a man of means, at no point challenges the biases of slavery. Neither, in all probability, did the readers of *The Talisman*. But Bryant subtly undermines that complacent acceptance. Herbert has the "best coffee in the world" brought to his palatial bedroom in the morning by Benzon's servant, probably a slave, and he admires the planter for the "great awe" in which his slaves hold him, an expression of an "instinct" bedded in their "inferior minds." When Herbert eventually dares ask whether the planter fears the slaves will make "a bloody attempt to shake off the burden of servitude," the reply reveals the brute mentality beneath Benzon's agreeable, gentle, sophisticated exterior. Military posts line the shores, he insouciantly states, and the oppressors enjoy the advantage of hatreds arising from skin color distinctions the slaves have drawn among themselves.

At the story's core are Indian adolescents plucked from their society and treated as curiosities while subjected to the "benefits" of Christianization. Here, too, Cuba reflects conditions in the United States. Despite Bryant's Jacksonian affiliation and his acquiescence to Indian Removal as historically inevitable, he recognized the injustice toward our native tribes and their politically imposed suffering. "Cuba" obliquely expresses that sympathy. Benzon's recital of ever more horrific deeds by the Indians is offset by evidence of a different nature. In telling of the fugitives' refuge in Guanes, for example, Benzon mentions that they "subsisted easily, and lived in a manner quite to their taste among the lazy settlers," fishing, hunting small game, loitering, napping in the shade, and harvesting and curing tobacco in times of need. But then government commissioners entered the area, and a herdsman, avenging "some dispute," informed against them; the three were then jailed, bound in heavier chains and condemned to forced labor. Managing to escape once again, they returned to the village and massacred its inhabitants, thereby triggering another round of escalated terror. Benzon never reflects on the debasing treatment that set the cycle in motion. Nor does he consider the implications of his own judgment on the very "race" whom the Indians slaughtered:

I hate the rascals, for they once stole from me the finest horse in the world, an English hunter which cost me sixty doubloons, and I was obliged to pursue my journey on a stunted, hard-trotting jade, which I purchased of a dingy mulatto who called himself a white man, and who had the conscience to ask me a hundred dollars for her. I dare say he stole the animal.

The most revealing point in Benzon's narrative occurs after two of the Indians have been killed, and the lone survivor commits three abductions. The first is of Anita, the comely daughter of a colonist. Aguarda, her fiancé organizes a rescue party. The hound on the scent leads them to an apparent dead end, and Aguarda, inflamed over having been misled, is about to shoot the dog when a movement overhead discloses the abductor's presence atop a rock. The Indian escapes, leaving the bound girl behind, unhurt. We soon learn that the Indian was about to kill the hound at the same moment Aguarda came within a pull on the trigger of doing the same – and both because they believed the dog betrayed them. This link between the two young males, stirred to violence by their human claims to the same beautiful same girl, is no coincidence. Benzon observes, in the opening sentence of the next paragraph,

Yet this man, in the midst of his hatred of the people of the island, and the bloody deeds with which he gratified his thirst for revenge, seems to have still felt some of those natural sympathies which attach us to our race, and to have yearned after the pleasure of seeing a human face, and hearing a human voice, in peace and kindness.

The second abduction, of Anita, a small girl he treats with the tender concern of a loving parent, reinforces the point. After several months she is rescued, but, Benzon adds, "not until she had contracted a strong attachment for Taito Perico, as he had taught her to call him." Taito is apparently a corruption of the Quechua *taita*, "Uncle" (a child's word for a close family friend); Perico is a common Spanish nickname for "Pedro," but various dictionaries also note that *perico* can also mean "parakeet" and "bully." Is Bryant playing with language to imply that underlying the wanton vengeance is a child's tutelary spirit? In the sole instance the Indian has a name, he discloses it to the girl. Is this a sign that the Indian can reveal himself only to an innocent child? Is his cruelty reducible to a parroting of the actions of the whites toward him and his people?

The third abduction advances that very interpretation. The Indian comes upon a group of boys picking fruit (much as, the reader has been told, "Pedro" had done for Anita). Suddenly, their "innocent laughter" stops. " 'El Indio! El Indio!' " one of them screams, and the boys scatter "like a flock of paroquets at the discharge of a gun." José Maria, an eight year-old boy, "trembling and powerless with fear," is the single exception. The Indian clutches the boy and rides off with him, showing no hint of malicious intent. Again rescuers pursue, led by Arias, the boy's uncle who is also an officer of Cuba's militia, and Cespedes, a man with a reputation for extraordinary valor. By accident, they discover José Maria, unharmed and unfettered, sitting against a tree. Arias orders his nephew to point to the Indian's location; when the boy obeys, the pursuers kill their startled prey. Arias orders his nephew to point to the Indian's location; when the boy obeys, the pursuers kill their startled prey. (At this point, readers might be starting to question their previous assumptions about this villainous savage and the nobility of his pursuers.)

With the terror lifted, the people rejoice. Signaling the restoration of law, a judicial tribunal will identify the corpse and certify that Arias was justified in shooting him. Benzon ends his narrative, intimating nothing but approval of the outcome. Almost as an afterthought offered for the sake of completeness, he scruples to mention, if only to dismiss, a theory that the "frightful savages" were not Florida Indians but members of a Mexican Guachmangos tribe. Herbert, also dedicated the whole truth, assures his audience that, despite "a degree of incredibility," the particulars of Benzon's story rest "not on the credit of my host alone." It is as if Bryant were saying to his readers: "I've shown you the ravages wrought by the worst criminals, animals without conscience, and then I've shown, beyond doubt, condign justice. Are you now content?"

The answer Bryant really wants is: "No."

Illumination of that answer is clearest at the end of Benzon's narrative, when he states he "ought not to conceal" the common supposition that the atrocities were committed, not by Florida Indians but by Guachmangos. Suddenly, his entire version of the story becomes a highly doubtable hypothesis, undercut by his own words.

I know not that there is any other reason for this belief than their fierceness, but I know that there is no other way of accounting for what became of those three savages from Florida than by supposing them to have been the ravagers in question.

What ought not be concealed is precisely what, unconsciously, he has been refusing to see all along.

Benzon assumes that the "multitudes" who gathered to view the Indian's body were drawn there by curiosity to see an evil-doer connected with the powers of darkness, but his report that they "spoke to each other" in "subdued tones" and with an "expression of awe that stole over their features" implies a contrary interpretation. The wax dripping from their candles that covers nearly the entire corpse bespeaks the kind of reverence shown a saint. Similarly, respect for the Indian better explains naming the mountain on which he was killed Loma del Indio than Benzon's assertion that it was "in memory of the exploits of Arias." Exploits *of Arias?* What killed the Indian was either an accidental misfire or, as everyone believes, the result of Arias's cowardly instinct "assailed by the ignoble passion of fear." Arias has fired his musket instantly, against a startled adversary armed only with a lance. Is this consistent with Benzon's praise of Arias as "a gentleman of the true stamp, and of that courage which shows itself not in words but in deeds"? Actually, it is the Indian who displays courage and honor: even while drawing his last breaths, he summons strength enough to grasp his lance with both hands, and, though lying on the ground, point it at his killer to show indomitable defiance. How do his enemies respond? Benzon notes that Cespedes, a *valenton* – that is, one who bombastically proclaims his valor – "valiantly sent another ball through him with one of his pistols." As if shooting a corpse were not sufficient "valor," Cepedes's slave then proceeds to slash the vanquished Indian's face with a houghing-knife, an instrument "used to hamstring the wild and furious animals of the herd."

By the end of Benzon's narrative, Bryant has artfully overturned all the justifications for the vindictive pursuit of the "savages." From the story's beginning it has been apparent that prejudice filters perception, but by the end it is obvious that prejudice has gone beyond distortion to inverting reality. When the Indian asks the abducted little girl to call him Taito Perico, does Bryant intend a caustic allusion to St. Peter, the founder of the Roman Catholic church that has "abducted" him from Florida? Perhaps not – after all, Pedro is a common name – but is "José Maria" – Joseph Mary – also a coincidence? Might ordering the boy to betray the Indian who is perceived as betraying his Catholic hosts be another instance of inversion – of Jesus, in effect, betraying Judas? And then there is the crowning irony in the Christian mission to destroy the three "savage" Indians that culminates in a double hanging, the dragging of the body through the streets behind a horse, dismemberment, and public display of the severed parts, all by the island's "civilized" Christians? Although it goes unmentioned in the story, Bryant was well aware that Cuba's Arawak native population had been slaughtered into extinction by a nation dedicated to the teachings of Jesus.

If "Story of the Island of Cuba" is not a perfectly wrought story, it is certainly a sophisticated innovation. Nothing quite like it would enter American literature until Melville's *Benito Cereno*, almost three decades later. It is tantalizing to imagine where Bryant might have taken this ingenious concept. Instead, his interest in the operation of stories reached elsewhere in the last of the *Talisman* volumes.

The Whirlwind

On Sunday, September 9, 1821, a number of whirling funnel-shaped clouds, estimated to be half a mile in diameter at their tops and slightly more than two hundred yards at ground level, wreaked destruction across the Northeast. The greatest damage was concentrated in the area around Lake Sunapee, New Hampshire, but remarkable feats of the wind's power were reported from great distances, as far as lower Canada. Newspapers throughout the northeast and at least down to Philadelphia carried the details of destruction to homes, barns, cider mills, orchards, crops, and woodlots. Among the grisly facts deemed most worth reprinting was the fate of Samuel Savary, aged seventy-two, ferried across six rods to have his brains dashed against a rock, and the burial of his family in rubble. A subsequent discovery of a young girl's corpse in Job's Brook added a poignant irony, provoking questions about God's goodness that did not need to be spoken aloud.

That Sunday, Bryant, home in Great Barrington, had just returned from an exciting two-week stay in the Boston area. He had read "The Ages," his Phi Beta Kappa poem, at Harvard's commencement, and five days later, he had deposited the manuscripts for his first poetry collection with his publishers. Surely news of nature's rampage stirred his sympathy, but even disasters soon fade from mind, and Bryant's attention, with a first child due in four months and a financially lean start in his legal career, was absorbed by personal concerns. Three years later, publication of William Austin's "Peter Rugg: the Missing Man" in a Boston Masonic periodical may have reminded him of the tornadoes that had struck his area in 1821. Austin's tale – about a stubborn, anti-social blasphemer who defiantly rides into a tempest, presumably sent by God as castigation, and is doomed never to arrive at his destination – was widely pirated and soon took on the character of myth.

Bryant surely read the story – it was almost impossible to avoid it – but if "Peter Rugg" sparked thoughts of attempting his own version of a tempest, they remained at the back of his mind. As editor of the *United States Review*, constrained to write a burdensome portion of its contents, however, he apparently entertained a similar notion for a fiction about the clash between the concept of a just God and the injustice of natural calamity, but he chose instead to pursue the idea that thrashed clumsily ahead to become "Narrative of Some Extraordinary Circumstances." Yet some vestige of the Savary family's fate, and particularly of the little girl in Job's Brook, persisted in his memory. Seven years after the tornadoes' indiscriminate destruction, the abiding questions it raised mingled with the Book of Job and the story of Elijah in 1 Kings 18:43-45 to take form in the last *Talisman* as "The Whirlwind."

The personal history recited by a Baptist preacher while riding with Francis Herbert from Wheeling to Lexington contains good reason to curse God. His father, like Job "a good moral man" whose farm afforded the family a "pleasant abode," was obsessed with studying the heavens to predict the weather and adjust the care of his crops accordingly. The practice usually went well, but when the weather "refused to conform to fixed rules, and failed to fulfill the promises it held forth," it disturbed his temper. To the son, the father seemed to be "questioning the providence of God, exerted in the great courses of nature.

As in the story of Elijah, drought brought ruin; rather than resign himself to God's will, the father continued to search the heavens. Suddenly, he foresaw dire events, and the next day, a "small, dark cloud, enlarging, blackening and advancing every instant" appeared in a clear sky. But instead of bringing life-restoring rain in answer to prayer as in Kings, this cloud was accompanied by crackling, "as of a mighty flame running among brushwood" – an echo of God's appearance in the burning bush to proclaim his identity as the timeless being of being who is not to be questioned. Instantly, a great wind swept from the forest and all nature bowed before it. Dropping his Bible, the father screamed for the family to run for their lives, but the whirlwind crushed the dwelling's timbers, killing everyone except the son who is now telling the story.

The unmistakable allusion to the whirlwind in the Book of Job is the key to Bryant's story, another bout with the question of how to understand God's punishment of the righteous. Here, the son sinks into bitterness, but after Baptist neighbors take him in and shower him with kindness, he slowly receives

...the consolations of the Gospel. I saw that the chastisement, though severe, was meant for good, and that the Lord, by removing all whom I loved, and separating me from the children of men, had enabled me to devote myself the more entirely to the work of reconciling my fellow-creatures to him.

"The Whirlwind" can initially seem a bit of a shaggy dog. To Herbert, their arrival at the home of a Baptist family arbitrarily prevents the preacher's account from having a satisfactory ending. He is an urbane New Yorker; presumably, he regards the proposition that study of nature's secrets should provoke God to demonstrate his inexplicability by destroying both a pious servant and his family as utterly absurd, and equally incomprehensible that the son should subsequently devote himself to humanity's reconciliation with that God. Dissatisfied by what he perceives to be an anticlimax, he laments having "had no opportunity of remarking on certain of [the tale's] circumstances which seemed to me a little extraordinary." Just as in "Story of the Island of Cuba," however, Herbert has missed the point. The preacher's appointment at the house will fulfill a commitment to perform a baptism. Unlike Peter Rugg, he has reached his destination. His journey – analogous to life's journey – ends in a beginning that is a continuation. To the preacher, the baptism affirms his faith in a God who, like being itself, defies reason. If Bryant himself could not muster faith in such a God, he nevertheless closes with a sign of faith in life's regeneration.

What makes the stand-off between the evangelical preacher and the author's persona at the story's end so intriguing is the preacher's similarity in several respects to Bryant. The fictional boy's home in a village not unlike Cummington recalls the Snell hilltop house, and the boy's scholar-father who studies nature to discern God's lessons closely resembles Peter Bryant. Like Dr. Bryant, the boy's father had gone to sea before returning to his town to win public office and the respect of the local citizens. The more resonant detail, however, is the son's close relationship with a loving sister who died young: Bryant's sister Sarah, dearest to him of all his siblings, had died in December 1824. In "Thanatopsis," his breakthrough as a poet and his most enduring claim to literary immortality, Bryant offered liberation from fear of a theistic God's wrath in the assurance that death meant nothing more than reduction to nature's materiality. Although the rationalist in Bryant never retracted that view, the ache of Sally's death stirred a desperate wish for a hereafter. His tribute to her, "Consumption," concludes in the couplet, "Close thy sweet eyes calmly, and without pain: / And we will trust in God to see thee yet again."

"The Whirlwind" apparently expresses a deep ambivalence in Bryant himself. As a personal statement, it presents a confrontation of faith and reason that drives the story yet cannot achieve resolution. The preacher's perfect faith and Herbert's inability to comprehend it cross, but Bryant has contrived no mechanism to make anything more of it than that.

The Indian Spring

Though "Rip Van Winkle" and "The Legend of Sleepy Hollow" may forever enjoy greater fame, Bryant's artistry in "The Indian Spring" surpasses Irving's more popular genius. Later giants of nineteenth-century American literature would compose short stories of comparable merit, yet only a dozen or so perch at the same high level of mastery. How astonishing, then, that it has been neglected by anthologists and has remained virtually unknown to even our most respected literary historians and critics.

Though cast, like "A Border Tradition," as a ghost story, "The Indian Spring" is so ambitious it resists that classification. Bryant's earliest thoughts about the possibilities for American Romantic fiction had emphasized the value of the supernatural as a way of compensating for the absence of an evocable past to engage the emotions. Here, the supernatural element is used as a tool to pry loose the fright of existential jeopardy. Throughout, the challenge is to solve a mystery: what are the limits to reality in the narrator's perception? The clues that emerge in the course of the telling shift judgment back and forth until, at the end, the narrator wakes: the terrifying experience was all a dream. But the story's resolution is not so simple: the reader also "wakes" – to the realization that the mystery has been a calculated misdirection. The discovery that concludes the story is not, finally, what was dream and what was not, but what Herbert's self-encounter reveals.

Consistent with the convention employed throughout the three *Talisman* volumes, the narrator, though not identified, is presumably Francis Herbert. Unlike previous Herbert incarnations (except in "Adventure in the East Indies") this one is the protagonist of the tale he tells. Addressing the reader in the introit, he draws a line between philosophy (by which he means dealing with empirically derived truth) and belief in the supernatural, and then asserts that the two sides of the line are not always distinct. Obviously, this is to prepare for a tale in which the two modes of knowledge collide, but it also initiates the similar pairings of opposites through which his tale will progress.

He and a friend set out on a walk through country in which newly cultivated areas border on the wilderness from which the settlement has been wrested. That concept of borders will persist. Herbert himself is a "cultivated," genteel fellow who sees nature as a source of beauty, not as a hostile force. Although he carries a musket, it is for show, not survival; indeed, he is disinclined to shoot an animal before it has enjoyed the bounty of the summer. Soon, however, his veneer of refinement – the "border" that defines him – will be imperiled.

Herbert, in fine trim, walks fast; his corpulent friend, unable to keep up, urges him to press ahead alone. Their separation is pivotal to the plot, but the difference in pace also serves to begin a process of destabilizing the perceptions of time and space. Coming to a glade, he sees a spring; lying on the ground near it, he lets his fancy create a scene of an Indian family carrying on its peaceful life. The "almost imperceptible" motion of an earth newt he sees crawling before him induces his own drowsiness. When he awakes (or, as the reader later understands, dreams that he awakes), he sees an Indian – "a real Indian," he insists – standing on the very circle of grass where he had just napped. To the startled nineteenth-century New Yorker, the Indian is somehow a living "incarnation" of the past. A spatial incongruity now begins to accompany the temporal disjointedness: although the two are "at least" a hundred paces apart, Herbert can see even minute details of the Indian, especially his eyes, as though they were immediately close. Something is awry: who is the intruder in the other's dimensions? Herbert's senses tell him it is the Indian, but his guilt tells him it is himself. Yielding to "an impulse to remove from so unpleasant a neighborhood," he hurries into what he feels is oppressive heat in his hasty escape – a manifestation of guilt that will continue to increase. The distance between them widens, but after averting his eyes for an instant, the Indian, though motionless, has made up all the ground Herbert had gained on him.

The pursuit magically ceases when Herbert sees a well, flanked by a log house. Glad to be free of his tormentor, Herbert asks the twelve year-old boy who is drawing water whether any Indians remain in the neighborhood. The boy confirms that all the natives had long since abandoned the area for the West; only one-eyed, "fat as a woodchuck" Jemmy Sunkum comes to the neighborhood, begging for hard cider. Just a few steps have released Herbert from the nightmarish unreality of the Indian in the forest and delivered him to the ordinary, white counterpart of the native family he had imagined at the Indian spring.

Thus reassured, Herbert resumes his walk, but a few rods on, the Indian reappears, just behind the forest's border – only to vanish again when Herbert peers across the clearing where the boy and his father hoe their corn field. When the alternation repeats, Herbert realizes that setting foot on soil "sown with European grasses" spares him the sight of the menacing figure: the avatar of a displaced race "could only haunt its ancient wilderness, and was excluded from every spot reclaimed and cultivated by the white man." Why, then, does Herbert reenter the woods, where his terror mounts with every step? With unintended irony, he explains that it offered the shortest route home.

Racing through a stretch of forest thickly strewn with fallen trees, he loses his shoe, his hat, his other shoe, his gun – each surrender of a token of white identity is in turn appropriated by the Indian. Herbert is in effect being pursued by a *Doppelgänger* embodying his guilt. The sun and the heat generated by his own body as he flees exacerbate his distress: he compares it to heading into the mouth of a fiery furnace – suggestive of entering hell. But his panic takes him, not to hell but back to the Indian Spring he had praised for its purity and absence of the corrupting toxins of civilization, and that had lured him with its promise of cool relief from the heat.

The significance of his circling to the exact spot where he had lain down to nap, and where, after he "awoke," the Indian first appeared to him, now becomes dramatically evident. Fleeing from the Indian has brought Herbert face to face with him. With a "desperate leap," he falls ahead to "where the pressure of my form still remained on the grass." At the same instant, he realizes that the Indian has also leapt. They land side by side, and immediately the "demon" locks Herbert in a "grip that shook every fibre of my frame." The story's principal pairs have fused into one.

After "an interval of insensibility" of indeterminable duration, Herbert wakes to the sight of the red newt, which has since crawled about a yard. With this sign of restoration of the coordinates of time and space, the nightmare ceases. Or does it? Herbert cannot completely dismiss the encounter as only a dream: "deeply and distinctly engraved on my memory," it has assumed the aspect of a different kind of reality, indistinguishable in its own way "from the waking experience of my life." Perhaps sensed more than understood, some recognition produced by the inevitable clash at the end has seeped below the level of consciousness to alter Herbert's concept of himself.

Possibly more than any other national literature, ours has fixed on the shock of a climactic self encounter in pursuit of the meaning of an American identity. (A few short story titles that spring to mind: Hawthorne's "Young Goodman Brown," Henry James's "The Jolly Corner," and Philip Roth's "Eli, the Fanatic"; of novels: Charles Brockden Brown's *Stephen Calvert*, Fitzgerald's *The Great Gatsby*, Faulkner's *Absalom, Absalom*.) "The Indian Spring" is squarely in that tradition, and as in most of the others, the radical element is guilt. Bryant had recently dealt with the interplay of guilt and fear in "Story of the Island of Cuba," where neither Benzon in telling his story, nor Herbert in listening to it, ever suspects that his perception of the "savage" Indian youths is a construct of the civilized whites' anxiety, a projection of their own inhumanity. "The Indian Spring" resumes that theme, specifically applying it to the dislocation of the tribes being urged by the Jackson administration at the time the story was being written. Bryant's tragic vision of American history is apparent on his majestic Indian's face – and in the pitiable drunk Sunkum "visibly stamped with the presentiment of the decline and disappearance of their race."

But Bryant's scope extends beyond the Indian agony to a more fundamental quandary. In *Letters from an American Farmer*, published in 1782, Crevecoeur had asked, "What is an American?" Much more than a rhetorical device for an ethnically disparate infant nation, the question went beyond principles and social conduct to the environment that would shape this new man Crevecoeur foresaw being cast when poured from the melting pot (a metaphor Crevecoeur coined). But this had rather disturbing implications. Alongside the benign effects, Crevecoeur also had to consider the Indian as the result of that evolution: logically, then, the new American would eventually shed his European heritage – all that had constituted his identity. In one way or another, this tremulous consciousness has continued rippling through observations on the unique nature of Americanness. In *Studies in Classic American Literature*, D.H. Lawrence wrote of the split in the artistic expression of the American mind that, though its exterior is cultured and well-bred, the "inner meaning" contradicts it: "You must look through the surface of American art and see the inner diabolism of the symbolic meaning, a half-baked mystic, listening to inner voices and watching for signs and portents." Nine years later, attempting a similar assay in a taxonomic survey that immediately proved highly provocative, Philip Rahv divided our writers into two camps: Palefaces (who wrote as extensions of European culture) and Redskins (the defiant, uncurried nativists). Although both Rahv's criteria and his assignments were hotly disputed for good reasons and bad, the intensity of the controversy showed that he had struck a nerve.

Bryant's story does not grapple with the defining qualities of American literature – not directly, at least – but it is driven by the same basic inquiry as to what it means to be an American that has agitated our writers. Our literature began with a rash of epics that accepted, self consciously, a charge to justify our existence as a people by explaining the meaning of America to itself as the exceptional nation. The forests behind the Atlantic shore were seen as a new Eden, an expanse accommodating a rebirth of history. Written a decade after that epic impulse had subsided, "The Indian Spring" exemplifies a slowly emerging mythic reconsideration that takes account of an original sin in the garden. Bryant's tale is not only one of the earliest ventures in our national myth-making but also among the most exquisitely wrought.

The Marriage Blunder

Bryant had extolled America's regional diversity as a bountiful resource and stressed the need to develop a national consciousness of the peculiarities of the different ethnic groups that lent their flavor to our composite identity, but he himself had limited his

American stories to his familiar Northeast. "An Adventure in the East Indies" had been pure invention, but despite its use of detail to enhance credibility, it did not evoke a complex reality beyond its characters' actions. "Story of the Island of Cuba" did strive for that more ambitious realism, and with great success it sustained the illusion of Cuban life, despite the author's never having been within a thousand miles of the Antilles. Perhaps that experiment emboldened him to set a story in Louisiana's Creole community he had referred to earlier in the decade as a worthy lode for the American writer.

Literary historians tend to mark the years immediately after the Civil War as the onset of realism and to point to the so-called local color movement as the populist, democratic rebirth of the short story (indeed, it is in this period that the short story finally sloughs off the label "tale" and acquires its more descriptive name). And so it seems if – looking backward from Bret Harte's essay "The Rise of the Short-Story" and his Western tales, and from the phenomenal rise of such writers as Sarah Orne Jewett, Mary Noailles Murfree, Mary Wilkins Freeman, Thomas Nelson Page, Rose Terry Cooke, and dozens of other trinomials – one sees only Melville's few tales, Hawthorne's Puritan morality fables, Poe's psychotic forays, and Irving's sportive Gothic fantasies. But that is not accurate history. To name but three, who happened to be Bryant's friends and colleagues, Richard Henry Dana, Catharine Maria Sedgwick, and James Kirke Paulding wrote stories that meet the criteria for local color realism, and they were by no means rarities. No writer of that decade, however, was more attentive to the importance of capturing local flavor than Bryant, and "The Marriage Blunder" surpasses all other stories of that field in conveying the regional distinctiveness of its characters. Even without first-hand exposure to Louisiana territory, Bryant had no rival prior to George Washington Cable and Kate Chopin in portraying it so convincingly – and it is arguable that his story is literarily richer than the short fiction of either.

"The Marriage Blunder" departs from his previous work in another respect as well. Before he had written his first story, perhaps before he had even considered the possibility, Bryant preached avoidance of reliance on plot, presumably because he thought its appeal meretricious. Scene and story, he would later write in "The Cascade of Melsingah," are mutually dependent and necessary, but he mistrusted "plots" as mechanical cleverness at the expense of the poetic qualities of mimesis and insight into the qualities of how lives were lived. "The Marriage Blunder," while sacrificing neither the evocative power of language nor the nuances of character, flies in the face of those early misgivings: everything in the story pivots on a delightfully absurd, titillating contrivance.

Bryant lays the ground expertly. "Herbert's" introit enlists confidence by wittily debunking the soapy platitude that marriages are made in heaven. On the contrary, he states, marriages, more than any other human decision, result from great calculation and study – and to support the thesis, he says he knows of only two exceptions. Initially, however, both couples appear to confirm the very bromide he disdains, not refute it. Richard, the ruggedly handsome, poor-but-ambitious youth, and Teresa, the pretty orphan he encounters, are storybook characters destined for one another, but they are hardly rash lovers: Teresa consults Father Polo, who, weighing their prospects, concludes that their industriousness and virtuous habits should overcome the disadvantage of their poverty, and the couple plan the wedding based on "rational" considerations. As one might expect, the older pair draw together for mundane motives. The widow Labedoyere needs to govern her estates through the conventional authority of a man, and in self-absorbed Monsieur Du Lac, she sees a suitable foil. Her strategy to win him panders to his hypochondria; he, flattered by what he believes is a common interest in his health, allows eros to reawaken and is eager to give it license. Both couples' expectations are directed toward the nuptial mass, and this, too, underscores their deliberation: the months of cold and then wet weather have forced a backlog of engaged couples waiting to marry, and the advent of Lent, when the Roman church forbids weddings, leaves only a few days open for the rite. Scheduling exchanges of vows will therefore require clustering the exchanges of vows.

All the tiles in place, celestial intervention can now smash them. Father Polo lacks one eye and is nearly blind in the other; the church is dim; the gusting wind forces the wedding parties to clutch their hoods; the fourteen couples press closely together; and the rain impels the celebrants into the protective embraces of friends and families who hurry them into the waiting carriages. Only when the young bride and groom find themselves in the homes of the wrong spouses do they realize what has happened. The simultaneously comic and perverse misalignment seems easily correctable, but the two older principals are not amenable to a quick reshuffling, and Polo, a strict interpreter of what legitimates the sacrament, sees no way of revoking the mistake that heaven has blessed. Nevertheless, although the blunder cannot be undone, the venerable curate offers a remedy: Du Lac and Madame Labedoyere are the obvious beneficiaries of the mispairing, hence they should settle half of their estates on the young lovers, with the marriages remaining as fate decreed.

Through the centuries, many (perhaps even most) marriages have been arranged on a pecuniary basis no loftier than that imposed by Polo. Even so, the adjudication does smack a bit of prostitution. Bryant sweetens Polo's medicine by sufficiently preserving the beloved priest's sight to enable him to officiate at the wedding of Teresa and Richard five years later, when the senior mates have conveniently died. He also palliates moral objection by inflicting authorial punishment on the undeserving old, obdurate husband and wife: the interior narrator, who tells Herbert the story, reports that both marriages produced by the blunder were unhappy – only to then add, as if in consolation for their misery, that each marriage bore two children. Such muddling helps preserve the charm of a tale that, if inspected through a less forgiving lens, might be open to moral question. One could ask, for example, why, if the accidental bride and benedict were sexually abstinent after discovering Polo's error, she did not file for an annulment. But to cavil over a detail like that would be comparable to condemning Mark Twain for not immediately sending the raft across the Mississippi to set Jim in the free state of Illinois instead of letting it float into slave territory. Why ruin a good story?

And it is, not just a good story but an exceptional accomplishment. Only Irving had approached commensurate success in writing understated, poignant humor, and no one did so while also dramatizing the slow, psychological reckoning with the consequences of the unintended marriages. Balanced against the sapid carnal opportunities granted by their stroke of good luck are the carefully assayed advantages of which fortune has robbed them; by lustfully claiming the former, they prove themselves fools, doomed to be punished by that which they covet. The cleverness of the chiastic plot captures the reader's fancy, but it is the characters' implied psychological machinations that engage readers with their humanity. Because "The Marriage Blunder" lacks the impressive thematic reach of "The Indian Spring," it is vulnerable to belittlement as merely entertainment, but the workmanship of that entertainment barely a decade into the modern history of the genre is of the highest order.

Glauber-Spa

On March 30, 1832, Bryant informed Gulian Verplanck, his friend and erstwhile collaborator now a Congressman, that the group of *Talisman* associates who had loosely organized themselves as the Sketch Club had "voted to have an Annual, – something more splendid than any which has yet appeared in this country." The ambition was indeed "splendid": the book, in two volumes, would be printed on quality stock and not only feature copper plate engravings by Charles Ingham, Asher Durand, and Robert Weir but also display its text within a format larger than of any previous publication of its kind. Would an invitation to join in an enterprise with the best artists and writers available entice Verplanck "to undertake the superintendence of the literary part"? Although originally one of those who talked of resurrecting, under a new title, the annual miscellany that its publisher, Elam Bliss, had been forced to let die, Verplanck had since become Chairman of the House Ways and Means Committee; with his mind directed to political strife, his possibility of contributing anything of his own to another annual was remote, and he had withdrawn from the project. The Sketch Club's offer, surely instigated by Bryant, was doubtlessly tempting, but practicality dictated that he decline once more. The responsibility thus fell to Bryant – where it probably would have resided in practice if Verplanck had acceded to the attempt of this amiable cenacle to include him in the venture, even if only in a largely nominal role.

Although Bryant had several matters requiring his attention, including preparations for a long absence to visit his brother in Illinois and to tour the Mid-West and Southwest, a letter to Verplanck from Baltimore dated May 23 states that "the first volume is printed and the second I suppose will be finished very shortly." But he was either mistaken in his assumption or an important change would soon have to be made. The title he mentions to his correspondent, *Hexade*, derived from the number of writers who had pledged to contribute: in addition to Verplanck and Bryant, Robert Sands, Catharine Sedgwick, James Kirke Paulding, and Bryant's assistant at the *Evening Post*, William Leggett. Actually, Verplanck had bowed out months before, but the identities of those in the collective authorship were ostensibly secret, and New York's rumors still had it that he was among the six. Neither Bryant nor Robert Sands, his lieutenant, saw fit to issue a correction – indeed, they helped foster the rumor, for the Harper brothers' commitment to publish the book had assumed Verplanck's participation. Retaining the title guarded against the risk of the publisher's reneging on their promise if it were known that the popular Congressman had backed out. But then for some reason – perhaps because one or more of the authors objected to continuing the deception, or because someone pointed out that it was a bootless and rather silly game – Hexade changed to Tales of Glauber-Spa (an expensive decision. If the book had already been printed, at least the first signature – i.e., the initial thirty-two pages – would have had to be destroyed and replaced.)

Curiously, none of the stories has any reference to Glauber-Spa: it occurs only in a headpiece consisting of what pretends to be an advertisement from the book's publishers and an appended letter to them from the owner of a spa where the stories were presumably written. Perhaps, all along, the intention had been to present the miscellany as the work of a literary group convened at the eponymous resort, and the new title simply took the name given the spa in the headpiece. That is possible, but rather unlikely. The reverse, that the headpiece was a last minute invention, contrived some time after May 23 to accommodate a new title, seems far more probable. Two factors support this hypothesis. First, the great discordance in tone and subject matter between the mocking, rough humor of the letter and the stories that follow implies a hurried effort at a quick fix for a pressing problem. The letter's focus on cholera is the second clue. When Bryant returned to New York on July 12, he found a city in the throes of a cholera epidemic. Significantly, Sharon Clapp's letter carries a July dateline, followed by a dash, which may indicate it was written in the last two weeks of that month. But the date of composition could be slightly later. In a August 23 letter to his mother, Bryant says with great relief that the worst of the disease has passed. The impulse to treat an escape from peril with humor is a common human reaction, and if Bryant did write the headpiece around the end of themonth, it would explain the haste evident in its composition: the book had to go to the printer for it to be in book stalls for Christmas season sales.

Several strands braid in the creation of this Glauber-Spa headpiece. In 1809, a notice had appeared in the Evening Post asking the whereabouts of one Dietrich Knickerbocker, who left manuscripts behind when he vanished from his hotel. If Knickerbocker could not be located and his bill remained unpaid, the hotel's proprietor stated that he would publish the papers to recoup his loss. The ruse spread concern throughout the city. When Washington Irving subsequently published A History of New-York as Knickerbocker's work, it sold at a brisk pace, and Irving's reputation was made. Tales of Glauber-Spa recycled the same hoax, launched from the same newspaper – of which Bryant was now, effectively, the managing editor. Sharon Clapp's letter offering the manuscripts abandoned by the writers who had stayed at his establishment and then bolted was a clever means to trade on the previous notorious joke, not, as in 1809, to fool anyone. Recent family experience supplied another major strand. Like many who could afford refuge from the city's heat and humidity, Bryant's wife fled to summer boarding houses in bucolic villages close enough to Manhattan to permit an occasional visit from her husband. In 1827, Francis and their daughter spent two months in the hamlet of Fishkill, close to the setting of "The Cascade of Melsingah," where the Verplancks had lived since colonial times. Springs in the area may have been part of the attraction, but whether they were or not, Francis was so unhappy over conditions at their inn that her exasperated husband offered to send enough money to move to a more pleasant establishment. That Bryant had his wife in mind in writing the story is attested by the comic repetition of "premonitory," one of her favorite words, and "valetudinarian," which became a recurrent term in the couple's banter.

One of literature's great classics lent a third strand: Glauber-Spa patently substitutes for Fiesole, the hilltop town where Boccaccio's Florentine story-tellers gathered while plague raged in the city below. But unlike Boccaccio's injections of wit into the relationships among his company, Bryant's humor is an extended burlesque: his spa, an extravagant humbug, mocks what a surge in the wealth of the upper middle class had made fashionable: a stay at mineral springs resorts, ostensibly for their medical benefits but often as a setting in which to vaunt. (The name Glauber-Spa points to Ballston Spa in New York's Saratoga County, the thermal bath most in vogue at the time. The town was a chief producer of Glauber's salt, or sal mirabilis.) And Sharon Clapp, the name of the spa's proprietor, nods to Sharon Springs (about thirty miles west of Albany), the poshest of the spas before Saratoga Springs lured away its clientele. (The allusion to venereal disease in the surname wryly suggests derision, possibly alluding to gossip that a well-known client had contracted gonorrhea while not taking the waters.) Bryant's target is the same pretentious nouveau riche class of New York he had lampooned in "The Legend of the Devil's Pulpit." Here, however, the humor takes a strikingly different form.

A new kind of humor had been gaining an audience over the previous decade, a humor spun from the brash, unsophisticated ways of the frontiersmen of the "Old Southwest," the "half-horse, half alligator" roughs who posed their American lack of sophistication against the schooled sons of the Enlightenment in Eastern cities. Bryant was one of three jurors who awarded first prize to his friend and future collaborator James Kirke Paulding for his broad stage comedy, *The Lion of the West*. Transparently modeled on Davy Crockett, it had huge success, first in New York and then, in a modified version, in London. Also in New York that same year, 1831, William T. Porter and his brother relaunched *Spirit of the Times*, a weekly men's periodical that would soon become the most prestigious platform for the Southwest Humor writers. Bryant was evidently not only aware of a phenomenon which was furnishing the very emphasis on America's diversity he had been trying to promote but also, perhaps because of his ties to Andrew Jackson, our first president from the West, a student of it. His trip into the nation's interior had a visit with his brother in Illinois as its objective, but it served as well to justify traveling through the country's southwest quadrant. Notably, on his return journey, he spent several days in Cincinnati at the home of Timothy Flint, the New England minister who, though not himself a Southwest Humorist, had been promoting interest in some of its more prominent figures. Although the Glauber-Spa tale is not set in the Southwest, it resembles that genre of humor in its key traits. Bryant seems to have been attempting to catch a wave.

Like many Southwest Humor pieces, Sharon Clapp's narrative is discursive; only the transformation of Sheep's Neck into Glauber-Spa holds it together as Clapp shifts from subject to subject. He himself occupies the classical position of the protagonist in Southwest Humor, the outsider: the archetypical crude male beset by a wife and daughters who pursue refinement and social advancement; the victimized bumpkin with whom we sympathize because we identify with his values; the fool who is smarter than those who exploit him. As in Southwest Humor too, the fun is often at the expense of orthography, and puns abound, some – as when Clapp, commenting on the razing of a newly renovated house because it was not in good taste, meekly retorts that it tasted good to him, or when he misunderstands Mrs. Clapp's mention of "divestments" and "future returns" as stripping off clothes and "footer returns" – extreme groaners.

Sharon Clapp's befuddlement over his wife's anticipation of achieving great wealth by having the spring on her property spurt through a barrel of potash, or the pact between two doctors to bring their rivalry to an end by splitting profits from their chicanery, or the depiction of chaos ensuing from the suspected arrival of cholera at the spa may not match J.J. Hooper's Simon Suggs tales, or Joseph Baldwin's *Flush Times of Alabama and Mississippi*, or George Washington Harris's Sut Lovingood's *Yarns Spun by a Nat'ral Born Durned Fool*, but Bryant's foray into tall-tale humor preceded these paragons by more than one, two, and three decades; indeed, it was published a year earlier than Paulding's *Nimrod Wildfire's Tall Talk*, often cited as a trailblazer in the genre.

Bryant's public image was hardly that of a man given to comedy, yet among his friends he was well-known for his wit and practical jokes, and his mimicery of various accents was much admired by a small group of friends. In late 1823 or early 1824, his intimates were surprised to learn that he had written a farce, entitled *The Heroes*, about a duel involving two Southern gentlemen. Writing as Sharon Clapp, he demonstrated that he had an undiscovered gift for humor. Despite the easy bids for laughs in malapropisms, misspellings, and misused pretentious language, he displays an occasional sign of comic acuity. Clapp's line about the new house his women have "obliged" him to erect – "They found the furniture, too, but I had to pay for it; and when it was in order, as they said, it was such a trumpery, bandbox-looking place that I could not spit in it with any comfort" – evokes instant commiseration from most male readers and is worthy of Mark Twain himself.

The Clapp letter is hardly a paragon of American humor, but it does show the extent of his literary daring. Among writers of his time, only Paulding showed comparable breadth, and none touched excellence as often within the variety he was bold enough to attempt.

The Skeleton's Cave

As Bryant rounded the bend in the Mississippi leading into Cape Girardeau, he fastened on the landmark that had lent the town its name. On leave from the *Evening Post* to visit his brother in Illinois in 1832, he had added a tour of the West to the trip. Cape Girardeau was its southwesternmost point. "Cape," as it was known, was one year shy of the centenary of its founding as an outpost in France's Louisiana expanse. Bryant, ever interested in local history, surely sought to learn about its past, but it was the dramatic promontory that sparked his imagination. Perhaps he immediately grasped a possibility in the juxtaposition of the town going about its business and the image of proud, towering indifference of the jutting rock. He had attempted to exploit a similar relationship in "The Legend of the Devil's Pulpit," only to become tangled in its lines. This time he confined himself to a simple idea, and perhaps because it was so simple, he studied it carefully, choosing to rivet his narrative to the interaction of a very small number of characters within enclosing circumstances. It developed into his longest story.

Seven years after he first turned to short fiction, Bryant was still exploring new strategies and means of exploiting its possibilities. He divided "The Skeleton's Cave" into chapters, each adorned with an epigraph as though it were a novel, but quite apart from the fact that its length is only about a half to a third of the usual minimum the term implies, the story is not a novel. In English, "novel" denotes a narrative with a mutual complexity of actions and events extending over a period sufficiently long to accommodate the plot. Bryant's story plays out over three days in one location, and in place of complexity he relies on the systole and diastole alternation of hope and despair that defines the chapters. Ostensibly an adventure tale, it actually progresses as a psychological investigation of its three characters.

In 1880, Émile Zola published *Le Roman experimental*, his manifesto analogizing fiction to a laboratory in which the novelist operates in the manner of a biological scientist. Zola argued for a writer of experimental fiction to replicate an empirically defined area, introduce the "organism" to be studied within its confines, subject that organism to stress, and objectively record his observations of the results. Zola's definition of Naturalism, precisely matches Bryant's "experimental" approach to "The Skeleton's Cave" – half a century before Zola. Bryant had previously shown an inclination toward Naturalism in "Adventure in the East Indies," where, anticipating a technique employed by Stephen Crane and Jack London in their most Naturalistic stories, the progression of details leads the reader to infer a character's thoughts. Bryant's subsequent "experimental" tale is less severe in that respect, but its foreshadowing of Zola's precepts is more encompassing.

The very first sentence of the introit squarely states the conflict the story will dramatize: "We hold our existence at the mercy of the elements: the life of man is a state of continual vigilance against their warfare." After expatiating on this condition, Bryant immediately opens the story with a picture representing this elemental struggle: three persons confronting a steep precipice, an obstacle to their advance. As though to emphasize the frailty inherent in nature, Bryant notes that the rock mass above them, cracked by the relentless elements along its seams and fissures, has surrendered its shards to gravity, rendering them piles of "shivered" fragments. A few trees have managed to take root, but the "ungrateful soil" restricts them to "dwarfish stature" and wild grape vines overrun them, winning the competition for the "warmth of the rocks and sunshine." What chance the weakened trees have for survival is choked by the celastrus that winds its "strong rings round and round the trunks and the boughs" in a killing embrace. As though vaunting its triumph, the celastrus then "clothed the leafless branches in a drapery of its own foliage." The adjoining sentence – "Into this open space the party at length emerged from the forest, and for a moment stopped" – springs the humans, by contrast susceptible and apparently overmatched, into this field of unceasing combat. Bryant then begins a new paragraph with the party's leader, an aged priest, pointing to a dark spot in the precipice: "Yonder is the Skeleton's Cave." Symbolically, the cave is the test that awaits them; its darkness, the mystery as to its outcome.

Next, the cast of this Naturalist drama is presented: two men of French ancestry and an "Anglo-American" young woman – each also emblematic of one of three stages of life. Father Ambrose, somewhere between sixty-five and seventy, obviously represents faith, but he is also the voice of reason. Le Maire, a Franco-American version of Cooper's Leatherstocking, is a self-reliant materialist, a robust middle-aged man of the senses. His niece Emily, "nineteen or twenty," is compared to a "wood-nymph" with a Grecian profile; Bryant asks the reader to imagine her "with just colour enough in her cheek to make it interesting to watch its changes, as it deepened or grew paler with the varying and flitting emotions which slight cause will call up in a youthful maiden's bosom." Like her cheek, Emily herself serves as a kind of litmus indicator eliciting the typical qualities of her companions. When, as the party contemplates a climb to the cave, Emily can see no way of reaching it, Father Ambrose directs her eye to the visible and hidden portions of the path, as though it were a pilgrim's road through life's difficulties. To Le Maire, she embodies vulnerability. When she begins to faint in crossing a two-foot wide chasm in the path, the hunter, "perfect" in his "self-possession," pulls her back from the abyss by exerting all the strength in his sinews. It is a signal moment, attesting his courage in his role as provider and protector.

The ordeal – or experiment – to study human behavior under stress begins with the three hikers entering the cave. At the sight of a huge rock over its entrance, Emily envisions the consequences should it fall, and she shudders. Shame for her girlish fear insures her silence, but Father Ambrose, sensing her trepidation, reassures her: "to suppose peculiar danger in a place which has known no change for hundreds of years is to distrust Providence." Every reader instantly recognizes of course that the rock will crash and seal the cave, but Bryant's purpose is less to foster anticipation than to insinuate the question of the existence of a benevolent God – or, indeed, any God at all – who can be understood through analytical reason. Ambrose (who had visited the cave many years earlier) next leads his companions into the chamber holding an ancient skeleton. Besides being an obvious *memento mori*, the relic is also mute comment on the folly of trusting Providence: after examining the bones, Ambrose concludes that the Indian had suffered a wound and then slowly starved to death. When a thunderbolt booms and an explosive crash announces the fall of the giant boulder, the intimation of the similar fate that awaits them, as the chapter closes, is unescapable.

Zola himself could not be more Naturalistic than Bryant in the study of the three characters that follows. Ambrose continues his homiletic reassurance, based on his confidence in divine goodness, but despond gnaws at that confidence, and he dares "expostulate" with God over the injustice of what seems Emily's certain death. Le Maire instinctively recoils from appeal to any power outside him. When he cannot control his circumstances, he is quick to fix blame on someone else – in this case, on Ambrose for having brought him into the cave.

He speaks of being married to his rifle, which attests his potency, and confronted with his impotence, he would use his rifle to kill himself so that the others might feed on his flesh. Repeatedly, he defines living itself in terms of the next meal; if he cannot eat, he will submit to being eaten.

The most affecting psychological portrait among the three, however, is of Emily, who provides the story with the key to its structure. The narrative's single break from the present recalls her recent memory of a "rustic ball" where she quarreled with her beau, Henry Danville. A moment's gay conversation with a handsome stranger had irritated Henry, and she, "to discipline him for this unreasonable jealousy," flirted all the more – which he answered with aloof withdrawal. Despite admitting to herself that her folly caused the rift, she expects him to ask her forgiveness: "he will soon sue for a reconciliation, and I shall then show him that I can be as indifferent as himself." For Emily, reality is simply a stage set for the drama her fantasy concocts, even should that reality be death's imminence. When Father Ambrose counsels prayer "to the great Preserver of men" as they lie on their beds of leaves, Emily imagines Henry heroically surmising their entrapment, climbing the precipice, and rescuing them, and herself then grandly forgiving him. But if that fantasy does not happen and she should perish, she tells herself, she will have the consolation of his misery: "He will bitterly repent the wrong he has done me, and the tears will start into his eyes at the mention of my name." Bryant closes this exquisitely dire comic scene with a poignant insight: "A tear gushed out from between the closed lids of the fair girl as this thought passed through her mind, but it was such a tear as maidens love to shed, and it did not delay the slumber that already began to steal over her."

The gears in the story's machinery turn it to the necessary concluding rescue, perforce involving Henry. Because that resolution is both determined and obvious, Bryant tries to thwart the reader's expectation by sticking a spoke in the gears: instead of ushering the end to the prisoners' agony, the removal of the rock that has doomed them ironically creates a new obstacle. But the spoke itself needs to be removed rather quickly. (The alternative would require either a pointless delay of the rescue or the characters' slow and dramatically uneventful death by starvation.) And so Henry, cast in the role of a dashing deus ex machina, appears below the cliff, spots the marooned party, goes back to the settlement for help, returns for the rescue, and proposes to Emily so Father Ambrose can marry them and they can have children – one of whom will be a companion to Le Maire in his advanced years. All in the course of three paragraphs.

The weakness of "The Skeleton's Cave" is all in this ending, not because of its breathless exertion to satisfy its audience's presumed wish for the characters to enjoy a happy future, but because the outcome is unrelated to the ideas and conflicts generated during the confinement in Bryant's "laboratory." The rescue resolves the young lovers' quarrel; it does not bear on the qualities the characters have demonstrated under stress, nor does it speak to the philosophical premise of life as a constant struggle for survival that Bryant raises as the backdrop to the operations of human will. Perhaps his readers saw in the ending a justification of Ambrose's tenet that the Maker rewards those whose faith does not falter, but the tale itself does not manifest human exception to nature's insentient laws.

Bryant initially approached fiction writing with a prejudice against plot, and the success of "The Marriage Blunder" notwithstanding, "The Skeleton's Cave" reveals that a change of method had not delivered greater agility in contrivance. His skill in extruding story through the mentalities of characters concentrated within static circumstances, however, is of an uncommonly high order, and his instinct for a concept of fiction unlike anything his countrymen had yet construed for the short story attests an unappreciated inventiveness.

Medfield

Having initiated his career in fiction by covertly drawing upon his own life for "A Pennsylvanian Legend," Bryant closed it with a transparent reference to his public involvement in a recent scandal. In 1831, New York's fractious politicians were split in two main camps, those who maintained loyalty to John Quincy Adams's alliance with Henry Clay, and those who joined with Andrew Jackson after his capture of the White House in 1828. Bryant, who had followed Coleman's lead in aligning himself with the Westerner, had emerged early in Jackson's administration as one of his chief supporters in the Northeast. Late in that first term, some of New York's anti-Jackson opposition convened a dinner to honor Tristam Burges, a prominent Rhode Island congressman. Someone raised a toast insulting the *Evening Post* for "stupidity and vulgarity," and Bryant quickly counterattacked with an editorial attributing the slur to William Stone of the rival *Commercial*

Advertiser. Stone, in a private note, answered that he had neither made the toast nor knew who had, but since Stone had sponsored the dinner and printed an account of it, Bryant scorned the denial as highly implausible. Stone returned fire with a "solemn" disavowal, "leaving the brand of a significant word spelt with four letters ... to blister upon the forehead of William C. Bryant if a blister can be raised on brass."

Not one to suffer being implicitly called a liar, Bryant coiled a cowhide whip in his hat and walked down to Broadway, where, as he expected, he encountered Stone. Withdrawing the whip from his hat, Bryant lashed it at his opponent; Stone retaliated with his cane, which shattered, revealing a sword hidden in its shaft. Companions and startled passers-by brought the duel to an end without serious physical injury to either combatant, but Bryant was soon writhing between keen embarrassment over his behavior and petulance that Stone had not paid for his scurrility with condign punishment. The next day, April 21, Bryant published an apology in the *Evening Post*.

"Medfield" stems directly from that episode. Bryant mounts the story in his customary manner, positioning the "author" in circumstances facilitating the introduction of an interior narrator, here the eponymous Charles Medfield, who, when asked to explain his transformation from quick-tempered pepper pot to a model of humility and forbearance, unwinds the tale that extends to the story's final page.

Physically, Medfield is an unmistakable Bryant self-portrait, not only in such telltale features as his "finely arched forehead" and the locks curling to cover where the hairline had begun to recede but also in such particulars as the tendency for his face to lapse into "an unsettled and expression" when his thoughts wandered in the midst of a group conversation – a trait occasionally noted by the author's friends and associates. It is also hard to miss that Medfield's service as a small-town magistrate mirrors Bryant's law practice and public office in Great Barrington, or that Medfield's "rational" approaches to politics and religion, as well as his propensity for advocating means of civic betterment, directly reflect Bryant. But the most salient similarity emerges in the literary profile of Medfield that Bryant provides at great length, from a proficiency in foreign and ancient literature to specific favorite authors and titles.

Although Bryant reworked his pique and turmoil in the Stone affair quite extensively, it remains the story's anchor. "I was now attacked in a newspaper with that coarse invective, too much indulged in by the press of this country," Medfield recalls. "I knew that the shaft came from the hand of a rival candidate, and I resolved I would send it back to his bosom with tenfold force." The correspondence to the venomous escalation between the two editors is exact. In the fiction, however, Bryant introduced a supernatural element to pose a philosophical issue regarding tolerance for insult: the ghostly touch of a hand, presumably that of Medfield's dead wife, repeatedly intervenes to subdue the wrath, that, in actuality, Bryant had exploded on Broadway. Medfield's desire for vengeance refuses to subside, despite the ghost's interventions, and it literally "consumes" him – just as it was doing to Bryant.

In real life, the vexed editor whipped Stone; in the story, the whipping is prevented. Medfield buys a horse from a man who tells him it is "the best creature in the world" except for "some caprices of temper" which can be easily corrected: "[Y]ou have nothing to do but to take a whip and whip the devil out of him." When that "caprice" manifests, and Medfield prepares to follow the instruction, the ghost stays his arm. The second instance of Medfield's recourse to the whip finally causes him to change his life. More than any preceding incident, the insolent tenant farmer's scornful reaction to Medfield's notice of eviction, followed by the threat to take the landlord to court to protect his rights, would seem to warrant some measure of retaliation. Through Medfield, Bryant is implicitly asking whether violence is ever justified by provocation. In the tale his surrogate tells, the answer is no. Deciding "to investigate the nature of the strange invisible shackles which confined me," Medfield feels, not the firm, gentle hand that had previously held him back, but the bones of a skeleton who is among a company of skeletons. Whether because it reminds Medfield of Christian accountability in a Day of Judgment or, more simply, because the inevitability of death changes his perspective, this memento mori produces a resolution "to abstain from the utterance of every thing unkind or angry, and from the doing of every thing which could give pain to a living creature."

On its surface, the story seems a sackcloth-and-ashes gesture of contrition and of resolve to strive for fundamental change – and so, apparently, it has consistently been read. But that is a misreading. Given the close relationship between the fiction and the facts from which it derived, one might expect to find some sign of Bryant's repentance

314

and an attempt, however unsuccessful, to mend his choleric ways as the redeemed Medfield had done? That sign is conspicuously absent. Indeed, his editorials in the *Evening Post* reveal just the opposite.

The apology Bryant printed the day after the clash on Broadway offers a better clue to his true feelings, but not for what its readers thought it said. Although cast as an apology, it did not, as one might think, apologize to Stone. It was instead an apology "to society," and at that, not quite an apology at all. What had provoked the incident, he reminded his readers, was having been subjected to "the most outrageous possible insult"; to have submitted to it, Bryant argued in lawyerly fashion, would have invited its repetition and even imputed validity to the charge. Yes, he had subsequently taken the law into his own hands, but only because "the outrage was one for which the law offers no redress"; hence he hoped, "if the propriety of my course be admitted, that the retribution will not be thought excessive." Clearly more justification than remorse, this strange, at best ambivalent apology reads rather like the "feelings of supreme and intensest scorn" Medfield says "came crowding to my pen, – phrases of the bitterest derision, coined by my very heart" that the invisible hand impedes him from sending. Like Medfield at that point, Bryant never does admit to having been wrong in opposing the insult with violence, and even in acknowledging the public incivility of his response, he posits that it is excusable and merits only a mild, nominal reproach.

The story is not as exculpatory as the unapologetic apology, but neither does it embrace Medfield's conversion to pacifism. The key to Bryant's intent comes in the final sentence: "In the month of June afterward, as I was looking over the columns of a newspaper, I saw announced in the obituary the death of Charles Medfield, of ————, aged 36 years." There has been no previous mention of Medfield's age, and nothing in his tale is age related. Why add this information at the very end? Why, for that matter, have him die at all, since nothing in either Medfield's long narrative or in his relationship with his friend invests the death with evident meaning?

There are two clues. The first is in a pair of poems published in 1825. "June" consists entirely of the comforting thought that he might die in that month. "A Forest Hymn," virtually a companion piece published at the same time, serves as a gloss on its sentiments: it extols retreat from society into nature's solitude, where "the passions," the enemies of "feeble virtue," are silenced, pride is laid by, wrath as the necessary agent of justice is dismissed, and where, the closing couplet states, "to the order of thy works / Learn to conform the order of our lives." The meditation could be a blueprint for Medfield's reformation. Can the apparent allusion to those poems in the story be coincidence? Of course, but the second clue, which is far more significant, weighs against it: Bryant was thirty-six in April 1831, when the Stone drama played out. Why is this, among the many other details tying author to protagonist, of particular importance to interpretation?

Paradoxically, Bryant fashions Medfield as his double in order to reject the course that his fictional alter ego ultimately chooses. The story presents two Medfields. The first is a skeptic, guided by his perception of truth and justice:

[M]y disposition has always been to examine and to doubt, rather than to admit and believe. An early fondness for mathematical studies gave my mind the habit of insisting, even too much perhaps for the common purposes of life, on strict demonstration of whatever was pro- posed for my belief. I took delight in sifting the grounds of a received opinion, and rejecting it peremptorily, when it seemed to me support- ed by incomplete evidence....[My general inclination was to believe too little rather than too much.

That this Medfield delivers Bryant's own self-assessment is evident. Although Medfield's tale focuses on the ghostly guardian's effort to curb his fiery temper, that flaw should not obscure the unreformed Medfield's reputation for "great judgment and equity, as well as benevolence." Even good qualities, however, can be reflections of prideful rigor. He knows himself to be egocentric, preoccupied with his rights as he perceives them, ready to answer any insult with an insult of his own and to repay scorn with vengeance. "In short," he says, "I was one of those men of whom if the whole world were composed, society would be a state of perpetual warfare, or at best an armed truce." (In short, allowing for a bit of self-critical exaggeration, a man not unlike Bryant himself.)

As Medfield recognizes, his "pugnacious spirit" was tolerable because it could occasionally be useful, but it also engendered a self- indulgent arrogance. Eventually this led to the two unpardonable acts with which Medfield concludes his account: firing an old black servant for nothing more than solicitously allowing his exhausted employer to sleep past his usual hour of awaking; and, in a clash of legal rights, disregarding the effect eviction of the tenant farmer will have on the family. The second, conspicuously alluding to Bryant's assault on Stone, culminates in his raising his whip against the man who has affronted him. Recoiling from the shock of seeing the hateful extensions of the same righteous traits that had contributed to his good character, Medfield embarks on a journey to remake himself into a creature consisting entirely of beatitudes.

Yet – in what is the most important (and most easily overlooked) statement in the story – Medfield wonders at the end whether he had not, after all, made a mistake. Circumspection, he grants, has brought complacency, "the sense of gratitude at having been preserved from odious and mischievous actions." But this tranquility has come at a huge price: "I confess to you that with this perpetual restraint upon my actions, this sense of a presence which checks and chastises what is wrong, I am far from happy. *I feel like a captive in chains, and my spirit yearns after its former freedom.*" (My italics.) Here, it appears, is the true meaning of the story's otherwise puzzling last words.

The Stone episode represented a genuine crisis for Bryant. Despite his rejection in "Thanatopsis" of a God of judgment and the prospect of an afterlife, young Cullen had been steeped in Christian faith, and he never did abjure any of its moral teaching. Whipping Stone, without ever expressing sincere remorse, violated fundamental Christian principles. What, then, did this make Bryant? His friend Richard Henry Dana, a traditional Christian deeply committed to theological inquiry, had warned Bryant against the contamination of spirit sure to ensue from stepping into the foul pit of New York journalism. The vicious contentiousness unleashed by the politics and commercial competition during this era went beyond anything Dana had envisioned, yet, somewhat to his surprise, Bryant found it invigorating. In 1832, the *Evening Post* was proving to be a sound investment: he was on his way to becoming a rich man as well as an influential force in the shaping of a nation. But still greater satisfaction poured from the fight itself, from the pugnacity in service to conviction with which he endowed the unreformed Medfield.

Essentially, the story turns on recognizing the concept of the double in the two Medfields: it is about the choice of a self. With the death of the thirty-six year-old alter ego, Bryant symbolically affirms his liberation from the captivity of guilt and shame. Ultimately, he comes down on the side of action – and of the risk of error to which action is vulnerable – over the seductive safety offered by passivity. Medfield chose to be reborn as a veritable St. Francis who eschews fishing, not only to spare the fish but also to avoid torturing the worm. Not Bryant. The unapologetic owner-editor can acknowledge his respect for that man, but the illusion of himself becoming a Medfield – of holding naively to a life consistent with the faith proclaimed in "A Forest Hymn" – died in the confrontation with Stone. The hard-driving, tough-minded, combative voice of the *Evening Post* came to terms with himself. The editor trumped the poet.

That "Medfield" has been read as a morality fable dramatizing the defeat of pride is ironic. Medfield does defeat his pride – and thereby extinguishes himself. In the end, that Christian teaching is not the value the story affirms. None of Bryant's previous stories – or poetry, for that matter – dares more in combining psycho-logical exigency with a philosophical reach into the very conditions of being. In effectively shrinking from life to avoid inflicting hurt on others, Medfield anticipates Melville's Bartleby, who prefers not to prefer the ineluctable terms of existence. The comparison with Melville becomes particularly striking as Bryant's regenerate protagonist approaches the end of his narrative. Immediately after conceding that his spirit yearns for its former freedom, Medfield strains to overcome that longing: "My sole desire and hope is, by the patient submission to the guidance appointed me, I may become fitted for a state where liberty and virtue are the same, and where in following the rules of duty we shall only pursue a natural and unerring inclination." At that point Bryant and Medfield divide. Submission to an appointed guidance necessarily sacrifices sole authority over one's actions; logically, absolute submission and absolute liberty are irreconcilable. The epiphany at which both the story and its author arrive is that in extirpating the sin of pride, of the sovereignty of individual will, from his conduct of life, Medfield has run from his own humanity. Bryant, using the writing of his story as a means of resolving the crisis the Stone affair, rejects Medfield's philosophical suicide.

At least part of the blame for the failure to appreciate "Medfield" as a profoundly serious fiction falls on Bryant. The emphasis on the mysterious hand implies a ghost story leading to a concluding explanation, but the ghost's influence is not actually germane to Medfield's choice. The story's meaning really rests on the choice of the friend who listens to his tale, but he is too insubstantial a character for the implications of his decision to register. Nevertheless, Bryant's last story is one of those works more important for the concept it aims to achieve than for the artistry in its realization. "Medfield" begins to wear a path into a metaphysical realm of fiction that Hawthorne and Bryant's Berkshire neighbor Melville would subsequently pursue. The pity is that a writer of such intelligence and literary talent then fixed his eye in a different direction.

The story's meaning really rests on the choice of the friend who listens to his tale, but he is too insubstantial a character for the implications of his decision to register. If the friend's role is perceived as providing an auditor, then the business about the supernatural restraint is repetitive and mawkish. But the powerful effect inherent in the conclusion really depends on recognizing the true identity of this friend who passively makes his case through Medfield's total self abnegation. It is a clever concept, but the story has not been engineered to deliver its impact. Nevertheless, Bryant's last story is one of those works more important for the concept it aims to achieve than for the artistry in its realization. "Medfield" begins to wear a path into a metaphysical realm of fiction that Hawthorne and Bryant's Berkshire neighbor Melville would subsequently pursue. The pity is that a writer of such intelligence and literary talent then fixed his eye in a different direction.

In a few short years, while simultaneously also working to confirm his standing as America's poet and establishing himself as a man of pivotal importance in a political era dedicated to an unprecedented democracy, Bryant had cleared ground for new modes of narrative. From a radical adaptation of the traditional Märchen to the rough-cut humor flowing back from the hinterland, from depictions of local peculiarities that would infuse the Local Color movement to the innovative techniques of having the teller reveal a story he himself had not recognized, from sentimental saga to the dissection of human behavior that would become the nucleus of Naturalism, Bryant was testing strategies to reinvent storytelling. And yet, in this naive time, no one seems to have been aware of the intimations of what he was doing. Perhaps not even himself.

Notes

Punctuation. In the editing of Bryant's stories, I have slightly modernized punctuation in order to improve ease of reading and, in some few cases, clarity of meaning. Principally, this involved sifting out unnecessary commas impeding the flow of a thought. In some places, commas replaced semi-colons – and vice versa. Dashes have been inserted where commas create a false series. Bryant himself felt unsure about punctuation and generally left it to the very last. He was also inconsistent in his practices.

Paragraphing. Here and there, I have broken very large blocks of print into paragraphs, not simply to better the aesthetic quality of the page but also to accommodate transitions that would normally warrant a new paragraph. It is evident, in some instances in the original printing, that paragraphs were compressed to save pages.

Orthography. The original spelling has been preserved, even when the spelling of a word has varied within the same story. The exceptions reflect the editor's judgment that the misspelling is not a variant but a typographical error.

Word order and omitted words.... where jumbled, I have sought to restore the apparent sense of the passage. Words obviously omitted have been supplied with brackets.

The Complete Stories

As the description in the title claims completeness, I should explain that I have chosen to omit the the installments of "Reminiscences of New-York" and "Phanette des Gantelmes" in *The Talisman.* In each, Bryant was a co-author (and it may be to these examples that his reference to dictation and cooperative effort apply). Though fictive, they are not short stories.

From Poet to Story Writer

Page 2. *Williams College :* A campus dispute among the president, the students, and the faculty that caused cancellation of classes surely played a part in Bryant's disappointment, but as reflected in his satirical poem *Descriptio Gulielmopolis,* delivered as his stay drew to an end, the general tone of the place was as lead to the spirit. Even so, he benefited from friendships with fellow students in what was a new social experience for him. Page 3. *Phi Beta Kappa :* Curiously, it was only when he was invited to deliver the American Scholar annual address that he discovered he had been elected to membership the previous year on the strength of his writing for the *North American Review.*

Page 4. *Catharine Sedgwick :* Evidently Miss Sedgwick's feelings for Bryant extended beyond admiration for a fellow artist. Some have even speculated that she never married because of her affection for Cullen, although that is probably not true.

It is an illustration of how tight the circles at society's upper levels were in those days that Catharine had boarded as a student in the Boston school run by the father of John Howard Payne. In my essay, "Appearing As Edgar's Father" (*Open Letters Monthly*, August 1, 2012), I argue that Payne may have been Edgar Allan Poe's biological father. During the Union College Easter recess, Payne may have had an affair with Elizabeth Poe, an actress then appearing at the theater around the corner from the Payne school.

Page 5. *Dana* : Dana's son, also named Richard Henry, was the author of *Two Years Before the Mast*, for which Bryant fought hard to obtain a publisher.

A Pennsylvanian Legend

Page 1. *A Pennsylvanian Legend* : Charles Brown, in his book, reports the title as "A Pennsylvania Legend" (*William Cullen Bryant* [Scribner/'s, New York, 1971] 142-43). The error occurs in other places as well, including Rufus Griswold's *Prose Writers of America* (New York. 1847). The title used here is that which appeared in the *New-York Review*, edited by Bryant and thus presumably correct.

Page 19. *toothless, old female domestic* : The reference may be to Hannah Cox, who is mentioned in Sarah Bryant's diary as "help" after Cullen's birth. I have found no reference to her in census records, but those records do not list Sarah Snell Bryant, either.

Page 28. *doit* : An old Dutch coin, worth about an eighth of a British penny at that time.

Page 29. *lotteries* : State lotteries were much in the news. In New York: the so-called Vannini lotteries, with thousands of winners for partial number matches, were conducted by Union College from 1823-24 and furnished much grist for charges of scandal.

Page 262. *Bridgewater emigrants* : A group from the Bridgewater area began settling Cummington in the late 1760s. By 1771, the community had grown sufficiently for a minister to join them. Ebenezer Snell established residence no later than 1774.

Page 265. *"They taught me, and it was a fearful creed"; "This grassy slope, this ancient tree."* : Both incomplete poems are printed in my *William Cullen Bryant: An American Voice* (Antoca, Hartford, VT, 2006), 31, 40. These poems reflect the importance of the tree and the brook in young Cullen's imagination. "The Rivulet," written two years before this story, shows the enduring symbol of life's renewal that the rivulet through the Homestead grounds in Cummington remained for him. It recurs in "An Evening Revery" (1842) and "The Stream of Life" (1845), among other works.

A Border Tradition

In WCB:AAV, 190, I deemed this story "a flaccid performance." Obviously, I have reconsidered that judgment.

Page 271. *slaves* : Although it comes as a surprise to many, the colony of New York had a substantial slave population. The Dutch were very active in the slave trade. Census data for 1750 showed colonial New York's population as 76,696 including 11,014 Negroes. Comparable figures for Massachusetts are 188,000 and 4,075. Source: http://www2.census.gov/prod2/statcomp/documents/CT1970p2-13.pdf

A Narrative of Some Extraordinary Circumstances

Bryant's full title: "A Narrative of Some Extraordinary Circumstances That Happened Some Twenty Years Since." Writing to his wife during their 1827 summer separation, Bryant said he drew upon "a story of a man killed in an explosion of fire and water from the ground like that which happened in Alford a few years since at Otis Patterson's farm." Frances Fairchild, Bryant's wife, was born in Alford, a few miles from Great Barrington, and Bryant courted her there, frequently by taking long walks into the countryside. Professor Fred Fagal has brought to my attention that there is a cavern in Alford known as the Devil's Den, and that local lore attributed mineral stains on a natural rock "altar" inside the cavern to blood sacrifices. Although the rock formation named the Devil's Pulpit in a subsequent story has sufficient allusive power in itself, the idea of devil worship in that tale may owe, in some small measure, to associations tracing to Alford. Perhaps the skeleton in "The Skeleton's Cave" also had a distant link to Bryant's strolls in Alford.

In his biography, Charles H. Brown refers to this story as his fourth, but he mentions only two prior efforts, and I have located no reference to a missing story between "A Border Tradition" and this one.

In a footnote in *Letters* 1, 248, William Cullen Bryant II and Thomas G. Voss also list that this was the fourth of his tales, but they nowhere indicate a title of a "third" story. They may have simply copied the count in Brown's biography, published three years earlier.'

Page 55. *Harrisburg Convention* : The Tariff of 1824 had hurt agriculture, and wool producers particularly harshly. A convention was called for Harrisburg, Pennsylvania, to which approximately one hundred delegate from the Northeast came, The result was a memorandum demanding greater protection, but its demands were superseded by the so-called Tariff of Abominations of 1828. The dates of the convention, which ran from July 30 to August 3, 1827, help date the

composition of the story, which Bryant apparently could not bring to completion until some weeks September.

Page 57. *the five points* : Refers to the religious controversy between the strict Calvinists and the Arminians regarding the question of compatibility of free will and predestination. Interpretation of the five points, later abbreviated in the acronym TULIP (Total depravity; Unconditional election; Limited atonement; Irresistible grace; Perseverance of the Saints ~ i.e., salvation once, and forever), generated great debate in western Massachusetts. In a letter to his brother John in 1831, Bryant wrote: "Four-day meetings, an expedient for the spread of fanaticism borrowed from the Methodists, were held everywhere, and when I visited Cummington, although the rage was somewhat cooled by the necessity the farmers found of attending to their business, prayer meetings were held at four o'clock in the morning at the village, and meetings in the day-time twice a week. People would trot about after prayer-meetings for the sake of listening to unprofitable declamations about the metaphysics of the Calvinistic school, who would never stir a step to furnish their minds with any useful knowledge."

The Legend of the Devil's Pulpit

Page 63. *Jersey* : The New Jersey setting is the western shore of the Hudson, a flat bank until it meets the abrupt rise of a sill of igneous rock. On the sill's western side, the ground slopes into the broad marshes known as the Meadows (or Meadowlands). Beyond the marshes, as Bryant notes, stretches a ridge of hills.

Hoboken, across the Hudson from mid to lower Manhattan, where Bryant's associate Robert Sands lived at the time of the story's composition, occupies most of the northern area of Hudson County that is near sea-level. Weehawken, named for the Leni-Lenape word for the great monolith Bryant describes, borders Hoboken to the north along the Hudson.

When colonized by the Dutch as part of New Netherlands, the area west of the sill attracted settlement because of its fertile soil and plentiful supply of furs. The part of New Netherlands west of the Hudson, known as Bergen, retained the name after cession of the region to the English. In 1840, its southern portion became Hudson County, long known as one of the most densely populated and politically corrupt counties in the United States.

From colonial times through the twentieth century, these unsettled marshes served murderers as a place to dispose of bodies without fear of discovery. On Halloween, 1938, Orson Welles located his radio presentation of an invasion from Mars on this site, causing a national panic, and television's David Chase incorporated it in the HBO success, *The Sopranos*. From 1976 to 2010, it was the home of Giants Stadium, which was then demolished and replaced by MetLife Stadium.

From Bryant's essay, "Weehawken": "Looking across the bay, you see, rising directly over the meadows, the first of the Weehawken bluffs, on the brow of which is the famous rock called the Devil's Pulpit, described in the first volume of the Talisman. Here, according to an old tradition, the devil used to preach every Friday to a congregation from New York, until driven off by Dr. M'Graw; the explanation of which is thought to be, that the spot was the haunt of a gang of smugglers, who circulated frightful stories, respecting the place, and who were at length discovered and broken up by the eccentric doctor.

———

"During the warm season great numbers of people resort thither from New-York, some of whom cross the ferry for the sake of a purer and cooler atmosphere, and others attracted by the beauty of the spot – *White muslined misses and mammas are seen / Linked with the gay cockneys glittering over the green* – and the wood nymphs are astonished at seeing stalls for selling ice cream and various liquid refreshments, set up in their sylvan recesses. – The American Landscape, No. 1, December 23, 1830 (Elam Bliss, New York), 7-8. (This was to be the first of a series, with etchings by A.B. Durand and E. Wade, Jr., but the publisher's financial circumstances and its lack of success with the public blocked continuation.)

Dutch Proverbs quoted:
Hy moet wel loopen die door de Duivel gedreven word – He must run, who is driven by the devil.
Het kleed make den man – Clothes make the man.
Spoedige klimmers vallen schielyck – Hasty climbers have sudden falls.

Page 64. The spiritual importance of the perception of nature, in his own life as in his writing, is attested by this passage, written soon after "The Devil's Pulpit":
"[The American Landscape] suggested the idea of unity and immensity, and abstracting the mind from the associations of human agency, carried it up to the idea of a mightier power, and to the great mystery of the origin of things.... there is in our scenery enough of the lovely, the majestic, and the romantic, to entitle it to be ranked with that of any country in the world. Little, however, has been done for it by the artist. With the exception of some of our most remarkable waterfalls and rivers, we have scarcely any delineations of our scenery, worthy of the name. .... The first number of the

American Landscape, now published, is the commencement of an attempt to supply, in some measure, this deficiency." *The American Landscape*, 6.

Page 65. *"I have one to tell, sir."* : Refers to "The Friend of Humanity and the Knife-Grinder," a humorous dialogue by politician and poet George Canning (1770-1827). The "Friend," upon meeting the tattered, bruised Knife Grinder, asks how he came to his lowly work: "Did some man tyrannically abuse you?" He then solicits some tale of mistreatment by some of the grinder's oppressors, assuring him that "Drops of compassion tremble on my eyelids," awaiting the "pitiful story." But the supposed victim of social injustice has no tale to tell, his appearance owing only to a scuffle while drinking at a tavern. He will, however, happily drink to the Friend's health, if he will give him sixpence for a beer. This incites the Friend to respond: "*I give thee* sixpence! I will see thee damned first, – Wretch! whom no set of wrongs can rouse to vengeance. Sordid! unfeeling, reprobate, degraded, spiritless outcast!" The dialogue concludes with a stage direction: "(*Kicks the knife-grinder, overturns his wheel, and exit in a transport of republican enthusiasm and universal philanthropy.*)"

In his note to the poem, Canning, then a member of the British cabinet and soon to be chosen Prime Minister, described it as: "A burlesque upon the humanitarian sentiments of [the poet Robert] Southey in his younger days, as well as of the Sapphic stanzas in which he some times embedded them."

Bryant may have read the poem in 1825, while editor of the *New-York Review*, as Canning's *Poetical Works* was published in that year. (It had previously been published in *The Gentlemen's Magazine* in December, 1797.) Also in 1825, it had been included in an anthology, *The*

Laughing Philosopher, published in London and edited by Charles Lamb and Thomas Hood. Bryant might have given the book attention because it included selections by a fellow American, Washington Irving. Canning's Sapphic burlesque evidently made a lasting impression: Bryant included it in his 1876 anthology *A New Library of Poetry and Song*.

Page 67. *George the Second* : The death of King George II occurred on October 25, 1760, sixty-eight years prior to publication of "The Devil's Pulpit."

Page 67. *dowlas* : A coarse linen cloth, mainly produced in the north of England.
Page 70. *macaroni:* a late 18th-century affected young English gentleman who flaunted foreign words and dress. Derived from the Italian *maccarone* – in this sense, a mixed heap; later, a dumpling – which was then applied to those who pretended to know Latin by placing Latin endings on Italian words. The word survives in American English at the end of "Yankee Doodle."

Page 74. *roquelaire* : Roquelaure: : An 18th century knee-length cloak.

Page 80. *scourge* : Refers to lines from Oliver Goldsmith's poem, "Retaliation":

Here Douglas retires from his toils to relax,
The scourge of impostors, the terror of quacks:
Come all ye quack bards, and ye quacking
/divines,
Come and dance on the spot where your
/tyrant reclines,
When Satire and Censure encircl'd his throne,
I fear'd for your safety, I fear'd for my own;
But now he is gone, and we want a detector,

The Cascade of Melsingah
The setting is in present-day Beacon, NY.

324

Notes

Adventure in the East Indies

Page 285. *first short story* : Twentieth-century research has shown that DeFoe was accurately reporting a presumed-to-be true account.

Page 286. *debunking* : Is this intentional on Bryant's part, or just another casual detail? The fact that it will recur at the close of "Story of the Island of Cuba" supports the former. In his poetry as well ~ e.g., in "The Knight's Epitaph" ~ Bryant deliberately rejects the Romantic haze of hero worship.

Story of the Island of Cuba

Page 115. *Malte Brun* : A supporter of the French Revolution, Danish-born Conrad Malte-Brun (1775-1826) championed freedom of the press in many pamphlets, for which he was indicted and later banished. As an exile in France, he began a treatise on geography, six volumes of which were published between 1803 and 1817. After Napoleon's fall, the disenchanted Malte-Brun became a zealous monarchist. Bryant reviewed his work on "universal" geography in the *United States Review*.

Page 116. *possess the best character* : The unedited version: "They come of a good stock—the virtuous, industrious, and poor inhabitants of Teneriffe and other Canaries, whom the occasional famines which afflict the islands named the Fortunate, after having driven them from Fuerteventura to the Grand Canary, from the Grand Canary to Teneriffe, and from Teneriffe to Palma, oblige to leave their native isles altogether, and would cause to emigrate in still greater numbers but for the severe laws which restrain their departure."

Parke Godwin suggests that WCB's acquaintance with this story "probably"

derived from his residence, "when he first came to New York," with "a Spanish family, which entertained many ladies and gentlemen from Cuba." Purely a guess, the supposition refers to the Bryants' time with the Salazars from March 1828 through May 1830 in three successive locations: Humbert, Hudson, and Varick Streets.

Page 118. *St. John's* : The third major island in the Virgin Islands, at that time a Danish colony.

Page 127. *vampires* : Refers to the bat, not to the Bram Stoker species.

Page 129. "The *chuso* is a weapon of about four feet in length and an inch in diameter. It is made of a very solid and heavy wood, hardened at one end in the fire and brought to a sharp point. The African negroes of Cuba throw it with great force and certainty of aim." (Bryant's note)

The Whirlwind

Page 147. The original published version reads: "In this I think he was wrong, as questioning the providence of God, exerted in the great courses of nature; but who is without his errors?"

Page 152. *white for the reaper* : The original published version reads: "were white for the reaper...." Under stress caused by extreme heat or cold, wheat can turn white. Perhaps the typesetter misheard (or misread) "white" for "ripe," or "right."

Page 292. *Lake Sunapee* : The most extensive account of the devastation was published decades later in an article, "The Great Tornado of 1821," by Fred W. Lamb (*The Granite Monthly*, [Concord, NH, 1911] XLIII, 358-65.) In a note, Lamb mentions the belief that Charles Dickens, on his American tour in 1842, heard accounts of the tornado. A story entitled "The Fisherman of Lake Sunapee," based on the event, was said to have been written by Dickens; it appeared in the British publication *Our Week* in 1863, but whether it was actually Dickens's work is highly doubtful. The story was reprinted in *The Living Age*, Volume 78.

The Indian Spring

Page 299. "Paleface and Redskin," (*Kenyon Review*, Summer, 1939), has had an influence incommensurate with the low degree of sophistication and discrimination Rahv shows in his essay, but the persistence of references to it reflects a basic cleft in the notion of an American identity. Although Bryant's Indian is not the "redskin" Rahv treats, he nonetheless represents a haunting sense of American cultural disjunction.

Leslie Fiedler, in his much-discussed *Love and Death in the American Novel* (Criterion, New York, 1960), revived Rahv's division with a different spin, portraying the dark-skinned double in a succession of archetypal American fictions as an expression of repressed homoeroticism (or, at least, a retreat from the feminine). Whether or not one accepts Fiedler's thesis – and I, in the main, do not – to the extent that it rests on a division in the American identity between the instinctive "savage" and the well-curried civilized, he could have found support (but of course did not) in Bryant's story.

The Marriage Blunder

Page 158. *Gaspar Gil Polo* : A sixteenth-century notary, born in Valencia, was a poet and author of one of the great Spanish romances, *La Diana enamorada*, a sequel to Montemayor's *Diana*. Polo's *Diana* may be the best continuation of a non-original work in European literature.

Cervantes lauded and imitated it, and an English version by Bartholomew Young may have been a source of material for Shakespeare in *Two Gentlemen of Verona*. Bryant may have encountered Polo's work during his stay with the Salazars in New York City; perhaps he was introduced to it by his friend, Lorenzo Da Ponte, Mozart's librettist. Da Ponte and Bryant, who briefly lived in the same boarding house, translated each other's poems (which Bryant published in his *Review*) and often discussed literary topics.

Glauber-Spa

Page 304. *ostensibly secret* : Attribution of this humorous piece to Bryant relies on internal and circumstantial evidence. His wife and daughters had spent two summer months of 1827 at a health resort in Fishkill, NY. Such places, capitalizing on the supposed medical benefits of mineral springs, had become as popular in the United States as they had been for centuries in Europe. Throughout his life, Bryant had been an exponent of "natural" healing and an ardent believer in nature's restorative powers; Sharon Clapp's letter turns a satirical eye to the craze. Although *Tales of Glauber-Spa* is not comic in its contents, the spoof is presented as the collection's headpiece.

The Harper brothers, noting the general success of the three publications of *The Talisman*, had tried to lure Robert Charles Sands, founder and editor of the *Atlantic Magazine* in the spring of 1824, assistant editor of the *Commercial Advertiser* (chief rival of the *Evening Post*) in 1827, and, later that year, Bryant's collaborator on the *Talisman*, to edit a similar book for their firm. The brothers were confident that they could market such a collection more advantageously than had Elam Bliss, a beloved man but regarded, with reason, as lacking business acumen. When Sands backed away from having editorial responsibility, the Harpers laid the proposal before Bryant, Sands' close friend, collaborator, and later Hoboken neighbor. Significantly, the firm would also issue Bryant's *Poems*, a collection they were confident had an excellent prospect of finally establishing his reputation as America's major poet. Of course, as Bryant's stories for Bliss had also won a measure of fame in that field, the experienced editor was the obvious choice as team captain for the new book. In that role Bryant bore responsibility for providing an integrating mechanism.

The name given to the fictional town refers to the apothecary Johann Rudolf Glauber, the developer of hydrate of sodium sulfate, known as Glauber's Salt.

Playing with the secret authorship while effectively ensuring that it would be disclosed, Bryant wrote, in the *Evening Post*: "But the newspapers, those inveterate enemies of secrecy, have undertaken to point out the several partners in the joint stock. To Miss Sedgwick they ascribe one story, 'de Bossu,' and whether from deference to her as a lady, or whether from their candid opinion of her intrinsic merits as a writer, thy have allotted to her the best tale in the collection. To Mr. Paulding they ascribe two stories, 'Childe Roeloff's Pilgrimage' and 'Selim'; to Mr. Sands, two, 'Mr. Green' and 'Boyuca'; and the remaining three tales they apportion between ourselves [Bryant and Leggett].

"Whether this ascription is correct or not so far as the others are concerned, is not for us to say; but, for ourselves, we may and do solemnly assert that we were never at Glauber-Spa in our lives; that we never had anything to do with Sharon Clapp, or his son Eli, or his wife, or his daughters; that we never tasted of either 'oxhides' or gin from the fountain at Sheep's Neck; and, finally, that we believe Mr. Clapp's story is a piece of sheer fiction, manufactured out of whole cloth,

and with no other object than 'to do' those respectable gentlemen, Mr. John and Mr. James Harper, out of a portion of their well-gotten gains."

The Skeleton's Cave

Page 308. Unfortunately the featured rock formation that induced Bryant to write the story was blasted in conjunction with laying railroad lines.

Medfield

Page 312. In his last story, Bryant finally shows some common ground in fiction with his good friend Richard Henry Dana. Medfield's moral turmoil, expressed in the ghostly hand that preserves him from acting on his impulses, is reminiscent of some of Dana's stories in *The Idle Man* (1821-22), a periodical Dana had launched to stimulate interest in psychological Romantic fiction. Dana's brother-in-law, the poet and painter Washington Allston, had written a novel, *Monaldi*, with a double self – one preternaturally good, the other evil. Though not published until 1841, it had been written much earlier. Bryant knew Allston, but any knowledge he might have had of Allston's novel would almost certainly have come through Dana.

Frank Gado, professor emeritus of American literature, was born and raised in northeastern New Jersey. Throughout his teaching career at Union College in Schenectady, NY, he focused on American fiction, with particular interest in its idiosyncratic features. As a consequence of having been awarded two Fulbrights to the University of Uppsala, he was among the first in an American college to teach courses on the great film auteurs. Among his publications are *First Person: Conversations on Writers and Writing* (interviews with Glenway Wescott, John Dos Passos, Robert Penn Warren, John Updike, John Barth, and Robert Coover); *The Passion of Ingmar Bergman*; and *William Cullen Bryant: An American Voice*. His essays have appeared in several books, most prominently, on Bryant in *Dictionary of Literary Biography: Antebellum Writers in Upstate New York*, and on the rise of American poetry during the first third of the 19th century in the *Cambridge History of American Poetry*. He has also edited and written introductory essays on works by Sherwood Anderson, Stephen Crane, James Kirke Paulding, and Charles Brockden Brown.

Gado now lives on a Vermont hilltop, where he ponders the plight of American higher education and reflects on the literary expression of the American mind. In concert with The Trustees of Reservations and the local board in Cummington, MA, he lends his efforts to promoting interest in the Bryant Homestead which overlooks the lovely roll of hills.